PRAISE FOR

"Fast-paced legal-intrigue gold that could be improved only by kicking off a new series."

—*Kirkus Reviews* (starred review)

"Twist-filled . . . John Grisham fans will be pleased."

—*Publishers Weekly*

"Justice has rarely been this compelling."

—Criminal Element

"Another simply riveting novel from Robert Dugoni, *Her Deadly Game* is original, deftly crafted, and a fun read from first page to last for anyone with an interest in murder mysteries and suspense thrillers."

—Midwest Book Review

"*Her Deadly Game* is one of the best murder trial tales to come along in recent years. It's superb."

—*Winnipeg Free Press*

"One of the best puzzle books ever! I raced through the pages, which are packed full of compelling characters and taut gamesmanship, desperate to learn the answer to this extraordinary thriller, which is both whodunit and how-dunit. I would follow Robert Dugoni anywhere."

—Lisa Gardner, #1 *New York Times* bestselling author

"I adore Robert Dugoni's legal thrillers, and *Her Deadly Game* is his best one yet. I loved Keera Duggan's strength and her heart, which shine through the pages, and I rooted for her every step of the way through this unputdownable story."

—Lisa Scottoline, *New York Times* bestselling author

"Absolutely riveting. A juicy tale that will leave readers hungry for more."

—Victor Methos, bestselling author of *The Secret Witness*

"Robert Dugoni has done it again—created a twisty puzzle-box story with one of the most satisfying, jaw-dropping endings I've read in a long time. Part murder mystery, part courtroom drama, and part character study of fascinating chess prodigy turned defense attorney Keera Duggan, *Her Deadly Game* will keep you reading late into the night."

—Angie Kim, international bestselling author of *Miracle Creek*

BEYOND
REASONABLE
DOUBT

ALSO BY ROBERT DUGONI

A Killing on the Hill

The World Played Chess

The Extraordinary Life of Sam Hell

The 7th Canon

Damage Control

The Keera Duggan Series

Her Deadly Game

The Tracy Crosswhite Series

My Sister's Grave

Her Final Breath

In the Clearing

The Trapped Girl

Close to Home

A Steep Price

A Cold Trail

In Her Tracks

What She Found

BEYOND REASONABLE DOUBT

ROBERT DUGONI

 THOMAS & MERCER

Text copyright © 2024 by La Mesa Fiction LLC
All rights reserved.

Published by Thomas & Mercer, Seattle

www.apub.com

Amazon, the Amazon logo, and Thomas & Mercer are trademarks of Amazon.com, Inc., or its affiliates.

ISBN-13: 9781662517990 (hardcover)
ISBN-13: 9781662500220 (paperback)
ISBN-13: 9781662500237 (digital)

Cover design by Jarrod Taylor
Cover images: © Katsiaryna Chumakova / Shutterstock; © Greens87 / Shutterstock

Printed in the United States of America

First edition

To my wife, Cristina, for giving me the best life a husband and father could ever ask for. You deserve all the credit.

It is better to risk saving a guilty person than to
condemn an innocent one.

—Voltaire

Prologue

Five Years Ago
Seattle, Washington

Erik Wei did not choose the South Lake Union restaurant for its eclectic ambiance, nor for the excellent food, nor even for its location—walking distance from work; he chose the restaurant because it was popular, which would ensure a crowd, even on a weeknight.

He chose it because he'd feel safe.

He made an eight-thirty reservation for two. Then he scanned his pass in the secure building lobby, registering the exact time he left the office. Once outside, Wei walked several blocks in the comfortable, seventy-degree temperature before he pressed the send button on his cell phone and deployed his text bomb to Jenna Bernstein, his CEO at Ponce de León Restorative Technology. He didn't want to be anywhere near the office when she imploded.

Wei worked as chief scientist at PDRT, one of the dozens of biotech companies centered in South Lake Union. He'd earned his PhD from the University of Washington in biotechnology and nanotechnology and had fulfilled his desire to work in "the neighborhood Paul Allen built." Allen, the deceased Microsoft cofounder and *Star Trek* fan, had formed Vulcan Inc. and used some of his billions to demolish old buildings and develop a state-of-the-art office and residential area, which attracted innovative start-ups and research institutions that might just change the world.

PDRT sat atop the list.

Wei's work cell phone buzzed. A text.

Where are you?

His text bomb had landed. Bernstein. Curt. Did not sound happy. He did not reply. His text had been clear about where he would be.

He tried to curb his imagination. He half expected to hear tires screech and see the black Escalade speed down the block and skid to a stop alongside him. PDRT security would jump from the car, hustle him inside, and whisk him away, never to be seen or heard from again.

But that only happened in the movies; didn't it?

He picked up his pace.

In his text, he had told Bernstein his concerns and his intentions, but he also gave her the chance to meet, should she have something to change his mind. She deserved that much. Bernstein had given her blood, sweat, and tears to PDRT, and she had given Wei's career a start.

She'd meet him at the restaurant.

He'd given her little choice.

If she didn't, he'd speak with the regulatory agencies. It would cost him his job, and he'd likely be sued for breaching the strict confidentiality clause in his employment contract, but he no longer cared. PDRT wasn't developing an app with bugs that could cause users minor inconveniences. PDRT sought to revolutionize medicine by commercializing tissue nanotransfection (TNT). PDRT's product, the LINK, had the potential to inject genetic material directly into a person's skin cells, thereby altering them, without invasive medical procedures. The applications were endless—curing or alleviating the world's deadliest diseases and regenerating failing organs. Heretofore, *Star Trek* science-fiction fantasy.

Then again, flip phones and MRI machines were once *Star Trek* science-fiction fantasies. Technology had made those fantasies realities.

PDRT boldly touted the LINK as the "Fountain of Youth," and the device had generated unprecedented excitement from pharmaceutical companies who desired to sell it, insurance companies hoping to dramatically cut their insureds' medical costs, independent investors looking to make millions, and the US military, which sought to quickly cure its wounded. Just twenty-two years of age and a new University of Washington graduate, Jenna Bernstein had procured $12 million during PDRT's first round of financing. The second round she received $150 million, the bulk coming from biotech and nanotech entrepreneur Sirus Kohl. For his financial commitment, Kohl became PDRT's COO and CFO and a 48 percent owner. Bernstein was currently in the process of raising an additional $450 million to bring the LINK to market.

There was just one problem.

The LINK didn't work.

Not as PDRT advertised.

Not even close.

It remained *Star Trek* science-fiction fantasy.

After eight years as PDRT's chief science officer, Wei had caught wind of Jenna's representations to this round of potential investors, and he could no longer stomach the "fake it until you make it" start-up mentality.

He entered the restaurant to the sound of crackling techno music from overhead speakers and the cacophony of animated voices from the mostly twentysomething crowd seated at metal tables or gathered at the bar. He smelled the familiar grilled shrimp quesadillas, smoked brisket enchiladas, and his favorite—tequila-lime grilled chicken. But he wouldn't eat tonight. His stomach wouldn't allow it.

The hostess—they all seemed young since Wei had celebrated his fortieth birthday—greeted him by name. "Good evening, Mr. Wei. Another late night?"

"Aren't they all?" he said.

"Seems that way," she said. "Will it just be you, again?"

Ouch. Forty and alone. He'd aged twenty years working ridiculous hours under intense pressure. "No. Tonight there will be two."

"A date?" A faint smile—or expression of doubt—creased the woman's lips.

"It's a working dinner."

"Of course. Right this way." She gathered two menus and led him into the lively restaurant, the tables nearly full. She appeared to be headed for the back. Wei stopped her at a table in the center of the dining area, though it was not yet cleared of dirty plates, used napkins, and silverware. "What about this table?"

"It's quieter in the back."

"No. This will be fine," he said.

"I'll get the busboy to clean and set it," she said.

Wei chose the chair facing the restaurant's picture window, which provided a view of the street. The hostess handed him the menu as a busboy quickly cleared the table, and a waitress set fresh silverware and asked if he cared for a cocktail.

He knew that Andy Saiki, the head bartender, worked tonight. Seemed he knew all their names and schedules. "Have Andy make me an old-fashioned," Wei said. "Tell him it's for me."

The waitress departed. Wei checked his watch: 8:23 p.m. The butterflies in his stomach fluttered again. He told himself he was doing the right thing.

Promptly at 8:30 p.m., the black Escalade stopped outside the restaurant windows. Wei sipped his drink. The head of PDRT's security team stepped down from the front passenger seat and looked up and down the block before opening the back door. Jenna Bernstein exited, seemingly all legs. She considered her Apple Watch, said something to her security officer, and entered the restaurant's front door. Several people seated at tables and standing at the bar turned their heads, recognizing the tall woman who'd recently graced the covers of prominent business magazines and been touted as "One to watch under thirty" and "One of the world's most influential people," but who rarely ventured out in public.

Wei stood as the hostess guided Bernstein to his table. He didn't want the CEO, nearly six feet tall in flats, to look down on him. She was dressed in blue jeans and a crisp white blouse. She carried herself as if she were much older than her peers—her demeanor decidedly serious and seemingly impervious to frivolity.

Bernstein gave Wei the cobalt-blue, ice-cold glare PDRT's employees said could cut diamonds before she sat across the table from him. The waitress offered a menu. Bernstein waved it away. She eyed Wei's drink, then said to the young server, "Water. With a lemon. No ice."

The waitress looked to Wei. He shook his head and handed her his menu.

Once alone, Bernstein wasted no time. "What is this about, Erik?" she asked, her voice controlled.

Wei cleared his throat. She knew what it was about. "I have concerns PDRT is rushing the LINK to market prematurely," he said diplomatically. Wei had told himself he wouldn't let Bernstein intimidate him. He was older by a decade and, because he'd started at the company's inception, he knew the LINK's capabilities better than anyone. He'd poured his own blood, sweat, and tears into the technology, and his reputation as a scientist was riding on the product's success. If he didn't get the concessions he sought, he'd quit. He wasn't about to let the LINK's inevitable failure taint his career.

"I read your text. Tell me why."

For the next half hour, Wei told Bernstein his specific concerns. She listened quietly, her intense gaze never wavering, not even for a moment.

"I can't not say something," he concluded. "People's lives could be at risk."

Bernstein sipped her water and set down the glass. "You're PDRT's chief science officer and chief biomedical engineer. If the LINK is not progressing to your satisfaction, why didn't you tell me about this before?"

He stifled an urge to scream. "In-house, we discuss what we are *striving* to achieve. I wasn't privy to your discussions with outside investors regarding the LINK's development. I only recently learned what you were representing to this third round of investors. Nothing, at present, can perform to the level you have represented. It is simply not yet scientifically possible. We may get there. I hope we do. But the LINK is not there, not at present. Far from it."

"Technology is constantly evolving. Look at the Apple iPhone and watch. Today's dreams become tomorrow's realities."

It was one of her sales pitches. "Yes, but the comparison isn't apples to apples. We're making representations that give people with illnesses the false belief they're being treated when they are not."

Bernstein sat for several seconds without speaking. Wei had done this dance before, in her office and in his lab. He'd spoken his mind. Now it was a game of chicken. He waited.

Bernstein let out a sigh and broke off her gaze. "Why didn't I know about this?"

Her words stunned him. "You didn't know?"

It seemed unlikely. Then again, given the strict compartmentalization at the company, another of PDRT's paranoid security measures, Wei didn't put it past Sirus Kohl to keep the LINK's progress, or lack thereof, under wraps from the sales team.

But from the CEO?

"I understood the technology was evolving and believed we were moving forward. I didn't know we were so far from being commercially viable," she said.

She sounded wounded and sincere. Could Kohl have misled her?

"What do you recommend?" Bernstein asked.

Wei breathed a sigh of relief, though still cautious. He knew of Bernstein's marketing genius. If anyone could save the company, she could. But this was an all-or-nothing proposition that could derail the multibillion-dollar idea.

"Pull back and tell this round of investors, all our investors, the truth. Tell them the dream is alive but requires more research and testing before it can go to market. Tell them we remain committed to the technology. Tell them the LINK will do all we've represented, but the technology is not yet there. We need more time for research and to conduct human trials. Investors won't want to jeopardize lives. They will appreciate that we're being prudent."

"That's the problem. This round of financing is critical. I've already raised close to three hundred million dollars in commitments. If I go back to those investors now . . . it will kill the deal. It will kill PDRT. We need to give our investors something more than a dream to make them believe our product will be commercially viable."

"It's not." Wei shook his head. Part of him empathized with the young entrepreneur. PDRT was her baby. "I'm sorry, Jenna. To go to market now would be morally and ethically unconscionable."

Bernstein sat back from the table. For the first time Wei could recall, she looked stricken, vulnerable. She'd always been poised and self-confident, the picture of calm no matter the turbulence of the waters in which she swam. She sipped from her glass and set it down.

"Who else have you told of your concerns?" she said.

"No one, yet," he said. "I hoped you would do the right thing."

Part I

Chapter 1

To those seated in the packed courtroom gallery, the jurors looked attentive, unbiased, and open to what Keera Duggan was about to say in her closing argument.

Keera knew better.

She'd spent six weeks reading each juror's facial expressions and body language until she knew each intimately. Juror number six, the housewife from Renton with two teenage daughters, smirked, still skeptical. Juror number five, the mother of four, rarely met Keera's gaze. She also had her mind made up. Juror number nine, the thirty-three-year-old mechanic from Belltown, glanced at Keera's client with an expression of disgust and disbelief, as if to say, *You might not be guilty, but, man, you are a stupid son of a bitch.*

Which meant Keera still had her work cut out for her. The evidence had gone in as she'd wanted. Her direct and cross-examinations had been better than good. Some had been excellent, even by her high standards.

All that was left was to give her closing argument.

Keera ignored those seated in the gallery, the judge, and the prosecutor. Her closing would be between her and the jurors. She brought a singular focus she had honed playing competitive chess, her attention always on the next move. Her father had taught her to think ahead. "Your next move is always the most important."

At the lectern, she thanked the jurors. "The judicial process could not go forward without a jury of the defendant's peers. This is the legal system upon which our country was founded, a system in which Mark Strickland comes before you presumed innocent. A clean slate. It was the State's job to prove, with solid evidence, Mark's guilt, *beyond reasonable doubt.*"

She strayed to the jury railing and looked juror six in the eye, as if to say, *But you didn't give him a presumption of innocence; did you?* The woman's smirk faded. Keera stepped down the row. "When first asked to defend Mark, I realized I was looking at his case through my eyes and my life experiences."

She paused and scanned the jurors. "That was wrong."

"For you to truly be a jury of Mark's peers, you must see this case not through your eyes and experiences but through the eyes of an eighteen-year-old young man, a college freshman away from home for the first time and living in a fraternity. Each of you agreed that you could do that. You each agreed that you would see this through Mark's eyes." Keera looked at juror five. This time, the mother of two sons met Keera's gaze. She was willing to listen.

Keera stepped to counsel's table and deliberately put a hand on her client's shoulder to let the jurors know: *This young man was not to be feared. He was not a pariah.*

"Mark had never rushed a fraternity. He had never been much of a partyer." She pointed to the witness stand. "Members of his fraternity sat in that very chair and told you how they had hazed Mark, a pledge. They told you the amount of alcohol Mark and his fellow pledges were forced to consume before the young women arrived."

She spoke to juror nine, the mechanic. "Mark and his fellow pledges wanted to become fraternity members. I know many believe the fraternity and sorority systems are antiquated and Neanderthal, that the system promotes an unhealthy perspective of young women and young men. But the system exists, through no fault of Mark's."

Keera paced and spoke of stories of hazing and of alcohol poisoning, even deaths, all around the country, and about young women being mistreated. She increased her volume to gain attention. "While you may be outraged and offended, it is not your job *in this case* to send the university system a message that you disagree with the presence of fraternities and/or sororities on college campuses. The university is not on trial here. The Greek system is not on trial here. Mark is on trial."

She moved to the middle of the jury box, emphasizing her words. "Your job here, the job you swore to do, is to decide whether the State has proven, beyond reasonable doubt, that Mark had intercourse with Beth after she asked him to stop."

Keera heard the hum of the 109-year-old building's air-conditioning system and smelled the buttery aroma of popcorn permeating from the ground-floor snack shop. Familiarity gave her comfort. "Beth Mendoza told you what she *believes* happened, but, given the amount of alcohol she said she also consumed that night, her recollection is not trustworthy." Keera read from a sheet of paper—the daily court transcript: "She testified, 'things are a bit hazy.'"

Keera lowered the transcript and tapped the railing with one finger. "So, what do we know *for certain*? What do we know to be *fact*?"

For the next hour, Keera went through the evidence, gently picking apart Beth's testimony and highlighting the testimony of others present at the party who said Beth went willingly into Mark's room. Then she said, "We don't know what happened *in* Mark's room. Some of you, I'm sure, wanted to hear from Mark. You wanted him to tell you what happened." Keera pointed to the bench. "But as Judge Constantino advised, every defendant has a constitutional right not to testify, and you cannot infer anything from Mark's decision not to testify, certainly not that he is guilty.

"So, I ask, ladies and gentlemen, have you heard evidence, beyond reasonable doubt, that Mark and Beth Mendoza had intercourse *after she told him to stop?* Or did two intoxicated college students—adults—have consensual intercourse, and one of them regretted it?"

Thirty minutes later, Keera had finished. The State took ten minutes to offer rebuttal. Judge Constantino read the jury instructions, then dismissed the jurors to deliberate. Keera, Mark Strickland, and his parents returned to a conference room at Duggan & Associates, where Keera's sister Maggie had ordered sandwiches and salads, as she had each day of trial.

"Your closing was brilliant." Mark Sr. bit into half a turkey-and-cranberry sandwich and munched on potato chips. The other two sandwiches on the table remained unwrapped. Mark Jr. paced near the conference room windows, looking pained. He flexed his hands as if to restore circulation. His mother sat quietly, gaze fixed on the tabletop, disappointment etched on her face.

"There's going to be anti-fraternity sentiment," Mark Sr. said. "I heard the same crap when I was in college. Everyone wants to condemn the Greek system, but no one wants to discuss the housing that system provides, the school spirit it fosters, the lifelong friendships and business relationships it forges."

Keera had suspected Mark Jr. rushed the fraternity at his father's urging. She also knew Mark Sr. hired her because she had successfully defended Vincent LaRussa for the murder of his wife. The senior Strickland believed a female attorney would play better to the jury.

Mark Jr., for his part, seemed like a good kid, truly contrite about what had happened. He steadfastly maintained he did not rape Beth Mendoza. He steadfastly maintained their sex had been consensual.

But Beth Mendoza sounded just as sincere that she had asked him to stop.

Mark Sr. placed his sandwich down and wiped mayonnaise and cranberry from the corners of his mouth with a napkin. "I'm saying this case is about much more than whether two young people willingly engaged in sexual intercourse."

"Then you missed the point of my closing," Keera said, not pulling her punches. "That is all this case is about."

She found the boy's father arrogant and insolent. But being a defense attorney didn't always give her the luxury of liking her clients.

"Right." Backtracking. "But everyone knows what happens in college." Mark Sr. gulped down his soft drink, then spoke as if out of breath. "People experiment with alcohol, smoke a little weed, and have sex. We all did it. It's a part of growing up."

"Rape is not a part of growing up. And it is not sex. It's a violent criminal act," Keera said.

"Right," Mark Sr. said. "But Mark didn't rape her. I just—"

"Dad." Mark Jr. stopped pacing. He turned to the table and beseeched his father. "Let it go, okay? Please. Just . . . let . . . it . . . go."

His mother looked like she had a stomachache. A tear rolled down her cheek.

Keera departed the conference room to catch up on other cases she had ignored, but also to get away from Mark Sr. This was not a case she had wanted, but Ella, her sister and the managing partner of Duggan & Associates, made it clear that while Keera's defense of Vince LaRussa had generated a lot of publicity and brought in new cases, helping the firm to claw a little higher out of its financial hole, it still remained in the red. Duggan & Associates no longer had their father's reputation to pull clients through the firm's doors. For decades, the Irish Brawler's victories in the courtroom spread his notoriety by word of mouth. But Patsy's drinking had caught up to him, and he was no longer the trial lawyer he had once been—though he could still turn it on for short bursts, like his brilliant cross-examination of Detective Frank Rossi in the LaRussa trial.

At present, Keera was Duggan & Associates' trial attorney, and as Ella liked to say about the LaRussa case, "One case does not a reputation make."

Nearing the day's end, Judge Constantino's clerk called. Keera expected the clerk to advise that the judge had sent the jury home, and it would resume deliberating in the morning. Instead, the clerk said, "The jury has reached a verdict."

Keera retrieved the Stricklands from the conference room, and they hurried from Pioneer Square back to the King County Courthouse. Mark Sr. peppered her with questions about what such a quick decision could mean. She dodged answering. A quick verdict was usually not good for the defense.

Inside the courtroom, the attorneys for the State and Beth Mendoza sat quietly, waiting. Judge Constantino entered the courtroom and retook the bench. Keera thought he looked harried, like he, too, hadn't expected the verdict this quickly. He asked the bailiff to bring in the jury. Keera felt the familiar rush of adrenaline. She read the jurors' facial expressions and their body postures.

She knew what was to come.

Judge Constantino spoke to the jurors. "Has the jury reached a verdict?"

Juror number six stood—not a surprise the jury chose her to be foreperson. "We have, Your Honor."

"Please hand the verdict to the clerk."

The clerk then gave the document to Judge Constantino, who briefly studied the form before handing it back.

"The defendant will rise," the judge said.

Mark Jr. looked stricken. He whispered to Keera, "I don't think I can."

Keera helped her young client to his feet. She told him to grip the table to keep from flexing his hands.

"The foreperson may read the verdict," Judge Constantino said.

The woman cleared her throat, then sipped from a glass of water and set it down. Seconds felt like minutes. "In the matter of the State of Washington versus Mark Thomas Strickland Jr. as to the count of rape, we the jury find the defendant not guilty."

Behind her, Mark Strickland Sr. let out an emphatic "Yes!" and pounded his fist on the railing, drawing a rebuke from Judge

Constantino. Mark Jr.'s shoulders slumped and he dropped back into his chair, tears streaming down his cheeks. Across the courtroom, Beth Mendoza also sobbed, but for a wholly different reason, and was consoled by the prosecutor and her parents.

Keera diverted her attention from the young woman, not wanting to see her pain.

Judge Constantino concluded matters and dismissed the jury. Juror number nine raised a fist to Mark. The young man ignored it. His father returned the gesture.

"Can we talk? In private?" Mark asked Keera, wringing his hands.

Keera shook her head. "I don't think this is—"

"It's important."

Keera warded off Mark Sr., who was clearly worried as to what his son might say, or admit, in private. She led her client from the courtroom to a familiar, windowless room, shutting the door. The room smelled of stale coffee.

Mark Jr. cleared his throat. "Thank you," he said.

"You're welcome, Mark."

She waited. Mark looked worn out, troubled. He wept. "My father told me not to say anything to anyone."

"I think that's good advice, Mark," Keera said.

"But I feel terrible about what happened—"

Keera raised her hand to stop him. Had Mark Jr. intended to rape Beth Mendoza? She doubted he did. But had Beth said no and Mark persisted? She also suspected that to be true, and that it had eaten at Mark's conscience every day.

Her father told her a defense attorney's job was not to find guilt or to exonerate. That was the jury's job. Trials were not about determining the truth, only what the evidence could support. Her job was to ensure the defendant's constitutional guarantees were respected. All well and good in theory. Seeing the result in practice, as here, was another matter altogether. A former prosecutor, Keera wrestled with the concept—and with her conscience. She still had to go home and live with herself. She wouldn't soon forget Beth Mendoza's sobs.

Mark Jr. also had to live with himself.

He'd been wrongly absolved, and guilt could be as crippling as serving time behind bars. Mark wanted to unburden his soul and to have someone, other than his father, tell him his sins were forgiven.

It wasn't going to be Keera. Absolving sins was not her job.

They'd both have to live with this verdict.

"I'm not your priest or your preacher, and I'm not your psychiatrist. Get counseling, Mark," she said. "Find someone to help you reach some resolution. I did my job. I have my own conscience to deal with."

Chapter 2

Seattle, Washington

Frank Rossi made a U-turn in the cul-de-sac, spinning the steering wheel with his left hand. In his right he clutched a cup of black coffee. He parked the Ford pool car behind two others just like it, as well as an ambulance, but no fire truck. He never understood why detectives had to drive separate pool cars to a crime scene. It would save gas if they met at the Seattle Police Department and drove together. And if they did, at least Rossi wouldn't always be the last to arrive.

He inhaled the aroma of his coffee, took a sip, and mentally prepared for what awaited him. He would never allow arriving at a suspected homicide to become routine. If it ever did, he'd retire, and at just thirty-eight, he hoped he had many more work years ahead.

He stepped from the car into an already warm June day. An older man and woman stood on the front walk to their home across the street. Rossi nodded, but they did not respond. Curiosity and concern brought them outside. Fear of becoming involved made them reticent to interact.

Rossi approached Chuck Pan, sergeant of the Violent Crimes Section's C Team, and Billy Ford, Rossi's partner. They talked in the driveway of a brick, two-story home with manicured landscaping. Behind them was a navy-blue Porsche Spyder. Nice car. Rare color. Pricey. Rossi knew cars. Rossi drove a 1969 Pontiac GTO. The first car he'd ever owned. During the past twenty years he'd restored it to immaculate condition.

Ford made a point of checking his wrist, though he didn't wear a watch. "Nice of you to join us," he said in his annoyingly cool, baritone voice that rolled like distant thunder. "Did you stop to get coffee for all of us?"

"You've been up for hours," Rossi said. "Both of you."

Pan woke Rossi with a 7:00 a.m. phone call, never a good thing when you and your partner are the detective team on call for the week. Rossi hadn't spoken to Ford yet this morning, but they'd been partners for several years. The man was also annoyingly disciplined. Ford started his day at 5:00 a.m. with a run—rain, sleet, even snow didn't stop him—a half-hour of meditation, and breakfast with his wife and their kids, whom he drove to school. He'd long been awake when Pan called.

Rossi was a night owl. Unmarried. No kids. Most evenings he didn't get to bed until midnight, usually unwinding with a good book. He crawled out of bed at eight, took a twenty-minute shower to wake, and grabbed a power bar for breakfast as he drove into the office, where he didn't speak until he'd had his first sip of coffee.

This morning, Pan had told Rossi a woman had made a 911 call of a dead body inside a home on Capitol Hill. The first responding officers reported the victim had been shot in the head. Red flags waved all around Rossi. A murder in an affluent neighborhood would bring out the press, the lookie-loos, and the brass, and each could be a major pain in an investigating detective's ass.

"Beat the ME," Rossi said to Pan and to Ford, not seeing the gray medical examiner's van. "And the MDOP." The King County prosecutor's office assigned a senior prosecutor from its Most Dangerous Offender Project to violent crimes. They believed the prosecutor's presence at the crime scene reduced detective mistakes that could handcuff the prosecutor at trial, as well as expedited things like search warrants. *If* you got the right prosecutor. Otherwise, they, too, could be a pain in Rossi's ass.

Rossi pointed to the Porsche with the vanity plate. EGREGUS. "Nice car," he said.

"Maybe for you," Ford said. "I see a backache waiting to happen." Ford stood six foot eight. "I bend down that far, I might not get back up again."

"That color's rare. You're looking at $170,000. And I might be a tad light."

"Spelled wrong." Ford pointed to the plate. "Should have an *I* and an *O* before the *U*."

"Leave it to you to look at a $170,000 automobile and only see the spelling mistake. Seven-letter limit."

"Let's get back to why we are all here." Pan looked and sounded annoyed. He wasn't. He knew Rossi and Ford's banter. He just needed to assert himself. Pan had short-man's complex. That, and his parents had named him Peter, a cruel fate for any kid to be linked to the iconic fictional character who wore tights. Rossi figured Pan grew up fighting. He now went by his middle name and shortened it to "Chuck" because it sounded badass. *Chuck Pan.*

Pan reiterated the basics. "Single victim. Male. Fifty-six years old. Shot in the back of the head in a room just off the kitchen. We can expect a crowd."

"Who made the 911 call?" Rossi asked.

"Adult daughter."

Thank God for small favors. At least it wasn't a child.

"Spouse?" Rossi asked. The spouse was always a suspect.

"Long divorced, according to the daughter. Ex lives in Southern California."

"Girlfriend?" Also always a suspect.

"Not at present."

"How long has it been since the divorce?"

"Daughter said it was 'complicated.'"

"What does that mean?" Rossi asked.

Pan's brow furrowed. "She said she'd explain it to us."

Rossi glanced at Ford. "Pretty ballsy. She in law enforcement or politics or something?"

"Lawyer."

Rossi looked again at the license plate. Definitely her car. "Anyone talk to the two people across the street looking over here but acting like they're not interested?" he said without pointing or nodding.

"Responding officers, but only briefly," Pan said. "They didn't see or hear anything. I'll get the next-up team to interview them and the other neighbors." They wanted to determine if anyone close by saw anything suspicious like an unfamiliar person or car in the area, or whether they heard a gunshot, what most civilians would equate to a car backfiring. They'd seek out any security camera footage as well.

Pan checked his watch. "I'm going back inside. I'll also call the ME and CSI and get an ETA. Billy will fill you in on the rest, what there is."

"The rest?" Rossi asked his partner.

"Media will be here," Pan said. "So do like Lady Gaga says and put on your poker faces." He marched through a door that led to a covered walkway between the garage and the house.

"Lady Gaga?" Rossi said to Ford.

"He's got a teenage daughter same age as my son," Ford said. "Though my son is into Kendrick Lamar."

"Never heard of him."

"We're not supposed to have heard of him. We're old."

Rossi looked again at the house and the car. "Who is this guy?"

"Victim? Sirus Kohl."

"Why do I know that name?"

"Most recently he was indicted by the US Attorney for wire fraud and conspiracy to commit wire fraud."

"Ponce de León . . ."

"Restorative Technology," Ford said. "PDRT."

"I would have got it . . . eventually," Rossi said. "The technology company in South Lake Union that went belly-up a couple years back."

"You got a mind like a steel trap."

"Am I wrong?" Rossi asked.

"Not wrong. Just incomplete. Five or six years ago, they tried the CEO, Jenna Bernstein, for the murder of the company's chief science officer, Erik Wei. He'd threatened to blow the whistle that the company was a sham, and got a bullet in the head."

"You looked that up on the internet before you got here," Rossi said.

Ford grinned. "Maybe."

"She got off," Rossi said, "that I remember. Patsy Duggan represented her. That was when he was still at his best."

"Bernstein testified," Ford said. "And made it appear Kohl had greater motivation to kill Wei."

"Reasonable doubt," Rossi said.

"Prosecution didn't see it coming," Ford said. "Bernstein and Kohl were supposed to be close. Lovers."

"That's the Irish Brawler," Rossi said, using Patsy Duggan's nickname. "You can fault his methods, but not his results."

"Maybe not you. You got a thing for the daughter."

"Keera?"

"'Keera?'" Ford imitated him. "You look as guilty as my son listening to inappropriate rap music in his room. Thought maybe something was there between you two . . . when she worked in the prosecutor's office. Thought maybe you rekindled that flame on the Vince LaRussa case."

"There was never a flame. And now she works for the opposing team, so . . ." Rossi changed the subject. "Let's get a couple more uniforms here, have them put up sawhorses at the cul-de-sac, keep the media and brass as far back as possible."

"Way ahead of you, partner. Backup should be here within five."

Rossi turned to the shrubbery behind the garage. "What's behind that wall?"

"Volunteer Park."

Ford reached into their go bag at his feet. He handed Rossi Tyvek shoe coverings and blue nitrile gloves and took a set for himself. After slipping them on, the detectives approached the uniformed officer holding the sign-in log and standing at the door in the covered walkway. Rossi signed his name and wrote his badge number. "You let the fire department trample my crime scene?" he asked.

"No need," the uniform said. "The guy was clearly dead. I told them to stand down, and they left."

"Good man. Pan said the daughter called it in. Where is she now?" If she was first on the scene, she was a suspect until they cleared her. Patricide involving a daughter killing her father was rare.

"Still inside."

"She live here?" Rossi asked.

"No," the officer said.

"Why is she here so early in the morning?"

"Said she and her father had a meeting to go over some legal matters. She called the house this morning to confirm, but the father didn't answer or respond to her text messages. Daughter said she worried something nefarious had happened to him."

"'Nefarious'? Too early to be throwing around four-syllable words," Rossi said, wondering why that would be the daughter's first thought.

"She's a lawyer," the uniform said.

"Heard that." Rossi glanced back at the Porsche. *Definitely hers.*

Rossi followed Ford into the house, checking the door and the jamb. No signs of a forced entry. They walked through a mudroom into what looked like a family room with an open-plan kitchen. Rossi made a mental note to have CSI check the appliances for fingerprints and the toilets for urine spatter. Killers had been known to use one or the other, sometimes both, before leaving a crime scene.

Pan stood in the family room alongside a second uniformed officer. Behind them hung a large flat-screen television and a picture window providing a view into the backyard. The air smelled stale, causing Rossi to glance at the appliances that shone as if never used. Rossi and Ford stepped around a high-backed couch. The victim's body lay facedown on a Persian throw rug alongside a glass coffee table. For reasons Rossi didn't understand, dead bodies seemed smaller. Sirus Kohl looked like a chubby young boy.

Rossi bent to a knee and got a strong metallic odor of blood. He visually scanned the damage to the back of the head where blood matted black-and-gray hair. His preliminary assessment was a 9-millimeter bullet. The size and pattern of blood spatter on the coffee table and the couch cushions indicated a shot delivered from a short distance, under ten feet.

Rossi stood as Ford introduced both of them to the uniform. Nick Price was a big dude with serious pipes stretching the fabric of his shirtsleeves. He appeared tough, and he was doing a good job acting unintimidated, but he also wasn't looking at the body. Dead bodies always unnerved—no matter how tough you were or how many you saw.

Price said he and his partner arrived at six thirty. "Daughter met us outside on the driveway and brought us inside—"

"Which door?"

Price pointed to the door Ford and Rossi had entered. "Back door. Once inside, we confirmed her father was dead."

"You have a look around the house?" Ford asked.

"Cleared it," Price said. "Empty. She said the victim lived alone."

"No signs of a forced entry anywhere else?" Rossi asked.

"Not that I saw and not that she reported."

"Nothing missing? Turned over?"

"No."

"Where is she now?" Rossi said looking about the room.

Price gestured. "In the office. Just off the foyer. She's working on something on the computer."

Rossi and Ford exchanged glances. Odd.

"I've asked for a couple of extra uniforms," Ford said. "Have them set up a perimeter at the entrance to the cul-de-sac."

"Roger that," Price said. He stepped outside, looking relieved.

Ford and Rossi walked through the kitchen to a white marbled foyer inside the front door. To Rossi's right, glass doors led into an office—parquet floor, dark leather furniture, bookshelves crowded with books, a large desk, a minibar, and another flat-screen television. A woman stood from the leather high-backed chair behind the desk. Rossi noted her business attire: navy-blue skirt and jacket, white shirt, pearls, black pumps. He estimated late thirties to early forties. Dark hair fell to her shoulders. She did not look to be wearing makeup, but she had what Rossi's mom would call "natural beauty." He guessed Middle Eastern descent.

"Are you the homicide detectives?" she asked before Rossi or Ford could introduce themselves or offer their condolences.

"Violent Crimes, yes." Rossi introduced them both. "You're the victim's daughter?"

"Sirus Kohl was my father. I'm Adria Kohl."

"We're very sorry for your loss." Rossi noted a sheet of paper on the desk. "Is that something you were working on?"

She looked back and picked it up. "A timeline of what happened this morning. So I wouldn't forget anything," she said.

Definitely a lawyer. Possibly in shock, or still processing what had occurred. Still odd. "We understand you're a lawyer?"

"That's right."

"Criminal law?"

"No. Business law and transactions."

Rossi nodded, then pointed to the sheet of paper. "Tell us what you recall?"

"I called my father at 6:10 this morning when he didn't respond to earlier text messages I had sent."

"You expected to hear from him?" Rossi asked.

"My father and I had an appointment at nine this morning. We had agreed to go over things before the meeting. He didn't answer his phone. I gave him some time, in case he was in the shower. I called again, and when he didn't answer a text, I decided to come over."

"You called his cell?" Rossi asked.

"He doesn't have a landline."

"Officer said you were worried about your father? Did he have health issues?" Rossi asked.

"No. Nothing like that. It was just . . . I don't know. Just a feeling."

"What kind of feeling?" Rossi asked.

"It wasn't like him not to answer his phone or respond to my text."

"How did you get in the house?"

"I have a key to the back door."

"What did you see when you entered?"

"I called out but didn't get a response. I went through the kitchen, then upstairs to his room. The bed was made. I should say, it didn't look slept in. The door to the master bath was open, but it didn't look like anyone took a recent shower. I came downstairs to see if his car was in the garage and saw his legs behind the sofa." She shook her head. "Then I saw the blood."

"Did you touch his body?"

"I don't know. The police officer asked me, but I don't recall." She paused to compose herself. Cleared her throat. Her voice quaked. "I called 911, and the dispatcher told me to step outside and stay on the line."

"Are you doing all right?" Rossi asked.

"No." She bristled and words shot from her. "I'm not doing all right."

"I meant, are you up to answering our questions?"

She looked between Ford and Rossi. "Sorry. Yes. I'd prefer to do it now while everything is fresh. That's why I made the list."

"The uniformed officer said you walked through the home. Did you notice any signs of a forced entry or robbery?"

"No. Nothing like that."

"Nothing out of the ordinary."

"I don't know 'ordinary.' This isn't my home or my father's home."

"What do you mean?"

"After PDRT went belly-up, and the US Attorney's indictment, I convinced my father it was best he rent, not knowing what was to happen."

"We understand your parents are divorced. Was it amicable?"

"Definitely not, but it was thirty years ago, and my mother lives in Palm Springs. The two haven't had contact since I graduated law school."

"Have you spoken to her?"

"Not yet."

"You said you and your father agreed to meet this morning before going to a business meeting. Can you elaborate?"

"My father was recently indicted by the US Attorney. He was once the COO and CFO of PDRT, Ponce de León Restorative Technology. I had arranged for him to meet the US attorney to discuss a plea agreement."

"What kind of plea agreement?" Rossi asked.

"My father had accumulated documentation to prove Jenna Bernstein, his business partner, played a much larger role in the company than she previously admitted."

"You mean when she testified at the Erik Wei trial?" Ford asked.

"That's correct. She made misrepresentations to investors about the LINK—the product PDRT was developing. She knew the LINK could not perform as she represented. At trial, she'd made it sound like my father withheld information from her, but it was the other way around. She made misrepresentations to potential investors and did not tell my father."

"What kind of evidence?" Rossi asked.

"Internal text messages and emails."

In Rossi's experience, probably neither person was telling the whole truth. But if Adria Kohl was telling them the truth, and if Jenna Bernstein had found out about Kohl's intent to meet the US Attorney and blame her, Bernstein had a serious motive to kill Sirus Kohl.

"Did anyone besides you and your father know about the meeting?"

"I don't know. I told my father not to say anything until we had an agreement in writing with the US Attorney. I don't know if he took my advice. Seems he didn't."

"What do you mean?"

She held up a cell phone. "This is my father's cell phone. You should know my father and Jenna Bernstein both used burner phones."

"Why is that?" Rossi asked.

"The LINK was a multibillion-dollar idea. PDRT took every precaution to prevent corporate espionage. Then, given what transpired at the trial, he and I agreed it would be best for him to continue using burner phones." She picked up her phone from the desk. "Here. This is the number he used to call me last night." She punched in a code, then scrolled to the last number called. "That's my cell phone. He called me last night at 9:17 p.m."

"And what was the purpose of that call?"

"To confirm the meeting this morning with the US Attorney, and that I would meet him here to go over things before that meeting."

"And you think he might have told someone, and that person killed him?" Rossi asked.

"See for yourself." She pulled up text messages on her father's phone. "These are the last text messages he sent before he called me."

Rossi read the string of text messages.

What goes around comes around.

What is that supposed to mean?

You shit on me in Wei's trial. Time to return the favor.

I don't know what you're talking about.

Yeah. You do.

I took my attorney's advice.

And I'll take mine.

Can we talk?

We'll see.

"My father purchased the phones from the Target store on University Way. He used a PDRT company credit card to make the purchases, and I kept a record of who got which phone. The second phone, the one responding to his text messages, was given to Jenna Bernstein."

"Why would he tell Jenna Bernstein what he intended to do if you told him not to?" Rossi asked.

"My father was bitter about what Jenna Bernstein intimated at the Erik Wei trial, that he had greater motivation to kill Erik. He felt she had betrayed him."

"Rumors are they were more than business partners; are those rumors true?" Ford asked.

"My father cared for Jenna, which is why he felt so betrayed."

Rossi pushed her. "And he was going to get even by providing evidence against her?"

She gave him a withering stare. "My father was a businessman. Meeting with the US Attorney was first and foremost a business deal. But he could also be vindictive." She shrugged. "Like all of us."

"Where are those documents he was going to give to the US Attorney?"

"I have them."

"We'll need copies of everything," Rossi said while Ford wrote a note. "And we're going to need your father's phone. We'll have a copy made of his emails, text messages, calls he made, and calls he received. Any other enemies who might have had a beef with your father?"

Adria Kohl scoffed. "Every person who invested in PDRT had a beef with my father, especially after Jenna Bernstein testified that it was my father who misled their investors and their board of directors. Half a dozen death threats were made against my father after the company imploded."

"Did your father report those threats to the police?"

"He reported them to the PDRT security team—Thomas Martin. I can provide a phone number."

Rossi nodded. "Do you know if there are any cameras on the property?"

"I believe there is a Ring camera on the front door. I don't know."

"What about computers?" Rossi asked.

"He had a laptop. Look, Detectives, I don't want to tell you how to do your job," Kohl said, which was usually how someone began a sentence when they were going to tell Rossi and Ford how to do their job. "But the person you need to talk to is Jenna Bernstein. She was looking at the possibility of going to jail for a very long time if my father had kept that appointment this morning." Her eyes shifted between Ford and Rossi as she spoke.

"We intend to speak with her," Rossi said.

"You let her get away with murder once," Kohl said. "Don't let her do so a second time."

Chapter 3

Keera bent over, hands on knees, breathing hard. She hated the start to a morning run, when her muscles remained tight and her motivation low, but she usually loved the finish. Her insides had warmed. Her muscles had relaxed, and she still felt that exhilarating runner's high.

Not this morning.

This morning, every step of the five-mile loop from her rented home in the North Beacon Hill neighborhood, around the periphery of Jefferson Park, and back had been a slog. In shape, she could finish the run in forty to forty-five minutes. She was not in shape. Trying back-to-back criminal cases had left little time for sleep, exercise, or much else. She'd run just a handful of times in the past three months.

She placed her hands behind her head, elbows wide, and sucked in deep breaths of morning air as she paced.

Her Apple Watch buzzed, again.

Call me. Now!

Her sister Maggie's third message. She'd previously sent:

Trying to reach you. Call me.

And:

Keera. Call Me!

Maggie served as Duggan & Associates' receptionist, paralegal, and alarmist. After Keera had obtained her second "not guilty" verdict, a four-week criminal trial against two doctors accused of drug trafficking in oxycodone and fentanyl, she was taking a much-needed vacation. She'd told Maggie she did not want to be disturbed, for any reason. She said Ella and Patsy could handle Keera's case files for a few days.

"Where are you going?" Maggie had asked.

"Nowhere. I'm tired, and I haven't exactly had time to plan a vacation. I'm staying home for a few days eating, sleeping, and exercising."

"A staycation?" Maggie said.

God, Keera hated that word. It sounded like a vacation for people too lazy to plan one—or unable to afford traveling. Unfortunately, both were partially accurate. She and Ella continued to rebuild Duggan & Associates' client list. And though her schedule didn't allow for it, she'd also been attending weekly AA meetings with Patsy, both to support him and to ensure he went. The family knew he would struggle to remain sober after a lifetime of binge drinking, and Patsy had already fallen off the wagon twice. Keera, on the other hand, hadn't had a drop of alcohol since she started attending the meetings, and she questioned whether she'd ever drink again. She didn't miss it, and she could think of no reason to throw gas on the genetic embers and possibly ignite a flame.

Her watch buzzed again.

Keera! Call me! Now!

Wow. Three exclamation points were a lot, even for Maggie.

Keera smiled at the thought of Maggie pounding the exclamation key on her keyboard until it broke. It would serve her right. Maybe she'd finally respect Keera's days off. Nothing else had worked. Maggie called Keera at all hours asking mundane questions easily answered—if

Maggie ever bothered to read the case file. She didn't. It was easier to annoy her baby sister. Doing it when Keera was on a "staycation" wasn't just laziness. It was a power play—a chance for Maggie to let Keera know she was ten years older.

Keera went inside the brick home and pulled open her refrigerator, then her freezer. She removed frozen strawberries, blueberries, a carrot, broccoli, peanut butter powder, and organic honey, blended the concoction, and shook half a dozen vitamins and amino acids from their bottles. In addition to cutting out the booze, she had cut out caffeine and promised to exercise more and eat better. She'd lost a little weight and physically and psychologically felt better, at least before she'd tried the back-to-back cases.

As she drank her concoction and popped her pills, her Apple Watch vibrated yet again. Her cell phone, which she'd left behind on her run, buzzed on the kitchen counter. If Keera didn't take the call, Maggie was liable to destroy the exclamation key on her keyboard.

She kept her voice upbeat and positive. "Hi, Maggie."

"Keera?" Maggie sounded momentarily surprised. Then she said, "Where have you been?"

"You mean while on vacation. After I left explicit instructions I was not to be bothered?"

"So, you did get my text messages!"

Keera imagined an exclamation mark at the end of that sentence. "Not to be bothered includes phone calls and text messages, Maggie. It means *do not bother*."

"Do you think I have nothing better to do than hunt you down for Patsy?"

Sometimes Keera wondered. She wasn't, however, surprised Maggie had invoked Patsy's name to justify her breach of instructions. "So, what exactly does Patsy want?"

"Did you read the morning *Times*?"

"Read as in print?" Keera didn't get a newspaper. If she wanted to read bad news, she read it on her phone. "Can't say I did."

"Patsy wants you to come in. Now."

Keera would not be easily swayed. "And what fire is burning, necessitating I interrupt my vacation and come into the office?"

"You didn't even go anywhere. You're at home. It's a staycation." Maggie drew out the word, presumably for emphasis.

"Next time my staycation will be without my cell phone or watch."

"PDRT is in the news again," Maggie said.

That got Keera's attention. She'd been a prosecuting attorney when Jenna Bernstein had been tried for the murder of Erik Wei. Patsy had defended Bernstein, who'd saved herself by sacrificing her company and her business partner, Sirus Kohl. The jury found Bernstein not guilty, but the strategy had also ended the multibillion-dollar company, and the billions of dollars Bernstein had been worth, at least on paper, had evaporated.

"I'm aware the US Attorney is going to try Jenna and Kohl for wire fraud and conspiracy."

"Then you don't know the half of it," Maggie spat.

Keera wanted to strangle her sister. Not only had she interrupted her stay . . . her time off . . . now she was withholding information. Another Maggie power play. "Fill me in, Maggie."

"I told you. Patsy wants you to come in, ASAP," she said and hung up.

❖ ❖ ❖

After a much quicker shower than she had planned, Keera pulled on jeans, her favorite kick-around sweater, which had frayed in all the right places, a black knit hat Ella said made her look like a thug, and forsook makeup. She didn't plan to stay at the office long.

She hit traffic, because Seattle always had traffic these days, but eventually she made it downtown to the three-story brick building in Pioneer Square. She walked past the lunch crowd seated on the Paddy

Wagon's patio. Liam, Keera's Irish suitor, waited several tables, too busy to notice her.

Inside the building owned by her father, Keera rode the cage elevator to the top floor and stepped out. Maggie sat at her desk, the firm sentry. She rolled her eyes and shook her head. "Is that what you're wearing?"

"I don't plan on staying."

"They're in the conference room," she said dismissively.

"They? Who is they?" she asked.

"Keera?" Patsy had leaned out the door to the room behind reception. He wore one of the suits and ties he kept in his office for court appearances and important client meetings. He clearly wasn't in court, so . . . But the blinds were lowered and drawn, preventing Keera from seeing who else was in the room.

Patsy stepped out, closing the door behind him. "Do you have a suit in your office?"

After her last trial Keera took her suits home to be dry-cleaned, thinking she wouldn't need one until at least the beginning of next week. "No. Why? Who's in there?"

"Never mind," he said, shaking his head. "Just get in here."

Patsy opened the door. Keera followed him inside but stopped short.

Jenna Bernstein sat beside her father, John, at the conference room table. Keera hadn't spoken to Jenna in years, and she hadn't seen her since Keera snuck into the back of a King County courtroom to hear the jury find Jenna not guilty of the murder of Erik Wei.

Chapter 4

Five years ago
Seattle, Washington

Keera slid into the back of Judge Harold Lubbock's courtroom after lunch, when the rumors began circulating in the prosecutor's office that Patsy was going to put Jenna Bernstein, defendant in the Erik Wei murder trial, on the witness stand. Walker Thompson, the state prosecutor, did not believe the rumor, calling it another Patsy ploy to distract and deflect. Keera agreed. Patsy knew better than to throw away a defendant's Fifth Amendment right not to testify, especially when the evidence against that defendant was circumstantial. The prosecution could not produce a witness to the shooting of Erik Wei, and they hadn't found the murder weapon, a 9-millimeter handgun, though they had established Jenna had at one time owned such a gun.

Others in the prosecutor's office reasoned Thompson, who had lobbied the PA for a shot at the famed Irish Brawler, had forced Patsy's hand—that putting the defendant on the witness stand would be a desperate act by a desperate man.

But Keera also knew underestimating Patsy was never a good idea.

Patsy tried cases the way he played chess, the way he'd taught Keera to play chess—methodical, calculated, and lethal. He *never* acted out of desperation, and he frequently made moves his opponents never anticipated.

Checkmate.

Game over.

Keera stepped to the last pew in the packed courtroom and took a seat. Moments later, Patsy entered with Mr. and Mrs. Bernstein, who moved behind the railing to the first pew but remained standing, talking with Patsy. Keera hadn't seen them in a decade or more. They'd aged. Everyone had.

The marshals brought Jenna in a side door. She wore a conservative, dark-blue skirt and matching blazer, but Keera couldn't help but see the young girl she'd gone to grade school with. Like everyone in Puget Sound, Keera had heard and read about the wonder kid who founded PDRT upon graduating college. The start-up had put Jenna on the cover of every local and national business magazine, made her a household name, and a billionaire on paper.

Until it all came crashing down amid allegations of fraud, conspiracy, and murder.

PDRT's fall from grace shocked the Lake Union biotech community to its core.

But not Keera. She had not been surprised.

Jenna joined Patsy and her parents, talking quietly, though Keera sensed an urgency in her father's facial expressions and body posture. Patsy did not look like the portrait of poise he normally was in a courtroom. Several times he shook his head. When he did, Jenna seemed to grow more animated. Patsy looked from Jenna to her parents and eventually gave a small, resigned shrug. Keera doubted anyone else in the courtroom saw it.

Judge Lubbock entered and called the court to order, then took care of housekeeping matters before instructing the bailiff to retrieve the jury. Once the jurors had settled, Lubbock addressed Patsy. "Does the defense wish to call any other witnesses?"

Patsy pushed back his chair, but he did not eagerly stand. This was a slow rise. "The defense does, Your Honor. The defense calls Jenna Bernstein to the witness stand."

Judge Lubbock looked up as if he'd misheard Patsy. Walker Thompson looked sucker punched, sitting at the State's counsel table. Murmurs ran through the gallery, and the jurors looked intrigued, even excited, at this unexpected development.

Jenna Bernstein rose when the bailiff called her name and walked to the witness stand looking poised and unconcerned. She raised her right hand and swore to tell the truth, the whole truth, and nothing but the truth, so help her God.

Keera doubted it.

Patsy quickly established Jenna's background, her education at the University of Washington, and her motivation for starting PDRT. It was the same story she told in the dozens of magazine articles written about her. An uncle had died from complications caused by Parkinson's disease. An aunt had developed Alzheimer's in her late fifties and spent thirty years in a memory-care clinic.

Patsy stepped forward. "Was there something else that also made PDRT so personal for you?"

"My mother." Jenna let out a held breath. Was this an act? It looked sincere . . . If you didn't know her. "My mother has developed a tremor in her hand."

The room became very still. "And did she receive a diagnosis?"

"She has Parkinson's disease."

Keera's eyes shifted to Mrs. Bernstein, seated in the front pew with her head down, weeping. John Bernstein put his arm around his wife's shoulders, consoling her. Keera wasn't buying the tableau, not entirely.

"If I rushed the LINK to market, in any way," Jenna said, "it was because I wanted to help my mother. I believe necessity is the mother of invention, and we needed a better way to treat these diseases and prolong quality of life."

Jenna testified that she studied medical laboratory science and pathology. She said she'd had plans to go to medical school and become a pathologist, calling it the bridge between science and disease.

"Then I read about tissue nanotransfection, and I realized if it could be successfully used in humans, it would revolutionize the medical industry and cure many of mankind's worst diseases. It could have saved my uncle and my aunt."

Patsy smiled. "The Fountain of Youth?"

Jenna returned his smile. "That was something the media imposed on PDRT, not something we promoted."

But not something PDRT refuted either.

The possibility of regenerating organs using new cells and prolonging life spans attracted investors along with a much-needed infusion of cash for the start-up. Who didn't want to live a long and healthy life?

Jenna testified she believed the formation of a company with top researchers to be the best avenue to getting TNT to the commercial market. She discussed finding investors for the capital needed to hire people knowledgeable in tissue nanotransfection, as well as those who could build a device to adapt TNT for human application.

"How would it work?" Patsy asked.

"In simplistic terms, the device, no bigger than a cuff link, is attached to the arm and allows genetic material to be delivered directly into skin cells through an electric charge. The charge creates pores in the skin cell membrane through which a specially designed DNA plasmid is delivered to reprogram the cells to perform a specific function, like delivering dopamine to Parkinson's patients, memory cells to Alzheimer's patients, and immunotherapy to cancer patients. It would virtually cure heart disease," she said.

Walker Thompson stood, and Keera wondered what had taken him so long. "This is all very interesting, Your Honor, but it's irrelevant. This is a murder trial. And I will add that before he died, PDRT's chief scientist, Erik Wei, met Ms. Bernstein to advise the LINK could not perform any of these pie-in-the-sky dreams."

"Counsel, I caution you to make objections and avoid the soliloquy, please," Lubbock said to Thompson. Then he directed his attention to

Patsy. "Mr. Duggan, counsel's objection is sustained. Let's wrap this up and get back to the point."

"The defense fully intends to do so, Your Honor."

But Patsy did not wrap it up quickly. He asked Jenna about the financing needed by PDRT to entice the best scientists, including Wei. Jenna talked about initially getting money from family friends and acquaintances, but when that wasn't going to be enough, she courted investors, including Sirus Kohl, and they agreed on $150 million for 48 percent of PDRT, with Kohl serving as CFO and COO.

"Is it fair to say Mr. Kohl became the science/product development person, and you were the money person?"

"That's fair to say, yes. My day-to-day responsibilities were to raise money to fund the research needed to develop the LINK and ultimately bring it to market."

"Did you accomplish that goal?"

"I thought we were getting close to achieving a commercial product ready for testing on humans."

"Was that not the case?"

"I was told it was not."

"Told by whom?"

"Erik Wei."

"Can you explain?"

Jenna told the jury of working at the office late and receiving a text from Wei, as Patsy put the text message back on the computer screen. In it, Wei said the LINK could not perform many of the functions currently being represented. Jenna testified she met Wei at a restaurant and was greatly concerned by what he had to say.

Patsy replayed videos from cameras located inside the restaurant. "Counsel for the State intimated your hand gestures and facial expressions indicate your conversation was 'animated.'"

"I *was* animated."

"Were you upset?"

"I was."

"At Erik Wei?"

"No. He was just the messenger."

"Who then?"

Keera leaned forward, realizing what Jenna was about to do. Walker Thompson looked like he was going to stand and object, but he didn't. He hadn't anticipated what was to come. He should have, but he hadn't. His failure to anticipate and to prepare would be his downfall.

"Jenna, you said you were livid. At whom?" Patsy asked.

"Sirus Kohl."

Sirus Kohl was not in the courtroom during the trial of his former business partner and lover.

"Why Sirus Kohl?" Patsy asked.

"Because what Erik Wei told me I was hearing for the first time."

Patsy made a face and took a step back, as if the Brawler had absorbed a blow, all part of the façade Patsy was so good at creating. He sounded incredulous, distrusting, and sought an explanation. "But you were the CEO. You were the person in charge. Are you telling this court no one had brought to your attention the LINK's failings?"

"Not to this degree; no."

"Can you explain to the jury how that could be possible?"

Jenna turned and faced the jurors. "In a technology company, a start-up, it is not uncommon for the founder's aspirations to exceed the technology's capabilities, at least at the company's formation. The founder's aspirations drive the innovations."

"Was PDRT's idea based on any scientific fact?"

"Absolutely. Researchers have been using tissue nanotransfection, TNT, in mice and have successfully reprogrammed cells to heal chronic wounds. The idea is exciting, but it needs private investment money for more research and to conduct human clinical trials. In the private sector we have to sell the idea to take TNT across the finish line."

"And that's where you come in?"

"I was the company face. The LINK, the idea, was my baby. But I was also young, and a woman. I wasn't a scientist. I had no experience in biomedical engineering or nanotechnology. I was just the person with the dream, the idea. I needed someone experienced in these scientific fields, as well as investment money. Someone who had clout to convince investors PDRT and the LINK had real potential, and who could, at the same time, take the proper precautions to protect the idea and keep others from stealing it. Sirus had been educated in biomedical engineering. He had invested in start-ups that had become commercially successful. He had money to invest. More importantly, he believed dreams and ideas could become reality."

Patsy gestured to the jurors. "Which meant what?"

"Sirus agreed to train me, transform me into a confident, competent, and capable chief executive officer."

"How?"

"We were together twenty-four seven. Working dinners, mostly in the office, sometimes out at restaurants. Sirus soon dictated just about everything I did from the moment I awoke in the morning. My workout schedule. What I ate. What I wore. My makeup. My hairstyle. My investment pitch. He had everything printed out. He said it was needed to convince investors to invest their millions in PDRT. I welcomed the tutelage. I wanted to succeed. I wanted PDRT to succeed. So much was riding on it succeeding."

"At some point did Sirus's instruction become overbearing?"

Another pause. Jenna blew out a burst of air. "Sirus asked me to move in. He said we didn't have enough hours in the day to do everything that needed to be done. At the time it seemed like the right thing to do. I'd have my own bedroom, bathroom, and office. We could commute to and from work together and discuss the day's strategy."

"At some point did things change?"

Jenna lowered her gaze to her hands. Tears trickled down her cheeks. Honest-to-God beads of water. "Yes. We became lovers."

"You did this willingly?"

"I thought I did. I mean . . . he never physically forced himself on me. We were working so many hours, I didn't have time for a relationship outside the office, and Sirus had said such a relationship could jeopardize the company."

"So, he dictated your love life as well?"

"In a sense I guess he did."

"Did your relationship change?"

"His prodding became more intense. If I overslept and missed my workout, he chastised me as lazy and called me fat. He would tell me I wore too much makeup. He would pull food away from me and tell me I had enough."

Walker Thompson stood yet again, his interruption like someone walking into a bedroom at an intimate moment. The jurors frowned. "Objection, Your Honor. Again, I fail to see the relevance in any of this."

But Keera did see the relevance. She had a good idea where Patsy was going. It was brilliant. It was Patsy thinking outside the legal box to implode Walker Thompson's case. Unorthodox and highly unusual, but brilliant. Patsy was laying the groundwork, Keera assumed, to have a mitigation specialist testify that Sirus Kohl, significantly older and experienced in business, had psychologically preyed on Jenna and PDRT, that he had targeted the company and had led Jenna into a personal relationship to control her. In chess terms, Patsy would argue Kohl made Jenna his pawn. In legal terms, it was called the "Svengali defense." It had saved the life of Lee Boyd Malvo—whose attorney argued Malvo had been under the control of John Muhammad in the 2002 DC sniper shootings. It also saved the life of Dzhokhar Tsarnaev, brother of Tamerlan Tsarnaev, responsible for the Boston Marathon bombings. But in both cases the defense was made during each trial's *penalty* phase, after both men had been convicted. Patsy was using it to explain to the jury how Jenna, the CEO, could not have known the LINK was unable to do what she was representing to investors—because Kohl had completely isolated her and compartmentalized the information she received, which was only through him.

Keera wanted to step forward and tell Thompson what was happening, but she couldn't.

She couldn't bring herself to do that to her father.

Judge Lubbock fixed his gaze on Patsy the way a person might stare at an impressionist painting, recognizing, if not understanding, the artist's brilliance. "Overruled. You may continue, Counsel."

"Jenna," Patsy said. "Did PDRT's investors or board of directors know of your and Sirus's relationship?"

"I don't believe so. The board would have considered it unprofessional and harmful to the company's overall reputation and credibility."

Jenna explained that if she and Kohl had a bitter split, it could create a toxic work environment, a conflict of interest, and influence their professional judgment and decision-making, compromising fairness and objectivity. As CEO and COO, she and Sirus had a fiduciary obligation to act in the best interests of the board members and investors.

"So . . . Jenna, knowing all of this . . . the potential impact to a company you started, your dream, why would you enter into that relationship?"

Thompson again stood and made the same objection, and this time Patsy used it against him to make a point. Patsy stepped forward and spoke as if perplexed by the objection. "Your Honor, this line of inquiry will prove to the jurors why my client did not know the LINK could not do the things she was representing, and therefore she had no animus to kill Erik Wei."

"Your Honor, she clearly has testified what Erik Wei told her that evening, that the LINK could not do the things she was representing, which the State contends is all the animus she needed to kill him."

"Both of you can refrain from giving your closing arguments," Judge Lubbock said. "Mr. Duggan, this has gotten far afield in the liability phase."

"Then I will pull it back into the infield, Your Honor."

"Do so," Lubbock said. "Or I will cut you off."

Patsy returned to Jenna Bernstein. "How is it the CEO of a start-up was not privy to Erik Wei's concerns prior to the evening you and he met at the restaurant?"

Here we go, Keera thought.

"All employee emails and text messages were on a private company server monitored by Sirus. Employees were repeatedly told all emails and text messages were to go through him. Sirus told me this was to prevent employees from disclosing company trade secrets or other corporate espionage. Sirus controlled the flow of information."

"But, as counsel for the State has just pointed out, you did meet Erik Wei, and he told you the LINK was nowhere near human trials or ready for regulatory review."

Jenna explained she was in the process of securing additional financing and Wei's threat would have killed her efforts. Patsy played the video from inside the restaurant. In it, Jenna abruptly pushed back her chair, nearly toppling it, and departed.

"You left in a hurry," Patsy said in his understated, deadpan demeanor that caused many in the courtroom to smile, including the jurors. "Where did you go?"

"I went to confront Sirus about what Erik had told me."

"Was Sirus upset?"

"Very."

"Who invested the most money in PDRT?" Patsy asked. "Who had the most to lose?"

Jenna sat forward, with a look like she had just realized the purpose of Patsy's questions, but it was an act. She'd known the purpose all along.

"Sirus Kohl," she said.

Chapter 5

Jenna and John Bernstein sat across the conference room table from Ella, who gave Keera a look, the way a mother might disapprove of her daughter's date attire. Keera wasn't thrilled with her choices either, not with Jenna dressed in an expensive, royal-blue, St. John pantsuit, pearls draping her neck and earlobes. Keera had worn casual clothes to spite Maggie, but the joke was on her.

"Mr. Bernstein. Jenna," Keera said, trying to sound pleasant and unconcerned. She'd followed Jenna's career from afar, curious but never convinced. More than once, a spark of jealousy hit her, but each time it did, so did a spark of doubt. She kept thinking it was all too good to be true, as it always had been with Jenna. Turned out PDRT was much, much more than too good to be true. Jenna's trial for the murder of Erik Wei had revealed the mammoth fraud PDRT perpetrated on investors and on the general public; a fraud Erik Wei had been prepared to expose, until someone shot him. Most in the prosecutor's office, including Keera, believed Jenna got away with murder.

After hanging up the phone with Maggie, Keera had run a search on Jenna Bernstein and Sirus Kohl on her laptop and learned that Kohl had been shot in his home on Capitol Hill. The article didn't say Jenna was a suspect, but clearly she was. The significant other was always a suspect, and the previous trial had revealed Jenna and Sirus Kohl to have been more than business partners.

And why else would Jenna be here, in her defense attorney's offices?

Mr. Bernstein came around the conference room table in slacks, a sport coat, and an open-collar shirt. Jenna's height came from her father, who was at least six four, but now showed the rolls of middle age. "I think we can do away with 'Mr. Bernstein,' Keera." He bent to give her a hug. "You're not a young girl anymore. Call me 'John.'"

Jenna followed her father. She, too, bent down, but unlike her father, she did so as if it took great effort to lower herself to Keera's level. The two exchanged an uncomfortable hug.

In school, Jenna had used her height and figure to intimidate or to entice. Her blonde hair, blue eyes, and curves turned heads everywhere she went. Men assumed she was older than her actual age, a notion she did not try to dissuade when it was to her advantage. It usually was. Jenna and Keera had competed for top grades to be their high school class valedictorian, an honor bestowed on Jenna after Keera received a B+ and Jenna an A in AP Calculus. Some said Jenna had cheated off Christy Johnson, who went on to MIT the following year, but like the murder of Erik Wei, the rumor could not be proven.

"How are you?" Jenna asked, sounding as if she hadn't a care in the world. "I heard you worked for Patsy now. We read about the Vince LaRussa trial. Horrible it turned out so poorly."

A backhanded acknowledgment—never a compliment—and a subtle dig. Not that Jenna's assessment wasn't accurate, given what transpired following the LaRussa not guilty verdict.

"Why don't we all sit down," Patsy said. He pulled out the chair at the head of the table. Keera shifted over and took the seat. Patsy hesitated before moving to sit beside Ella. Jenna and John Bernstein returned to their seats. Behind them, the western-facing conference room windows provided a view of Elliott Bay and the V-shaped wakes left by ferries and pleasure boats. Framing the vista were the snow-covered Olympic Mountains.

"This is a nightmare, Patsy. It's déjà vu," John said, wasting no time. Unlike Jenna, he looked harried and sounded upset. Sitting through the criminal trial of his daughter accused of murder had taken a toll. In addition to the extra weight, his hair had thinned and turned white. Worry lines etched the corners of his eyes and mouth. Now Jenna faced federal charges by the US Attorney for fraud and conspiracy, a white-collar crime not within Patsy's or Keera's expertise. Something else was going on, and Keera suspected that "something" had to do with Sirus Kohl's death.

Keera looked at Patsy's hands. He'd developed a tremor since giving up drinking, and now he often kept his hands folded in his lap. "What's going on?" she asked.

Jenna answered. "The police came to my condominium today."

"Why?" she asked. She wanted to hear from Jenna what had happened.

Jenna arched her eyebrows. "You haven't read the paper or heard the news this morning?"

"I was just about to leave on vacation," Keera said, not wanting to admit she was staying home. "So . . ."

"Sirus Kohl was shot to death in the house he rented on Capitol Hill," Ella said.

"The police came and asked me questions," Jenna said. She didn't look or sound concerned or upset.

"What questions?" Keera asked.

"Where was I last night *and* early this morning? Could anyone vouch for my whereabouts? Did I own a gun?"

"You didn't respond," Keera said.

Jenna shook her head. "The only thing I said was 'If you have questions, speak to my attorney.' I gave them Patsy's name. Then I called—"

Keera raised her hand and cut Jenna off. "Don't say another word."

Together, Jenna and John Bernstein said, "What? Why?"

Ella lowered the pen she'd been using to take notes.

"If the police consider you a suspect in Sirus Kohl's death, and they wouldn't be asking you questions if they didn't, then you are here for our professional help—"

"I don't know if—" Jenna said.

"It hasn't gotten that far," John said.

"It doesn't matter. If Jenna is here now for our professional advice, then I'm going to have to ask you to leave the room, Mr. Bernstein."

"What?" Jenna and her father said again in unison.

"You can't be in here. Jenna's an adult, and the attorney-client privilege does not extend to a parent. If you remain in the room, anything Jenna says to us will be discoverable by the State, should there be any further court proceedings."

"She's right," Ella said to Patsy. She looked chagrined she hadn't considered the issue.

John Bernstein also directed his attention to Patsy, who appeared embarrassed. "Patsy, we can work around this; can't we? If it ever gets that far. I mean, I'd just say I wasn't in the room."

"No," Keera said, retaking control. "That would be a lie. Under oath it would be perjury. Patsy and I would be ethically obligated to prevent you from saying that."

"This is ridiculous," John said, again looking to Patsy.

"It's not, John," Patsy said.

Jenna's gaze remained fixed on Keera. She looked as though she was searching for a solution to the problem, a way to one-up Keera.

Not this time.

Jenna smiled faintly and gently touched her father's arm. "It's okay, Dad." John turned to his daughter. "Keera is an attorney, and if she says that's the law, then we have to abide by it. She's only trying to be of help."

John looked again to Patsy, who said, "I'll have Maggie take you down to the Paddy Wagon. You can have a cup of coffee and something to eat."

"I'll leave," John Bernstein said, getting to his feet, "but I won't eat." He walked around the table. "They can't stop Jenna from telling me everything discussed once we leave; can they?" His rhetorical question made him sound like a petulant child.

"That's up to you and Jenna," Keera said. "But if she does, neither of you should tell us. We also have an obligation not to allow Jenna to perjure herself, if she's ever asked under oath if she revealed our advice to anyone."

Again, Jenna gave Keera a glacial stare.

Patsy escorted John Bernstein to the door. "Come on, John, Maggie will take good care of you."

Ella closed her notebook. "And I've got calls to make and other matters to attend. Now that Keera is here, you're in good hands."

The two men and Ella left the room, leaving Jenna and Keera alone, as when they were children. With Jenna being an only child, and Keera's siblings out of the house before Keera hit double digits, the two had seemed a perfect fit to be friends, then Jenna shattered that illusion.

Now, the two women forced smiles across the table, but Keera knew Jenna wasn't happy. This conference room, and the law, were Keera's domain. The wonder kid who was going to change the world did not control this situation, as she had always sought to do when the two were younger.

And not being in control had always bothered Jenna.

"It's been a long time," Jenna said.

"Since the winter of our freshmen year in college, I think. When we went skiing," Keera said. It was intended as a piercing comment, but if the arrow struck, Jenna didn't flinch.

"No. I saw you in the courtroom during my trial," Jenna countered.

Keera knew Jenna had seen her, though she'd never acknowledged Keera's presence. "As a prosecutor I was prohibited from interacting with you—or Patsy for that matter."

"I forgot you were a prosecutor," Jenna said, then revealed she hadn't. "You had a relationship, I believe, with someone in the office, an older man?"

Keera had no idea how Jenna knew of her failed relationship with Miller Ambrose that led to her exit from the prosecutor's office, but she had always been adept at finding out and using a person's vulnerable information.

"I was so grateful to Patsy for everything he did for me in the Erik Wei trial. He was magnificent," Jenna said.

"*Is* magnificent."

"Of course."

"Did you get the detectives' names who came to speak to you?" Keera asked.

"I have their cards." Jenna removed two cards from a small purse, placed them faceup on the table, and slid them to Keera.

Billy Ford and Ian Bressler.

"Do you know them?" Jenna asked.

Keera nodded. "They're good detectives." But that wasn't her first thought. Her first thought was that Billy Ford was Frank Rossi's partner. Or had been. She wondered what was up.

"Honest?"

"I don't follow."

"If they learn a suspect is innocent, will they go away, or persist like the two detectives in the Erik Wei matter?"

"They're honest . . . if they're certain the person is innocent."

The conference room door opened. Patsy smiled as he entered, but it was forced. "Well, he isn't happy, but I think I got him settled down."

"Thank you, Patsy. I know my father will take your counsel," Jenna said.

Never subtle.

"Has Jenna filled you in on the morning's events?" Patsy asked, retaking his seat.

"Not yet," Keera said. "But before you do, Jenna, is it your intention to retain Duggan & Associates to assist you in this matter, should it go further?"

"Yes, of course." She turned to Patsy. "I want you to represent me, if it comes to that."

Patsy shook his head. "My days as lead trial attorney are behind me, Jenna. Keera handles our trials now. I sit second chair when asked."

"I feel comfortable with you, Patsy. Keera doesn't have your . . . experience." She looked at Keera. "No offense."

"None taken," Keera said, and she meant it. Few attorneys had her father's trial experience or his skill. Certainly not her. Not yet. Patsy had defended hundreds of clients in trial and counseled hundreds more. His well-earned nickname, the "Irish Brawler," signified his bare-knuckles trial style. Keera had gained a similar reputation playing in dozens of chess tournaments. An opponent could anticipate and prepare, but preparation went out the door after the first move. After that, you had to adjust, grind, and scrap, or you'd find your king toppled. She tried cases the same way.

"Keera has skills I no longer possess," Patsy said. "And she's a woman, which I think will play well to a jury, again should the matter ever get that far. Let's hope it doesn't."

"From your lips to God's ears, though I haven't been very lucky lately. I would like your word you will be involved," Jenna said.

Jenna was no longer stroking Patsy's ego. She was placating her own. She always sought a concession, no matter how minor, a victory to which she could cling.

Patsy obliged her. "I'll be involved."

Jenna's glare found Keera. "And I want your assurance, if this goes forward and if I'm charged, you will do what is necessary to get me off."

Keera thought it interesting Jenna talked as if she would be charged. "The best trial attorney in the world won't guarantee they will get a client off. Especially if the client is guilty."

"Tell that to O. J. Simpson," Jenna said, the corners of her mouth lifting.

"Are you O. J. Simpson, Jenna?" Keera asked, matter-of-fact.

"Keera," Patsy said.

Jenna put up a hand. "No. It's all right." She smiled as if unbothered. She was. "To answer your question, Keera, no. I'm not O. J. Simpson. I didn't kill Erik Wei, and I didn't kill Sirus Kohl, but somebody wanted me convicted for killing Erik, and having failed, they have killed Sirus. I'm aware the spouse, the girlfriend, or the ex-girlfriend is always a suspect."

"Prime suspect," Keera said.

"Prime suspect."

"Then, *if* this goes further, I will make every effort to ensure you are not *wrongly* convicted," Keera said.

The two women stared across the table at one another in an uneasy truce. Jenna blinked first. "I guess I'll have to take you at your word."

"That makes two of us," Keera said, except Jenna's word could never be trusted.

Chapter 6

Rossi stepped into the covered walkway between the house and the garage and sucked in a breath of fresh, though warm, air. He had talked through the progression of his investigation as lead detective with the CSI sergeant and explained what he wanted the CSI detectives and videographer to do inside the house. CSI would use total station survey equipment to create a crime scene diagram to scale. Arthur Litchfield, the medical examiner, had also arrived and now had control over Kohl's body. The latent fingerprint and DNA experts were in a holding pattern.

At every homicide scene he had worked, Rossi took a moment to step away and remember that the victim had been a living, breathing human being, not just the lifeless piece of evidence on the floor, and that someone had deliberately and, given the gunshot wound's location, cowardly taken that life.

Rossi also took time to consider the laminated card he and Ford kept in their go bag. The card itemized a checklist of tasks to be performed to thoroughly process each crime scene. He didn't want to overlook anything. "Routine" did not exist when it came to murder; each case had to be processed individually or you'd miss something, possibly screw up the prosecution, and find yourself back working patrol.

Ford stepped outside and approached Rossi. He held a laptop computer in his large hands. "I'd swear you were a closet smoker the way you disappear."

"Just thinking about what you said about Jenna Bernstein," Rossi said.

"Calculating?" Ford replied. He could size up a person in a word or two and was usually spot-on. Ford's other superpower was his ability to play almost any musical instrument and any song, without sheet music. If Ford heard a song once, he could play it. "Didn't shed a tear when we told her the news. Eyes didn't even water. She and Kohl worked together eight or ten years; didn't they?"

"Lived together as well, according to the daughter," Rossi said. "I thought you might say 'cold.'"

"Might have, but almost as quick as I got out my first question, Bernstein said she had nothing to say, and we could talk to her attorney, Patsy Duggan."

"She has been down this road before," Rossi said.

"I'd say that road is well traveled," Ford agreed.

"Is that the search warrant?" Rossi nodded to the computer.

"First pass," Ford said, handing it to Rossi.

After the CSI team and their sergeant had arrived, Rossi sent Ford and Ian Bressler, one of the two next-up detectives, to talk to Bernstein before news of Kohl's murder broke. Bernstein lived just ten minutes away in a condominium complex on Lower Queen Anne. Upon his return, Ford had told Rossi the building had a security guard on duty, and he had noticed security cameras in the lobby, in the elevators, and on Jenna Bernstein's floor. Ford had asked the guard for the security footage from last night and early this morning, but the guard got nervous about violating the tenants' rights. Ford told the guard to secure the video and ensure it did not get erased or recorded over, that he'd be back with a search warrant signed by a superior court judge. The guard provided Ford with a company business card.

"Looks good to me. Let's run it by the MDOP when he or she gets here," Rossi said, handing back the computer. "What did you think of the daughter?"

Adria Kohl had reluctantly departed after Rossi had told her the police would control the house for at least another day, and that he would contact her to get back into the residence to retrieve her father's belongings.

Ford mulled the question over a bit, then said, "Vindictive. She's definitely out for blood."

Rossi smiled. "You're good."

"I know."

Rossi had no superpowers, though Ford did say Rossi had "grim persistence." Seemed appropriate for a homicide detective, but more a necessity than a superpower. He was like a machete, hacking at the thick jungle vines in search of a beam of light. It wasn't going to get him laid, as his buddies liked to say, but it had always got the job done. "Not sure she was more angry her father had been murdered or that Bernstein had walked on Erik Wei's murder," Rossi said.

"She clearly thinks Bernstein is guilty on both accounts," Ford agreed.

"Let's follow up on her," Rossi said. "Just to be sure."

"Her father was a wealthy man," Ford suggested.

"Maybe," Rossi said. "But I'm assuming he invested heavily in PDRT and lost most of it when the company went tits up." Rossi came from a family of accountants and had majored in accounting in school. He had decided he didn't want to sit at a desk in an office crunching numbers all day, but numbers remained his thing. Not a superpower. Not by any means, but better than most. "Let's find out." He made a note in his spiral notebook.

Footsteps drew their attention. Rossi had the word on the tip of his tongue, but Ford beat him to the punch. "Ironic."

"Walker Thompson," Rossi said, as if having a hard time believing the prosecutor had been assigned to this investigation, given what had happened in Wei. Then again, Thompson might have asked for the assignment.

Ford's word for Thompson was "Cowboy," but that was just too easy. Thompson lumbered up the driveway in the same rolling gait John Wayne had made famous. He was also tall, favored jeans and boots and long-sleeve, button-down shirts, and had a rugged, outdoor complexion.

Thompson motioned to the street corner where a crowd that included reporters had gathered behind sawhorses. "So much for working in anonymity." He even had a twinge of a Texas drawl, though he'd been born and raised in San Francisco.

"Didn't take the media long to put it all together; did it?" Ford said.

"No, it did not." Thompson spoke from authority. Patsy Duggan had made the Jenna Bernstein trial a circus. Knowing the media would be intrigued by the young, driven entrepreneur's fall from grace, Duggan had embraced and welcomed the attention, and he'd said the PA had picked the low-hanging fruit and rushed to trial without evidence. He cited the lack of an eyewitness and of a murder weapon and said the State's case was all circumstantial evidence. He even changed Jenna's wardrobe from her traditional, dark-colored pantsuits to light-colored dresses that softened her appearance and made her look like a young housewife. The press and the public ate it up. Spectators had packed the courtroom and the overflow courtroom broadcasting the proceedings to watch the slugfest. When the jury found Bernstein not guilty, there were as many shouts of outrage and disbelief as there were of amazement and wonder.

The more recent US Attorney's indictment had again put Kohl and Bernstein back in the judicial crosshairs, but not like this investigation threatened to do—murder always trumped business shenanigans.

"Street cameras?" Thompson asked.

"Next-up team is working it," Rossi said.

"Who's the ME?"

"Litchfield," Rossi said. "Initial cause of death is single gunshot wound fired from a distance of four to ten feet. Likely a 9-millimeter slug. No evidence of a struggle. No abrasions or bruising on his hands or arms."

"He wasn't trying to get away," Thompson said.

"More likely he turned his back, and the assailant shot him," Rossi said. "The killer didn't want to look him in the face." He thought again of the daughter. "Seems consistent with the lack of any evidence of a forced entry."

"The killer let himself in, or Kohl let him in. Same as Erik Wei; isn't it?" Ford asked.

"Same," Thompson said softly, as if recalling a bad memory that he had tried to forget. "Including the caliber of the weapon . . . if Litchfield is right about a 9-millimeter slug causing the wound. Jenna Bernstein owned a 9-millimeter handgun, though we never found it."

"Likely at the bottom of Lake Washington," Ford said.

"Kohl's daughter doesn't think so," Rossi said.

"Meaning?" Thompson said.

Rossi and Ford showed Thompson the text messages on Sirus Kohl's cell phone about the meeting that morning Kohl had with the US Attorney. "Daughter said Kohl called her last night and confirmed the meeting was going forward this morning, and she told him not to say a word to anyone. Call log on her phone confirms his call."

"But he didn't take her advice?" Thompson said.

"Doesn't look like it," Rossi said. "I sent Billy and Ian to speak to Bernstein. Find out if she could account for her whereabouts last night."

Thompson's interest had clearly been piqued. He turned to Ford. "Yeah? She have anything of interest to say?"

"'Talk to my attorney,'" Ford said. "Noticed a security camera in the lobby of Bernstein's building, though. And in the elevator, and on her condominium floor. Asked the security guard on duty to see the security video, but he got squirrelly and said I'd have to talk with his home office. Took a first pass at a search warrant." Ford handed Thompson the laptop.

Thompson read the document, but Rossi and Ford had put together dozens of such warrants and knew the key was to provide an affidavit showing probable cause, that the evidence sought was potentially relevant to a crime under investigation, and that it was needed to aid in identifying a suspect. "Looks good to go," Thompson said, handing back the laptop. "Let's get a judge on the phone."

Thompson would be strategic about which superior court judge he wanted them to call. The judge who issued the warrant was automatically disqualified from being the trial judge—if the investigation got that far. The PA didn't want to burn one of his first trial-judge choices.

After discussing a few names, Thompson said, "Let's call O'Neil," meaning Judge Thomas O'Neil.

Ford attached the recording device to his cell phone, plugged in the earpiece, and called Judge O'Neil's cell. When the judge answered, he explained the circumstances. O'Neil swore him in as the affiant of the facts to justify issuing the warrant, and Ford read what he had typed and said an urgency existed to get the security video. "We want to secure them before they're lost," Ford said.

O'Neil said, "All right, Detective, I'm orally granting the search warrant. Have a written copy sent to my chambers and I'll sign it ASAP."

Ford hung up, then sent the warrant in an email to Mark Upson, the C Team's "fifth wheel," and asked him to run it over to the judge's chambers to get it signed, then get the video from the building. "Fifth wheels" were detectives either on their way to retirement or waiting to get a permanent position as one of the sixteen Violent Crimes detectives working in four-person teams. Upson was on his way to retirement and a lot of golf, but unlike some others who saw the position as a place to hide out until their final day, he remained diligent.

Rossi and Ford also told Thompson that Adria Kohl was convinced Bernstein killed her father and Erik Wei.

"Bernstein had several billion reasons to kill Wei. Did the daughter say why she thought Bernstein would be motivated to kill her father?" Thompson asked.

Rossi showed Thompson the text string on Sirus Kohl's cell phone to another burner cell phone assigned to Jenna Bernstein.

Thompson nodded his head, his lips pinched tight. "Doesn't come out and say that exactly. Can we confirm the other phone belonged to Jenna Bernstein?"

Rossi said they would. "What led you to Bernstein the first time?" he asked. Rossi had just passed the detective exam and hadn't been involved in the first trial.

"I'll pull the Erik Wei file and send it over," Thompson said, "let you have a look for yourself. Did Litchfield give you an estimated time of death?"

"Nothing definitive yet," Rossi said. "But his initial assessment, based on the degree of livor mortis and the presence of rigor mortis, is six to twelve hours. And we know Kohl called the daughter at 9:17 last night to confirm the morning meeting. At least there's a call registered on his cell phone."

Lividity was indicated by red, blue, and purple splotches to the skin caused by blood settling to the body's lowest parts after the heart stopped pumping. It became fixed at six to twelve hours. Rigor mortis—joints and muscles stiffening—occurred one to two hours after death and could last for days.

"So last night or early this morning," Thompson said.

Ford said, "With all due respect, could Bernstein have been innocent in Wei?"

Thompson shook his head. "As Gil Garcetti said after the jury found O. J. innocent: 'The killer just walked out the courtroom door.'"

Chapter 7

At a break, Keera asked Ella to have Maggie order lunch.

"Why don't you ask her?" Ella asked.

"I'm not speaking to her at the moment."

"I'm not getting involved—"

"And ask her to send John Bernstein home."

"Fine, but the two of you need to get your shit worked out," Ella said. "Do you want me in the conference room?"

Keera diplomatically told her no. She didn't want it to appear like her oldest sister watched over her.

It was bad enough having her father in the room, though she and Patsy had an established work relationship.

Patsy was like a net to a trapeze artist. He'd catch Keera if she fell, and soften the blow. She knew Jenna. Too well. Keera also wanted Patsy present to witness what was and was not said. If Jenna was charged, again, then Keera would have another decision to make—whether to represent her. The case would likely generate even more interest than the Vince LaRussa case, which the firm could certainly use, not to mention the legal fee would be substantial. But Keera didn't know if she wanted to go down that path and let Jenna back into her life—on any level.

They tuned the conference room's television to a local news station. Reports of Sirus Kohl's killing trickled in. At least one reporter said Kohl had died of a single gunshot wound and the police were treating it as a homicide.

"Did the detectives say how Sirus Kohl died when they came to your condo this morning?" Keera asked Jenna.

"We never got that far."

"Do you own a gun?" Keera asked, though she suspected she knew the answer from the Wei trial.

Jenna spoke to Patsy. "I did, a Glock 9 millimeter, but I left it behind when I left Sirus's home."

"You don't know where it is?" Keera asked.

"No one knows," Patsy said.

To Jenna, Keera said, "Do you know?"

"No. I don't."

"I assume the police searched for it in the Wei matter?" Keera asked Patsy.

"They did. But they didn't find it in Kohl's house. The prosecutor insinuated at trial that Jenna had gotten rid of it to prevent ballistics from matching it to the bullet that killed Wei."

"Did you?" Keera asked bluntly.

"Did I what?"

"Did you get rid of the gun to prevent ballistics from matching it to the bullet that killed Erik Wei?"

"No." Jenna looked and sounded upset. "As I told Patsy, after I spoke to Erik and learned Sirus had been lying to me about the LINK's capabilities, I grabbed a handbag of clothes and quickly moved out of his house. I didn't have any reason to take the gun."

"When was the last time you saw it?"

"When Sirus locked the gun in the safe in the bedroom."

"Why did you have a gun?"

"Sirus purchased it for me for protection."

"From whom?" Keera tried to keep skepticism out of her tone. She'd read about the extreme security measures PDRT employed in magazine articles profiling the company and Jenna, and then in the investigative pieces written after Wei's murder and Jenna's arrest. Private security accompanied both Jenna and Kohl wherever they went.

Jenna said, "I was on the cover of every business journal and touted as being worth billions of dollars."

An image Jenna likely wanted portrayed. Having private security lent credibility to that image. "Let's talk about last night and this morning," Keera said. "Can you account for your time?"

"Some of it."

"Start from the time you got up."

"I spent most of the day on a friend's boat on Lake Washington. It's one of the few places I can go and not be harassed since the US Attorney filed the federal court action."

Keera obtained the friend's name. "What time did you get home?"

"I was back in the condominium around four or five."

"Do you have to sign in or out?"

"Not as a resident; no."

"Did you stay home?"

"No."

When Jenna didn't continue, Keera looked up from taking notes, as did Patsy. "Where did you go?" Keera asked.

"I went out for a walk."

"When and for how long?"

"A few hours. Between seven and sometime after ten."

Jenna did not provide any details of where she had gone. "Did you go alone?"

"Yes."

Keera felt like she was pulling teeth. "Where did you go?"

Jenna paused. "I walked to Volunteer Park and back."

Keera and Patsy exchanged a look. Volunteer Park was on Capitol Hill, where Kohl had been living, according to the news reports. Keera said, "Why did you go there?"

"I was hungry, and I wanted to get some exercise after being on a boat all day. Wednesday evenings Volunteer Park has food trucks. As I said, I can't go into restaurants any longer. I walked to the park, bought a burrito from a food truck, and walked around eating it before returning to the condominium."

"Which food truck?"

"Bitchin Burritos."

"Did you get a receipt?"

"No."

"Did you use your phone or a credit card to pay?"

Jenna shook her head. "I paid cash."

Which was no longer the norm. Not paying with her phone or a credit card could be used to infer that Jenna acted surreptitiously; at least that's what any good prosecutor would argue. "Would they remember you? Do you go there regularly?"

She shook her head. "Probably not. And no."

"Did *anyone* see you? Did you speak to anyone?"

"You should know that I disguise my appearance when I go out, Keera."

"A disguise?" This was going from bad to worse.

"I'm a marked person since the trial, and especially after the federal indictment." Her statement was a decent rebuttal to any argument that Bernstein had deliberately tried to hide her identity to kill Kohl. "I can't sit at the condo every night by myself doing nothing. I like to walk this time of year when it stays light so late."

"Does your condominium complex have security cameras?"

"In the hallways on each floor, in the elevators, and in the lobby."

"They would have video of you coming and going."

"I assume."

Billy Ford would have the same thought as Keera, and he would get the security footage. In fact, having already been to the condominium complex, he was likely already in the process of doing so. When he did, he'd find Jenna had attempted to disguise herself before heading out on a walk to a park very close to the murder. Keera turned to Patsy. "We need to get JP on it ASAP," she said, meaning JP Harrison, a former SPD detective and now the firm's private investigator on big cases.

"I'll make the call when we're done."

"What kind of disguise?" Keera asked Jenna.

"Nothing elaborate; I just put my hair in a ponytail and tuck it up under a baseball cap. And I wear large sunglasses to hide much of my face."

"You've done this before?"

"Whenever I go out walking."

Keera made a note to also have Harrison determine if the security guards at the condominium complex could confirm Jenna's statement that she wore a disguise whenever she left the building. She'd also have him talk to the employees at Bitchin Burritos to determine if anyone saw and remembered Jenna.

"Look, I can tell by your tone that you're frustrated, but what do you want me to do?" Jenna said. "Had I known Sirus was going to be killed, I never would have left the condominium. I know the building has security cameras. And I certainly would not have walked to the park in a disguise; why would I do something so blatantly obvious it focuses any investigation on me?"

Keera had the same thought but for a different reason. She wondered if Jenna had thought through her actions as a way to justify her leaving the condo in disguise, but to also argue she'd never be so stupid, or blatant. A good prosecutor would counter that the disguise was clearly not intended to fool the security guard or the cameras inside the building. It was intended to conceal Jenna's identity from anyone she might encounter outside the building.

"It's fine," Patsy said, mollifying her.

"It isn't fine," Keera said, glancing at her father before reengaging Jenna. "You have to realize that going out alone—to an area close to the murder, wearing a disguise—does not look good."

"Of course I know it doesn't look good, but I told you I can't go out to a restaurant."

"Why not order in?" Keera said.

"I don't want to become a captive in that condominium," Jenna said, voice rising. "The footage is what it is. I can't change it. Besides, Patsy was able to get a not guilty verdict despite the restaurant having a video of my meeting with Erik Wei the night of his death."

"You had a very good reason for meeting Wei. You don't have a good reason for going out last night to Capitol Hill. Or do you? If you do, I need to know what it is."

"Meaning what?"

"Meaning did you have any other reason to go out?"

"You act like you don't believe me."

"Whether I believe you or not is irrelevant. What's relevant is what the jurors will believe, and they're going to have a hard time believing what you've told us. 'I was hungry, so I put on a disguise and walked very close to the site of the murder to get something to eat.' The prosecutor will list the number of restaurants you passed on your walk."

Jenna sat back, clearly uncomfortable being pushed. "I told you the reasons I went out."

"Did you take your cell phone when you went out for the walk?"

"Why is that important?"

"Cell phones provide geolocation records and reveal where the phone, and presumably the owner, has been over the course of a day. The police know this. They'll get a search warrant for those records and others for your phone and determine exactly where you went."

"I didn't bring my cell phone."

Jenna's story was becoming less and less credible. Who went anywhere this day and age without their cell phone? "Why not?"

Jenna sighed. "I walk for peace and quiet. I didn't want the distraction of a phone."

"But you said you feared for your safety. Your cell phone would have provided you a means to call for help, if you needed it."

"I guess I didn't think of that," Jenna said.

"It is what it is, Keera," Patsy said. "We'll deal with it if we have to."

Keera bit her tongue. While her father was correct, she didn't like him coddling Jenna. Jenna needed to know Patsy could not be counted on to pull a rabbit out of his hat every trial. Neither of them was a magician.

They spoke well into the afternoon before Keera sent Jenna home, telling her she'd be in touch, not to talk to anyone, and to direct any inquiries from the press, or the police, to her or Patsy.

Later, in Patsy's office filled with trinkets from appreciative clients during forty years of legal practice, Patsy read from a checklist he'd taken during their meeting. "I'll get ahold of JP—"

"Dad?"

"Ask him to find out from his contacts at the police department what they know and suspect. We'll want to—"

"Dad!"

He looked up. "What?"

"Don't you think this is all just a bit too coincidental? Jenna and Kohl are indicted, her gun is missing, and she just happens to take a walk, in disguise, to the very neighborhood where Kohl was shot and killed?"

"The two of them being indicted isn't evidence of a motive for murder. Her gun went missing years ago, and she has a legitimate reason for walking in disguise."

"To Capitol Hill?"

"Jenna isn't an idiot. She knew her building possessed security cameras and would detect her in a disguise and record when she left and returned. As she said, why would she have been so obvious?"

"Maybe that's exactly why she was so obvious, Dad. So we could argue she never would have been so obvious had she intended on killing Kohl. She's very smart, always has been, and she clearly could have thought this through."

"We can't change the facts. Better we know them now."

They couldn't. They could only make inferences and arguments. "As soon as Rossi and Ford get that security footage, and if it matches the ME's estimated time frame for Kohl's murder, she becomes suspect number one."

"She's already suspect number one. If they bring charges on evidence that flimsy, I'll beat them again."

"*You'll* beat them?"

"You know what I mean."

"Don't you think you're being a tad blind here because you've known Jenna since she was a schoolgirl? She's not a little girl anymore, Dad, and she wasn't so innocent back then either."

"I know that, kiddo, all too well. But Jenna needs defense counsel, and it's what we do. Let's gather evidence and wait and see what the prosecution does."

"People in the prosecutor's office remain convinced she killed Wei, Dad, and but for your brilliance she'd already be in prison."

Ella popped her head in Patsy's office door. "Thought I heard you two arguing."

"Just two attorneys debating the evidence," Patsy said.

"Okay, then maybe you can agree on what we're going to charge Jenna for the consultation today."

"Nothing," Patsy said.

"Nothing?" Keera and Ella said at the same time, their voices rising in question.

"If this matter goes further, we'll all invest plenty of hours to bill. Until then, we're not going to charge a family friend."

"She's not my friend," Keera said. "And you haven't seen the Bernsteins since the trial."

"You know what I mean."

"No. I don't."

"Okay, enough," Ella said, always the mediator. "The last time you billed them the family rate for the entire defense. Please tell me we're not doing that again."

"We'll deal with that if and when the time comes," Patsy said.

"We'll deal with it now," Keera said. "We will bill them what we billed Vince LaRussa."

"The case came in to me, Keera," Patsy said.

"Then you try it. I am not working for free."

Patsy glared at her, but it was not the glare he'd once possessed, the one that withered opposing attorneys or witnesses. He was not what he once had been, and it pained him because he knew it. He couldn't try this case, were it to come to that, and Keera believed it would.

"Let's table this discussion and talk about it more in the morning," Ella said. "Keera, go home. I'm sorry about your vacation, but—"

"Yeah, I know," she said. "Everyone's sorry, but here I am." She left Patsy's office wondering if she was stewing over what they'd charge Jenna, or the fact that Jenna was, once again, back in Keera's life.

Chapter 8

Rossi watched as Ford disconnected the call and slid his cell phone back into his jacket. He flipped his laptop open and put it on the hood of one of the pool cars, speaking to Rossi, Thompson, and Pan.

"Upson just got the security footage from the condominium complex and says we're going to want to see it ASAP." Ford angled his laptop computer screen for everyone to see. "First file is the security footage from the camera in the hallway outside Bernstein's condominium. The second is from the camera in the elevator, and the third from the camera in the lobby."

He hit play, and the men watched the black-and-white video. A running clock in the upper right-hand corner indicated the time in hours, minutes, and seconds. After a few moments, a door opened and someone stepped into a carpeted hallway. A woman. She walked toward the camera.

"Is that Bernstein?" Pan asked.

"That's her unit," Ford said.

Rossi had been paying attention to the time in the computer screen corner: 7:23:48 p.m. Ford paused the video, and they all looked more closely at the image of the person on the screen. It looked like Bernstein, but it was hard to be certain. The person in the video wore a ball cap, her blonde hair tucked beneath it, large sunglasses that obscured much of her face, and baggy clothes—what looked like a dark-colored sweat suit and tennis shoes.

"She's got her hair pulled up," Ford said. "Sunglasses."

Ford hit play again, and they watched the woman walk to an elevator bank. When the elevator arrived, she stepped inside. Ford opened the second file and cued it to the time Bernstein, if it was Bernstein, had stepped into the elevator. She was alone. The second tape had better lighting.

"Is that her?" Rossi asked Thompson.

"Definitely looks like her," Thompson said.

When the elevator stopped descending, Bernstein stepped out.

The third file was the security tape from the building lobby. Again, Ford cued it, and they watched as Bernstein exited the elevator. This camera was farther away, but the video showed her crossing a marbled lobby past the security desk, which was unstaffed at that moment. The front door opened, and she exited onto the street.

"She could have left to work out," Pan said, "given the way she's dressed."

"Or she went for a walk or a run," Rossi said. "Maybe a guard recalls seeing her on other occasions go out similarly dressed to work out."

"It's been warm out, and she isn't going for a run in those glasses," Thompson said. "It looks to me like she's trying to hide her identity; doesn't it?"

It did, but nobody, except Thompson, was willing to say that just yet. Detectives were trained to consider more than one alternative so they didn't rush to a judgment and get bitten in the ass. Rossi had been paying attention to the time in the corner of the video. Bernstein left the building at 7:27:52 p.m. "Regardless, that's within the window Litchfield estimated for the time of death," he said.

Ford said, "Upson's email says there's more. Let me fast-forward to the time mark he gave me."

Ford did so, stopping the security tape that again showed the lobby, this time at 10:17:32 p.m. After a beat, they watched Bernstein, still dressed in the same clothing, but no longer wearing the hat or the glasses, enter the lobby and cross to the elevator bank. The footage showed her getting into the elevator and returning to her condominium unit.

Ford stepped back.

"Let's be certain it's her," Thompson said. "Talk to the security guards at her building. Show them the tape. As you said, maybe she's gone out dressed like that before."

Rossi said, "I'll have Upson also call Wash-DOT and the City of Seattle to determine what traffic cameras exist in that area, and get him and the next-up team to search for business cameras in that neighborhood. Maybe we can pick her up outside the building, determine where she went."

"Could she have parked close by?" Pan asked.

"Building is high-end. It has underground parking, accessed from the elevator in the lobby," Ford said.

Rossi said, "We should also find out how far it is from her condominium to Kohl's home on Capitol Hill."

"My wife and I used to live over there. It's no more than a couple of miles."

"So, walkable," Thompson said.

"Let's be specific," Pan said. He directed his attention to Rossi. "Get Upson started searching for cameras. Make sure she didn't get into a parked car, or have somebody pick her up—a cab, Uber, something."

"On it," Rossi said, making a note. "And the next-up team is canvassing the houses along Federal Avenue and talking with the owners to determine if they heard or saw anything, or if any of their homes have cameras that might have picked someone up."

Pan turned and looked at the house. "Daughter said there's a Ring camera on the front door."

"We'll ask TESU if we can pull up the footage from her father's phone or computer," Rossi said, referencing the Technical and Electronic Support Unit. He addressed Ford. "And let's get a subpoena to Jenna

Bernstein's cell phone provider, determine if her phone was anywhere near the park or in the vicinity of Capitol Hill last night."

Detectives had the ability to track cell phones in different ways, depending on the type of phone. Network-based tracking, Wi-Fi-based tracking, and GPS all could pinpoint the phone's location at specific times to various degrees of accuracy, but only if the phone was turned on and had GPS and location services enabled.

"What about the home across the street?" Thompson asked. "The one with the two lookie-loos?"

"Bressler and Kennison talked to them," Ford said, referencing the next-up detectives. "They have a Ring camera on the front door. But those two trees"—he motioned to the trees planted in the sidewalk—"block the camera. The coverage doesn't extend beyond the front walk."

Rossi turned and looked to the back of the property. At the end of the cul-de-sac was an easement with a sign. "Did you say Volunteer Park is behind that wall?"

Ford nodded, and Rossi left the group and walked to the back of the property, then to the easement—a dirt trail that led directly into the park. When he returned, he said, "If Bernstein walked into the park, she could have come out that trail and avoided any security cameras on the houses along Federal Avenue."

"Are there any security cameras in the park?" Thompson asked.

"Not likely," Rossi said, scribbling additional notes, "but we'll confirm."

The men took a collective breath. No one spoke, not immediately. Rossi was wondering whether it could be this easy, maybe the grounder he and Ford kept seeking, but he shook that thought as way too premature.

Thompson said, "Let's sit down again after we get Sirus Kohl's burner phone records and determine what Upson learns about possible cameras picking up Bernstein after leaving her condominium. Anyone think of anything else?"

"Let's also subpoena Adria Kohl's phone records," Rossi said. "Just to confirm what she's told us."

"She said her father had received threats," Ford said.

"Look into those as well. I want to eliminate any other potential suspects," Thompson said. "If we charge Jenna Bernstein, I don't want Patsy Duggan intimating this is retaliatory because she got off in the Wei trial, or that we somehow rushed to judgment and didn't consider other suspects. People threatening Kohl will be at the top of that list."

"Patsy isn't handling trials any longer," Rossi said. Thompson, Ford, and Pan all gave him a long look. He backtracked. "At least I don't think so. I mean, given the LaRussa case." Keera had told Rossi her father was no longer trying cases. Reading between the lines, Rossi concluded that the booze had finally caught up to Patsy.

"His daughter?" Thompson said. "She defended Vince LaRussa."

"What is his daughter's name again?" Ford hid a smile, poorly.

"Keera," Rossi said. "Keera Duggan."

"Well, if the LaRussa verdict is any indication, especially given what transpired after the trial, she's as formidable as her father," Thompson said. "I'm told she kicked Miller Ambrose's ass."

"That was our case." Rossi indicated himself and Ford. "I sat alongside Ambrose at counsel's table. Keera Duggan is very good. Intuitive. Thinks outside the box."

"Like her father," Thompson said. "Apparently the apple didn't fall far from the tree; did it?"

Chapter 9

Minutes after Keera had left her father's office and returned to her own, Ella knocked on Keera's door and stepped in. Keera didn't wait for Ella to speak. "Are you kidding me?" she said, gathering her briefcase. "I gave up my vacation to come in here and work for free? That's bullshit, Ella."

Ella closed the door and kept her voice low. "I understand you're frustrated," she said in the parental voice she had used when Keera was a child.

"I'm not frustrated. I'm upset. I'm pissed. Maggie pulls a power trip and doesn't tell me who is in the office, and then Dad wants me to work for free."

"I'll figure something out. We can back bill your time for today. God knows we need another big case, and this will be very big, if she is charged."

"She'll be charged," Keera said. "Based on what she's told me so far . . . and hasn't told me."

"You think she's withholding information."

"I know she is."

"How?"

"Because I know her. With Jenna, the truth is always a moving target. I'm more concerned about how she is going to pay going forward. PDRT is dissolved, and with the federal lawsuit pending, you can bet she's spending what money she and her parents have on white-collar criminal defense lawyers and experts."

"John inherited money," Ella said. "At least that's what Jenna told us five years ago. But I also know her parents took out a mortgage on their home and sold their summer house on Lake Chelan to pay for Jenna's defense in the Wei case."

"Well, I'm not doing this pro bono," Keera said. "If she can't pay the same rate we charged Vince LaRussa, she can get somebody else. And Patsy can't do it. Not a case of this magnitude."

Ella folded her arms. "What's going on? I thought you and Jenna Bernstein were friends."

"We were never friends."

Ella gave her a quizzical look. "So what is it?"

Keera put her briefcase on her desk. "Maybe it's because I know Jenna. I don't believe she's innocent in the death of Erik Wei, and I'm not buying her story this time either."

"Okay, assume you're correct. You've represented guilty parties before, and you will again. It comes with the territory, Keera. You told me you believed Mark Strickland was guilty. So why is this one bothering you so much?"

Ella was right. Keera had represented Mark Strickland though she'd suspected he had been guilty, but she hadn't felt good about doing so and endured a few sleepless nights because of it—a holdover from her years as a prosecutor, perhaps. She wasn't in the mood to capitulate, however, not at this moment, and not for Jenna Bernstein.

She sat on the edge of her desk and motioned to one of the two chairs. "I'll give you a snapshot of who Jenna Bernstein is."

Ella sat.

"Mom and Dad were significantly older parents for my class."

"They struggled with that. They wanted you to feel included with your friends," Ella said. "They wanted you to have all the things we had experienced."

"I know. And I've realized, over the years, that they weren't close to the Bernsteins, but they tried initially for my sake."

"What do you mean?"

"It *seemed* a perfect fit, Jenna being an only child, and all of you having moved out of the house by the time I was ten. That's when I started playing chess, to have some connection to Dad."

"You were a prodigy."

"I don't know about that. I just know I grew to love it for more than the connection it gave me to Dad."

"You were just a kid. You didn't understand when Dad went on a binge."

"I understood that he was like a different person when he drank, and I was scared of him. I used to think that maybe if I kept him occupied . . . I don't know. Maybe chess was also a bit of an obsession. But Dad loved that I loved it. I know it sounds silly, but I felt like he'd stopped drinking—"

"Wishful thinking, Keera."

"A child's wishful thinking," Keera agreed. "Anyway, back to my point. One summer weekend we were invited by the Bernsteins to their home on Lake Chelan, and I brought along my chessboard so Dad and I could play. Jenna saw it when I was unpacking and said she wanted to play. I told her I would teach her, but she said she didn't need me to teach her."

"Did she know how to play?"

"Rudimentary, at best. The first game, I beat her in five moves. More to teach her a lesson, like Dad use to do to me when I got cocky. She asked to play again. Again, I easily beat her. I told her I could teach her some things, but she just kept saying she wanted to play again, a third time, then a fourth and fifth. With each loss she became angrier, but she kept insisting we keep playing."

"She was always determined to succeed."

"It was more than that, Ella. She *had* to win."

"Had to?"

Keera nodded. "I was only ten, but I figured her out that quickly. I grew tired of playing and tired of her attitude. I wanted to get outside and swim in the lake—the Bernsteins had a large bouncing trampoline with a slide just off their boat dock—but Jenna refused to stop, and I finally realized the only way I was going to leave that room before dark—"

"You let her beat you."

Another nod. "And when she won, she said, 'I knew I could figure it out. It's not hard. You were just lucky.'

"Then *I* got angry. I said, 'Let's play again.' But Jenna refused, upended the board, and ran from the room."

"Hmm . . . ," Ella said.

"I know what you're thinking. You're thinking it's just child's stuff."

"It does seem harmless."

"There's more. I no longer wanted to play with Jenna. I wanted to go home. I went and talked to Mom, who was reading a book on the dock, and I told her what had happened. She told me to let it go; that Jenna was probably just embarrassed I was so much better than her. She applauded my decision to let Jenna win and said it was too beautiful a day to waste."

"Sounds exactly like something Mom would say."

"I changed into my swimsuit and, when I got outside, Jenna was already on the trampoline, jumping up and down. Mom and Dad and the Bernsteins had gone inside to make lunch. I swam out to the trampoline, but when I grabbed a handhold to pull myself up, Jenna jumped on my fingers until I let go, and I slipped back into the water."

Ella's eyebrows knitted together.

"When I came up, Jenna said 'Sorry,' with this impish grin, and I tried again."

"Let me guess. She jumped on your fingers again."

"This went on repeatedly. I kept telling her to stop. I told her it wasn't funny, that I was getting tired. I swam around the trampoline trying to find a different way up, but she just followed me. I started to have trouble staying afloat, but I was also determined not to swim back to the dock. I was determined to get on that damn trampoline."

"But I assume Jenna was just as determined to keep you off?"

"The harder I tried to get up, the more physical she became," Keera said.

"Physical how?"

"She'd pinch and hit my hand. She dug her nails into my skin and drew blood. She would sit down on the trampoline, put her foot in my face, and push me off."

"Jesus," Ella said and made the sign of the cross—one of their mother's habits. "That goes a bit beyond normal behavior, I would agree."

"I hated to let her win, but I was so tired by this time I was no longer sure I could swim back to the dock. I tried anyway, and I had swum about halfway, then got a leg cramp and went under. I came up and called for help. I recall, vividly, Jenna dropping to her knees on the trampoline and watching me sink under the water and struggle back to the surface again and again and again. She just watched, Ella. She just knelt there, watching."

Ella remained silent, though with a look of morbid curiosity, as if she didn't want to hear what happened next, though she knew, obviously, Keera had survived.

"I heard a loud splash and felt someone lift me up. Dad. He swam with me back to the dock, and Mom wrapped me in a towel. I was crying so hard Mom took me into the other room for a moment to get me to calm down. When she closed the door, she asked me what had happened, and I told her.

"She said it was probably just a game, but then I removed the towel and showed her the scratches on my hands and arms and the scrape mark on my neck. I also had red splotches where Jenna had punched and kicked me. Mom got this horrified look I'll never forget. I know now it was the look of someone who is trapped and doesn't know what to do."

"You were at their house, enjoying their generosity. Mom likely wanted to leave, but she was unable to come up with a suitable excuse."

"I think so too. I remember Dad came into the room, still a bit rattled from having to save me, and Mom showed him the marks on my arms and neck and told him what had happened. Dad and Mom talked for a while and decided that Mom would bring it up after lunch. They agreed that Mr. and Mrs. Bernstein should know. When Mom brought it up, Mrs. Bernstein asked Jenna why she wouldn't let me on the trampoline."

"What did she say?" Ella asked.

"She said it was just a game. She said we were playing King of the Hill and I lost, and I was just being a poor sport. She said we could play again, and she'd let me be king of the hill. But it wasn't just what Jenna said. It was the way she looked at me, smiling very sweetly but with this gleam in her eyes. I don't know how to describe it. Even now. The other thing that struck me then, and still to this day, was how easily Jenna lied, how convincing she sounded."

"Did it appease her mother?"

"It did. Even though Jenna never apologized. She never said she was sorry. When I said I didn't want to play anymore, Mrs. Bernstein said, 'Don't be a poor sport. Jenna said she'd let you be the king of the hill.' And Jenna said, 'She's sulking because I beat her at chess.'"

"I started to respond, but Mom touched my leg under the table."

"Her sign to stop us from saying anything."

Keera nodded. "She looked across the table at Dad. I could tell from the looks on their faces they both knew Jenna could not have beaten me. And I had told Mom I'd let Jenna win just so we could go outside to play."

"They knew then that she was, in essence, lying to her parents."

"After dinner, I asked Dad if he wanted to play chess, but when I went to set up the game, I noticed the queen was missing from Jenna's side of the board. I looked all over the room, thinking maybe it had fallen under the bed when Jenna upended the board, but I never found it."

"You think she took the queen, so nobody else could play the game," Ella said.

"I think she took the queen so she would finish as the winner," Keera said. "She always had to finish as the winner."

"Did you tell Dad?"

Keera shook her head. "But I think he suspected what had happened. He found a piece of driftwood, did a little carving, and we used it as his queen. That night, Mom had me sleep in their room, not with Jenna. She told the Bernsteins I wasn't feeling well. In the morning she used that as an excuse for us to leave early. I don't think the Bernsteins bought it, not entirely, but they also didn't try to talk us into staying."

"Did the Bernsteins ever invite you back?"

"I don't know if they ever invited us again, or if they did and Mom and Dad declined."

"But you didn't go back."

"I never did," Keera said. "But here's something else I've thought about over the years. This was the fourth grade, and Jenna had switched schools that year. And Mom and Dad were older parents, not a first choice for a young couple seeking friends."

"You're wondering why they chose you to invite to Chelan?"

"I've wondered if, maybe, it wasn't the first time something like that had happened."

Ella didn't respond so Keera continued.

"It's not the only time Jenna did something like that, Ella, far from it. So as I said, she was never my friend, and the Bernsteins were never family or friends. So why did Dad cut them a deal on his fees? Why does he want to cut them a deal now? I don't understand."

"My turn to tell a story," Ella said.

Keera nodded. "Okay."

"I don't know how much this might have played into it, or what you even remember, but back when you were in high school, Dad's drinking got worse."

"I remember. He showed up drunk at one of my chess tournaments. It's the last time I played in a competitive tournament."

"He'd also apparently shown up drunk at several school functions, and parents had complained to the administration. The principal called Mom and Dad in and told them going forward that they would have a zero-tolerance policy if Dad's behavior continued. They said they would be asked to leave . . . *you* would be asked to leave the school."

"I didn't know this," Keera said, thinking of her mother and how her father's drinking had pained her. It must have been humiliating and embarrassing.

"Mom didn't want you to know," Ella said. "She didn't want you to be embarrassed. Anyway, Dad stopped for a while, but as you know well, it's never for good."

"All too well."

"The school had a casino night and auction to raise funds, and Dad got busy here at the office. He told Mom he'd meet her there. Apparently, he started drinking, and by the time he arrived at the school parking lot, he was drunk, smashed his car into the back of another car, and passed out."

"Why didn't I ever hear of this? Mom?"

"No. Because of John Bernstein."

"What do you mean?"

"He, too, arrived late to the auction, and he saw and heard the crash. He went to Dad, who'd cut his head on the steering wheel, realized he was drunk, and got Dad in their car. He drove him home, got him bandaged, and put him in bed. When he went back to the school he spoke to Mom, who you can imagine was more than a little upset. She told John they were going to kick you out. John went to the parent who owned the other car, explained that Dad had been late and in a rush . . ."

"He left out the part about Dad being drunk."

Ella nodded. "He said Dad had some bumps and bruises and had hit his head, and John had driven him home. He said Dad wanted the person who owned the car to know that he would pay for all damage. When the administration asked about it, suspecting Dad had been drunk, John told them the same story. And you got to stay at Forest Ridge."

Keera was starting to understand. "Dad feels he owes John Bernstein."

Ella nodded. "For you. Because of what John did. He saved you and Dad the embarrassment of being asked to leave the school."

Keera sighed. "The firm isn't in a position to be cutting anyone any deals, Ella. Not yet. We're not out of the red."

"I know. And I'll make sure that doesn't happen. I'll bill Jenna for your time today and moving forward. If Patsy wants to work for free, that's his business."

"It's not his business, Ella. Not anymore. We're all partners. It's *our* business, and we can use the money this case is going to generate."

"If Jenna is ultimately charged."

"As Mom used to say, 'Trouble seems to follow that girl.'"

"You think she'll be charged."

"I think the prosecuting attorney will proceed with caution, given what happened in Wei. He might take it to a grand jury first to be sure they have their ducks in a row before filing formal charges, but he'll ultimately charge her."

In Washington State, the prosecutor, without the accused or defense attorneys present, could introduce evidence to a group of people and ask them to determine if enough evidence exists to bring the accused to trial.

Ella stood and pulled open the office door. "Keep track of your hours. I may have to do a little creative billing. Now go home."

She closed the door behind her.

Keera took a deep breath. She let her anger pass before she sat down at her desk. Though late in the day, she called JP Harrison's cell number.

"I thought you were on vacation," he said, his British accent pronounced. Harrison had worked on both of Keera's recent defense verdicts. "This wouldn't have to do with a certain killing of a certain person on Capitol Hill this morning; would it?" Harrison had also worked for Patsy on the Erik Wei murder case.

"It would," she said.

"Thought it might."

"Need to meet. You available tomorrow morning?"

"Pick your poison."

"Eight a.m."

"Ouch. Will have to cut my date short."

"Send her home at seven," Keera said. "Tell her to make her own breakfast."

"Someone is in a foul mood."

"You don't know the half of it. I'll see you in the morning."

"I'll bring tea and crumpets."

"At your own peril. I'll take a tall decaf latte."

"Thought you weren't drinking coffee?"

"I've cut out caffeine . . . And two sous vide egg bites."

"Sounds boring."

"I'm on a diet."

"You? Why are you on a diet?"

"I have to work off all the rich food I dreamt of eating while I was supposed to be on vacation."

Chapter 10

Early Thursday evening, Frank Rossi's cell phone rang on his way to his pool car. He'd shut down the house and arranged to have uniformed officers sit on it until morning, when the latent fingerprint and DNA experts would return to finish their work. Her name appeared on his cell phone's caller ID—the same cell number Keera Duggan had used when she worked in the King County prosecutor's office for roughly five years upon graduating law school. She and Rossi, then a new detective, had cut their teeth together prosecuting cases—misdemeanors and minor felonies. He thought maybe something existed. Chemistry between them.

Keera let him down easily. Made it sound like she didn't date where she worked. He could respect that. Then the rumors started about her and Miller Ambrose, her boss in the prosecutor's office, and Keera's eventual defection to Duggan & Associates, a move that indicated the Ambrose rumors had been true. Rossi figured her rejection of him wasn't about her place of employment at all but about him. It hurt. He could have been bitter. He could have taken it to heart. But where would that have gotten him? As his father liked to say, *If you take shit to heart, you die with a heart full of shit.*

Rossi just let it go.

Then he and Billy pulled the Vince LaRussa case, and Keera was back in his life again. And Rossi came to better understand that Keera hadn't willingly left the prosecutor's office. She'd been forced to leave when Ambrose made her life difficult. Rossi had to smile when Keera pulled a Patsy Duggan in the LaRussa trial and surprised Ambrose with something no one saw coming.

Chip off the old block?

In Rossi's mind, Keera was the block.

He answered her call looking up at the fading blue sky. A flock of birds buzzed overhead, in and out of Volunteer Park, chirping happily, a sharp contrast to the brutal murder that had occurred in the home just hours before. The temperature remained comfortable.

"Let me guess. You're calling to check on my golf game. It sucks, but it sucks less than it sucked last week."

"A lot of suck in there, Frank. That can't be a good thing."

"You *have* seen my golf game." She laughed, and it brought a smile to his face. "No? That's not the reason for your call? Okay. Guess number two. You represent Jenna Bernstein, and she tattled on my partner for showing up at her condominium door asking about her whereabouts last night and early this morning."

"Is that the time frame you've received from the ME?"

"I'll never tell," he said. He wondered if Keera knew Bernstein had left her building and perhaps had an airtight alibi as to where she had gone. If she did, Rossi didn't exactly expect her to say so, not in an initial conversation. Keera was just feeling around the edges, trying to ascertain what the police might have. "Why? Are you calling to tell me she has an airtight alibi and selfies beside the Eiffel Tower? I'd be open to receiving them, though you can photoshop yourself anywhere in the world now. My mother is convinced I recently spent a week in Rome looking for a nice Italian girl after I sent her a picture in front of the Colosseum. I said I looked all over Rome, but there was nary a girl to be found."

"Not that I wouldn't like to pursue that line of inquiry, Frank, because I doubt there was nary a girl to be found, but what gives with Ford talking to Jenna Bernstein? Is there more I need to know?"

He sensed she was sitting on information. "What gives is: Sirus Kohl is dead, and we're treating his death as a homicide. I'm sure you've seen the news by now."

"I have. Tragic. Do you have some evidence my client could somehow be involved?"

"So, she's *your client*? Not Patsy's?"

"Patsy is cutting back. I'm taking on the trials. You know that."

He did. "Too early to tell, Keera, but Billy and I received a tip to chat with her. Billy tried, but she wasn't in the chatting mood. Told him to speak to her lawyer, and Billy backed off. Patsy represented her in the Erik Wei matter; didn't he?"

"You know he did, and you know she was found innocent."

"Nope. She was found 'not guilty beyond a reasonable doubt.' The two are not the same. But you know that."

"What kind of tip?" Keera asked.

There was the reason for her call. "The kind I can tell the prosecutor but not the defense attorney."

"Can you put my client at the scene?"

More direct now. "Does she have an alibi you're willing to share?" Rossi asked again. If she did, he expected Keera would at least hint at it. If she didn't, it made him more convinced Jenna Bernstein didn't leave her building and attend some function with a dozen people who could vouch for her whereabouts. So where did she go at 7:27 in the evening?

"What *can* you tell me?" Keera said, getting to the point and still not offering an alibi.

"Off the record, single gunshot wound." Something he was certain she already knew.

"That was on the news."

"I know."

"Do we know the caliber weapon?"

"Not definitively."

"ME's best guess?"

"Not for public disclosure. We haven't arrested anyone." Meaning if they did arrest someone, the caliber of weapon would be something they used to confirm they had the right suspect.

"Do me a favor?" she said.

"If I can." He couldn't and she knew it, but she figured it didn't hurt to ask, and he figured it didn't hurt to be polite.

"Let me know if you find anything on my client."

"Too broad and too vague. I will suggest to the PA, however, that we let you know if we plan to arrest your client and give her the chance to turn herself in before we do, maybe avoid another media circus." It was his not-so-subtle way of saying they were seriously considering Jenna Bernstein, and another chance for Keera to tell Rossi they were barking up the wrong tree.

She didn't. "Who's the MDOP attorney?" Keera asked. "Will he allow it?"

"Walker Thompson," he said. He listened for a reaction but didn't hear one. "And yeah, I think he will. If it gets that far." Would it? "Thompson is a decent guy."

"Let's hope it doesn't," she said. "Get that far." Again, no alibi provided.

"That's out of both our hands, Keera."

"Thanks, Frank."

"Anytime, Keera."

Rossi disconnected and paused. The conversation reminded him why he'd enjoyed working cases with Keera, but then they had played on the same side. She played the game well, always with a reasoned approach. Maybe that was enough—to admire her from afar. Not for his Italian mother, but . . . Best to forget what might have been and deal with what was. He was a homicide detective. She was now a defense lawyer. And ne'er the two shall meet.

Keera finished the call and sat back, staring at the chessboard on her kitchen table. On her bookshelf, Alexa played a mix of music, an afternoon playlist—not hers. She didn't have the time to put one together—or the desire.

She knew nothing more than she had known before she'd made the call, but that wasn't her purpose for calling Rossi. Her purpose was to put the police on notice she was involved, maybe determine if they were sitting on anything. She smiled. Frank was too smart for that. He wasn't about to slip. Was *he* sitting on something? Hard to tell, but it sounded like he was. He kept prompting Keera to provide him with an alibi for Jenna Bernstein. Problem was, she couldn't, and each time he asked, and Keera didn't provide one, let Rossi know Jenna didn't have an alibi.

Did Rossi and Ford know Jenna had been near the murder, or was she just the logical first suspect as the ex-girlfriend and business partner? Had they already obtained the security tapes? Likely Rossi sent Ford to talk to Jenna so he could evaluate Jenna's reaction to the news of Kohl's death *before* the news broke and Jenna had time to prepare herself. Ford also would have looked the building over, specifically for security cameras, a tenant register—evidence that might tell the detectives Jenna Bernstein had left the building. Then they'd put all their efforts into finding out where she went—checking security cameras on buildings and homes in that area and traffic cameras at intersections. They'd eventually determine Jenna was on Capitol Hill. The question then was whether Thompson would charge her, or would he be reticent and proceed more slowly. Walker Thompson was a good attorney, thorough and resilient, but also relatable and likeable. He wouldn't implode his own case, like Miller Ambrose had done in the LaRussa matter. And he didn't prosecute cases he didn't believe he could win. In the PA's office Thompson had been certain he'd convicted Jenna Bernstein for the murder of Erik Wei. Didn't work out that way, though he remained convinced he'd put on enough evidence to prove Bernstein's guilt beyond a reasonable doubt.

But Rossi was right. Thompson didn't lose that case. Patsy had won it.

Beyond reasonable doubt?

Keera wondered.

Chapter 11

North Beacon Hill
Seattle, Washington

Keera spent all of Friday morning on her hands and knees, working in the garden beneath the picture window in the front yard of her rented home while waiting for JP Harrison to arrive and fill her in on what he'd learned. She wanted to stay busy, and, like everything else in Keera's life when she tried cases, she'd ignored the flower beds, now overgrown, and the lawn, which had turned brown. Keera was no gardener, not like her mother, but the rental lease did put the responsibility of the yard upkeep on her, the tenant. She'd picked up plants from a local nursery to spruce up the garden but had not yet had time to plant them. She hoped the recent hot weather hadn't killed them, and that, like the lawn, the plants would recover with a little TLC, water, and fresh soil she'd bought at the local hardware store, which had the faint odor of fish.

Mostly she was just killing time.

Keera usually arranged for meetings with Harrison outside of the office to keep Maggie, always on the hunt for a new relationship, from drooling on him. This time she'd done so to spite her sister. A juvenile act, certainly, but she wasn't about to go into the office and give Maggie the satisfaction of knowing she'd also ruined Keera's weekend.

She had set Harrison to task securing the security footage at Jenna's condominium building, as well as asking him to obtain the names of

PDRT employees, investors, and board members, and to determine anything and everything that was going on at SPD and the prosecutor's office related to the investigation. Having been an SPD homicide detective, Harrison still had friends and contacts in the department and in the prosecutor's office. He'd been well liked and respected, and since retiring on a full pension and becoming a private investigator, he'd respected those contacts. He never told Keera or Patsy how he gathered some of the information he obtained. And they had learned not to ask.

Keera heard the thump of heavy rap music and looked to the street as two white, teenage boys, who looked too young to drive, cruised past the front yard in an older-model car with the windows down. She wiped sweat from her forehead and checked her watch. Harrison had called her just before noon and said he wanted to talk in person, which meant he'd learned something of interest.

Shortly thereafter, Keera heard the familiar throaty engine of Harrison's Verona-red, 1972 BMW. It sounded like a boat engine. Today it would save her from more yard work.

She got up and watched Harrison park at the curb, ever so slowly so as not to hit the curb and damage the hubcaps. The car glistened as if he'd just driven it off the showroom floor. If reincarnation existed, Keera wanted to come back as Harrison's car. He cared for it better than most men cared for their wives, gently caressing it and providing it with whatever it needed. It never failed to shine.

Harrison stepped from the car and gave Keera his electric, one-hundred-watt smile that must have made his dates swoon. The bachelor, now in his mid-fifties, had retained a youthful look that he attributed to eating right and working out six days a week. A tall, good-looking Black man, he had a wardrobe as stylish as his car. This afternoon, Harrison wore fashionable blue jeans; leather shoes; no socks; a white, untucked polo; and a blue blazer.

Harrison approached along the brick walkway, stopping to stare at the flower bed. "I think they're dead, Doctor."

Keera sighed. "I thought I might be able to save a few."

"The optimist sees opportunity in every difficulty."

"Did you just make that up?"

"God, no. That's the esteemed Sir Winston Churchill."

She changed subjects. "You said you had something for me? I assume it involves Jenna's walkabout the other night?"

"It does."

"Let's go inside," Keera said. "I made lemonade."

"Gardening *and* making lemonade? You're becoming domesticated, Ms. Duggan."

"Bite your tongue," Keera said.

Inside, Keera put her garden gloves on the dining room table and poured two glasses of lemonade from a pitcher in the fridge, handing one to Harrison. He took a sip. His face pinched.

"Too tart?" Keera asked. "I didn't want to use any artificial sweetener."

"Honey," Harrison said. "I don't mean you. What bees make. My mother used it to sweeten her tea."

He set down his glass, pulled out a chair at the dining room table, and sat. Then he removed his laptop from his leather satchel. "FYI, Ford and Rossi have the security footage from the condominium complex. The guard on duty said Ford came by yesterday and asked for it, but he told them to go through the corporate office. Ford returned with a signed warrant."

"Figured as much. Not wasting any time."

"Definitely not. They seemed to have fixated on your client."

So, Frank Rossi had known that Jenna had left the building, as Keera had suspected, when he and Keera spoke early yesterday evening.

"I met with Ms. Bernstein, and together we charted her walk from her South Lake Union condominium to Volunteer Park on Capitol Hill. I then put in a call to the Washington State Department of Transportation and the City of Seattle to check for traffic cameras to confirm what she told me. I walked the route looking for those cameras and security cameras on businesses and homes. Would have been much easier if she'd just brought her cell phone. Who goes anywhere nowadays without their cell phone?" Harrison said.

"Makes her look like she left it behind because she knew her phone could be tracked," Keera said.

"The disguise doesn't help either," Harrison said.

"I'm not as worried about that," Keera said.

"No?"

"It's like a chess sacrifice," Keera said. Patsy used them frequently in trials. The opponent believes he's scored a point with a piece of evidence, but Patsy deliberately gave up the piece to launch a stronger attack.

"And what would that sacrifice be in this instance?"

"The prosecution makes a big deal about the disguise, as if it is an important piece of evidence needed to convict. When they do, I tell the jury, *Of course Jenna went out in disguise. She was a pariah in the community, possibly even a target. She wasn't going to put her safety at risk.* The jurors accept it as logical, and I argue it creates a hole in the prosecutor's evidence needed to convict. It also creates empathy for Jenna."

"Tactical," Harrison said.

"Can be fatal if it's done correctly . . . or incorrectly. I'm doubting Walker Thompson will fall for it again."

"'Again'?"

"In the first trial, Sirus Kohl was the sacrificial pawn. Patsy . . . and Jenna shifted the motive for the killing of Wei to Kohl."

"And what about Ms. Bernstein leaving her phone at home if she believed she could be a target . . . ?"

"Still working on that one," Keera said.

Keera knew from discussions within the PA's office that Thompson had wanted to cross-examine Jenna after Patsy put her on the stand. Thompson wanted to show that Jenna knew she was making misrepresentations to PDRT's investors, but he had no emails or text messages to prove she did know—the lone text message on the topic had been the one Erik Wei sent her the night of his death. Board minutes at meetings Jenna attended also did not raise the subject of the LINK's failings. Thompson made the tactical decision not to attack Jenna and give her further opportunity to elicit juror sympathy. He also decided not to complicate a simple argument by subpoenaing Sirus Kohl to testify as to what Jenna knew. Without documents to back up whatever Kohl might have said, Thompson knew Patsy would have torn up Kohl, made the entrepreneur look like he was simply trying to save himself, had a grudge against his former lover, and befuddle the issue further. In the process, he would have turned Jenna into a martyr. Thompson decided to stick to the simple argument that, regardless of what Jenna knew or didn't know leading up to her meeting with Erik Wei, he clearly informed her the LINK could not do much of what she had represented, and that he would implode the entire company if she proceeded. Jenna had three billion reasons—the paper value of her stock—for killing Wei.

"Thompson tried a good case. His closing was strong, under the circumstances. Patsy created just enough reasonable doubt to get Jenna off," Keera said.

"We know that?"

"Patsy spoke with several jurors after the trial and, as was the common conclusion reached in the prosecutor's office, those jurors didn't necessarily believe Jenna to be innocent. They believed Kohl *could* have been the person who pulled the trigger, and if that were true, then there had to be reasonable doubt; didn't there?"

"Shrewd," Harrison said.

He hit play on his computer, and they watched the black-and-white video footage from the condominium complex until Jenna left the building lobby.

"She leaves the building at 7:27 p.m.," Harrison said. "I picked her up outside on building security cameras, walking east on Republican Street." He pulled up pictures of Bernstein, in disguise, on his laptop at various points of her walk. "She turns left onto Eastlake, continues over the I-5 freeway, then eventually will make a slight right onto Belmont

Avenue. Here, let me show you." Harrison brought up a map with a blue line he'd used to mark Jenna's walk. "She said she turned left on Bellevue Place, then left again on Boylston Avenue." He clicked the mouse pad, and again brought up images of Bernstein walking along the designated path. Each picture noted the camera's location by address. It also noted the time the picture had been taken. As Jenna had said, the path was in the direction of Volunteer Park.

"She turns right on East Prospect, and that's when we lose her," Harrison said.

"Nothing showing her entering Volunteer Park?" Keera asked.

"The last traffic camera is at the intersection of East Roy and Broadway. That's it." If the State couldn't put Jenna in the park, it made the prosecution's case that much more difficult. But Harrison wasn't finished. "However . . . as Ms. Bernstein advised, Wednesday is food truck night in Volunteer Park during the summer months, which attracts a crowd. No public cameras to speak of, but . . ."

"Somebody with an iPhone?" Keera asked.

Harrison shook his head. "No. Nor is there a public camera in the park. I imagine everyone would scream invasion of personal privacy, until someone got robbed or shot, then those same people would bitch about the lack of cameras. But that's my own personal diatribe. I won't make you stand beneath my soapbox and listen."

"I think you just did."

"Did I?" He laughed.

"No public cameras, but . . . ," she said, to get him back on track.

"I wondered if it was possible one of the food trucks had a camera, you know for theft and such. I made a call to Bitchin Burritos and determined they did, a camera pointed right at their line of customers." With his accent, "Bitchin Burritos" sounded like a delicacy. "They even have a sign that says: 'Smile. You're on *Candid Camera.*'"

Harrison pulled up the photograph.

"Oh shit," Keera said. Jenna stood in a line, looking directly into the camera. "They'll be able to put her in the park." She leaned closer. "What is she looking at?"

"I presume the menu above the truck window at which the customer—not me, mind you—orders their grub. Why? What do you think she's looking at?"

"It looks to me like she knew the camera was there and is looking directly into the lens, to document her alibi that she walked to the park to eat."

"You're dripping cynicism," Harrison said. "That would require some extensive, premeditated planning; would it not?"

"Not for Jenna," Keera said.

"We may need a bucket to catch your drips, Ms. Duggan."

"Doesn't it seem more than a coincidence she would just happen to be in the general location at the time of the murder?"

"Bad luck, no doubt," Harrison said.

"The worst luck, I'd say."

"Oh no, the worst luck is yet to come."

"More?"

"I'm afraid so. Take a look." Harrison pulled up a map of the park. "I circled the house Kohl was renting and marked a red line indicating an easement through the park." The easement came out directly at the back of the property. "I took a ride out to the house following my discovery and walked the path. If someone did not want to be noticed, then wearing a disguise and walking through a park without cameras to an easement leading directly to the back of the house would certainly be a way to do it," Harrison said. "Perhaps the question we should be asking isn't *Could she have done it?* Perhaps the question is *Why would she do it?* Not to be the bearer of yet more bad news, but a source says the US Attorney and Kohl were talking about a deal."

"What kind of deal?"

"I don't know specifics yet, but my source says Kohl was going to testify against Bernstein in the federal case, say Bernstein knew about the misrepresentations and fraud, in exchange for his receiving a lighter sentence."

"How reliable is your source?"

"Very."

Keera gave it some thought. "I doubt it's something I can confirm."

"Why not?"

"Thompson would not have missed documents substantiating what your source is telling you in the first trial—that Jenna knew of the LINK's failings—had those documents existed. He would have used them to cross-examine Jenna and prove to the jury she was lying. And it's even more doubtful the US Attorney will talk to me and tell me what evidence Kohl intended to produce against Jenna with their case against Jenna still pending."

"Wouldn't the lack of documents make Kohl's testimony all the more pivotal, and therefore killing Kohl all the more imperative?"

She nodded. "It would."

"Let me ask you something. You don't seem to like this woman much. Am I warm?"

"Burning up."

"Why not?"

"Jenna and I grew up together. Our parents started out friendly, I think more for each of us than themselves."

"Meaning?"

Keera explained that her siblings were out of the house and Jenna was an only child.

"Enemies?"

Keera gave Harrison's question some thought before answering. "It was never that blatant. Jenna was always more subtle. I only know a few people who would outright say they didn't like her, myself being one, but I also don't know anyone who would call her a friend. We had a saying in high school. 'Nobody likes Jenna as much as Jenna.'"

"A narcissist?"

"Definitely, though I'm not sure that's adequate either. Even when Jenna was doing something for you, you had the feeling you were being manipulated, that you'd regret it later, because she'd call in that favor when she needed it."

"Sounds like you're describing a sociopath."

Keera nodded. "I've certainly considered that possibility."

"Can you back it up?"

Keera could. "Better I tell you a few stories," she said.

"I do love a good story," Harrison said and sat back.

Keera told him about Lake Chelan, and he seemed genuinely concerned and intrigued. Then she said, "Later, in high school, my friend Loren and I wanted desperately to see the band Coldplay, who was coming to KeyArena on their concert tour. The problem was the show was sold out. I looked at the secondary market prices, but they were going for amounts way out of our league. Jenna overheard us discussing this in the school cafeteria and said her father knew a guy at KeyArena and could get tickets. The problem was: You never knew when Jenna was telling the truth and when she was fabricating for dramatic effect. Jenna liked nothing more than to be the center of attention, the person who could solve everyone else's problems. As I said, the caveat was Jenna always expected reciprocation, which could often be a bitch. I had learned to never ask her for help, with anything, because I didn't want to be obligated to her. But Loren couldn't help herself. She basically pled with Jenna to get tickets, and each time Jenna would respond with something noncommittal like: 'I told you my father's working on it' or 'I haven't talked with him for a few days.'"

"She was stringing your friend along."

"It got to the point, as it always did with Jenna, that I regretted she had even overheard us. Finally, early February, when I'd given up hope and had resigned myself to not going . . ."

"She got the tickets."

"No. She said her father *could* get them, but the price was eighty-five dollars each, which was forty-five dollars over the ticket price. When I questioned her, she said the tickets were more expensive because they were on the floor."

"Too crowded for me," Harrison said. "Never my style, but . . ."

"But this was also typical Jenna, always seemed to do what no one else could, but at a price. I still had doubts, and the cost was more than I wanted to pay, but I was working part-time at the firm and had the money. For me, the bigger question was whether I wanted to be indebted to Jenna. I didn't."

"But you really wanted to see Coldplay," Harrison said. "A dilemma."

"I agreed to front Loren the money, and I agreed to drive all of us, including Jenna's friend, Michelle.

"Later, as I was walking to class, I saw Jenna standing in the hallway. What I remember, distinctly, is she closed her locker, turned, and made eye contact. She didn't smile, and it wasn't an expression of acknowledgment, but it was a look I had seen before."

"Meaning what?"

"The look meant *I got you*. And it made me shiver."

"The plot thickens."

"Anyway, Jenna made a big production when the tickets arrived— like the moment in the movie *Willy Wonka* when Charlie finds the golden ticket in the chocolate Wonka Bar. Jenna reveled in the attention, as she always did."

"I would have bet it was all bullshit."

"I'm not done yet."

"Tension, like a good thriller."

"When I picked up Jenna and Michelle the night of the concert, I got out of the car to thank Mr. Bernstein, but Jenna hurried out and said he wasn't home, though his car was in the driveway."

"She didn't want you talking to her father? Why? Do you think she overcharged you for the tickets?"

"I'll shorten the story. Jenna held all four tickets all the way to the door, and when I asked for a stub for a scrapbook, she wasn't going to give me one. Then, finally, she handed one to me and I noticed the price—forty dollars. She was quick to add that the price didn't include all the service fees."

"What did you do?"

"I let it go. I didn't want to ruin Loren's night or mine. Money has never been that important to me, but it has always been important to Jenna," Keera said. "Anyway, the concert was great, and after it ended, Jenna wanted to get something to eat, but Loren had a curfew. Jenna, however, wasn't taking no for an answer. She said, 'You owe me for scoring the tickets.'"

"And there it was," Harrison said. "Payback."

Keera shook her head. "That would have been far too benign for Jenna. I suggested Dick's."

"Never heard of it."

"A man of your refined tastes would not have. Dick's is Seattle's iconic drive-up hamburger stop. It's ridiculously inexpensive and fast, which would have allowed us to eat for just a couple of bucks and get Loren home on time. Jenna vetoed the idea. She wanted to go to a diner in the University District because a certain waiter worked there. When the hostess finally seated us, it was eleven fifteen.

"The waiter was this tall, good-looking guy about our age. Jenna flirted with him the moment he came to take our order. He was a sophomore at UW and a member of a fraternity. Jenna gave him her best smile and asked if they had any parties we could attend. And he said they had parties, but during the week: 'To keep you high school girls away and avoid any trouble with the intra-fraternity council.'"

"I can't imagine that went over well."

"No, it didn't, and an unhappy Jenna was never a good thing. When the bill came, Jenna snatched it from the table, slid from the booth, and walked toward the cash register at the front of the restaurant. I figured she wanted to stiff the waiter his tip because he had rejected her."

"She had other ideas?"

"After several minutes, when Jenna hadn't returned, Michelle's cell phone rang. Then she said she had to go to the bathroom and got up. Shortly thereafter, my cell phone rang. It was Jenna."

"Where was she?"

"With Michelle, outside in the parking lot at a window, holding my car keys and laughing. She said, 'Dine and dash.' I tried to get her to come back and settle up, but she refused. Loren and I didn't have near enough to pay the bill. So after debate we slid from the booth and bolted for the back door. By this point, the restaurant manager and waiter knew something was up. Jenna had pulled the car from the parking slip, pointing it toward the exit. I made it out the door, but the waiter grabbed Loren. I wasn't going to leave her."

"What did Jenna and the other girl do?"

"They left."

"In your car?"

Keera nodded. "And for good measure Jenna flipped off the waiter as she drove away."

"What did she do with your car?"

"She drove Michelle home, then had Michelle follow her back to my house, where she parked the car and left the keys under the floor mat. The night manager called my father, and when he got to the diner, his expression of disappointment just about killed me."

"A daughter disappointing a father. Always painful."

"The manager said he had a daughter of his own, and he didn't want to see us get a police record, which I don't know would have happened, but it was enough to scare us. Anyway, as Patsy paid the bill, the waiter said to me, 'It wasn't your idea; was it?' When I said it wasn't, he said, 'You need some new friends.'"

"I would agree."

"On the drive home I told my father I'd pay him back, but he said it wasn't about the money, and it wasn't."

"Certainly not. Were the other girls punished?"

"Loren was grounded."

"But not Jenna?"

"My dad wanted to call her parents, but I talked him out of it."

Harrison nodded. "You took the high road and sacrificed yourself."

Keera shook her head. "No. I didn't want to get Jenna angry and give her a reason to retaliate—and she *would* retaliate. I wasn't scared of her, but I worried about Jenna ruining Loren's senior year."

"You did take the high road."

"I realized that no good came from being indebted to Jenna, but something bad always did, and I vowed to never again be indebted to her."

"Which raises another question."

"Which is?"

"Will you take her case . . . if they charge her?"

"They're going to charge her, JP." She pointed to the screen. "This just about ensures it." Keera wasn't going to tell Harrison about John Bernstein saving her senior year and protecting her father or about the firm still running in the red. "As much as I don't like it at times, and as much as I don't like Jenna, this is my job now, to provide a defense, even to the reprehensible."

"You don't sound like you're convinced."

"I know," she said. "Because I'm not."

"As I said, the plot thickens."

Chapter 12

Seattle, Washington

Keera spent Sunday morning on a long run and, upon returning home, enjoyed a breakfast of granola with fruit, orange juice, and mint tea. She needed to eat healthy again after weeks of eating fast food on the go. Her cell phone rang. Ella.

"I'm calling to remind you it's the first Sunday of the month." The first Sunday meant a family dinner at their parents' home in Madison Park. "I have you down to bring the salad."

"I'm on vacation," she said. "I only came in Thursday because you and Patsy asked me to."

"Nice try. Maggie already outed you for being on a staycation."

"What difference does that make?"

"You know Mom's rule. You're not in a foreign country. You're not having a life-threatening medical emergency. And you still have a pulse. You're obligated. And your responsibility this month is salad."

Keera stifled an urge to scream and contemplated stabbing Maggie in the hand with her dinner knife.

She ran errands she'd put on hold, and played a game of chess online with a new opponent who went by the moniker White Walker, clearly a *Game of Thrones* fan.

Late that afternoon, Keera put her large wooden bowl in the back of her car behind the driver's seat. The bowl contained lettuce. In separate plastic bags she'd brought grape tomatoes, chopped walnuts, hard-boiled eggs, and fresh bacon bits. In a jar she'd brought homemade vinaigrette dressing. She didn't put the dressing on the salad because Maggie complained it made the lettuce wilt. She didn't include the accouterments because her family members couldn't agree on the time of day if they were all staring at a stopped clock, let alone what they liked and disliked on their salads.

She drove to her parents' home. Maggie had parked her older model Toyota in the driveway, indicating she was on setup duty, the only explanation for her being early, or even on time. Keera, not wanting to get trapped by the other late arrivals, parked in the street.

She pushed open the front door and stepped inside to an array of fragrances coming from her mother's kitchen—garlic, parsley, white wine, and others. Her sister stepped from the kitchen into the hallway leading to the dining room. She carried forks and knives in each hand. Maybe Keera could trip her.

"What are you doing here early? I thought you were on staycation," Maggie said, a haughtiness in her voice.

"Tough to be on stay . . . Tough to be on vacation when people at work don't respect your days off."

"Talk to Patsy and Ella. I do what I'm told."

Maggie played the I-do-what-I'm-told card when it benefited her. Otherwise, she strutted around reception like the managing partner. Try to get a box of staples or roll of tape past her and you had to answer twenty questions.

Keera said, "You could have told me it was for a client meeting, and that everyone was in business attire. You could have told tell me it was Jenna Bernstein."

Maggie pointed the fistful of knives at Keera, and Keera was less than certain it was only for show. "Next time, maybe you'll answer my text messages, rather than make me hunt you down."

"I was on vacation. Why is that so hard for you to understand?"

"What's your problem with Jenna Bernstein anyway? Wasn't she your little pal after Ella and I moved out?"

"That implies you were ever my little pal. As I recall you largely spent your days either ignoring me or complaining I was annoying."

"*Was* annoying?"

Keera was about to unload an f-bomb when their mother quickly came from the kitchen. "What is all the yelling about?"

"The queen bee is upset she had to come into work Thursday," Maggie said.

Maggie could not be reasoned with when she got like this. She'd say the sky was green just to argue. "I was on vacation," Keera said.

"Then why did you go in?" their mother asked.

"Patsy told me to track her down," Maggie said. She went into the dining room to place knives and forks at each setting but not before adding, "She was at home."

"Did this have to do with Jenna Bernstein?" Their mother didn't react with horror—or even surprise. She let out a sigh and said what she'd always said about Jenna. "Trouble seems to follow that girl; doesn't it? Is she being charged?"

"Not yet," Keera said.

"But Patsy wants you to defend her. He told me. How do you feel about it?"

The question was rhetorical. Her mother knew how Keera felt about it because she'd lived through Keera's relationship with Jenna. "Like I'm taking an acid trip down bad-memory lane."

"Have a little grace, Keera. This must be horrible for Jenna's parents."

"Where is Patsy?"

"In his den," their mother said. "I think he's watching the Seahawks."

"Sunday night? Shawn and Michael must be thrilled to be missing the game," Maggie said from the dining room, referencing their two brothers. "This should be an eventful family dinner."

"They can record the game and watch it when they get home. Like their father is doing," their mother said. "This is my time, and I won't compete with sports." She took the wooden bowl.

"You didn't put walnuts on the salad; did you?" Maggie said. "They give me canker sores."

"What's for dinner?" Keera asked their mother.

"Chicken cordon bleu."

"Put a handful of walnuts in Maggie's chicken for me."

She found her father reading a book in his leather recliner and listening to piano music played through the ceiling speakers. The air had the faint odor of cigars, which Patsy had given up many years ago at her mother's insistence, and the smell of alcohol, though Keera deduced that was likely a merciless memory. When Patsy agreed to give sobriety a go, she and her mother had removed and thrown out every bottle of alcohol in the house, including the wine.

"Thought you'd be watching the Seahawks game."

Patsy closed the book and raised his hands. "Don't tell me the score."

"I don't know the score."

"Your mother is making me record it. I want to watch it as if I'm watching it live, without knowing the outcome."

"You could have just made an executive decision and cancelled the family dinner."

"Bite your tongue. These dinners are sacrosanct to your mother. I wouldn't dream of depriving her."

"I think you mean you wouldn't dream of *defying* her."

"That too. The woman scares me," he said with a chuckle.

"Good, then I won't disrupt your sacrosanct game or Mom's sacrosanct dinner. I need to talk to you about some things."

"Jenna Bernstein?" Patsy inserted a bookmark, closed the book, and set it on the side table beneath the lamp.

Keera sat on the leather ottoman. "But first . . . How are you doing?" It was always her first question since Patsy's go at sobriety.

Patsy gave her a wan smile. "I'm hanging in there, kiddo. Haven't fallen off the wagon again. Thought about it. Think about it just about every day. If this murder of Sirus Kohl goes anywhere, it will be a good diversion."

"But also a lot of stress."

Her father waved it off. "I don't feel stress in the courtroom." Funny thing was, neither did Keera. Once the preparation was completed and she stood for the first time, her stress went away, like when she'd played in chess tournaments.

"Have you heard anything?" Keera asked.

"No. You?"

Keera shook her head. "Talked to Frank Rossi, though."

"He and Ford pulled this case?"

She nodded. "Rossi wouldn't tell me anything specific but said he'd suggest to Walker Thompson to let Jenna turn herself in. If it comes to that."

Patsy smiled. "Thompson?"

"That's what he said. How do you feel about it?"

"Mixed. He could be gun-shy given the prior trial. Then again, he could see this as a second bite at the apple."

Keera then told him what JP Harrison had discovered, including that Sirus Kohl had a meeting scheduled with the US Attorney the morning he was killed. Her father had the same reaction Keera had—that if Thompson had documents implicating Jenna, he would have used them in the Wei trial, which made Kohl's testimony significantly more important, but certainly suspect.

"Sounds like they're lining up their ducks to charge her," he said.

Keera agreed. She paused, uncertain her father would answer the next question. She hadn't been working at the firm when Jenna was tried, and her father might not feel it appropriate to talk about that case with Keera. Then again, if it came down to Keera having to defend Jenna, she'd need all the information she could get.

"Something bothering you? Other than the obvious?" her father asked.

"The obvious?" she said.

"Your mother reminded me that you and Jenna had your issues."

"I'd prefer she remembered Jenna had the issues, and I was part of the fallout. You recall the dine and dash?"

"Too well."

She got up and walked to the wall where a cabinet hung, opened it, and took darts from the dartboard. She and her father had epic games when they didn't feel like playing chess. She stepped back and tossed the blue dart. A six. She was rusty.

"Why did you put her on the stand, Dad?"

Patsy held out his hand. "Give me the red." He took the darts and positioned himself to the board. "Let me ask . . . Why do you want to know?" He tossed his dart and stuck it inside the triple circle of number twelve. "Still got it."

"Because it goes against almost everything we're taught about how to try a case, especially one based on circumstantial evidence. It's risky. Too risky. Even for a risk-taker like you." Keera tossed the second blue dart, and it also landed inside the triple ring for the eight.

"True," Patsy said. "But that isn't why you're asking; is it?" His second dart landed in the inner circle. A double bull's-eye worth fifty points, if they'd been playing.

"I was in court that day."

"I remember."

"It was clear to me, maybe because I know you and Jenna so well, that you didn't want to put her on the stand." Keera stuck her third dart inside the number sixteen's triple ring. "Did Jenna convince you?"

"'Convinced' isn't the right word. I counseled against it, but Jenna was adamant she wanted to tell the jury her story. She was convinced she could persuade them. Her mother and father agreed." Patsy's third dart was for just two points.

"They always did give in to her," Keera said, retrieving the six darts. "Or Jenna would make them pay for it."

"Jenna believed she could convince the jury she was innocent, and she did," Patsy said, sounding resigned.

"No." Keera shook her head and handed Patsy the red darts. "You convinced the jury she was 'not guilty beyond a reasonable doubt.'"

"Kind of you to say, kiddo, and I'd like to believe that was the case, but I also spoke to some of the jurors after the trial. It was Jenna's testimony that persuaded them." Patsy stuck the first dart in the triple ring for the number seven. Twenty-one points. "They believed her."

Keera let out a breath, her arm at a ninety-degree angle, and stuck her dart in the triple ring of the number eleven. "People have always believed her. That's the problem."

"But not you." Patsy's second dart was for only ten points.

"I never bought the argument Sirus Kohl controlled her," Keera said. "Not then and not now." She put her second dart in the double ring of the number six. "I've yet to meet anyone who could control Jenna—not even you," Keera said. "She'll do what she wants when she wants. You remember that time I went skiing?"

"I remember you were home for Christmas break. You tore your ACL."

"Do you remember how?"

"I'm sorry, kiddo, I don't. The booze was heavy back then, especially around the holidays."

Keera reminded Patsy that she had been home from Notre Dame and met Loren, who was home from Colorado, in a bar downtown. Keera had grown up skiing. Loren had taken it up in high school and, living in a skier's paradise, she wanted to get better. They agreed to go the following day. Jenna, also in the bar, overheard them and weaseled her way in. Keera had little interaction with Jenna after the Coldplay incident, but saying no to Jenna was never easy.

When Keera picked up Jenna the following morning, she was already in a foul mood. She wanted new Völkl skis for Christmas, and her father wouldn't indulge her. "I ended up pulling over and telling her I wasn't going skiing if she was going to be a shit all day."

"Sounds like something you would say," Patsy said.

Jenna spent the ride talking about herself, all the dates she'd been on, living in her sorority, the fraternity parties. She said she'd also got an internship at Hewlett-Packard for the summer, though she was majoring in business, not computer science. When Keera questioned how she got the internship, she'd said she just showed up for the interview, and it wasn't her fault if Hewlett-Packard thought she was majoring in computer science.

By the time they'd reached the slopes, Jenna had already exhausted them.

"We got into an argument because Jenna wanted to avoid the crowds and ski the runs at the top of the mountain, but Loren wasn't comfortable. I agreed to ski with Loren and hoped Jenna would go up without us, but she stayed and complained all morning. After eating lunch in the lodge, Jenna assured Loren she could find easy runs up top—cat tracks—so Loren could get down the mountain. Loren finally relented."

"Jenna wore her down," Patsy said.

"As was her way," Keera said. "At the end of the day, Jenna took us to an area of the mountain that, I realized, too late, didn't provide an easy way down. The only way down was ungroomed snow on a double black diamond run with steep moguls that were icy from the lack of direct sunlight.

"When I got angry at Jenna, she acted like she'd made an innocent mistake, but I knew she was lying and called her on it. She showed no empathy for Loren. None. She just took off."

"I don't remember this," Patsy said.

"Loren was terrified. I told her to follow my tracks, that I'd lead her down. Long story short, I caught an edge, twisted my knee, heard a pop, and slid down the mountain, losing my poles and skis. I didn't stop sliding until I reached the bottom. It being the end of the day, there was no one around to help us, but eventually we made it down to the medical tent. Half an hour later, Jenna showed up with some guy. They'd been drinking in the bar. I was too angry to talk, but Loren unloaded on her. She told her what happened and said, 'What is wrong with you?' And 'What psychological disorder do you have?'

"Jenna never apologized, Dad. Instead she blamed Loren. I was so angry I told Jenna to find her own way home, that she was on her own, the way she'd wanted it all day. She wasn't even fazed. She left with the guy, still without any apology."

"I'm sorry, honey."

"That's not it, Dad. I watched her leave the ski slopes that day, and when she reached the ski racks, she grabbed a pair of black Völkl skis, the type she had tried to get her father to buy her. Then she turned and looked back, as if to determine if anyone saw her. But later I realized that wasn't why she looked back."

"Why do you think she turned?"

"She wanted me to know she was getting her way, again."

"She's paid a heavy price for it, kiddo. And I suspect from what JP has determined, she isn't out of trouble yet."

"I know. And I wanted to ask if you think that's why she's come to you a second time, because she thinks she can get her way again?"

"Crossed my mind, but . . ." He shrugged. "I'm an old man now. My ego isn't what it once was." He stuck his third dart in the outer ring of the bull's-eye for twenty-five points.

"Didn't mean to imply—" Keera said, but her father waved off the apology. "Did you subpoena Sirus Kohl's phone messages to determine if he also received Erik Wei's message?" She wondered if, as Jenna had intimated, Sirus Kohl could have killed Wei. She missed the inner ring for double bull's-eye with her third dart and received just eleven points.

This time Patsy retrieved the darts. "I didn't. But I did establish that Sirus Kohl had access to all PDRT employees' emails and text messages. So he could very well have seen Wei's. The name and the recipient would certainly have caught his attention."

"But we don't know for certain he saw it, or if he did, when?" Keera asked.

"We don't." He handed her the three blue darts. "For points this time?"

"Sure. Jenna said she confronted Kohl about Wei's threat to expose the company. Did you ever try to confirm she did that?" Keera's first dart stuck the double ring for the number fourteen for twenty-eight points.

"Sirus Kohl wouldn't talk to me, and I didn't seek to depose him because I didn't see how he would help my case. He could only have hurt me if he produced documents showing Jenna knew before she met with Wei." His first shot was for nine points. "Damn."

"Jenna testified that Mrs. Bernstein had been diagnosed with Parkinson's disease. That surprised you when Jenna brought it up on the witness stand; didn't it?"

"It did."

Jenna's second dart garnered just eight points. "Did you ever determine whether she had Parkinson's?"

Patsy shook his head. "Again, wasn't my focus." His second shot hit the triple ring of number eleven for thirty-three points. "Forty-two to thirty-six, my lead. Why are you bringing all of this up now?"

"I don't believe her, Dad. For all the reasons I said before." Her final dart hit just outside the outer ring, which would have been worth twenty-five points. Instead, she scored twenty.

"You think she killed Kohl?"

Keera thought of Jenna's facial expression when she grabbed the skis. "I don't know, but if she did, she got away with murder. And two times might be more than I can stomach."

"We don't know she's guilty." Patsy lowered his dart. "Listen, kiddo. I know this is new for you, being a defense attorney. And I know you have reservations after what happened in the Vince LaRussa case, getting him off, but it isn't your job to get *anyone* off. Including Jenna."

"I know." She'd heard her father's speech about a defense lawyer's job being to defend the accused's constitutional right to a fair trial—that the jury found guilt or innocence.

"But if Jenna is accused, and if you decide you don't want this case, that's your decision. I'll respect that, and I won't judge you one way or the other. First and foremost, I'm your father and I want what's best for you."

"I know, but the firm—"

"Will endure, with or without this case. We'll all just have to work a little harder. But if I can offer something?"

"Sure."

"I found that it was defending the difficult cases when I learned the most about myself—who I was as an attorney and as a person. I never compromised my principles. I never lied. I never allowed a witness to lie. I always respected the judicial system, regardless of the outcome. And I lost a lot of cases, Keera. Certainly as many as I won. That's true of every defense attorney. But I can say I gave every defendant my very best, and in doing so, I hope I preserved the integrity of the judicial system. One I believe in." He smiled. "Come on. Let's finish the game. It's almost dinner." He looked at the dartboard. "I need fourteen points to tie."

Patsy tossed his final dart. Sixteen points.

Keera smiled. "Don't have a big ego anymore, huh? Not about winning?"

Patsy gave her a wink.

"Hey?" Ella walked in.

Patsy quickly turned and said, "Don't tell me the Seahawks score. I'm recording the game."

"Why would I know the Seahawks score? Mom said the two of you are talking shop and to tell you to wrap it up and come for dinner. Are you talking shop?"

"Not anymore," Keera said.

Shawn, Keera's oldest brother, appeared behind Ella. "You watching the game in here?"

Patsy opened his mouth to speak.

"The Seahawks are down two touchdowns in the third quarter," Shawn said.

"No," Patsy moaned and dropped his head. "Why did you tell me the score? I'm recording the game. You know your mother won't let me watch it on Sunday dinner night."

"Who records games anymore?" Shawn said. "You can watch it on your phone." Shawn held up his phone for Patsy to see.

"Technology is killing me," Patsy said.

Chapter 13

The following Monday, Rossi stopped at Park 90/5 to meet with the various experts from the Washington State Patrol Crime Lab. Park 90/5 was the name for the city of Seattle's two-story industrial complex located on Airport Way South.

The news of Sirus Kohl's murder and speculation as to his killer had picked up a head of steam over the weekend and become a freight train rolling fast down the social media tracks. Two prominent influencers speculated Kohl's death was related to the US Department of Justice's fraud-and-conspiracy action against PDRT's CEO and COO. They speculated Kohl killed himself rather than go on trial and face at least a decade in prison. Litchfield's ME report said the location of the bullet hole in the back of Kohl's head made suicide decidedly impossible, unless he was a contortionist. He wasn't.

More disconcerting were rumors that Kohl had struck a deal with the US Attorney in exchange for providing damning information about his former business partner and lover, Jenna Bernstein. It was a little too on point for Rossi's comfort. Neither influencer cited any specific authority to support either theory, but that didn't stop millions of followers from jumping on the train and enjoying the roller-coaster ride.

SPD's public information officer held two press conferences to essentially say nothing. The mayor and chief of police held a conference to also say nothing, but to appease those living on Capitol Hill, they assured the public they were working hard to catch the killer. They added that any suggestion the police department was focused on a specific individual was premature. It was a delicate dance, Rossi knew. Say too much and the media would hint the speculation had legs. Say too little and it would accuse the police department of being incompetent and allowing a killer to roam the Capitol Hill neighborhood.

All of which trickled down the brass tree trunk to Rossi and Ford. In private, the message to them was clear. Get their asses in gear and gather information necessary to make an arrest before the public outcry worsened, along with persistent criticism of SPD. Rossi and Ford had met with Bressler and Kennison, the next-up detectives, and they worked the phones all weekend.

Kennison and Bressler had obtained security footage from cameras mounted on several homes on Federal Avenue, but a review did not reveal any unknown person or car in the vicinity of Kohl's home at the time of the shooting. No neighbor had claimed to have heard the shot or to have seen anything. They turned their attention to expediting receipt of the call detail records, or CDRs, from the various cell phones. Mark Upson worked tirelessly to determine where Jenna Bernstein had gone when she left her condominium building.

Rossi stepped from his pool car and climbed the stairs to the metal door at the back entrance. He entered a code on the keypad, heard the familiar click, and pulled the door open, letting himself in. Rossi had worked a CSI rotation for the better part of two years coming through the detective ranks. He gained valuable experience in the different forensics, including DNA profiling and bloodstain pattern analysis, toxicology, latent fingerprint analysis, procuring and analyzing digital evidence, and identifying firearms and toolmarks.

Rossi greeted those he knew as he walked the hallways. He would meet first with Barry Dillard, head of Washington State Patrol Crime Lab's firearms and toolmarks division. Dillard came to the crime lab out of college, where he had been, of all things, a literature major. Bright and well read, but largely underqualified for many jobs that paid well, he applied for a crime lab position advertised in the *Seattle Times* and soon realized he liked to blow things up more than read Emily Dickinson, Mark Twain, and F. Scott Fitzgerald. Dillard rose through the ranks swiftly. His motto soon became: "Why speculate when you can simulate?" Detectives loved him because he provided fact-based evidence. The years had passed, and Dillard's once blond hair displayed streaks of gray, and crow's-feet etched the corners of his eyes and his mouth, but his love for the job had not waned.

Rossi knocked on the section's door and stepped inside. Dillard and other analysts worked at stations with specialized microscopes and other instruments needed to examine firearms, bullets, and cartridge casings. Ballistics imaging systems captured high-resolution visuals of fired bullets and their casings. Other stations allowed for chemical analysis and detection of gunshot residue, though the latter was now used sparingly and considered largely unreliable. Another station contained a reference collection of firearms and their unique characteristics.

Since they didn't recover a gun at Sirus Kohl's home, Rossi had asked Dillard to compare the bullet that killed Kohl to the bullet that killed Erik Wei, hoping to check it off his to-do list. The two greeted one another, and Dillard gave Rossi a tight-lipped grin and handed the detective his multipage report. Rossi, well familiar with the report's formatting, skimmed it, noting Dillard had microscopically examined the bullet for unique features like rifling marks—distinctive, spiral-shaped impressions—recessed areas called "grooves," and raised areas called "lands" cut into the surface of a bullet as it spun through the barrel of a particular firearm. Dillard had then measured the width and depth of the lands and the grooves to determine the twist rate—the distance the bullet needed to travel down a barrel to complete one full rotation—as well as noting whether the bullet spun clockwise or counterclockwise. He looked for striations, scratches, and irregularities to the bullet due to imperfections in the gun barrel. All of this made the markings on a bullet as definitive as a human fingerprint, unique to each firearm.

"Mumbo jumbo. Yadda, yadda, yadda," Dillard said and held out his hands like a magician. "The two bullets match."

Rossi looked up from the detailed report and felt his pulse quicken. "They match?"

"Visually and microscopically," Dillard said. "No doubt about it. No question about it. Those two bullets were fired from the same 9-millimeter handgun."

This changed things.

Dramatically.

Rossi had thought it possible, but unlikely, the bullets would match. That they did match made it ever more likely the person who killed Wei had also killed Kohl. And Jenna Bernstein owned a 9-millimeter handgun and had a motive to kill both men. Problem was, Bernstein had already been acquitted of killing Wei, and double jeopardy prevented the state from prosecuting her twice for the same crime.

Rossi thought of his conversation with Adria Kohl at the home on Capitol Hill. Speaking of Bernstein, Kohl had said, *You let her get away with murder once. Don't let her do so a second time.*

"Shit," Rossi muttered. The brass would be all over him and Ford. Why couldn't they get a grounder every once in a while? Between the LaRussa investigation and the way Sirus Kohl's murder investigation was shaping up, he felt like the bull's-eye on an archery target.

He thanked Dillard and went to the latent fingerprints and DNA department. Neither department had found Jenna Bernstein's fingerprint or her DNA in the home. Both had been obtained from her following her arrest in the Wei case. They had found Sirus's and Adria's fingerprints, which they had obtained to eliminate prints found inside the home, as well as others they could not identify, meaning the prints weren't in IAFIS—the Integrated Automated Fingerprint Identification System maintained by the FBI.

Rossi would check in with the other departments by phone. He departed with the ballistics report, driving to the secure parking garage on Sixth Avenue and hurrying into the Justice Center. It was alive with activity, the sound of voices talking: detectives on telephone calls and newscasters on the twenty-four-hour news stations from the televisions mounted to the ceiling. He smelled the roasted coffee beans but ignored the temptation and first stopped to speak to Andrei Vilkotski at TESU.

"Ford beat you in," Vilkotski said.

"He told you to say that; didn't he?"

Vilkotski twitched his eyebrows dramatically like Groucho Marx. "I'll never tell. I gave him the forensic imaging I took off the laptop hard drive you provided, as well as the call detail records for the mobile numbers you provided."

Though Rossi and Ford did not have both burner phones, Rossi had submitted an expedited search warrant to the service provider for the call detail records for the two cell phones that exchanged text messages the evening Sirus Kohl was killed, as well as for Adria Kohl's cell.

Rossi exited and hurried to the C Team's bull pen. Ford sat talking with Chuck Pan.

"What's going on?" Rossi asked, removing his jacket and placing it in the locker next to his desk.

Pan said, "I'm getting heat from the brass."

"Tell them to up the police budget and hire more detectives," Ford said.

Pan ignored him. "They're getting questions from the mayor's office, who is getting questions from influential neighbors and organizations on Capitol Hill."

"Tell them we're making progress," Rossi said diplomatically. He leaned against the workstation table in the center of the four desks. Cubicle walls separated their bull pen from the other three Violent Crimes bull pens. "We don't want this to look like a rush to judgment. We need to be careful, given what transpired in Wei. Tell them that also."

"I'm just letting you know," Pan said. "But given the outcome in Wei, let's be sure to dot all our i's and cross our t's."

"But still make an arrest quickly," Ford said, shaking his head, his tone cynical.

"Stopped by the firearms section on the way in," Rossi said, deciding to pull off the Band-Aid quickly and get past the pain. "Barry says the markings on the bullet that killed Sirus Kohl match the markings on the bullet that killed Erik Wei. Same gun. No doubt about it. He's one hundred percent certain."

Pan and Ford did not immediately respond. They, too, knew this piece of evidence complicated matters—a lot. Not only could they not prosecute Jenna Bernstein a second time for the murder of Erik Wei, if they did prosecute her for the death of Sirus Kohl, the defense would, in all certainty, bring a motion to prevent the introduction of any evidence from—or even the mention of—the Wei trial, rightfully arguing it to be irrelevant and highly prejudicial. In other words, Dillard could comment on the markings on the bullet that killed Kohl, but he would be prevented from saying those markings matched the markings on the bullet that killed Wei.

That was the technical fallout.

Even more troubling was the conclusion Rossi had reached on his drive into the office, a conclusion that Ford and Pan were now reaching, based on their facial expressions. It seemed more than likely Bernstein killed both men, if the gun was the one that had belonged to her.

The question was, where was it?

Perhaps not wanting to dwell on the matter, Pan said, "Well, we'll have to deal with that. What else do we have?"

"The daughter sent over emails between her and the US Attorney prosecuting Kohl and Bernstein for wire fraud," Rossi said. "Billy and I went through them over the weekend."

"Anything?"

"The emails confirm the daughter was in contact with the attorney and looking to make a deal for her father." Ford handed Pan a thick packet and offered a summation. "She also sent over the messages her father intended to turn over. The messages aren't exactly clear Jenna Bernstein knew the LINK could not perform as she was representing. Certainly not definitive. They indicate Bernstein was being told TNT could treat chronic wounds and reprogram the skin cells of mice into heart cells."

"But I also read Bernstein's testimony in Wei," Rossi added. "And she made it very clear she wasn't a scientist and relied on them heavily."

"So she could plead ignorance," Pan said.

"Basically," Ford said. "The daughter, Adria Kohl, was probably pitching to the US Attorney that her father's testimony would be instrumental in explaining the documents and in implicating Bernstein."

"Making it more urgent to his killer that he be prevented from making that deal and testifying," Pan said, flipping through the packet of documents, skimming most but stopping to read a few. "What kind of deal was Kohl seeking?"

"In exchange for her father's testimony, she wanted the US Attorney to agree to her father serving one year of home confinement," Rossi said.

"And the US Attorney's response?"

"She confirmed Adria Kohl set a meeting for that morning, but she had not yet seen any documentary evidence, and was anxious to speak to Sirus Kohl and hear what he had to say," Ford said. "She said from her perspective the meeting's purpose was to determine what Sirus Kohl had in mind, and get a better idea about the information he possessed, whether it was good enough to convict Bernstein."

Pan put down the packet. "Adria Kohl needed the US Attorney to hear from her father."

"While the emails and texts don't implicate Bernstein per se, they do indicate Bernstein pushed Kohl, and not the other way around," Ford said.

"How so?" Pan asked.

"On more than one occasion, Kohl told Bernstein to slow down and pull back what she was telling investors, without specifics. He told her the human trials could take years, as could regulatory approval."

"And her response?"

"To paraphrase—that was *his* problem. Her problem was securing more financing to pursue more research and conduct those human trials," Ford said.

They turned to Upson, who walked into their bull pen smiling like the Cheshire cat.

"You smiling because you got lucky this morning?" Ford said. "Or do you have some good news for all of us?"

"Conference room. Thompson will be there. I called him."

"What's going on?" Ford asked.

"It's a surprise."

"I don't like surprises," Ford said.

"You'll like this one."

"Okay, but nobody better jump out from behind anything wearing a clown mask."

"No jumping," Upson said. "No clowns."

Chapter 14

Harrison held the passenger door of his BMW open for Keera in the parking lot of Duggan & Associates' Pioneer Square offices. "You know this is the independent woman era," she said. "You don't have to open the door for me." He didn't have to, but Keera loved his chivalry and would have been disappointed if he didn't.

"Bite your tongue," Harrison said. "My mum would have me boiled in oil if she ever saw me disrespect a woman in such a way."

"Well, we can't have that; can we?" Keera said sliding in.

Keera listened to jazz, a saxophonist, as Harrison closed the door and moved to the driver's side. The inside of the car smelled like vanilla and reminded her of her mother baking cookies after school.

"This music is beautiful," Keera said.

"Kamasi Washington," Harrison said. "My respite from the insanity of this world."

In addition to Harrison holding open her car door, Keera had never seen him put his feet up while wearing shoes, even if they were working late in the office. He said no shoes on furniture was a superstition that dated to the Black Death, the devastating fourteenth-century pandemic that killed millions in Europe. Much later, scientists learned the plague had been spread by fleas and ticks.

Harrison had arranged for Keera to speak with one of PDRT's former employees. Keera had also asked him to track down PDRT's biggest investors and determine their whereabouts the night and morning of the murder. She was anticipating that Rossi would learn of Jenna's walk-about, and Thompson would charge her. If so, she hoped to find others for a possible SODDI defense—Some Other Dude Did It—though she continued to wrestle with whether to represent Jenna at all. She moved forward with the knowledge that she could work the investigation, then turn everything over to another defense lawyer—should she decide to bow out. But she was already steeling herself to the idea of taking the case. She wasn't sure why, not 100 percent. She respected what Patsy said, about learning more about himself defending the difficult cases, but that wouldn't be the reason she took it, not entirely. Nor would the reason be because the firm needed the case financially. Keera also didn't want to back down from the challenge, much like she'd never backed down to opponents in chess tournaments, but that desire wasn't entirely her motivation either. She couldn't deny the fact that a part of her wanted to defend Jenna because it would mean that, for once, Jenna would have to shut up and take someone else's advice. For once Jenna wouldn't be in charge. Keera would run this show. And, maybe, a part of Keera wanted Jenna to know that while her life was once again spiraling down the toilet, Keera's was succeeding, quite well, thank you. Ego? Sure. Retribution. No doubt.

Maybe Patsy was right. Maybe Keera was already learning more about herself than she cared to admit.

As they drove, Harrison told her he'd spoken to half a dozen PDRT investors, all of whom professed to have airtight alibis he continued to check out.

They crossed the 520 bridge over Lake Washington and traveled the 405 freeway to the city of Kirkland, a residential neighborhood in transition, like most cities in the region. Newer, larger, and more modern homes existed among the original two-bedroom bungalows that housed workers when Kirkland had been an industrial town focused on shipbuilding.

"She was squirrelly on the phone," Harrison said. "Reticent to say too much. I'd say proceed slowly." He referred to Isabelle Blowers, who had worked on the marketing team at PDRT.

"Squirrelly in what way?" Keera asked.

"Nervous about being sued. I'll let her explain."

Harrison pushed from the car before Keera could ask him to clarify. Together they climbed concrete steps to a walkway and smelled the green, thick sod leading to a wooden porch with a designer railing. The house might have been modest in size compared to the McMansions going up, but upon closer inspection it appeared to have been significantly and recently remodeled. The windows were vinyl, the wood siding free of nicks and scars and freshly painted a grayish blue. Charming.

Keera pressed the doorbell and noted a Ring camera. What sounded like a small dog barked inside as the door pulled open.

"Isabelle Blowers?" Harrison said in his most charming British voice.

Tall and thin, Blowers had long brown hair, still wet from a shower, that extended down her back. She had applied minimal makeup, eyeliner and lip gloss. She stood barefoot in blue jeans and a pink T-shirt. Unable to get the tiny black-and-white mottled dog to be quiet, she bent and picked it up, grabbing its snout.

"Sorry," she said.

"We spoke on the phone," Harrison said, introducing himself and Keera. "Thank you for taking time to talk with us."

Blowers stepped back and invited them inside. She then went to another room carrying her dog. "Let me put him away or he'll bother us all," she said.

Like the exterior, the interior looked and smelled new. The hardwood floors, what looked like fresh oak and smelled recently finished, glistened beneath throw rugs, and the kitchen appliances and fresh white paint sparkled in the glow of LED lights. A staircase led to the second floor.

"Your home is lovely," Keera said. Hoping to put Blowers at ease, she'd dressed comfortably in blue cotton pants and a collarless white shirt.

"It should. It cost a small fortune," Blowers said, "but still cheaper than buying a new home. We're glad to get the remodel behind us. You represent Jenna Bernstein?"

She pronounced Jenna's last name different from how Keera had always understood its pronunciation. She asked, "You said 'Bernstine,' not 'Bernsteen.' Why is that?"

Blowers shrugged. "I thought the same thing when Mr. Harrison spoke to me on the phone. I thought maybe he'd mispronounced her name, but that seemed unlikely, if you're representing her. 'Bern-stine' is how everyone at PDRT pronounced her name because it's how Jenna introduced herself." Blowers chuckled, though without humor. "She had this gimmick. She'd say, 'It's Bern-stine, rhymes with *Einstein.*' Sounded pathetic then. More so now."

It sounded exactly like something Jenna would say.

"We used to mock her," Blowers said. "We mocked Sirus Kohl too. Though not to either's face. We'd say, 'It's Kohl, sounds like coal, which is what you'll get in your Christmas stocking this year.' His nickname was Ebenezer."

So, no love lost between Blowers and her former employers. "Can we sit for a minute?" Keera asked.

Blowers led them into a living room with a light-blue fabric sofa and side chair, wooden coffee table, and shaggy white rug. In the corner nook was a playpen, a miniature table, and two chairs, and children's books and toys on shelves.

Keera sat on the sofa and faced Blowers. After declining coffee or tea she said, "How long did you work at PDRT?"

"Before we begin, I need to ask, can I be sued for talking to you?"

"I don't see how," Keera said. "But why do you ask?"

"Because that was always the threat to anyone who worked at the company and quit . . . or was let go."

"Can you explain that a bit more?" Keera asked, still not clear.

"Unfortunately, I can. Provisions in our employment contracts prevented us from having discussions with anyone about PDRT—the LINK, the company structure, its policies, just about anything. The contracts also had a strict no-compete provision that broadly defined competitors, which severely limited who we could work for after terminating employment. Oh, and a non-disparagement clause prevented us from saying anything negative about the company to the press or on social media. The provisions were onerous, and PDRT used them as hammers. The threat of being sued was always prevalent."

"When you say PDRT, who do you mean?"

"Mostly Sirus Kohl and his daughter, Adria. As general counsel she drew up the employment contracts, though Sirus handled much of the hiring and firing. We saw employees get escorted out the door without even being allowed to gather their personal possessions. They'd have to later retrieve them from security. As a result, most of us didn't keep anything personal in our cubicles, not even family photographs. The workspace was very sterile."

Keera hoped to put Blowers at ease by telling her PDRT had been dissolved when the US Attorney stepped in, and the company's patents were taken over by an equity firm. "No entity exists that could sue you, or anyone else." The dissolution had also wiped out Jenna's billions entirely.

"I read about that. We all did."

"'We'?"

"Those of us who worked there and who have remained friends."

"You still speak with other PDRT employees?" Keera asked.

"We used to meet surreptitiously once a month when we worked together. After the company went under, we've gotten together a few times. We called it the PDRT support group."

"You seem nervous," Keera said.

"I am nervous."

"Why?"

"Well, I don't want to get sued."

"That can't happen," Keera reassured.

"Maybe not, but someone killed Sirus Kohl, and the police aren't saying much."

"Why does his death make *you* nervous?"

Blowers leaned back. "After Erik Wei, it makes us all a little nervous."

"The PDRT support group?"

"We used to describe the atmosphere at the company as 'oppressive paranoia.' It permeated every department and impacted all of us who worked there. The company would cater lunches and dinners and have company parties Friday afternoons during the summer, but it never felt genuine, not like they were attempting to foster camaraderie or teamwork."

"What did it feel like?"

"It felt forced. Another way to keep us working long hours at our computers and desks. We all worked late because you were conspicuous by your absence."

"Did corporate keep track of your hours?"

Blowers nodded. "We scanned our passes each morning and when exiting the building. If you forgot your pass, you didn't get in. And yes, they checked. If you got in late or went home early, you were likely to get an email or phone call from Sirus asking why. It's why we all went to the parties—not necessarily because we wanted to go, but because we wanted to be seen. We were afraid not to go, that it would be a mark against us, that we wouldn't be viewed as a team player."

"You felt obligated," Keera said.

"We all felt as though we were always being watched and evaluated, which in a sense we were."

"In what way?" Keera asked.

"In every way," Blowers said. "From the moment you walked in the front entrance until the moment you left each night."

"Can you explain what it was like working there?" Keera asked, getting the impression Blowers wanted to vent a bit.

Blowers crossed her legs underneath her on the sofa, a yoga move. "It started from the first interview," she said. "You weren't interviewed at the company; you were interviewed at a coffee shop, or a restaurant. Only after you'd been vetted were you invited to PDRT's offices for further interviews. Even then you only saw the inside of a conference room. They didn't want anyone there who wasn't subject to the employment contract clauses. After being hired, you were expected to stay in your department and not wander. Personal cell phones were prohibited in the building, and the cell phones the company provided employees had the camera disabled."

"You couldn't take pictures?"

Blowers shook her head. "Laptops were also company owned, and again, no camera. We had to leave both the phone and the laptop on our desks at night. We were given work email addresses and only allowed to use those in the office. Social media access at work was forbidden. The internet was on a private, internal IP system, and we were told our internet searches and our emails and social media posts outside of the office were also monitored, and if anything violated the employment agreement we would be terminated and subject to a lawsuit."

"You agreed to these provisions? The employees agreed to them?"

"*Agreed* isn't exactly how we put it. It was mandated as part of our employment contracts."

"But you signed the contracts. Why?"

"One, the pay at PDRT was significantly higher than at other companies. And two, none of us knew the extremes to which things would be taken until we were in it knee-deep. A lot of start-ups have onerous employment clauses, especially technology companies, but the enforcement isn't serious. It's more a forewarning."

"You mentioned people who quit or who had been fired being threatened with a lawsuit?"

"All the time. One day the person was there, and the next he or she was gone. We'd see their laptops and their phones stacked on their desk and say, 'Another one bites the dust.'"

"But why would Sirus Kohl's death make you nervous?" Keera asked.

"Someone killed Erik Wei because Erik threatened to blow the whistle that the entire operation was a sham. Now Sirus, who knew more than anyone about the company's inner workings and about the LINK, is dead. Seems like someone doesn't want some information to get out, even now."

It did seem that way. "Did you know about the misrepresentations regarding the LINK?"

"No," she said shaking her head. "No idea. As I said, PDRT was rigidly compartmentalized, and that limited how much each employee knew about the other divisions. My development team was tasked with helping launch the LINK, but we had no independent knowledge about what the LINK could and could not do. I know that seems crazy, right?"

"Wouldn't the scientists talk about it at work?" Keera asked.

Blowers shook her head. "We weren't even allowed to go to the development floor. All the literature we used to promote the company and the LINK was written for us by management."

"Who did you deal with in the company administration?"

"That would have been Sirus."

"Did you interact with Jenna Bernstein?"

"No," she said emphatically. "We were told by Sirus we were not to take problems to Jenna, that she was busy securing financing."

"You didn't email or text her?"

"I didn't; no." She got a slight grin on her face.

"You were going to say something else?" Keera asked.

"No." Blowers shook her head.

"I'm here to listen."

"We considered it a blessing," Blowers said, a wry smile still on her lips.

"Considered what a blessing?"

"Not being able to communicate with Jenna Bernstein."

"Why is that?"

"Because no good came from interacting with her."

Keera could certainly relate. "Can you give me a specific?"

"The company would hold meetings to build morale and camaraderie, and Jenna and Sirus and his daughter would encourage us to voice concerns we had or problems at the company, but if you were smart you kept your head down and your mouth shut and hoped she didn't notice you."

"What would happen if you spoke up?"

"My experience? You were shown the door."

"You saw Jenna interacting with Sirus Kohl at these lunches and dinners and social functions?"

"We all did. We all watched closely because we'd heard the rumors it was more than a business partnership."

"You heard they were romantically involved?"

"That's what we'd heard. Can't say I ever saw anything to indicate anything more, but it wasn't a well-kept secret."

"You never saw signs of affection between them?"

"I didn't."

"Did you ever see any moments of dislike between them?"

"I'm not sure how you might categorize 'dislike'? But Jenna would get this look on her face, and in private we used to say, 'If looks could kill, Kohl would be a dead man.'"

Not good, Keera thought. "Did you follow the Erik Wei murder trial?"

"Every day. It was real-life drama."

"What part in particular?"

"Every part, but I guess if I had to pick something, I'd pick when Jenna got on the stand to testify. I read about it in the paper, and we talked about it in our PDRT support group. We were certain Jenna was going to be found guilty."

"Why were you so sure?"

"Because she had the motive to kill Erik. It was her company. No mistake about that. Yeah, Kohl was the largest investor, and he ran the day-to-day operations, but Jenna *was* the company. She was on the cover of all the magazines and doing all the interviews. And if it was successful, she was going to be worth a fortune."

"She claimed she didn't know the representations about the LINK were exaggerated."

"Yeah, I read that she said that," Blowers said. She sounded skeptical.

"You don't believe it?"

She shook her head. "No. I don't."

"Why not?"

"Like I said, Jenna was PDRT. It seemed highly unlikely she wouldn't know the product she was representing was so far off from reality."

"Could Kohl have kept the information from Jenna?"

"Again, I read . . . We all read Jenna's testimony in the paper that Sirus controlled her, that he did a . . . a 'mindfuck' on her."

"You don't think that likely?"

"I think you should talk to my friend Lisa Tanaka. She served as PDRT's controller and had a lot more interaction with upper management than I did."

"Was she also in the PDRT support group?"

"She was," Blowers said. "I almost asked her to come over for moral support. She lives close by. We used to commute to work together."

"Will she talk to us?"

Blowers smiled. "She'd like to. Very much."

"You've already spoken to her."

"Last night."

"Why is she eager to talk to us? She's not nervous about potentially being sued?"

"Not again," Blowers said.

Chapter 15

Ford, Rossi, and Pan joined Thompson in the conference room. Upson stood at the front of the table with his laptop connected to a projector. Behind him was a pull-down projection screen.

"First," Upson said. "As you know, we obtained the geo records for Adria Kohl's phone the night her father died." The detective put up documents on the screen to illustrate his presentation. "As she told you, she remained at home. At least her phone remained at home. At roughly six o'clock the following morning, we traced the phone to her father's rented house on Capitol Hill."

Rossi started to mentally cross off Adria Kohl's name from his list, then stopped, something preventing him from doing so, though he was not sure what. Instead, he put a check mark at the front of her name and circled it.

"We then did a thorough analysis to document Jenna Bernstein's whereabouts the night of the murder," Upson said, "starting with the security footage from her condominium complex. I spoke to the security guard who worked that night and showed him the footage. He said he couldn't be sure it was Jenna Bernstein, and they don't require residents to log in or out, just visitors."

"It's her unit," Ford said.

"Doesn't necessarily mean it's her," Thompson said.

"Can I continue?" Upson asked, making it clear he wasn't finished. "I measured the height of the guard desk, then had CSI calculate the height of the woman on the tape based on the height of the desk. The woman is six feet—Jenna Bernstein's height, which is not typical height for a woman."

It was a smart deduction by Upson. As the footage ran, he narrated Bernstein leaving the building, then each traffic and business camera that picked her up as she walked. Despite his skepticism, Rossi could feel his pulse kick it up a notch when Bernstein did not get in a taxi nor an Uber, and she didn't walk to a nearby workout facility. The path Bernstein walked was in the direction of Volunteer Park.

With each new picture on the screen, placing her closer to the park, Rossi felt his tension rise. As a detective got closer to a suspect, the anticipation of an arrest rose, but so, too, did the pressure to find enough evidence to convict.

"This is a picture from the camera at the intersection of East Roy and Broadway, near the park's entrance," Upson said.

Close but . . . "But nothing showing her entering Volunteer Park?" Rossi asked, which was the question on everyone's mind.

They all turned their attention from the screen to Upson, who was clearly enjoying what might be his last days in the lights before retirement. He put up another photograph of customers at an elevated counter and said in his low-key manner, "This is Bitchin Burritos, one of the food trucks in the park."

"Holy shit," Pan said. "That's her."

"She ordered food at 8:08 p.m." Upson spoke to Rossi. "It's just a short distance on park paths to reach the path you identified leading to the home Sirus Kohl rented."

Rossi tempered his excitement and tried to quiet the many questions firing in his brain. Jenna Bernstein was smart. She'd clearly know her complex had cameras, and she had to know the disguise would not hide her identity. She also had to know about traffic cameras and security cameras on commercial buildings and residences.

Why would she do it?

Why would she put herself in the crosshairs with a flimsy disguise and walk to a park so close to the home, *and* allow herself to be photographed at a food truck? Maybe she had no other plan and, upon receiving Kohl's text messages, she panicked?

"What about her path home? Can it be documented?" Pan asked.

"Not the path," Upson said. "But the building security tapes document her return at roughly 10:17 p.m."

Rossi struggled to slow his thoughts and assimilate the information. He knew Ford was doing the same. Homicide investigations needed to proceed step-by-step to prevent overlooking something and making a fatal mistake.

"There's more," Upson said. "We also got the GPS records for Bernstein's cell phone for that evening."

Upson put up a map with a red dot signifying the condominium building, then a photograph of the same red dot in the same location at 8:00 p.m., then 8:30 p.m., 9:00 p.m., 9:30 p.m., and 10:17 p.m.

"Her phone never left the building?" Ford asked.

"Doesn't look like it," Upson said.

"Who doesn't bring their cell phone with them when they go out walking?" Pan said. "Especially a woman, alone at night."

"Who could be a target, given recent news of fraud and misrepresentation," Ford said.

Rossi looked at the check mark he'd placed beside Adria Kohl's name. It was the same reason he hadn't scratched her name off the list. Her phone stayed home that night, but that didn't necessarily mean she had.

"Bernstein knew her cell phone records can be checked for GPS coordinates from the Erik Wei trial, learned from it, and left her phone behind," Thompson said, offering an explanation.

It wasn't a bad answer, but if that was true, couldn't Bernstein have come up with a better plan than to put on a ball cap and glasses and walk to Capitol Hill? Rossi shook his head. "Does anyone else feel like this is too easy?"

The other four in the room turned and looked at him.

"I mean she had to know her building had security cameras; didn't she? She's smart. She knew she couldn't evade them."

"That's the reason for the disguise," Ford said.

"She's six feet tall," Rossi said. "A ball cap and glasses don't exactly hide her identity, Billy, any more than they would hide yours. Especially when the tape shows her exiting her condominium unit. And Duggan will dismiss the disguise. She'll say Bernstein wore the hat and glasses to conceal her identity because of the recent indictment for fraud. That she was a target."

"Maybe," Pan said.

"No maybe. You can count on it," Rossi said. Keera would never let something like this go unexplained.

"I agree," Thompson said. "If she's anything like her father."

"Then Bernstein goes to the one food truck that happens to have a camera documenting its customers?" Rossi said.

"Is it the only truck that had a camera?" Pan asked Upson.

"Appears to be. I didn't check them all after I found the one."

"All I'm saying is you might be overthinking this. You might be giving her too much credit," Pan said to Rossi.

"Am I?" Rossi asked. "We just speculated she knew her phone could be traced so she left it in her apartment, but she didn't know we could document her leaving the building using the security footage?"

"We aren't the only ones who know about her walk to Volunteer Park," Upson offered. His comment again got everyone's attention. "The owner of Bitchin Burritos said I was the second person to ask about the same woman. He said the first person asking was a well-dressed Black man who came by the business the day after the murder, asking the same questions about whether the food truck had cameras and kept the recording."

"JP Harrison," Rossi said, familiar with Harrison from the Vince LaRussa trial. "He's a PI for Duggan & Associates."

"Former SPD. Good detective," Pan said. "We worked together."

"Then Duggan knows what we know," Thompson said. "She knows her client received text messages from Sirus Kohl, and she knows Bernstein left her building and walked to Volunteer Park shortly thereafter."

"Almost as if Bernstein is baiting us, daring us to charge her again," Ford said, looking at Thompson.

Rossi weighed the ramifications of what Upson had found. He knew the others were as well. They could put Jenna Bernstein close to the murder scene, though not at the scene. They had documentary proof Sirus Kohl reached out to her, even hinted at what he intended to do, though the text string did not provide specifics. Still, Bernstein—if it had been Bernstein who responded on the cell phone text string, and that certainly appeared to be the case—was clearly worried and asked to get together and talk.

Had that been the reason for Bernstein's walkabout? Was he over-thinking it? Had she put on a hat and glasses because it was the best she could do given the time constraints? Had she walked to Kohl's home to convince him not to strike a deal with the US Attorney and, when she failed, shot and killed him?

"Who did he call after that text string?" Thompson said, going through the documents Upson had provided. He recited the number when he found it.

"That was the call he made to Adria Kohl," Ford said, also flipping pages. "She told us her father called her that night between nine thirty and ten to confirm the meeting in the morning with the US Attorney."

"Proof he intended to go forward," Thompson said. He took a breath and sighed. Thompson now had evidence Jenna Bernstein had both a motive and an opportunity that fit within the medical examiner's window of time for when the murder had occurred.

The question on everyone's mind, but which no one would say, was whether Dan Butcher, the King County prosecuting attorney, would have the cajónes to pull the trigger and again charge Jenna Bernstein with murder.

Rossi thought about what Ford had said, about Jenna Bernstein possibly baiting them. Ordinarily he would have dismissed that thought. But he'd also read the Wei trial transcript, and he wondered whether Patsy Duggan put Jenna Bernstein on the witness stand or whether Jenna Bernstein had insisted. If the latter, it made Ford's hypothesis all the more probable. Jenna Bernstein, emboldened by the outcome in Wei, thought she was smarter than everybody else.

And that was a trait held by most sociopaths.

Chapter 16

Isabelle Blowers made a phone call, and Lisa Tanaka was indeed eager to meet Keera and Harrison. She suggested the 203°F Coffee Company at The Village at Totem Lake. Keera hadn't been to Totem Lake in years and was amazed by its transformation, which centered around The Village, a high-density residential and retail complex that took the place of what had been a strip mall. They drove past multiple apartment complexes with ground-floor bookstores, coffee shops, restaurants, retail shops, a movie theater, banks, a pharmacy, and workout and health-care facilities.

"I never understood the appeal of living, working, eating, and exercising on top of each other," Harrison said. "Makes me claustrophobic just thinking about it."

"Convenience," Keera said as Harrison maneuvered up one parking aisle and down another, looking for a safe place to park his baby, so it didn't get dinged.

"Convenience is boring. Give me chaos," Harrison said. "Only thing missing is a funeral parlor and cemetery. It reminds me of that movie *The Truman Show*."

Keera knew the movie. Jim Carrey lived inside a fake reality where everything was convenient. "Is that why you're parking far enough away to hail a cab to the coffee shop? Chaos?"

"A little exercise will be good for both of us."

"A little?"

"Humor me."

The coffee shop interior was white, neat, and orderly. The glass counter displayed quiche, croissants, and muffins, and the smell of the baked goods and the coffee was more than a little tempting to Keera. A board on the wall advertised espresso macchiatos, cappuccinos, cortados, and Americanos. Keera, who had given up caffeine, detected the rich, bitter aroma and was tempted to order a decaf but declined when Harrison asked.

"Bet you they serve the coffee with designs in the foam," he said.

A woman stood from a rough-hewn wooden bench in the corner and maneuvered around a small table to greet them. "I saved a couple of chairs," Lisa Tanaka said after introductions.

"Thank you for making time to speak to us," Keera said.

"I work in one of the buildings here and have an apartment close by." Tanaka had black hair showing strands of gray and falling to her shoulders. She was petite, her hands almost girlish in comparison to the large mug of coffee.

Harrison gave Keera a look.

"They have good coffee, if you'd like a cup."

Keera again declined. Harrison went to the counter.

Keera and Tanaka sat across from one another. Tanaka set her cup of coffee on the table between them. Steam wafted off the surface.

"Isabelle said you represent Jenna Bernstein. Is this for the US Attorney's suit for fraud?"

"No," Keera said.

"Sirus Kohl's murder, then?"

"There have been no charges against anyone, but given the circumstances, we are involved. Our firm represented Jenna in the Erik Wei trial."

"Oh," Tanaka said with a clear bite to the word.

Keera decided to bring out the elephant in the room. "We understand you don't care for Jenna."

Tanaka smiled. "No, I really don't."

"I appreciate your honesty." Keera almost said, *Neither do I.*

"I think she's a spoiled, narcissistic bitch who, when she doesn't get her way, attacks."

Keera wasn't going to argue. "You had some specific run-ins?"

Tanaka sipped her coffee and set the mug down. It looked from her reaction like the coffee was hot. "I did. I quit. I grew tired of the corporate paranoia, the unreasonably long hours, and the lack of appreciation. I also couldn't stand the lying."

"Let's start at the beginning. You were the controller?"

"That was the position I was hired to perform, but it's hard to prepare financial statements, estimate cash flows, and provide accurate and timely information to investors when you can't get the information out of corporate management."

"Who in particular?"

"Jenna Bernstein and Sirus Kohl. If you talked to Isabelle, then you know how tightly they controlled every aspect of the company. Especially the financing. I was given piecemeal financial information on a need-to-know basis but asked to prepare these rosy financial projections for distribution to PDRT's investors and board of directors."

"Who did the asking?" Keera asked.

Harrison returned with his coffee and a smug smile indicating he'd been right about the design in the foam.

"Kohl provided me with financial profiles, but Jenna had her hand in it. She'd review my financial analysis and practically rewrite the whole thing, making it look a lot more positive, but then she wouldn't sign it. She wanted me to sign the analysis. She said it was part of my corporate duties. If I balked or called the document into question, she'd say every start-up goes through rough patches at the initial stage, and it's common to 'fake it until you make it.' She said PDRT investors were sophisticated, that she'd spoken to each and every one of them and had conveyed the financial picture clearly and honestly. She said all were aware the financial analysis was brighter than reality, but necessary for the company to continue to bring in additional investors to move the LINK to production. That, of course, was a lie, as the US Attorney's suit can attest."

"You didn't agree?"

"Making the projection brighter is one thing. Creating a supernova is another. I got tired of fighting her on it and finally refused to sign the documents. If she wanted to put her ass on the legal line, fine, but I wasn't going to do it. I didn't care what they paid me. I was constantly stressed out. When I started losing my hair in the shower, my husband took me to see a psychiatrist who diagnosed me with situational anxiety. He recommended I quit for health reasons. I advised Jenna and Kohl in an email, told them I would be making a disability claim, and gave them my two weeks' notice. When I showed up to work the next day, security told me I'd been locked out. I couldn't even retrieve my personal belongings. I was told they would be delivered to me after they'd been gone through to ensure I wasn't taking any corporate secrets."

"Why did you get sued?"

"Because I got pissed and fired off an email telling them if I didn't get back my personal belongings immediately, and my severance package in full, I'd let our investors know the financial analysis they had been receiving was utter bullshit, and I'd alert the regulatory authorities, and file a claim for discrimination and retaliatory firing."

"I take it that didn't go over well," Keera said.

"They sicced Kohl's daughter on me, the pit bull. I received a multipage letter telling me they would sue me for breach of my employment agreement, claim my disability was manufactured, and, if I went to any regulatory agencies, they would respond that I had prepared the financial analysis and signed those statements verifying they were accurate and that PDRT management and investors had relied on them as accurate. The letter came from Adria Kohl, but it had Jenna Bernstein's fingerprints all over it."

"How do you know?"

"Because I worked closely with her and saw her do similar things to other people. I knew her buzzwords. She insulated herself by setting things up to make it look like mistakes were always some other person's fault. Never hers. Right down to blaming Sirus Kohl for Erik Wei's death. That was quintessential Jenna. The minute I read of her testimony in the newspaper I cried because it brought back memories of everything she did to me. All the threats."

"You think she set Kohl up?"

"I have no doubt that's exactly what she did, because she'd done it to me and to others. I read about the . . . what was her defense again?"

"Svengali," Keera said.

"Yeah. Such bullshit. Such utter bullshit."

From behind the counter a woman called out a name for an order.

"You don't think Sirus Kohl controlled and manipulated her?" Keera asked Tanaka.

Tanaka's eyes expanded. "From my perspective? Not a chance. From my perspective Jenna controlled Kohl. He doted on her. He was always at her side, making sure she was okay. He made sure she ate, she worked out, and she went home at a reasonable hour."

"Some might say that was evidence he was manipulating her by controlling her."

Tanaka shook her head. "Some might, but those of us who actually worked there, and who saw their interaction, called Kohl her labradoodle. Not to be unkind, but Sirus was short, overweight, and not exactly good looking. Jenna was tall, had a knockout figure, and a multi-billion-dollar idea."

"You didn't see the two of them as compatible," Keera said.

"To the contrary. Kohl was exactly Jenna's type—rich. Rich and vulnerable. People thought Kohl was this tough guy, but the tough guy was just a façade Jenna made him wear around the employees. Hell, her personality was also a façade."

"In what way?"

"In every way. The way she dressed, wore her hair, all her buzzwords." Tanaka spoke with an affected voice. "'Start-ups don't start up on their own. They take a team of dedicated employees.' It was all to create an image that she was important and about to forever change the face of medicine."

"But once she had Kohl's money, why continue the charade? Why move in with him?"

"It wasn't just the money. She was this twenty-two-year-old woman with an undergraduate degree and a billion-dollar idea. She didn't have a clue what she was doing. She needed Kohl's knowledge, his resume. He'd invested in biomedical companies and hit it big. She needed investors to believe if Kohl thought this highly guarded product had legs, then it must be something groundbreaking."

"Why do you think he put up with her then?" Keera asked.

"If he was in for a penny, he was in for a pound. Do you follow me?"

"He was in too deep to pull out," Keera said. "Too much money invested."

"Once Jenna had his money, she had all the control. He needed to make the company work or he was going to lose a fortune. If she told him to do or say something, he was going to do it and say it. But not just because his money was at stake."

"What other reason?"

"I think he genuinely loved her."

"Then you don't believe he manipulated her?"

Tanaka made a face like her coffee had turned bitter. "No one manipulated Jenna Bernstein. No one. In my opinion? I think she did a number on Kohl, made him believe she was too good for him, and he was lucky to have her. In my opinion he was like a lovesick teenager trying to appease his sociopathic girlfriend."

"You believe she's a sociopath?"

"Yeah. I do. And other former employees would agree with me. When we learned Jenna had moved into Kohl's home, we figured Kohl was done for. She'd have her claws in every aspect of his life, and Sirus would have no respite from the psychological abuse."

"Like what?"

"I believe she constantly made him think if he didn't do as she demanded, she'd leave him. Rumors of other men were persistent throughout the time I worked there."

"Any in particular?" Keera pushed, noting Tanaka had said "I believe."

"Yeah. The guy who owned the security company. He was with Jenna seemingly twenty-four seven and had the perfect excuse if anyone called him or her out. He could say he was just doing his job staying close to Jenna—a job Sirus had asked him to perform. What better cover was there?"

Keera again pushed for specifics. "Any incidents in particular to support your conjecture?"

"As a matter of fact, yes," Tanaka said, and she sounded like she had been waiting for Keera to ask. "I was at the office late one evening . . . most evenings. Anyway, I went down to Jenna's office to talk with her and I heard soft voices inside. Moaning and groaning. I froze at first. Thought it was Jenna and Sirus. Then curiosity got the better of me and I just listened for a moment. The next thing I knew the door opened and there stood Thomas Martin, the head of security at TMTP, an independent contractor that provided security services. He served as Jenna's bodyguard. Both he and Jenna looked more guilty than a dog with your chewed-up shoe. Martin was tucking his shirt into his pants. The buttons were undone down to his navel and his hair was mussed. Jenna looked like she'd been ridden hard. She said something like 'Oh. You're still here.' As if I would be anywhere else."

"Did you tell anyone about it?" Keera asked.

"I wasn't going to. I mean it was awkward. Really awkward, given Jenna was living with Sirus and his daughter was general counsel. But then I decided, this was wrong. What Jenna did was her own business, but when her actions were unprofessional and could damage the company, then it wasn't just her business."

"What did you do?"

"I went to Adria Kohl's office, and I told her what I had heard and what I saw. I said Jenna's personal life and her relationship with her father wasn't any of my business, but her actions were completely unprofessional and if any investors found out it could be damaging to the company."

"What was Adria Kohl's response?"

"Measured. She appeared stunned, then hurt. I mean, this was her father. She asked me if I had discussed what I had seen and heard with anyone else, but of course I hadn't, and I told her I wouldn't. She told me she knew how uncomfortable it must have been for me to tell her, but she was glad I did. She thanked me and said she absolutely agreed with me. She said she would talk to Jenna and let her know her actions were inappropriate."

"What about the head of security, Thomas Martin?"

"All I can tell you is he stayed on. I still saw him around all the time."

"He wasn't fired?" Keera asked, surprised.

"No. I don't even know if he was reprimanded."

Odd. In a company that seemed quick to fire, why wouldn't they terminate the contract for the security services if a bodyguard is sleeping with the CEO? "Any other incidents?"

"Not that I personally witnessed, but others said . . . PDRT would hold these blowout parties and the investors would often be there. Employees would see Jenna and . . ." She addressed Harrison. "You know when a woman is flirting—the excessive touching, the head tilt, the grin? Jenna would do it with investors in Sirus's presence, and he did not look happy about it."

"Angry?"

"I'd say more hurt than angry."

"Did you ever see them argue?"

"No," she said, shaking her head.

"Isabelle Blowers said PDRT sued you?" Keera said. "What came of the lawsuit?"

"It was costing me a small fortune, so I finally ignored my attorney's advice and called Adria Kohl directly. I told her that if PDRT didn't back off and pay me my disability and my severance, I'd let the investors know Jenna and her bodyguard were sleeping with one another."

"And?" Keera asked, thinking the threat could be dismissed as the untrue weapon of a disgruntled employee, which might have been why Martin wasn't terminated. Why give him an axe to grind?

"My attorney got a dismissal in the mail within a couple of business days of my telephone call."

A good indication Tanaka's perception of Jenna and Martin had been accurate. So again, why wasn't he fired? "Let me ask you a question. You obviously don't like Jenna."

"I don't, but what I'm telling you is the truth."

"I don't doubt it. But why didn't you ever go public with the information about her manipulating the financial projections? Why not take your knowledge to the IRS or other administrative agencies?"

Tanaka smiled, but it had a sad, you-have-no-idea quality to it. "The US Attorney," she said.

At first Keera didn't understand, then it dawned on her why Tanaka still feared Jenna. "You think Jenna is going to blame you in the US Attorney's lawsuit. You think she's going to plead ignorance to the fraud and the conspiracy and blame you for the misrepresentations because you signed the documents."

"I haven't slept well these past few months. Not since Adria Kohl called me."

"Adria Kohl called you?"

"Unbelievable gall, don't you think?"

"What did she want?"

"She wanted me to testify in the US Attorney's case about what Jenna had me do—how she had manipulated the corporate documents."

"What did you tell her?"

"I asked her what assurances she could provide me that Jenna wouldn't blame me for the fraud."

"Did she give you any assurances?"

"She said her father was going to testify. She said he would tell the US Attorney Jenna had lied at the Wei trial, that she knew her representations about the LINK were false. She said Sirus would back my testimony that Jenna had me change the financial projections."

"What did you tell her?"

"I told her I was scared of getting involved, and scared of going to jail. I told her I didn't trust Jenna Bernstein."

"What did she say?"

"She said she was working out a deal with the US Attorney. She said that, in exchange for Sirus providing such information, she would ask for immunity for him and anyone else who came forward. I told her if she could swing that deal, I would consider talking to the attorney."

"But then Sirus Kohl died," Keera said.

"And I'm back on my anxiety meds and looking over my shoulder and around doors," Tanaka said.

They spoke for more than an hour. Keera thanked Tanaka, provided her with a business card, and said she might have more questions. Then she and Harrison departed.

Back in the car Harrison gave Keera a look. "She seems convincing, but she also clearly has a grudge and the potential of going to jail if she didn't cooperate with Adria Kohl."

"Which could make what she has to say unreliable, except . . . Adria Kohl dropped the lawsuit. Wouldn't that be an indication Tanaka is telling the truth about the corporate projections being Jenna's doing—and about the relationship between Jenna and her bodyguard?"

"Doesn't sound like Sirus Kohl was controlling Jenna; does it?" Harrison said.

"No one ever could," Keera said. "Not even Patsy." They let that thought linger. Then Keera said, "But we have a bigger problem."

"The US Attorney?"

"Adria Kohl was getting her ducks lined up to save her father by having him and other employees testify against Jenna. That confirms what I said before: the documents Kohl said she had assembled to prove Jenna knew of the misrepresentations aren't convincing. Adria Kohl is an attorney. If the documents aren't enough on their own to establish what Jenna knew and didn't know, then all she had was her father's word, and Sirus Kohl could be largely discredited as trying to get even for what Jenna did to him at the Wei trial. Adria needed an independent source to confirm what her father would tell the US Attorney to get the immunity deal."

"And to have Jenna convicted," Harrison said.

"It might not have been enough to convict, but it certainly would have been enough to try," Keera said.

Chapter 17

Rossi and Ford drove to Auburn, Washington, just off a Highway 18 exit. The area was mixed residential and commercial, with single-story rambler homes and industrial complexes. The industrial complex that housed TMTP Security was located behind a cyclone fence with rolls of razor wire strung along the top. While debate raged within the prosecuting attorney's office whether to charge Jenna Bernstein or to bring the evidence before a grand jury first, Rossi and Ford wanted to learn more about the threats allegedly made to Sirus Kohl following the Erik Wei trial and the US Attorney filing its federal court action.

Ford stopped the pool car at a fence. A security guard stepped from a booth and approached their vehicle in a navy-blue uniform with patches on the sleeves, thick-soled black boots, and an equipment belt holding a Taser, pepper spray, and walkie-talkie. Popeye arms stretched the fabric of his short-sleeved shirt, and reflective sunglasses shaded his eyes.

"Look at this robocop," Ford said from his driver's seat. He was already unhappy because of the traffic and had a thing about what he called "rental cops" and "law enforcement dropouts." He likened them to paranoid militia members preparing for Armageddon and just itching for a fight.

"Play nice, Billy."

"Help you?" the guard asked, his tone and expression flat.

Ford held up his detective ID and badge. "Got a meeting with TMTP Security."

"And who at TMTP would you be meeting with, Officer?"

"It's 'Detective,'" Ford said. "And that would be none of your business."

This set the man back a step. He aimed his sunglasses at his clipboard. "Do you recall the time of your appointment?"

"Now," Ford said. "It's why I'm sitting in the car speaking with you now."

Rossi leaned across the car interior. "The name of our contact is Thomas Martin. Appointment is at eleven fifteen."

The guard scanned a clipboard. "You're not on the list of approved guests."

Ford held up his badge. "Look again."

"I can't let you—"

"I set up the meeting this morning," Rossi said. "Perhaps you can call someone at the company to confirm. I'm Detective Frank Rossi. This is Detective Billy Ford."

The guard pivoted and returned to his booth.

"Why do you pacify those guys?" Ford asked.

"Because I don't want to waste time talking to him out here."

"Bunch of white supremacists looking for any reason to start shooting people."

"That sounds kind of racist, Billy. I am white, you know."

"It ain't racist if it's the truth. And I said white *supremacist*."

The guard returned. "Sorry for the confusion and the delay, Detectives. Mr. Martin neglected to call and put you on the list." He pushed a button on his utility belt and the gate rolled back. "Take a left at the end of the first building. TMTP is in Building C. It will be on your right."

"Thank you for your help, Officer," Rossi said.

"Officer?" Ford said, rolling the pool car into the complex.

They pulled up to a cinder-block building. The only thing stenciled on the glass doors was the address. "Understated," Rossi said as they got out.

"The Ku Klux Klan didn't advertise their hoods either."

"You do have a bug up your ass," Rossi said.

Rossi pressed a button and, after identifying himself to a camera over the door, they were let in. The interior smelled musty, like a gym in need of a better ventilation system. Behind a reception desk a wall displayed a stenciled drawing of a growling, muscled man with a crew cut bursting through a concrete wall. On his bulging sleeves was the TMTP Security patch.

"So much for subtlety," Ford said.

Rossi greeted a receptionist who said, "Mr. Martin is on his way out."

A lean, fit-looking man came through a secure interior metal door dressed in a black formfitting T-shirt, black tactical pants, and black boots.

"Detective Rossi? Thomas Martin," he said extending his hand. Rossi shook it and introduced Ford. "Sorry about the mix-up at the gate. We're in the middle of our six-week training of new cadets and I neglected to alert them you were coming. I hope it wasn't too much trouble."

"It's all good," Rossi said. "New cadets?"

"We put prospective hires through a rigorous physical and mental training camp, not unlike at the police academy. We try to eliminate those with the wrong disposition."

"Who would that be?" Ford asked.

"The cowboys who just want to knock heads. That isn't what we're about. Come on back. You can see our tactical course on the way to my office."

As they walked through an open warehouse, Rossi considered military training ropes, nets, towers, and other obstacles. Martin explained he had served in the army—Special Forces—along with his business partner, Tim Peterson. When they got out, they were looking for a profession. "There was a need for well-trained, highly skilled, private security. We don't employ the security guards you find in malls. Mostly we do corporate contracts, providing security to prominent executives and their families."

Of which quite a few existed in Puget Sound. The tech industry had made billionaires out of some and millionaires out of many more.

Martin's office on the second floor was also understated. He had photographs on the wall and what looked like military medals in display cases. Rossi noted a wife and two small boys in a picture frame on his desk. The children, blond, resembled their mother. A large picture window looked down into the warehouse obstacle course.

"Where are the recruits?" Ford asked.

"Taking a psychological assessment. If they pass, they will undergo interviews to evaluate stress management, emotional stability, decision-making abilities, and ethics and empathy."

"Sounds thorough," Rossi said.

"We push them to weed out those who can't make the physical standards, and a handful more that fail the psychological assessment." Martin moved behind his desk and gestured to two chairs. "Take a seat. This is about PDRT?"

Rossi and Ford sat. "You provided security to the company?" Rossi asked. He and Ford had agreed that Rossi would take the lead.

"At the company headquarters, and to two of its officers," Martin said.

"Which officers?"

"Sirus Kohl and Jenna Bernstein."

"What did the security entail?" Rossi asked.

"For the company?"

"Start with that."

Martin rocked back and forth, his leather chair creaking. "We performed background checks on new hires. We checked for drug use and criminal convictions and checked out their references and past work history . . . if any issues existed at prior places of employment. We reviewed social media postings for red flags such as drug and alcohol use. We also provided security in the building lobby. Employees were required to scan a pass to be admitted and when leaving. Guests had to be on a designated register and escorted onto and from the floors."

"And what was the security you provided for Sirus Kohl and Jenna Bernstein?" Rossi asked.

"Twenty-four seven."

"That seems extreme," Ford said.

"We kept security at the front gate and at the back of Mr. Kohl's home, which overlooked Lake Washington and could be accessed by boat, or someone swimming. We also provided a car service to and from work, and to wherever Mr. Kohl or Ms. Bernstein desired to go—restaurants, for instance. We checked out and secured meeting locations, beforehand, and scanned their corporate headquarters several times a week for bugs and cameras and other forms of corporate espionage. We also scanned their internal internet."

"Did you ever find a threat—of any kind?" Ford asked, sounding skeptical.

"We recommended rejecting certain hires for various transgressions, and we identified instances in which an employee broke company contractual policies regarding social media."

"Which was what exactly?" Rossi asked.

"Disparaging the company and/or disclosure of corporate secrets."

"Who did you report these violations to?" Rossi asked.

"Contractual violations were reported to Adria Kohl. She was general counsel. Other violations were reported to Sirus Kohl."

"Did you report to Jenna Bernstein?" Rossi asked.

Rossi detected a subtle pause before Martin said, "Not on security violations, no. We did, however, transport her, as I mentioned."

"Did you get involved in the lawsuits Adria Kohl brought against employees who quit or were fired?"

"We gathered evidence if they violated their employment contracts."

"And you gathered the evidence necessary to . . . what, intimidate those employees?" Ford said.

Rossi had worked with Ford long enough to know he was doing something similar to what the border patrol did to individuals who fit a certain terrorist stereotype seeking to drive across the border. They asked questions intended to provoke and rattle the person. A person under stress, like those sitting in a car atop explosive dynamite, or who had illegals, or drugs, could display physical manifestations when put under pressure.

Martin smiled. He, too, seemed to know what Ford was doing, and he sounded eager to prove he'd passed the psychological assessment. "We just gathered the information. We didn't act on it."

"Any threats from any disgruntled former employees?"

"Some. Those who were sued had no love lost for the company or for upper management."

"Any threats issued by any of those employees?"

"Yes."

"How did you handle those threats?"

"We assessed whether they were viable and reported the threat to local law enforcement. Most were just angry and blowing off steam. Police would pay them a visit and that would be the end of it."

"Any employee threats to reveal that the company product, the LINK, was fraudulent?" Rossi asked.

"Nothing that specific; no."

"How specific?" Rossi asked.

"The threats were more along the lines of a disgruntled employee bad-mouthing the company atmosphere as oppressive and intrusive, rather than revealing anything about the corporate products."

"Any lawsuits go to trial?"

"Not that I'm aware of. Like I said, most employees didn't want the fight."

"Did you find that odd, given what eventually transpired about the company's product being fraudulent?"

"Wasn't really for me to consider the nature of the threat. My job was to assess if the threat was viable and provide proper security measures."

"Okay, but did you find it odd in light of recent events?" Rossi pushed.

"I guess I didn't give it much thought."

"Were you aware Erik Wei threatened to expose the LINK as fraudulent?"

"Not until after the fact."

"After what fact?" Rossi asked.

"After he was found dead, and Jenna Bernstein was tried for his murder."

"Did that make you rethink some things about the company or its officers?"

Martin sighed and gave a shrug. "Of course it makes you rethink things."

"What exactly?"

"Well, I was on the security detail that drove Jenna Bernstein to her meeting that night with Erik Wei."

Interesting, Rossi thought. "Did she say anything to you about the meeting's purpose?"

"No."

"What was her demeanor?"

"Quiet. Ms. Bernstein never said much in the car. Nor Mr. Kohl, for that matter."

"Did she seem angry? Upset?"

"I'm not sure—"

"Your company does psychological assessments," Ford said. "Based on your perception of Bernstein and anything she said, what was your impression?"

"She clearly seemed upset. Especially when we picked her up after the meeting."

"You picked her up?" Rossi asked.

"That's right."

"Where did you take her?"

"I took her to Sirus Kohl's home on the lake."

"Did you go into the home?"

"No."

"Did you have any further interaction with her that night?"

"Yes. She called for the car service and asked to go back to an apartment she kept in South Lake Union."

"You drove her?"

"I did."

"And her demeanor on that drive?"

"Upset."

"Angry?"

"I don't know about angry, but definitely quiet."

"You said she was always quiet in the car," Ford said.

"Upset," Martin said.

"Crying?" Ford asked.

"No."

"Did she say *anything*?" Ford asked.

Martin paused. He seemed to be choosing his words. Rossi and Ford knew it best to wait him out, whether he could be having a crisis of conscience. Finally, he said, "She said, 'I'm not going to take the fall.'"

"You recall her saying those words? Or something like that?" Ford asked.

"Those words," Martin said. "As I said, she didn't speak often in the car. I paid attention when she did."

It sounded to Rossi like Jenna Bernstein had already decided to blame Sirus Kohl for the LINK's failure. Then again, she could have meant she wasn't about to let Erik Wei take her and her company down.

"Did you have any further interaction with her that night?" Rossi asked.

"No."

"She didn't call and ask to be taken anywhere else?"

"No."

Rossi had reviewed the trial transcript in the Wei murder. Jenna Bernstein could not account for her time after leaving Kohl's mansion and returning to her apartment. She claimed she stayed in and turned off her cell phone to avoid Kohl's numerous telephone calls.

"Were there any threats made to Kohl or Bernstein, or both?"

"Yes. Adria Kohl asked to have security increased for her father during the Wei trial. She said he had received death threats, and investors were becoming increasingly hostile."

"Did you ever see any of those death threats in writing?" Rossi asked.

"No," he said, shaking his head.

"You took her at her word?" Rossi asked.

"Why would she make up something like that?"

"I'm not saying she did," Rossi said. "I'm wondering if you have any documents with the names of any of those persons who made threats?"

"Benjamin Cooper was one."

"The hedge fund guy?" Ford asked.

"Out of New York," Martin said. "He invested a large sum of his own money and some of his clients' money. He wanted blood."

"Did you pursue any of his threats to determine if they were viable?"

"No. Our job was to ensure our clients were secure."

"Meaning Mr. Kohl?"

"And Ms. Bernstein."

"She never moved back into the mansion, though, did she?"

"She didn't; no."

"Did she arrange to have security at her apartment complex?"

"She didn't; no. But Mr. Kohl did."

"He paid for her to have security after she left his house?"

"Yes."

"For how long?"

"Until Ms. Bernstein was acquitted and PDRT was dissolved."

Rossi and Ford exchanged glances. That seemed odd. Why would Kohl continue to provide security after the woman tried to blame him for the murder?

"Even after Jenna Bernstein testified against him in the Erik Wei murder trial?"

"Even then," Martin said. "Or I should say up until then."

"Who was your primary contact at PDRT?"

"Jenna or Sirus could call me or my team directly. They had my cell."

"Not Adria Kohl then?"

"We didn't provide any security to Adria, no."

"She wouldn't have had reason to call you."

Martin paused and Rossi noticed he did. Then Martin backtracked his answer. "Only maybe if there was a hire and we were doing background checks on a potential candidate or candidates."

"Wasn't that primarily within Sirus's domain?"

"It was, but on occasion, Adria would step in. If Sirus was busy."

"So, intermittent."

"Yeah. And there were a few lawsuits against former employees. She might call about those also."

They asked Martin several more questions before Rossi thanked him for his time, and Martin walked the two of them to the front door.

Back inside the pool car Ford said, "What was that all about?"

"What?"

"The questions about Adria Kohl and who was his primary point of contact."

"Adria Kohl's cell phone had a number come up repeatedly during a short span of time, calls she made and received at odd hours—well after work hours. Phone calls but no text messages. I was curious about who it was, and asked her who the number belonged to. She said the number had been assigned to Martin. I asked why she would be speaking to him."

"What did she say?"

"She said she was Martin's primary contact within PDRT."

Ford said, "What do you think about that, then?"

Rossi shrugged. "Probably nothing, but . . . just kicking over stones for now."

Chapter 18

Keera instructed Harrison to drop her at the law firm. It was after hours, but only for those who worked nine to five. That didn't apply to lawyers Keera knew. Certainly not to her. Being in back-to-back trials, out of the office on an aborted staycation, and now running down witnesses with Harrison, the work in her other cases had piled up. She'd need to catch up or get further behind.

Harrison got out of the car after parking.

"You're walking me to the door?" Keera asked.

"Thought I'd try the restaurant," Harrison said. "Have a drink and something to eat, relax for a bit, before heading home. Care to join me?"

"You don't have a date awaiting you?"

He smiled. "You and your sister have an inflated impression of my dating life."

"One you've never discouraged."

"It seems to give you joy, needling me. In truth, I like my solitude, especially on weeknights."

"Thanks for the offer, but I better go upstairs and find out if there are any fires burning. I'll leave you to your fortress of solitude."

She rode the elevator and walked past reception, thankful Maggie was not seated at the desk. When it came to leaving work, Maggie was more accurate than Greenwich Time. She didn't stay a second longer than necessary. Keera grabbed a power bar and a bottle of water from the lunchroom and walked the hall to her office.

The lights in Ella's office were off, but not Patsy's, creating a wedge on the carpeted floor. These moments, just before Keera pushed open the door and determined whether Patsy was sober, in the process of tying one on, or already on his couch sleeping off a binge, were always high anxiety for her and for her sisters. The fact that Patsy was currently sober only increased her anxiety. Every day was another step forward, but a setback would be like the dreaded Go to Jail card in the Monopoly game. Do not pass Go. Do not collect $200. Start over.

She knocked on the door. Her father sat at his desk, readers perched on the bridge of his nose, a multipage document in his hand. "Hey, kiddo. What brings you in here this time of night?"

"You know," she said, feeling a sense of relief, then quoted one of his sayings. "You're never really out of the office." Lawyers brought their cases home with them and on vacations. It likely contributed to the higher-than-normal rate of substance addictions and divorces. "Why are you still here?"

"I have a hearing tomorrow morning," Patsy said. From beneath them, Keera heard the sound of music coming from the Paddy Wagon. "Listen. I'm sorry if we screwed up your vacation. It was never the intent. In hindsight, Ella and I should have handled the meeting, then filled you in on the details."

"Water under the bridge," she said. "You got a minute?"

He set down the document and removed the readers, holding the stem in his hand. "Always got a minute for you. What's on your mind? Though I bet I can guess."

She sat across from him. "JP and I tracked down some former PDRT employees, and they had quite the story to tell, and not the story Jenna is telling."

He leaned back. "Fill me in."

Keera told Patsy about her conversation with Isabelle Blowers and about the oppressive culture at PDRT.

Patsy said, "I know some people who started at Microsoft back in the early eighties, and they'll tell you the same thing about the work environment. They'll tell you Bill Gates would fly off the handle in meetings and humiliate employees who didn't have answers to his questions. It made the work environment difficult, but it also made the company hugely successful. Those people who endured are multimillionaires many times over. The buck stops with the guy at the top. So does all the pressure of succeeding and failing."

"There's more." She told him of her conversation with Lisa Tanaka. "There's being a hard-nosed businessperson and there's lying. It sounds like Jenna lied about the financial projections, and, according to Tanaka, she set it up so that if anyone ever questioned it, Jenna could blame Tanaka, say that was her domain. It sounds an awful lot like her misrepresentations to investors about the LINK; she set it up to blame Kohl as controlling her and the flow of information within PDRT."

"Sounds like the controller had an axe to grind. Maybe she's protecting herself."

"Maybe. Maybe for a good reason. PDRT pretty much destroyed her life for months. Even now, she's afraid to get involved. She's afraid Jenna will blame her in the US Attorney's suit, say Tanaka presented knowingly false financial profiles to PDRT investors. It sounds to me, Dad, like Jenna was using PDRT's secrecy and compartmentalization to insulate herself from liability."

"Well, it will be something we have to deal with . . . if the prosecutor decides to charge her."

Keera felt her frustration building. Her father was like a horse wearing blinders. She got up from the chair and paced. "Doesn't it bother you?"

"What exactly?"

"She's lying to us. She manipulated you in Wei, and she'll do so again."

Her father remained calm. "I don't have knowledge she manipulated—"

"Tanaka isn't the only employee to tell me Kohl didn't tell Jenna what to do, that he wasn't controlling her. They said Jenna manipulated Kohl, and she used him for his financing and his background to give the company credibility. Once he'd made such a substantial investment, he didn't have much choice but to go along with what Jenna wanted. There's even speculation Jenna had an affair, maybe more than one, while she lived with Kohl."

"If it's speculation, it won't get admitted into evidence, Keera."

"Maybe not, but I'll know she's lying, and I'll know she's using me and you—your reputation—to get her off, again."

"We represent guilty parties all the time."

"I don't like being manipulated, Dad. I didn't like it when Jenna and I were young, and I don't like the idea Jenna manipulated you in that first trial, and she will do so again if given the chance."

"I'm a big boy, Keera. I can take care of myself."

"Why didn't you have the mitigation specialist testify in the first trial?"

Patsy stared at her, as if wondering how much Keera already knew.

"You introduced a Svengali defense in the liability phase—not at sentencing—to argue Sirus Kohl had so manipulated Jenna that she would make misrepresentations to investors without question, but you never put on the mitigation specialist to support her testimony that Kohl did in fact control Jenna and how he did it. Why not put a professional psychiatrist on the stand?"

"I didn't think we needed the testimony. Not after Jenna testified. She was very convincing."

"But was she honest, Dad? Did Kohl manipulate her?"

"Nothing in the Erik Wei trial will be admissible, Keera. A jury will never hear a word about it."

"I need to know, Dad."

"No. You don't." He said it without hesitation. Without equivocation.

"I need to know who my client is."

170

"You know who she is. You grew up with her."

"Exactly. And the incidents the employees are telling me about confirm what I already know about Jenna, that Sirus Kohl didn't manipulate her. That it was the other way around. Why didn't you have the mitigation specialist talk to me—or to Loren Kawolski—when she did her psychological assessment of Jenna?"

"Where is all this coming from?"

"It's something I've been considering since Jenna came into the office, whether I want to defend her. You had a psychiatrist evaluate Jenna and, I assume, talk to those who knew her, but not me and not Loren. Why not?"

Patsy didn't immediately answer, but his silence spoke volumes.

"You controlled the flow of information to the mitigation specialist to control the conclusions and opinions she would render; didn't you?"

"That's my job. That's every attorney's job."

"You didn't get a fair and unbiased opinion of Jenna Bernstein. You got the opinion that would help you, if she was convicted and you needed it."

"Again. My job."

"You had no idea who you were representing, except all the things I had told you. That's why you tried to talk Jenna out of testifying in court. You didn't want her to testify because I'd told you Jenna was a liar."

"I wouldn't have let her testify if I had known she was going to lie."

"Because you remained blissfully ignorant by limiting the information provided to your expert."

Patsy stared at her, his expression defiant but also vulnerable. "I asked the expert only to comment on the pertinent question: Could Sirus Kohl have manipulated Jenna such that she made representations not knowing they were false?"

"Hypothetically. Not in reality."

"We're talking semantics."

"I want to read the mitigation specialist's report."

"I don't see what purpose it would serve."

"What purpose?" Keera couldn't believe her father would ask that question. "How about, I want to understand my client, Dad. I want to understand who I am dealing with. I want to know if I need to be concerned."

"What would you have to be concerned about?"

It was as if she didn't know the person sitting across the desk from her. Where was the attorney who could anticipate several moves ahead and have a response to each move? "Have you forgotten everything that happened when I was a child? In high school? The winter I came home from college?"

"That was a long time ago, Keera."

"Two people have been murdered, Dad. Two people have been shot in the head. The gun is missing. The one that belonged to our client. And you ask what am I concerned about? How about whether my client has a propensity for violence? How about the integrity of this law firm? I'm not going to allow her to use me."

Patsy stared at her for a moment. Then, slowly, he opened the bottom drawer of his three-drawer desk and removed a thick document stapled at the top. He handed it across the desk to Keera.

So he had deliberated deceived her. "You removed it before you gave me the case file."

"I shouldn't have. I'm sorry. I worried you'd make an unfair judgment."

Keera shook her head. "An unfair judgment? My perception of Jenna comes from knowing her since we were ten, Dad. The real Jenna. Not the hypothetical one. Not the one masquerading as CEO of a billion-dollar company. The one based on fact. I spent twelve years with her. Who were you protecting by removing the report? Me or Jenna?"

"That's not fair, kiddo."

Keera held up the report. "And this is fair, Dad? Removing the file before I have the chance to read it?" She stood, not wanting to hear another one of his excuses. His actions spoke volumes. "Damn it. The moment we start working together and things are . . . You pull this crap."

"Keera—"

"No." She turned back to him. "Don't try to pacify me. I'm not a kid anymore. I don't need to hear excuses, and I don't need to have things hidden from me to protect me. You want to protect me? Then be honest."

"I have been honest."

"Have you? Then why didn't you tell me Mr. Bernstein saved me from being kicked out of Forest Ridge the night you drove into my high school parking lot drunk and hit a parked car?"

Patsy froze.

She shook her head and sighed. She shouldn't have brought it up. Her anger had gotten the better of her. But now it was out in the open. "Yes, Dad. I know about that."

"I didn't . . . I didn't want to see you have to change schools your senior year. I thought it would hurt your chances of getting into Notre Dame."

"But you didn't stop drinking; did you? You didn't stop then, and you didn't stop drinking after you embarrassed me at my chess tournament, showing up drunk and making a scene. You never stopped. You told me you cared about me, but if you cared about me, you would have stopped. If you cared about me, you would have given me this report and trusted me to decide for myself what it means."

"Keera, that's not true. Of course I care about you."

She moved to his office door. "As for the Bernsteins, you got their daughter off for murder. I'd say you're square. You don't owe them anything. Going forward I will make the decisions whether I want to represent Jenna or not."

She stormed from the office and went downstairs to the Paddy Wagon. Liam greeted her, but she saw JP sitting at a table in the back, by himself. "Thanks," she said. "I'm meeting my private investigator."

"Can I get you a drink or something to eat?" Liam asked.

"No," she said, though at the moment she craved a Scotch and could feel the pull of the bottle. "I'll seat myself, thanks." She walked to JP's table. He looked up when she approached. "You really are eating alone," she said.

"As I said . . . And you look upset."

She dropped into a chair across the table from him. "My father and I just had it out."

"About?"

She told him about the mitigation specialist and the report.

"If it's any consolation, Keera, attorneys limit the information provided to experts all the time to direct the flow of their investigation and the opinions and conclusions they reach."

"I know that, JP," she said.

Liam returned, bringing her a soda water with lime and a garden salad. "In case you get hungry," he said and gave her a quick smile.

After he left, JP smiled. "He fancies you."

"I know," Keera said.

"You don't feel the same?"

She shook her head.

"So tell me, are you upset your father withheld the report, or does this have more to do with your dislike of Ms. Bernstein?"

"Both, if I'm being honest. I shouldn't have said some things I said to Patsy, but . . . I was upset. It wasn't fair. This is what I'm worried about, JP. My mother always said about Jenna, 'Trouble always seems to follow that girl,' and those of us who were around her suffered for it. It's only been a few days but already there's trouble, and I'm fighting with my father about some things that happened years ago."

"You could call him."

"I need to calm down first. The thing is, Jenna used my dad. He took the case at a reduced rate to repay a favor, and she abused that favor."

"Are you upset because you think she killed Erik Wei?"

She nodded. "In part. And because she got away with it. She always gets away with it—since we were children. She's lied her whole life and got away with it."

"At times at your expense."

"At times, yes. But it seems my father has, I don't know, conveniently forgotten all the lying, and Jenna's propensity for violence—like the occasion in Chelan I told you about."

"Let me ask you something. You said Jenna has always been a liar and a cheat and she always got away with it."

"It's true."

"Is it?" Harrison raised his eyebrows.

"You don't think she is?"

"She might very well be, but from my perspective, she hasn't gotten away with anything. From my perspective she's either been in trouble or trying to avoid it all her life. In the Erik Wei trial she wasn't convicted, not in court, but certainly in the public eye. She faces prison again if the US Attorney is successful, and she's now the prime suspect in a murder trial. I wouldn't call that winning, Keera. Not in the slightest. And I'm just wondering if . . . well, it has to have been hell on her parents. Maybe your father wasn't thinking of Jenna. Maybe he was thinking like a parent and trying to give Jenna some grace for her parents' sakes. Maybe your father didn't cut Jenna a deal. Maybe he represented her because he saw and knew what it was doing to her parents, a pain he could certainly relate to, having his own daughters. I don't have children, but I can imagine it was horrific for the Bernsteins, and I can imagine your father has tremendous guilt for his illness."

"You think I'm being too hard on Jenna."

"That's not up to me to decide. I'm just saying that, whatever the outcome in this matter, whether Jenna is convicted or not, Patsy will still be your father. He will always be your father, Keera. And you will always be the apple of his eye."

"Ella is the apple of his eye."

"Au contraire. He talks about you in ways I've never heard him talk about Ella or Maggie, or your two brothers for that matter. Your father loves you. He's ill, but he's trying to make amends. Will he make mistakes because of his illness? Of course. I'd say show him a little grace.

"As for Ms. Bernstein, you're no longer the little girl trying to get up on the trampoline. You control whether you're going to let her problems impact you or impact your relationship with your father. Not her. She can no longer hurt you unless you let her."

Chapter 19

Renton, Washington

The following morning, Keera drove to Valley Medical Center in Renton, Washington, a sprawling, multibuilding complex. She'd thought about calling home, but she didn't want to talk to her father over the phone. She'd do it in person when she got back to the office. JP had been right. It was time she stopped acting like the child whose father repeatedly disappointed her, or who got kicked off the trampoline. She controlled both situations, as well as whether she wanted to continue to be a victim. She didn't. Her father's alcoholism was a disease, an illness he was struggling hard to deal with. Jenna was a sociopath, maybe a psychopath, but Keera no longer had to let her troubles impact her private life, or her relationships, if she chose not to.

She stepped off the elevator and spoke to reception. They ushered her to the sterile office of psychiatrist and licensed clinical social worker Cynthia Talmadge.

Talmadge greeted Keera at her office door. Rather than sit behind her desk, she offered Keera a seat on a couch and sat in a gray chair to Keera's right. The office was otherwise spartan, with generic photographs, what looked like watercolors of plants. A fake tree rested in one corner. Talmadge controlled what her clients learned of her private life. Very little, it appeared.

Talmadge, with dark-brown hair, freckles, and large-framed glasses, looked young, but Keera knew from the file that Talmadge was in her late forties and well respected as a psychiatrist and mitigation specialist. She had worked for the defense on several high-profile trials across the country, was successful in helping convicted defendants avoid the death penalty and having others committed for treatment rather than sent to prison. The fact that Patsy had retained Talmadge indicated he anticipated Jenna would be convicted and further anticipated he would need to use Talmadge's testimony at the sentencing to argue Jenna had been influenced by Sirus and seek some form of leniency. But it hadn't turned out that way.

"You're Patsy's daughter," Talmadge said. "I can see the resemblance."

"That's the Irish in us," Keera said. "Thanks for speaking with me. I'll try not to take up too much of your time."

"I'm happy to do so," Talmadge said. "I enjoyed working with Patsy."

Maybe, Keera thought, but she might not like what Keera was about to insinuate. Keera also wasn't surprised Talmadge had been available on short notice, though she was incredibly busy. She doubted her sudden availability was due to her liking of Patsy or for the money—Keera had agreed to pay Talmadge's hourly fee. If Talmadge was like most doctors Keera had deposed, or cross-examined on the witness stand, especially those who testified professionally as expert witnesses, Talmadge had an ego when it came to her professional opinion and diagnosis. Keera suspected Talmadge's interest related more to Keera telling her she wished to discuss Jenna Bernstein. The local and national news had been filled with articles and stories about the US Attorney's criminal suit alleging Jenna and Kohl were guilty of fraud and conspiracy, as well as the more recent news that Sirus Kohl had been murdered. Talmadge would never say it, but she was likely interested in whether the conclusions she had placed in her report had been wrong or at least hadn't painted the entire picture of Jenna Bernstein. But Keera wasn't going to get anything out of Talmadge if she opened with a question like: *Dr. Talmadge, any chance your diagnosis and the conclusions in your report are incomplete or inaccurate?*

She'd have to be subtle.

"I read your report," Keera said. "I wanted to talk to you in greater detail and get a better understanding of your opinions and conclusions."

"Okay." Talmadge was well-versed in testifying both in depositions and in court, and though Keera spoke to her in an informal office setting and about someone Patsy had represented, Talmadge would be cautious in what she had to say, and likely say as little as necessary. Keera wasn't going to trap her. She lobbed her an easy question to get her comfortable.

"Could you tell me what Patsy retained you to do, specifically?"

"I was to evaluate Jenna Bernstein and determine if she could have been susceptible to manipulation by Sirus Kohl such that she remained in the dark about the company she founded, and specifically the product she was representing to investors, the LINK."

"In other words that the misrepresentations she was making to investors were actually Sirus Kohl's misrepresentations?"

"Yes."

"Had you ever been asked to render such an opinion in the liability phase of a trial as opposed to after the accused was convicted?"

"No. This was a novel legal theory your father was pursuing."

"And how did you make your assessment?"

"I spoke to Jenna at great length on several occasions."

"About what in particular?"

"About her background and her personal history. Where she grew up, her upbringing, whether she had siblings, whether her parents were married or divorced, family dynamics. Significant relationships she had in her life—past and present. I asked where she went to school, and about events in her childhood that significantly impacted her or that might have influenced her behavior."

"Good or bad?"

"Both. I asked about incest, rape, or other trauma, perhaps inflicted by a relative or adult family friend, which is more common than most people believe. I asked about drug and alcohol use, and criminal convictions."

"And how did you know she was giving you honest answers to your questions?"

Talmadge glanced away before reengaging Keera, a tell Keera had picked up studying her chess opponents. Talmadge was worried. "I also interviewed family members and relatives, friends, colleagues, teachers, coaches in high school, religious personnel from her high school, and anyone else who might have relevant information. I reviewed her school transcripts, medical records, and looked for criminal records."

"And did you do anything beyond interviews to evaluate Jenna's psychological and social functioning? Did you conduct any tests?"

"I administered several psychological tests. The results should be in the file."

"In conducting your interviews, did you speak to Sirus Kohl?"

Another pause. "I did."

"For what purpose?"

"To better evaluate the significant impact Kohl had on Jenna, especially her work life."

"What did you determine?"

"When they met, Kohl was considerably older and had significant more business experience, especially in biomedical science and engineering. Jenna relied on him heavily."

"So did Kohl become Jenna's business mentor?"

"I believe he did."

"Nothing wrong with that, is there? Having a more experienced mentor teach you the ropes."

"Not in and of itself, no."

"But in this instance . . . ?"

"Jenna and Kohl's relationship progressed beyond a business relationship."

"They became lovers."

"Yes."

"And you believe that was unhealthy?"

"Any relationship in which the man and woman are separated by significant years has the potential to be unhealthy."

"It isn't just the difference in years, though; is it?"

"No. Not just the years. But the potential for the relationship becoming codependent increases if one is young, naïve, or both."

"Did you find Jenna to be naïve?"

"No. I assessed her as being very mature."

"But you still believed the relationship to be unhealthy?"

"I believe it became unhealthy."

"In what respect?"

"I concluded Kohl preyed on Jenna because she needed his funding and expertise, then he isolated her from much of her family and friends. I concluded he molded her into an image he wanted, under the guise of caring for her and looking out for her best interests. I concluded he had a borderline personality disorder."

"And how do you believe he molded her?"

"He had Jenna work long hours and also isolated her from the workforce at the office. He had her move into his house. Further isolation. He told her when to go to bed and when to wake up. He told her what to eat and how much to eat. He put together workout schedules for her, dictating what exercises she should perform and for how long. He used sex in an unhealthy manner, as a reward for Jenna following his script. She was not allowed to use social media, or to send emails or text messages, under the guise that eavesdroppers could steal corporate secrets. At home and at work, Sirus was always present, and he had access to her phone and to her text messages. He isolated her more and more."

"And you concluded that Jenna would therefore tell PDRT investors exactly what Sirus Kohl told her about the capabilities of the LINK, without question?"

"That was a conclusion I reached."

"And who told you about Kohl's manipulation?"

"Both of them."

"Sirus Kohl told you he was manipulating Jenna?"

"No. No, of course not. But he confirmed he asked Jenna to move into his home and made the meals and set the proportions she ate. He also put together a workout plan for Jenna and had her chart her progress."

"Which isn't, of itself, a negative thing; is it? It could be a loving thing; couldn't it? Given how much Jenna was working, he could have tried to take some of the load off her shoulders, make her life easier?"

"Potentially. But he also became abusive when Jenna did not meet his expectations."

"That came from Jenna; yes?"

"Yes. Sirus Kohl denied any physical or verbal abuse."

"When you interviewed PDRT employees did they tell you Sirus Kohl was ever abusive to Jenna?"

"No. They didn't, but they did say he was omnipresent, very doting on her."

"So again, not necessarily a bad thing they witnessed."

"Not necessarily."

"Anyone other than Jenna tell you Kohl was abusive?"

"Other than her? No."

"Did anyone ever tell you the compartmentalization at PDRT was not Kohl's doing, but rather it was Jenna's idea?"

Talmadge hesitated. "No."

"What did you learn from Jenna's childhood and upbringing?"

"She was an only child. Her parents were firm but never abusive."

"Did anyone ever suggest Jenna was spoiled?"

"Not anyone I spoke with."

"Did anyone you spoke with suggest Jenna was manipulative?"

Talmadge froze, displaying the hint of a smile though not a trace of amusement. "I did have some teachers suggest Jenna could be very persuasive when she wanted something."

"Manipulative?"

"No one went that far; no."

"Fair to say your opinions and conclusions were based upon what you were told, in large part?"

"In large part."

"Was I on that list of school colleagues to speak with?"

"You? No, not that I recall."

"Loren Kawolski?"

"I don't recall that name."

"Who provided you with the names of Jenna's school and employment colleagues to interview?"

"Mostly Jenna, her parents, those persons I spoke with."

"Did you do any independent . . . digging?"

Talmadge chuckled. "I can assure you my assessment was very thorough and not limited or restricted in any way by Patsy."

"Did any of these people you interviewed tell you Jenna was a habitual liar?"

Talmadge eyes narrowed. "I don't recall that."

"Pathological?"

"No."

"Did they tell you they believed Jenna manipulated Sirus Kohl for his money and his expertise to give PDRT credibility and make it easier to attract other investors?"

"No one."

Talmadge was starting to squirm.

"Did they tell you she had affairs with other men while living in Kohl's house?"

"No." She sounded more and more cautious.

"You concluded Jenna was charismatic."

"To be twenty-two years of age and doing what she was doing, one would have to be charismatic."

"You mean to get others with greater experience to invest their millions in your fledgling company?"

"That's part of it."

"That would take someone very charming, wouldn't it?"

"Charm would be one factor."

"Being highly persuasive would be another, wouldn't it?"

"I wouldn't argue with that."

"Did Jenna ever express to you she had loved anyone?"

"I don't believe she had any other significant relationships."

"No expression of love."

"She loved what she did. She loved her work."

"Did she ever express sadness about the death of Erik Wei?"

"I'm sure she did."

"I didn't note anything in your report to document she did. Your notes indicate she claimed innocence. She believed she'd been set up by someone. But I never noted any sadness or sorrow."

"Then I guess she did not."

"Did you speak to any employees of PDRT who had been fired or who'd quit their job?"

"I spoke to employees."

"Did any express concern they could be sued if they said anything negative about their employment?"

"Some did, yes. It was the nature of a start-up with a billion-dollar idea. Security was necessary."

"Did you conclude from any of these employees that their firing had been rather callous?"

"In some instances. But it was Sirus Kohl who did the hiring and the firing. He and his daughter."

"Not Jenna?"

"No. That was not part of her duties or responsibilities."

"Did she ever express any fear about her situation, about possibly going to jail?"

"She was very confident she would win."

"What did you think when the US Attorney recently charged Jenna with making fraudulent statements about her company and its product?"

"I wasn't surprised."

"No? Why not?"

"Because Jenna told me during our interviews Sirus Kohl had lied to her. He gave her false information to provide to the investors so they would invest, and she did so. She had no idea the statements she was making were false because she had come to trust Kohl to the point she would say whatever he told her to say."

"You took her at her word."

"At the time I had no information to indicate otherwise."

"And if I provided you with information now, that it was Jenna who instituted the compartmentalization at the company, that Jenna was involved in the hiring and firing of employees, and Jenna was fully aware the representations she made about the LINK were fraudulent, would that change the opinions you rendered in your report?"

"I'd have to rethink things, certainly."

"If I put you in touch with people who told you Jenna was manipulative and a compulsive liar, that she lacked empathy for others and could be callous and indifferent to the suffering of others, would that change the opinions you offered in your report?"

"Yes. It would."

Talmadge had no doubt determined that Keera wasn't interested in the superficial. She wanted to know exactly who Jenna was. If she didn't know Jenna, then she could not fully represent her. She had to know who and what she was dealing with.

"If the portrait I just painted were proven to be true, what might your conclusion be?"

"Hypothetically?"

"Hypothetically."

"The person you've described—manipulative, deceptive, charming, without empathy for others, or remorse or guilt for what they've done—those would be a classic sign of someone with an antisocial personality disorder."

"A sociopath."

"Yes."

"And if that person engaged in criminal behavior—such as murder?"

"A psychopath, potentially." Talmadge again paused. "But I can assure you if Jenna were a psychopath, it would have come out in my assessment of her. A person can't hide something like that from someone clinically trained to spot all the clues. There would be inconsistencies between what they were telling me and what they had actually done in their lives."

"Unless," Keera said.

"Unless what?"

She needed to give Talmadge an out—a reason why her assessment of Jenna in her report was inaccurate but not her fault. "Unless they controlled the flow of information with which you had to work. It sounds like Jenna did just that."

"That would take extensive planning months in advance . . . years actually. In my experience that would be highly unusual."

"But not impossible?"

Talmadge became more combative, not willing to believe someone could have pulled the wool over her eyes. "I've never come across anyone so calculating. People with an antisocial personality disorder are bound to make a mistake, to slip. No one could carry on with such behavior without being caught. There would be some signs."

"Let me ask, is the position of CEO of a company consistent with someone who may have an antisocial personality disorder?"

"You mean is it a profession someone with that disorder might aspire to? Yes. Someone with an antisocial personality disorder is often highly intelligent and highly driven and wants to be in control."

"Jenna's aspiring to be a wealthy CEO of her own company would fit within the profile."

Talmadge paused and smiled again; this one, though, seemed sharpened and purposeful. "It would," she said. "But so, too, is the profession of lawyer."

Touché, Keera thought.

Chapter 20

Frank Rossi and Billy Ford had split the list of PDRT's investors who, according to Thomas Martin, made threats against Sirus Kohl, and had been working the phone lines. Rossi spoke with Benjamin Cooper, one of PDRT's largest investors. Cooper was likely emblematic of what Rossi and Ford could expect. Cooper had so much money he believed he was above the law, and therefore he didn't fear speaking his mind to a homicide detective working an investigation into the murder of a man who had lied to Cooper and the other investors, costing them millions of dollars. As soon as Rossi announced who he was and the purpose of his call, Cooper got on the line to give Rossi an earful. He called Kohl just about every name in the book, and he went so far as to say he hadn't shed a tear when he heard the news Kohl had been killed. Figured a guy like Kohl got what was coming to him. He was also all too glad to admit he'd threatened Kohl.

"I meant it, too, and I know a lot of other people hated that son of a bitch," Cooper said. "And with good reason. Look, we all make bad business investments. Hell, it's part of the process. For every business idea that hits, you have five or six that don't. But nobody likes to be lied to, Detective. Nobody likes to feel like somebody pulled a fast one and left you holding the bag. But it wasn't me who killed him. I was in Paris, France."

"Business or pleasure?" Rossi asked. He had Cooper on speaker, so Ford could hear the conversation. Billy had turned down the volume on the overhead television.

"You can't go to Paris and not have some pleasure. That's just plain wrong. But since you're asking whether I can document this alibi, I can. I can have the flight plan sent to you and the name of my pilot and his staff. I can also provide the person's name with whom I was doing business in Paris."

Rossi would ask Mark Upson to run down Cooper's alibi and any loose threads that might indicate Cooper went out of town to secure his alibi but had someone else pay Kohl a visit.

But, again, Rossi didn't think so.

Cooper was arrogant, but he wasn't ignorant, and that likely applied to the other investors as well. In fact, Cooper sounded quite rational about his hatred of Kohl. He wasn't going to put billions of dollars at risk, not to mention opportunities to fly to Paris for a croissant or to Barcelona for empanadas, to get even with someone for his loss of a few million dollars.

Rossi also knew from his accounting education that, to a guy like Cooper, losing millions was like losing a couple hundred bucks. And people with that much wealth also had the system rigged. Cooper's team of accountants would write the money off as a bad investment and offset it against his taxable income, further reducing his overall tax liability. His hedge fund investors would do the same. Cooper did, however, confirm a lot of hatred existed for Kohl and for Bernstein, but by a group of people with more money than God and, like Cooper, not about to throw it away for a prison cell.

Rossi disconnected the call and rocked back in his chair, then looked up at Ford.

"Isn't this job fun, partner?" Ford asked.

"Like a root canal. Got me thinking though."

"That's a first."

Rossi rolled his eyes. "Funny." He sat up. "It could be another explanation why Jenna Bernstein went on her walkabout in disguise."

"What explanation?"

"She was a pariah. She'd been threatened. That's the kind of argument I can see Keera Duggan flipping on Thompson. She'll flip it on him, make the jury believe the State is making much ado about nothing. I saw her do it to Miller Ambrose."

Rossi's cell phone rang. He picked it up and checked caller ID. "Speak of the devil. Thompson."

"Put him on speaker," Ford said.

Rossi did so.

"We've filed a charging document and obtained an arrest warrant for Jenna Bernstein. I assume you want to bring her in?"

"I told Keera Duggan we'd give Bernstein the chance to turn herself in," Rossi said. "Avoid a circus at the courthouse."

"Fine. But it has to be today."

Chapter 21

As Keera drove back to the office after her meeting with Cynthia Talmadge, she kept the radio off and considered what had transpired. Talmadge had taken offense at Keera's suggestion that Talmadge, an accomplished and renowned psychiatrist, might have been manipulated by Jenna. But Talmadge would only have felt that way if the hypotheticals Keera had presented—especially given recent events—had a ring of validity. If Talmadge believed Keera's suggestion was wrong or ridiculous—that she could not have been manipulated—she would have dismissed it as the musing of an uneducated and uninformed mind.

She hadn't.

Keera also thought again about why her father had done what he had done, limiting the information Talmadge had to evaluate, which was what every good attorney might do to secure a favorable expert opinion. In light of what JP Harrison had said to her the prior night, she wondered if Patsy did what he did not just to get the opinion he wanted, but for Jenna's parents' sake. As JP had pointed out, they had gone through pain and suffering only parents would know. And Patsy did not have the hindsight Keera now had after the US Attorney's suit for fraud and conspiracy—and the murder of Sirus Kohl. He also had not interacted daily with Jenna the way Keera had when they'd been young. He didn't know her, not the way Keera knew her. She wondered if Patsy had tempered Talmadge's opinions to save the Bernsteins the pain of hearing a psychiatrist classify their daughter as having an antisocial personality disorder. Maybe Patsy, like her mother, had been showing the Bernsteins some grace.

Her cell phone rang. The office. Keera connected expecting Maggie, but it was Ella. "Is Patsy with you?"

Keera felt the familiar, nauseating pit in her stomach flare, one she felt each time any of her siblings had asked that question. The pain got so bad during high school that Keera saw the school nurse about a possible ulcer.

"No," she said. "He was working late on a motion for a hearing in one of his cases."

"That's why I'm calling. The court called the office looking for him."

"He didn't show?"

"I said he had violent food poisoning and asked that the motion be postponed." Food poisoning was a reliable excuse for an alcoholic because it was a twenty-four-hour ailment. Ella had used it more than once. "I have Maggie out checking his regular haunts."

"Did you call and ask Mom?"

"No. And I'm not going to. She's been so happy to have him sober. If he is on a bender, do you have any idea what could have set him off?"

Keera thought of their conversation last night in Patsy's office. She'd been hard on him, suggesting he'd been more concerned about Jenna than about his own daughter. Could that have put him over the edge? Inched him back to the bottle? Her phone clicked. She was getting another call. Frank Rossi.

The pit in her stomach deepened.

"I've got another call, Ella. I need to take this. Let me know if you run Patsy down and whether he's okay."

She accepted the call from Rossi but didn't want him to know she still had his cell phone and name in her contact list. "This is Keera Duggan."

A pause. Then Rossi said, "Keera, this is Frank. Frank Rossi."

"You have good news for me, Frank?"

"I'm afraid not. I'm calling to let you know an arrest warrant has been issued for Jenna Bernstein for the murder of Sirus Kohl. I told the powers that be I had agreed to give your client a chance to turn herself in. With the media attention this case has and will generate, I convinced them it was the right thing to do."

Keera felt waves of conflicting emotions. She felt the press of a high-profile case that would require long and arduous hours and create stress for the entire office, but one that would also be lucrative. She also thought of the Bernsteins and what this would mean for them, to sit through another murder trial. They were good people. This news would be devastating.

"How long does she have, Frank?"

"It has to be today."

"This will leak. It always does. I, too, would like to avoid a circus."

"I'll arrange for you to enter through the sally port on Jefferson Street rather than the public entrance on Fifth Avenue. I'll meet you in the pre-booking area with the charging document in the next hour."

"Does it say anything of interest, Frank?"

"You know."

"Yeah, I do." Meaning the charging document would say very little. "First degree?"

"Premeditated," Rossi said.

"I'll call you when we're on our way in."

"Keera?"

"Yeah."

"I don't have a lot of flexibility on this."

"Walker Thompson?"

"I just don't."

"I'll call," she said and disconnected.

Keera took the next exit and turned into a park-and-ride parking lot. She shut off the engine and took a deep breath. Her father always had impeccable timing. This was another example. They had an agreement in place—she and him. He'd try to remain sober on his own. If he couldn't, he had agreed to check himself in to the same rehab facility in Eastern Washington her brother Michael had checked in to for professional help. Keera knew Patsy's health was more important than a legal case, even one as big as this one was certainly going to be, but she couldn't help but think, were she to take the case, that this time she'd be flying on the trapeze, high above the crowd, without a net.

And this time she'd be representing a client who was most likely a sociopath, possibly a psychopath, but most certainly a pathological liar. One who would make it beyond difficult for Keera to discern the truth, let alone do her job.

She picked up the phone, took another breath, and pressed the numbers on her cell phone keypad.

Bernstein had been eerily calm when Keera arrived at her condominium to deliver the bad news. It was as if she had anticipated it. "Where's Patsy?" she'd asked.

"Indisposed."

"What does that mean?"

Keera wondered if Jenna's fixation on Patsy was because she believed she could better manipulate him. "It means he's not available. I'll handle what's about to transpire."

"After that?"

"We'll see." She then told Jenna to remove her jewelry and leave behind anything of value. Jenna's parents would gather it and keep everything in a safe deposit box until, and if, Jenna was found not guilty.

"I assume, as in Wei, that I won't get out on bail?"

"Highly doubtful. Even if entertained, the amount would be set extremely high."

"How high?"

"A million dollars, minimum." Keera paused, waiting to hear if Jenna had that kind of money, which seemed unlikely. Jenna's speculated wealth had been on paper only, not reality. When a court dissolved PDRT, its minimal physical assets were sold to pay creditors less than a penny on the dollar. Jenna and all the investors walked away without a dime. "The court will also consider other factors besides money."

"I'm aware," she said testily. "I'm not a flight risk, and I'm not a threat to the community."

"The murder took place in a home in a wealthy residential neighborhood. The media attention is going to be even more intense than in the Erik Wei trial. Judges are elected officials, and the one assigned to your arraignment will consider that when deciding whether to release you."

"They can't bring up the Erik Wei trial; can they? I was found not guilty."

"They can't bring it up, but we can't erase the media attention it generated, or a judge's memory." She didn't tell Jenna that many judges were former prosecutors, or that the assigned judge would note, as had many in law enforcement, that Jenna had not technically been found innocent. Keera said, "I can make arguments that weren't available to Patsy, but let's not get ahead of ourselves. Detective Rossi only gave us an hour, and I want you to turn yourself in before this afternoon."

"What happens this afternoon?"

"The district court is in session at two o'clock, if the prosecutor is going to proceed with a hearing on probable cause to hold you. They could waive it, but I doubt they will."

"Why not?"

"Given the outcome in the Wei trial, I think the prosecutor, especially if it is Walker Thompson again, will want to use the finding of probable cause as validation that your arrest is not a witch hunt or motivated by the Wei trial outcome. Frankly, I'm surprised he didn't take the evidence before a grand jury, for the same reason."

"Is it . . . a witch hunt?"

"I don't know the State's basis for probable cause—the evidence they accumulated to charge you—but I assume they learned of your walk to Volunteer Park the night of the murder. I'll ask for the police file to be produced right away."

"Can *we* bring up the Erik Wei trial?"

"I can, at the probable cause hearing and at the arraignment, but it's a double-edged sword, Jenna. We say your arrest is a witch hunt because they didn't convict you. They say the Wei matter supports their argument you're a danger to the community."

"I was found innocent."

"Judges are only human."

Keera considered her watch. "I prefer to have the probable cause hearing today, before the media attention builds."

"I won't waive my right to a speedy trial."

"We don't need to decide that now."

"I don't want to be in jail any longer than is absolutely necessary," Jenna said. "In the Wei matter, Patsy said forcing the prosecutor to trial quickly reduces the time the prosecutor has to gather evidence."

Maybe so, Keera thought, but it also reduces the time she had to review that evidence, talk to witnesses, and cobble her own case together, should she decide to do so. She hadn't. "Do you want me to call your parents to prepare them while you're getting changed? You don't want them to find out through the news media."

"Yes," she said. "But tell them I'm going to be acquitted. Tell them I'm innocent."

"I'll tell them," Keera said, though with a caveat. She'd tell them, *Jenna says she's innocent.* Keera wasn't about to make that promise.

An hour later, Keera drove Jenna Bernstein into the King County jail's sally port. Rossi met them and advised Bernstein he needed to handcuff her.

"Is that necessary, Detective?" Keera asked.

"It's procedure, Counselor."

All very professional.

Rossi advised Bernstein she was being booked for the first-degree murder of Sirus Kohl. Upon Keera's advice, Bernstein said nothing.

Rossi took Keera and Jenna inside the jail. Jenna was photographed and fingerprinted. The booking officer already had much of Jenna's needed information: her full name, date of birth, and other personal information Jenna either confirmed or updated.

Female correctional officers then asked Jenna whether she was pregnant, had any allergies, and the medications she took. A psychiatric nurse evaluated her for suicidal thoughts. The process of going from being a free citizen living in a high-rise condominium to the confines of a jail cell could be jarring, but Jenna showed no indication she was intimidated.

At Keera's suggestion, Jenna had worn nothing but a black sweat suit, white T-shirt, and sandals. Jenna was led into a room under the watchful eyes of a female correctional officer. She would strip naked, and everything she owned, including her underwear and bra, would be seized. She'd be provided regulation underwear, a red jumpsuit, and mud-brown, plastic sandals. Given that she'd brought nothing but the clothes on her back, the logging of her personal property went quickly.

As Keera had predicted, Walker Thompson chose to go forward with a probable cause hearing in the district court on the ground floor of the King County jail, and Jenna was placed in a holding cell.

Given the case's high profile, as well as Jenna's notoriety, Keera could imagine an intense discussion had occurred in the King County prosecutor's office about the advantages and disadvantages of using a grand jury, as well as whether Walker Thompson should again be the prosecutor who tried Jenna. King County prosecutor Daniel Butcher would be cognizant of the witch-hunt argument—that Thompson trying Jenna a second time could be viewed as a personal vendetta. Thompson had likely countered, in his calm demeanor, that he'd tried a good case in Wei. He didn't likely say he wanted another shot at Patsy, but like all good prosecutors, Thompson was competitive. He didn't like having the Erik Wei black mark on his trial record. Whatever the arguments he had advanced, Thompson had prevailed.

Keera entered the cramped, windowless courtroom on the first floor and sat alongside other private defense attorneys and public defenders. Without comment, except for a brief and professional greeting, Thompson provided Keera with the charging document. It was short and said little—the probable cause standard was extremely low and easily met—though more than Keera had known up to this point. With no time to meaningfully attack the evidence, she scribbled one-sentence arguments in rebuttal. The charging document stated Sirus Kohl had a deal with the US Attorney to provide evidence to support the charges of fraud and conspiracy against Jenna. Kohl had an appointment to meet with the US Attorney the morning he was found shot once in the back of the head at close range. The ME had concluded the death to have been a homicide. Bernstein, according to the charging document, was made aware of Kohl's intention to provide evidence against her and had tried to change his mind. This was new information, but no evidence or further details were provided. The police could place Jenna Bernstein in the vicinity of Kohl's rented home on Capitol Hill the night of his murder. Kohl was killed with a 9-millimeter handgun, the same caliber handgun Jenna Bernstein was known to have owned, the location of which was unknown.

Bernstein's case was the fourth case called by District Judge Tanya Rodriguez. Keera took her shots. She argued the statement Jenna was made aware of Kohl's intentions was too vague to constitute probable cause. She argued that while Jenna did at one time own a 9-millimeter handgun, she had not possessed that gun in years, and the probable cause statement did not provide evidence she did. She also argued that the police placing Jenna "in the vicinity of the home" where the murder took place was not equivalent to her being in the home.

But she was swimming upstream against the strong current favoring probable cause. No district court judge would be inclined to release a high-profile defendant accused of first-degree murder. The safe finding was to hold Jenna over for arraignment.

Judge Rodriguez did, and Jenna Bernstein, the young woman once estimated to be worth billions, was again taken away in handcuffs, given two sheets, two towels, and a blanket, and assigned a room in 7 North, the jail's medical and psych unit, where she would sleep behind glass, and correctional officers would monitor her twenty-four hours a day.

And as Keera watched Jenna be escorted away, she thought again of what her mother had always said: *Trouble seems to follow that girl.* She thought of what JP Harrison had said about Jenna not having won.

Far from it.

Chapter 22

Keera left the King County jail and hurried back to her office, arriving in late afternoon. She hadn't called Ella to determine if her sisters had found Patsy and if he'd been on a binge. Bad news would come soon enough, though she still held out hope she'd find her father at his desk working, and she hated herself for doing so.

She had her answer the moment she stepped from the caged elevator onto the third floor. Behind her desk, Maggie looked harried and upset. She glanced up at Keera and rolled her eyes, then shook her head.

"That was a beautiful trip down memory lane, let me tell you. Loved hunting him down in all his old bars."

"Thanks for doing it, Maggie," Keera said, not knowing what else to say.

Maggie sighed and looked defeated, as if their father had finally worn her out. "Has to be me; doesn't it? It isn't going to be Shawn or Michael, and Keera and Ella are too busy with *real* careers."

"I'm sorry," Keera said, well-versed in not feeding Maggie's pity parties. "How is he?"

She gestured over her shoulder and blew out a breath. "See for . . ." She started, then wept, a response unlike Maggie. Maggie didn't cry. She got angry. She became sarcastic. But she didn't cry.

Keera stepped around the desk and hugged her sister. Maggie stiffened at first, not expecting it, and then said, "I made the mistake of getting my hopes up."

"We all did, Maggie. We all hoped maybe we'd have the good Patsy for how many more years he has left."

"Oh, he'll live forever," Maggie said, easing from the hug, her fire and brimstone returning. "He's damned near pickled. It's the rest of us whose lives he's taken years from."

"Did you or Ella tell Mom?"

She shook her head. "Ella's arranging for a family intervention tonight and intends to remind Patsy he agreed that if he couldn't remain sober, he'd get help. He'll likely be combative and refuse to go."

Keera didn't think so. This wasn't the Patsy of their youth. This wasn't the Irish Brawler of old. Age, and years of drinking, had shaved the sharp edges off the man she'd grown up with. The Irish Brawler would never give in. He fought until the final bell. But this Patsy, while still able to summon flashes of the combative fighter, didn't have the stamina, the will, or the desire. Keera sensed from conversations with her father these past few months that he was embarrassed, not for himself, but for her and, to a lesser extent, for Maggie and Ella. Keera was different, as JP had said. It wasn't just their ages that separated her from her siblings. She had been Patsy's baby girl, and maybe he'd seen Keera as his last chance to be the father he'd always wanted to be, but for his illness. It might also have been their bond over chess, the hours they had spent playing the game, and the hours Patsy spent tutoring Keera and helping her to become a champion. He took a father's pride in her outshining him, and he expressed deep regret his illness had screwed up "what might have been" for him and for her.

Show a little grace, Keera.

Like Mr. Bernstein had done that night when he rescued Patsy and, as a result, Keera. He could have called the police. He could have told the truth to the parent whose car Patsy had smashed, but instead he'd showed her father a little grace.

Keera walked down the hall to Patsy's office, and again her anxiety of the unknown spiked. The hall wasn't any longer than the other halls in the office, but it seemed longer at moments like this—her dread building with each step. As a child she'd felt genuine fear. Her father was Dr.

Jekyll and Mr. Hyde. Patsy could be compassionate, caring, funny, and loving one moment, then transform into someone Keera didn't know or recognize. It had scared and scarred her—all of them. As an adult, she no longer feared Patsy. She even felt sympathy for him. It was difficult for a child to see their parent vulnerable, helpless, and remorseful.

Now, she felt empathy. Maybe enough to grant him a little grace.

She knocked lightly and pushed open his office door without an acknowledgment. Patsy sat on the edge of his leather sofa, his hair unkempt, his suit wrinkled, tie askew. He had his head bowed and his hands clasped. The fading sunlight streamed through the window behind him, making him look like a penitent begging for forgiveness. He tilted his head, but only a fraction, and shifted his eyes to Keera before again dropping his gaze.

Of all the many times Keera had witnessed Patsy post-binge, this incident hurt the most. Her father looked utterly and completely defeated.

"Hey," she said stepping closer. He reeked of alcohol, a smell she'd come to despise. "How are you feeling?"

He shook his head and let out a gasp of air. Then he burst into tears.

She didn't want to look down on him, not literally, and spun around a chair and sat. "Can I get you anything?"

Another headshake. She handed him a box of Kleenex from the corner of his desk. He threw back his shoulders, as if to stretch his back, and let out another gasp of air. Keera felt his pain in her heart.

"Dad," Keera said. "I'm sorry about last night. I'm sorry for the things I said. I hope—"

"Don't," he said quietly. "Don't make excuses for me."

"I just—"

"It was nothing you did or said, Keera. It never is. Never has been. This is my doing. No one else's. If it hadn't happened this morning, it would have happened tomorrow or the next day, or the next."

She didn't understand. She'd never understood. "Why, Dad? You were doing so well."

He chuckled a sad laugh. "I wasn't. I was a tightrope walker over the Grand Canyon. I was on pins and needles every moment, knowing

I was going to slip. Wondering how far I would fall and how much it would hurt. Let me tell you, it hurts like hell. I've let your mother down, your sisters, and your brothers, but mostly I've let you down, Keera. You were the one who got me to go to the AA meetings. You were the one at my side. You . . ." He sobbed, speaking between gasps. "You were the one I hurt the most."

She'd never heard him be this honest, and that pained her even more—to know how much it hurt him to have hurt those he loved. "It's okay, Dad."

"It isn't," he said. "I know I hurt you. I took competitive chess from you. I felt like you were my second chance, then my third, and I blew them all. I blew them so very badly."

She needed to change the narrative. She needed to help her father, to get him to allow them to help. "It's not over, Dad. Not by a long shot."

"I'm weak, Keera. I'm a weak, drunk, old man."

"No," she said. "You're the Irish Brawler, Dad. I've looked up to you my entire life."

"Why?" he said, crying harder. "Why would you do that?"

"Because you were the best, Dad. And I wanted to be the very best, like you. And because I wanted you to be proud of me. I wanted to make you proud, Dad. I wanted to show you I understood all those chess lessons you gave me weren't just about chess. They were about life." He raised his gaze to her. "You taught me how to persevere, to never give in, and to never give up. You gave me life skills. That hasn't changed, Dad. That will never change. You have an illness, Dad. You need help. We all have something, Dad. Each of us is dealing with something."

"I know," he said softly.

"If you had cancer, people would understand. But they don't understand alcoholism. I do, though, Dad. Your family understands it's a disease and you need help."

"I agreed."

She hated to take advantage of him in a time of weakness, but she pressed ahead, for his good. "Ella is arranging a family meeting, Dad. They all think you're going to fight them on this. Don't. If you really meant what you just said, about being sorry, about letting me down, then do this for me. Go to Eastern Washington. Check yourself in. Get the help you need."

"I'm afraid, Keera."

She reached out and held his hands. "This is a place set up for people just like you, people who have an illness and need help. It's a validation of your illness, Dad."

"I'm not afraid of going," he said.

"What then?"

"I'm afraid of going and failing, getting drunk again. What do I do then, Keera? Who do I turn to then?"

Keera hadn't expected his answer. It stunned her because she didn't have a reply. Nobody did. He knew it, too, because he looked up at her and gave a pathetic shrug as if he was already conceding the inevitable.

"I don't accept that, Dad. I won't accept that you're going to fail. That would be like starting a chess match expecting to lose. You taught me better. You taught me to expect to win and to have a strategy to make it happen. You need to go into the treatment facility with the belief you're going to win and have a strategy to make it happen."

"I've lost at chess, Keera. And I've lost trials."

"But you never stopped playing. And you never stopped trying cases. You never went into anything expecting to lose. Even after I beat you four games in a row you would set the board believing you could win. Am I wrong?" She smiled.

"You used to let me win so you could go out and play," he said returning her smile.

She shook her head, still smiling. "I'm not saying I did, or I didn't. I'm just saying you always believed you had a chance. That's what I'm asking of you now, Dad. I'm asking you to go to this facility believing you have a chance to succeed, and if you take a step back, I'm asking you to reset the board and just keep trying."

"When did you get so smart?"

"I had a good teacher, Dad." She stood. "Come on. I'll have Ella drive you home to discuss this with Mom and to give you both time to pack and get on the road in the morning."

"Okay," he said. She turned and walked to the door. "Keera?" She turned back. "Any word on Jenna Bernstein?"

She knew if she told him of Jenna's arrest he'd be inclined to stay, feel an obligation to help her. If he left early in the morning for Eastern Washington, he'd miss the morning news and likely be on the road before the hurricane hit. She remembered from Michael's stay at the facility that it did not allow outside distractions. No televisions. No newspapers. No personal computers or cell phones. And if, by some chance, Patsy learned of the trial, hopefully by then he'd be too far away to do anything.

That thought was sobering.

Keera was about to step into the ring without the Irish Brawler at her side.

Now, she really did feel like the trapeze artist performing without a net. She shook the thought. She wasn't about to fall.

"No, Dad. No word yet," she said.

"You don't have to take this case, Keera. I know who Jenna is. I took the first case for her parents, but you don't have to."

Keera wouldn't take the case for Jenna or for her parents, nor because their firm needed the money, nor even for Patsy's belief in preserving the judicial system. She'd take the case because she'd meant what she said. She wanted to be the best, just like he had been. And because she suspected her father was right—that she'd learn more about herself defending the most difficult cases rather than the easy ones. She wouldn't run from Jenna Bernstein. She hadn't run when they'd been young, and she wouldn't run now. She'd defend her, but she'd do it her way. And in the process, maybe she'd learn a little bit more about Keera the defense lawyer, as well as Keera the person.

"Thanks Dad. I'll do my best, if it comes to that, and I'll make you proud."

"I already am," he said.

Chapter 23

The following day, the court administrator called Keera at the office to advise that Jenna Bernstein's arraignment would be held at noon, but not in the traditional arraignment courtroom on the twelfth floor of the King County Courthouse. It had been moved to 854E, the same court-room in which Vince LaRussa had been arraigned, to accommodate the anticipated crowd. As with LaRussa, the court had also established an overflow courtroom with closed-circuit televisions.

Keera glanced at a copy of the *Seattle Times* on her computer. The story of Jenna Bernstein's arrest had made the front page, above the fold.

PDRT CEO Bernstein to Be Arraigned

in Killing of Business Partner Sirus Kohl

Maggie had been fielding phone calls and reciting a script Ella had written for her that basically stated: "Ms. Duggan will not be issuing any statements."

"Good for business," Harrison said as he lowered into a chair across from Keera's desk.

"Ella's thrilled," Keera said.

"Not you."

Keera nodded to the two-page document Harrison held in his lap. "The prosecutor says there's evidence Jenna knew about the deal Sirus Kohl sought with the US Attorney, which gives them a motive, which I'm sure is why they pulled the trigger without going to a grand jury. I need you to find out what they have and who they've been talking to."

"What does your client have to say?"

"She's not saying much of anything, and I'm not certain she'll tell the truth when she does."

"That's a problem. When can we anticipate receiving the police file?" Harrison asked.

"Sooner rather than later. Walker Thompson isn't Miller Ambrose. He won't play games. As soon as I get it, I'll make you a copy."

"Do you have any idea who the arraignment judge will be?"

"That's a closely guarded secret. I won't know until he . . . or she takes the bench."

"Sorry to hear about Patsy," Harrison said.

"Thanks. I'll miss not having him in court."

"Can we get into the house where Kohl was murdered?"

"I talked to Rossi first thing this morning. The house has been closed since the murder. He said he'd see about getting us access today after the arraignment."

Harrison stood. The shade of his linen jacket and pants was a faint yellow. "I'll see you in court."

"You're coming?" Keera asked.

"Wouldn't miss it." He grinned and walked out the door.

Moments later Ella entered. "Was that JP leaving?"

"Let's hope Maggie doesn't drape herself around his leg."

"I doubt it. She's still pretty upset from the other day. How are you?"

Keera shrugged.

"Yeah. Me too."

"How are Dad and Mom?"

Ella grimaced. "Quiet. Resigned. Hopeful. Take your pick."

"It was kind of Michael to drive them over," Keera said. "Isabella isn't going with them; is she?"

"I told Michael that Dad might start drinking on the drive over if she did," Ella said. "Mom too."

Michael and Isabella had met in rehab, which seemed to be the only thing they had in common. Shawn, the oldest sibling, said if going to rehab meant having to spend the rest of his life with an Isabella, he'd rather be drunk.

"Had Dad heard about Jenna Bernstein's arrest?" Keera asked.

"If he did, he didn't say anything."

Keera rocked back. "What about a fee, Ella?"

"I sent a contract to the Bernsteins with the same fee Vince LaRussa paid, six hundred and fifty dollars an hour."

"And . . ."

"Not a peep of complaint. Got the signed contract back within the hour. Listen, I want to talk with you about something else. With news out that you're representing Jenna Bernstein, I anticipate things are going to pick up to a level we haven't experienced since Patsy was in his prime. With Dad indisposed, and you knee-deep in trial, we're going to be under the gun here. I can't handle it all. We're going to need help handling the cases you and I can't get to."

"Maggie bitching?"

"No. She'll step up. You know Maggie likes nothing better than to feel important. I'm talking about preparing and responding to motions, making court appearances, talking with clients. Things Maggie can't do."

"You have anyone in mind?"

"I have a couple of candidates I'd like to bring in for an interview. You don't have time."

As the oldest daughter, Ella had always been the most responsible. She had to grow up fast in a house where things could get bad in a hurry.

"Both are highly recommended. Just want to make sure you don't have any objection to my making the decision."

"Does this mean the next time I'm scheduled to go on vacation, I'll actually have one? If it does, then I'm in favor."

Ella smiled, but it quickly faded. "Listen, Keera. About Jenna Bernstein. If you don't want this case—"

"I'm taking the case, Ella."

"Don't feel compelled for the firm. We'll get by."

"I don't. And that's not the reason I'm taking it."

"What is?"

"Something Dad said, and something I realized. I need to put Jenna behind me. I can't do that if I run from this case. Win or lose, I need to try it. My way."

Just before noon, Keera stepped off the King County Courthouse elevator onto the eighth floor and was greeted with voices echoing off the marbled floor and high ceiling. She'd avoided the local and national media clustered at the building entrance by entering from the tunnel that connected the administrative building and the courthouse, but she couldn't avoid those reporters huddled on the eighth floor. They pressed cell phones under her chin as she crossed the lobby, and cameramen filmed her walking to the courtroom.

"How will your client plead?"

Keera answered as she walked toward the set of double doors. "Duggan & Associates will represent Ms. Bernstein. She will plead not guilty."

"Will Patsy Duggan be in court?"

"No. Patsy Duggan has other commitments."

"Mr. Bernstein said this is a witch hunt by the prosecuting attorney against his daughter because of what happened in the Erik Wei matter. Do you have a comment?"

Jenna had told the Bernsteins not to talk to the press. "Jenna Bernstein was found not guilty by a jury of her peers. That's our judicial system. The prosecuting attorney understands that. I have not had time yet to evaluate the police evidence against Ms. Bernstein. Until I do, I'll have no comment."

"Sources are saying Sirus Kohl had reached a deal to provide evidence against Jenna Bernstein in the US Attorney's action for fraud and misrepresentation. Do you have any comment?"

The question was unexpected. Keera stopped and looked at the reporter. "Can you identify the source?"

The reporter didn't respond.

"I'm not going to speculate. I suspect we will all know more about the case against Ms. Bernstein shortly. From the defense's perspective, Ms. Bernstein denies all charges against her and is eager to appear in court to prove her innocence. Thank you."

Keera disappeared through the tall entrance doors. A King County courthouse marshal held one of the second set of doors to the courtroom open for her and she slipped inside.

Spectators filled the gallery on both sides, seated shoulder to shoulder in the pews, a few standing at the back of the room. She recognized some press members, but not all, which meant national media was also covering the arraignment. People loved stories of a fall from grace, and few, if any, had reached Jenna Bernstein's heights or had fallen as far. The trial would get a lot of play.

Walker Thompson sat at counsel's table working, a young female attorney seated beside him. Keera did not recognize the attorney from her years at the PA's office, but bringing a woman to the team was a smart move. Another woman, with a dark complexion, stood just behind the railing dressed in an expensive suit. Keera suspected this was Adria Kohl, Sirus Kohl's daughter.

Thompson stood and shook Keera's hand while peering over her shoulder, no doubt searching for Patsy. Keera set her briefcase on the table closest to the jury box and removed the motion she and Ella had worked on late the previous night and early that morning, arguing Bernstein should receive bail. The arguments were unconventional, though not new. A lot would depend on the judge. Keera wasn't optimistic.

She handed a copy to Thompson, who read the caption and made a cynical face, then turned and spoke to Mr. and Mrs. Bernstein standing at the railing. While doing so, she considered Mrs. Bernstein's hands and noticed them shaking, a quiet tremor. Maybe Jenna had not been lying. Maybe her mother did have Parkinson's.

"Is Patsy going to be here?" John Bernstein asked, the question seemingly on everyone's mind.

Keera shook her head. "No. Patsy had to take some time off from work for a medical issue."

"How long will he be out?" John asked, sounding worried. Both he and Mrs. Bernstein looked concerned. When parents knew you as a little girl, the image was difficult to get them to forget. They wouldn't easily see Keera as an attorney and defender of their daughter.

"That's not yet known, but we anticipate it will be a significant amount of time." Whether Patsy would ever return to work and, if so, in what capacity, was unknown. Work was likely a blessing and a curse for him—it kept his mind and body busy but also created high levels of stress.

"Is he okay?" Mrs. Bernstein asked.

"We're hoping he will be," Keera said. "Thanks for asking."

"Do we know yet who the judge will be?" Mr. Bernstein asked.

"We're about to find out," Keera said, catching the bailiff entering the courtroom from the door behind the bench. "All rise. Judge Evelyn Greene presiding."

At first blush, pulling Greene as the arraignment judge was a good start. She had been a defense attorney for nearly forty years before being elected to a seat on the bench, and she had known Patsy well. However, Patsy always cautioned Keera that sometimes judges would bend too far in the other direction to appear unbiased.

Greene remained standing and leaned forward, palms on the desk, elbows locked, studying the attorneys and the crowd. With straight gray hair hanging down past her shoulders, half-lens reading glasses perched on the tip of a prominent nose, and a thin face, she looked like a stork. She was known in the prosecutor's office as an intellectual judge who studied the briefs submitted and gave reasoned, rational decisions.

"Be seated," she said, her voice deep. "I wanted to take a moment before the accused is brought in. You all realize we are not in the traditional arraignment courtroom. Those of you in the gallery have the right to be here, but, having said that, I will remind everyone . . . counsel, family, members of the media, and spectators, that this is a court of law, and this hearing is to arraign the defendant on charges brought by the state. No evidence will be admitted today. If anyone disrupts this courtroom, for any reason, I will have the correctional officers remove that person forthwith. I hope I'm clear." She turned to the bailiff. "Please have the correctional officers escort in the defendant."

A moment later, one female and two male officers escorted Jenna into the courtroom. She entered in white scrubs with "ultra-high security" stenciled on the back of her shirt. Again, this was customary for someone accused of murder and who could be a suicide risk. Jenna was handcuffed at the waist with a belly chain. Keera had neglected to tell Bernstein to stand tall and not be afraid to look spectators in the eye. She didn't need to. Either Patsy had ingrained that instruction in her during the Wei trial, or it came naturally to Jenna.

Jenna's gaze darted to the empty chair at the table. "No Patsy?" she whispered.

"No," Keera said.

"Be seated," Judge Greene said. "And let's get started. Mr. Thompson?"

Walker Thompson rose from his chair and walked in his slow roll to the side of counsel's table. He, too, wore half-lens reading glasses. "Your Honor, number twenty-two on today's arraignment calendar. The State of Washington versus Jennifer Lynn Bernstein. Walker Thompson and Cheryl McFadden on behalf of the State."

Keera stood and stepped to the space between the two tables, dwarfed by the much taller and broader Thompson. "Good afternoon, Your Honor, Keera Duggan of Duggan & Associates on behalf of the defendant. A notice of appearance has been filed."

"The court notes defense counsel's notice of appearance. The court also notes the presence of Ms. Bernstein. Ms. Bernstein, you are charged with the crime of murder in the first degree. How do you plead?"

Bernstein was caught off guard. So, too, was Keera. Arraignments often allowed the prosecutor to read the charging document into the record. Judge Greene had clearly circumvented that.

Bernstein stood, regained her composure, and with certainty said, "I'm not guilty."

"Very well. 'Not guilty' has been entered into the court record. Does the defense wish to discuss the issue of bail?"

"The defense does, Your Honor. We have a motion."

"The State opposes," Thompson said.

"Ms. Duggan?"

Keera provided a copy of her motion to the clerk, who stamped it, then provided it to Judge Greene. "Your Honor, the defense recognizes the seriousness of the charge against Jenna Bernstein, but believes bail is necessary and should be set. Ms. Bernstein enters this court with a presumption of innocence. The fact that this arraignment is taking place in a ceremonial courtroom, with an overflow room for spectators, is indicative of the high level of interest in both Jenna Bernstein and the allegations being made by the State. Given Jenna Bernstein's notoriety, we are concerned about her safety in the King County jail while she awaits trial, especially given that the King County jail remains overcrowded following the Covid years. Given Ms. Bernstein's notoriety, and the largely vitriolic publicity surrounding her and her former company, PDRT, she will be a target. Moreover, because of her circumstances, she is not about to go out wandering Seattle's neighborhoods.

She also is not about to flee. She has strong ties to the Seattle community. Her parents are present in the courtroom this afternoon." Keera gestured to the Bernsteins, and they stood. Then she turned back to the bench. "She attended high school here and college at the University of Washington. Her friends and support system are all in the state of Washington. Moreover, given what has previously transpired, the defendant has no income and no savings. She will willingly surrender her passport. She is not a flight risk. As to being a danger to the community, Ms. Bernstein does not own a handgun despite insinuations in the charging document."

Greene shifted her attention to the other side of the courtroom. "Mr. Thompson?"

"Your Honor," Thompson said in his affected drawl. "The King County jail has safely hosted many prominent defendants and can and will do so again." His tone was almost parental. "Defense counsel admits the defendant is prominent in the community and has been the subject of negative publicity. I would submit, given those circumstances, that she would be safer in the King County jail than out on the streets of Seattle. Moreover, her notoriety and bad publicity did not prevent her from leaving her condominium and walking about Seattle, albeit in a disguise, prior to her arrest.

"As to being a flight risk, the defendant could easily alter her appearance—again—and while counsel contends her client has no income and no savings, the State has submitted evidence the defendant was, at one time, estimated to be worth several billion dollars and had procured more than six hundred million dollars from investors for her company, PDRT. There has been no finding, by any court, as to where all that money went, and therefore it can't be assumed that the defendant is penniless. Moreover, this crime was both heinous and occurred in a heavily populated residential neighborhood. The victim was shot in the back of the head, indicating the act was premeditated, calculated, and brutal. Other than her parents, defendant has no relatives in Seattle and does not belong to any civic organizations."

Judge Greene lowered her gaze to the motion in front of her and remained silent for several moments. She appeared to be contemplating the two arguments, which was better than Keera had anticipated. She considered her motion for bail as largely perfunctory, to appease Jenna and her parents, but with little chance of success.

Judge Greene raised her gaze and spoke to Keera, much to Keera's surprise. "What would you propose as a means to keep your client safe, while satisfying the State's concern for the general public's safety?"

Keera knew overcrowding in the jail continued to be a trigger issue since the Covid outbreak, which had shut down the court system for nearly a year. The chief judge had mandated that courts fast-track trials to alleviate overcrowding in the jail, but it had only been partially successful.

"Your Honor, the defendant lives in a secure condominium complex in downtown Seattle with a security guard at the front desk and surveillance cameras in the hallway, the elevators, and the lobby. She will not be walking around Seattle as the prosecutor insinuated. We would propose defendant be fitted with an ankle bracelet and confined to her condominium."

"Mr. Thompson?"

"Again, Your Honor, this is not the first time the court has dealt with a defendant of notoriety. I am unaware of any prior defendant accused of first-degree murder receiving such preferential treatment."

With the judge seemingly leaning in Keera's direction, she pushed, hoping to tip her to the defense's side. "Your Honor, I would hardly call confinement and being closely monitored preferential treatment," Keera said. "If, at any time, Ms. Bernstein were to violate the terms of her court-ordered confinement, for any reason, she will submit to the jurisdiction of the King County jail."

"Ms. Bernstein was confined to the King County jail during her trial for the murder of Erik Wei," the judge said.

"Yes," Keera said. "But that was before Covid and the overcrowding problem, and before the US Attorney's federal lawsuit accusing Ms.

Bernstein of misrepresentation and fraud to PDRT investors and the general public, making her notorious."

Greene addressed Thompson. "She would be confined, Counselor. I would ensure the State has access to the cameras within the building and that Ms. Bernstein wear an ankle bracelet to ensure she does not leave the building."

"Your Honor, there's no precedent for granting home confinement in a murder-one case." Thompson sounded exasperated, and with good reason.

"Not under ordinary circumstances," Greene said, still looking to be debating the various issues. "And this is not an ordinary case or ordinary times." After another long moment, Greene continued, "I'll make my ruling. The defendant shall pay a bail bond of two million dollars, to be deposited to the court repository. Upon doing so, she shall be confined to her condominium and monitored with an ankle bracelet. Ms. Bernstein, you understand you are required to surrender your passport and your driver's license?"

"Yes," Jenna said.

"And that you cannot leave your building, for any reason?"

"I do."

"And if you violate the court's confinement order, for any reason, you will forfeit the bail money and be jailed in the King County jail until adjudicated. You understand that also?"

"I do."

"Then I am going to grant the defense's motion for bail under the terms set forth in my order. Defense counsel will prepare that order based on this morning's hearing and present it to me for approval by the end of the day."

Keera never had a case with bail set so high, but she wasn't about to protest. She'd done something this morning she never thought possible. She turned to Mr. and Mrs. Bernstein, who also looked stunned by the amount, but pleased by the result, knowing from the first trial, perhaps, when Patsy did not secure bail, that Jenna had pulled a rabbit out of her hat. John Bernstein gave Keera a nod.

"Anything else from the State?" Judge Greene asked.

Thompson, still looking visibly stunned, said, "No, Your Honor." He did not sound happy.

"Ms. Duggan?"

Keera leaned over, turning her head and whispering to Jenna, emboldened by the morning events. "Since you're not going to be confined to the King County jail, I would suggest you waive your right to a speedy trial."

Jenna shook her head. "I want this behind me as soon as possible."

Keera didn't agree, but it was what it was. "Your Honor, Ms. Bernstein does not waive her constitutional right to a speedy trial and requests the court set a case-scheduling conference to be held within the next seventy-two hours to set this matter for trial. Defendant further requests the court hear its motion to discover the police evidence forming the basis for the charges leveled against her."

Thompson said, "Your Honor, the State has no objection to the setting of a case-scheduling conference and will have the police file delivered to defense counsel this afternoon."

"Very well. Thank you, Counsel. If there is nothing else? We are adjourned." Greene rapped her gavel once and left the bench.

Jenna turned to Keera. "Am I free to go?"

"Not until bail has been posted and you have been fitted with an ankle bracelet. Then the marshals will escort you to your condominium."

Keera wasn't sure what she had expected, a thank-you perhaps, but she should have known better. She knew Jenna better.

Jenna simply turned to the officers, who reapplied her handcuffs and escorted her from the courtroom.

Chapter 24

Late afternoon, after Keera ensured bail using Jenna's parents' home, and Jenna was fitted with an ankle bracelet, she escorted Jenna back to her condominium along with the US marshals. As a condition to her bail, Jenna's visitors were limited to King County jail visiting hours, except for Keera, who could meet with Jenna at any time as counsel of record. All visitors were required to sign in and out, and the State had access to the register to ensure the conditions of parole were being met.

Jenna's focus had been on Patsy, where he was and whether he would defend her. Keera provided vague responses to Jenna's questions to protect his privacy. "I told you, Jenna. He's going to be away for some time. He needs to take care of some medical issues."

When Keera didn't elaborate, Jenna became specific. "His drinking?" she asked.

"That's not something I'm at liberty to talk about, and I won't," Keera said, refusing to let Jenna get under her skin. "For the time being you're going to have to be happy with my counsel."

"Will he be back for trial?"

"I don't know, but as we both told you, Patsy has cut back trying cases. And, since you refused to waive time, I suspect the trial judge will set the trial quickly."

"Do we know who that judge will be?"

"No. But it won't be Judge Greene. The arraignment judge is never the trial judge. We'll know soon enough." She could have said: *We won't be that lucky again.* But she refrained. "Before we go further," Keera said, "I want to discuss my representing you."

Jenna didn't verbally or physically respond.

Keera pressed on. "After I get the evidence, I will make a decision on how best to defend you. I will discuss that with you, but I will not allow you to dictate the defense. Is that agreed?"

Jenna looked insulted. "Meaning I have no input in my own defense?"

"I'll listen to you, but when it comes to how best to try this case, my decisions will be final."

"Or?"

"Or I withdraw now and help you secure other counsel."

Jenna looked to be chewing nails. "You don't leave me much choice."

"On the contrary, the decision is entirely yours," Keera said. And she meant it. If Jenna told her to walk, she'd do so without regret. What she wouldn't do was allow Jenna to manipulate her.

"Agreed," Jenna said.

"And if I find that you've lied to me, I will withdraw from representing you. Is that also agreed?"

Again, Jenna's jaw clenched. "Agreed," she said.

"Good. Then I'll get started," Keera said.

Keera left the condominium and returned to her office, but only briefly. She met briefly with the two lawyers Ella wanted to hire to help out on her case files, and she filled in Ella on what had transpired in court that morning, much of which Ella already knew. Apparently, the news of Keera having secured bail for a murder-one suspect was circulating throughout the courthouse, the prosecutor's office, and the defense bar. Most thought it an unsubstantiated rumor, until the news media broadcasts confirmed it.

Keera ignored her phone, told Maggie to take messages, which didn't make her sister happy, and escaped the office with JP Harrison. They drove to the Capitol Hill house Sirus Kohl had rented. As JP drove, Keera read the police report in her lap, not having had any time to yet read it while getting Jenna settled and checking in at the office.

"Getting bail for a murder-one suspect? I haven't heard of any attorney doing such a thing. Not even Patsy," Harrison said, looking over at her with a wry grin.

"It wasn't any novel argument," Keera said. "Covid has forced a number of changes in everyday life, and the court has had to adjust. Were it not for the overcrowding and the backlog of cases set for trial, not to mention lawyers claiming a lack of due process for their clients and filing motions for pretrial release and for speedy trials, I don't think we'd be having this conversation."

"Doesn't matter. The news has already spread that you pulled off something not even the Irish Brawler accomplished."

"Let's not get ahead of ourselves. We have a long, arduous road to travel."

"For a client who is a piece of work; isn't she?" Harrison said. "Bail in a first-degree murder case and she never even said thank you."

"You noticed," Keera said.

"I noticed," Harrison said.

"That's Jenna. But I'm not going to let her get under my skin." She told Harrison about her threat to withdraw if Jenna lied to her, and about Jenna agreeing to abide by Keera's decisions.

"Will she?"

"We're going to find out."

Frank Rossi waited outside the Capitol Hill home. Harrison parked his BMW in the driveway beside an SPD pool car. The day was again glorious, with a high blue sky and the weather temperate. The peace and quiet of the neighborhood belied the violence that had taken place inside the home.

"Has anyone been inside the home since you were here, Frank?" Keera asked after greetings.

"No. The owner would like to get it rented, though he recognizes that could be difficult, given all the publicity."

Rossi led them to the side door and removed the crime scene tape from the jamb. Keera and Harrison slipped on blue nitrile gloves and Tyvek shoe coverings. Harrison examined the doorjamb and the door.

"You didn't note a forced entry in your police report," Harrison said.

"We did not." Rossi pushed the door in and stepped aside. "I'll leave you two to your work. Call me when you're wrapping up, and I'll return to lock up." He started down the driveway.

"Frank," Keera said. Rossi turned back. "Thanks," she said.

He gave her a nod before continuing to his car. When Keera turned to go inside, Harrison considered her with a queer expression.

"What?" she asked.

"Nothing." A thin smile creased his lips. "So, no signs of forced entry?"

"No," she said.

"What *was* of interest in the police report?"

"Still going through it, but for one, Barry Dillard concluded the bullet that killed Erik Wei and the bullet that killed Sirus Kohl were fired from the same 9-millimeter handgun."

Harrison, who had worked the Wei murder for Patsy, gave Jenna a knowing look. "Somebody still has the gun," he said, stating the obvious.

"Now I know why Patsy pays you the big bucks," Keera said. "It definitely adds another wrinkle to an already complex case; doesn't it? But we don't know that it was the gun Keera once owned, or a different gun."

"You'll keep the Wei killing out, I assume?"

"I don't see the relevance, and admission would be highly preju-dicial, especially given that Jenna was found not guilty of that crime.

I'll bring a motion in limine to prevent the State from mentioning or alluding to the Wei investigation or the trial, including any mention of the gun. I expect it will be granted. But it certainly makes you wonder; doesn't it?"

"Indeed, it does. And our client? I assume she still claims she hasn't seen the gun since she moved from Sirus Kohl's house."

"She does."

"You get started," Keera said. "I want to go through the rest of the police report in greater detail."

The home held the metallic odor of blood, which stained the carpet in the television room and was spattered on the furniture. For the next few hours, Keera remained seated on a barstool at the kitchen counter studying the police report while Harrison measured the blood spatter and took copious photographs. Keera better understood what had led the police to arrest Jenna. The call detail records between two burner phones, purchased from the Target store in the University District and assigned to Sirus Kohl and to Jenna, included text messages between the two. On the night of his murder, Kohl had at least hinted about the deal he had with the US Attorney.

What goes around comes around.

What is that supposed to mean?

You shit on me in Wei's trial. Time to return the favor.

I don't know what you're talking about.

Yeah. You do.

I took my attorney's advice.

And I'll take mine.

Can we talk?

We'll see.

The police also had detailed Jenna's walk to Volunteer Park shortly after she received the text messages, as Keera had known they would. And they had Bitchin Burritos' photograph of Jenna in the park.

"She gets the text messages on her phone, then does a walkabout to Volunteer Park, very close to the murder site," Harrison said, reading over Keera's shoulder. "I can see why they've moved forward, and why they didn't think they needed a grand jury. But they do have a problem."

"They can't place her inside the house," Keera said. "At least not yet. No witnesses. No fingerprints. And no DNA."

"And no weapon," Harrison said.

"And no weapon."

"Circumstantial, certainly," Harrison said, sitting on the adjacent stool. "I suspect they'll argue the obvious—what are the odds Jenna just happened to take a stroll to Volunteer Park to get food on the night Sirus Kohl was murdered?"

"Even money, especially after she has a text tête-à-tête with Kohl about his going to the US Attorney," Keera said.

"About that," Harrison said. "Why would Kohl alert her? I'm presuming Jenna also could have gone to the US Attorney with information Kohl knew the LINK wasn't commercially ready. So why would he let her know his intentions and have her maybe try to beat him to the punch?"

"Your presumption isn't entirely accurate. I doubt the US Attorney would have accepted that deal from Jenna. They already had enough evidence to get Kohl," Keera said. "He handled the company's day-to-day operations and the LINK's progress. It was Jenna they didn't have, yet. And the documents Adria Kohl produced to the State, which she planned to take to the US Attorney, aren't definitive about what Jenna knew and didn't know. I can argue they're subject to interpretation, and the State's interpretation is biased."

"What does Jenna have to say about the text messages?"

"I haven't asked her yet."

"And she didn't offer anything either?"

"No, she didn't," Keera said.

"Hmm," Harrison said. "Why would she not tell you?"

"I don't know. It could be she didn't send the texts, that someone else has that phone and set her up, or it could be Jenna's always had a problem with telling the truth," Keera said, and wondered if Jenna was already lying to her.

"That won't help your case." Harrison rose from his barstool seat.

"Kohl made a call shortly after the string of text messages to a different number. The police say that call was to his daughter, Adria, to confirm he intended to go forward with the meeting in the morning."

"You sound skeptical."

"Just wondering why he would feel the need to confirm the meeting."

"People get busy. Plans and schedules change."

"Or maybe he hadn't been definitive about wanting the meeting."

"What do you mean?" he asked.

"The PDRT employees we've spoken with paint Kohl entirely differently than Jenna painted him. Rather than controlling Jenna, they paint him as doting on her. What if those employees' perceptions are more accurate? What if he truly loved Jenna and remained uncertain about fingering her for the misrepresentations?"

"Even after she pointed the finger at him for Wei?" Harrison sounded skeptical.

"I've seen men do some crazy things when it comes to love," she said, thinking of Miller Ambrose and his inability to accept the fact that Keera had broken up with him.

"As have I," he said.

"And Jenna is a master at manipulation."

"Any indication Kohl called Jenna, or that she called him?" Harrison asked.

"No. None. Just the text messages."

"Seems odd; doesn't it?" Harrison said. "Seems the Jenna you describe as having known would have done more than send text messages to convince him not to make the deal."

"The Jenna I know certainly would have. But . . ."

"What?"

"As you said, I doubt Jenna and Kohl were on speaking terms after she testified in Wei. Maybe she realized there was no point trying to speak to him?"

"Or maybe she did try to talk to him in person," Harrison said.

"The reason for her walk to Volunteer Park?" Keera said. She gave it some thought, then added, "It does seem more like something the Jenna I know would do."

"The prosecution will certainly make that argument," Harrison said.

Keera made a mental note, then resumed flipping through the police report. "The police also sought CDR records from Adria Kohl's telephone," she said, referring to the call detail records. "Those records confirm Sirus Kohl made a call to Adria Kohl's cell phone at 9:17. Seems like overkill."

"What do you mean?" Harrison asked.

"I mean they could pull any text messages or email between the two of them from Sirus Kohl's phone," Keera said.

"Yes, but why not confirm through her records? Adria Kohl found the body," Harrison said. "She was the person Sirus Kohl last telephoned. If it were my case, I would want to eliminate her. Any indication they did?"

"Eliminate her as a suspect?" Keera asked. "What motivation would she have had to kill her father?"

"I don't know, but investigations are as much about eliminating suspects as they are about gathering evidence to convict, and in this instance, I would think Walker Thompson would want to eliminate any and all persons who you—or Patsy—might point the finger at. You want me to look into it, study her phone records?"

For law enforcement, getting phone records required appropriate legal authorization and the use of specialized tools to access the GPS data associated with the phone. Keera suspected Harrison, who no longer was technically "law enforcement," worked with experts who specialized in digital forensics and mobile-device tracking and employed certain techniques and tools of questionable legality to obtain the records. She just didn't want to know how he did it.

"Look into it. Let's be sure. And find out what you can about her relationship with her father, and if she has any siblings." She closed the file. "You about done here?"

"Yeah. Not much here."

Keera checked her watch as she slid from the barstool. "I'll call Frank."

"He still has a thing for you," Harrison said as they moved toward the door.

"Frank?" Outside she put her hand on Harrison's arm for balance and removed her shoe covers while making a face and shaking her head. "No."

"You don't think he does? Or you're not interested?"

She handed Harrison her shoe covers and gloves. Harrison closed the side door to the house and made sure it was locked. "We don't exactly play for the same team anymore," Keera said, slipping on her sunglasses.

"So, you're not interested?" He removed his gloves and shoe coverings.

"I'm busy building a defense practice and focused on keeping people out of jail. He's busy being a homicide detective and focused on putting people in jail. I'm not sure how that would ever work."

"So, you're not interested."

"It isn't realistic, JP. I'm being practical."

He opened her car door for her. "People have made unrealistic situations work before. If they both really want it."

"Who are you, George Cervantes?"

"George Cervantes?" He put on his sunglasses.

"He's a celebrity matchmaker they call 'the pretty boy.'"

"Ouch. You think I'm a pretty boy?"

"I meant it as a compliment."

"I must be getting old. I've never heard that name. Besides, you're not exactly a celebrity, not yet anyway, though you're getting more print than most."

She looked up at him as she lowered into the car. "You really think Frank still has a thing for me?"

"Don't ask me. I'm no George Cervantes."

Chapter 25

The following morning, Keera returned to Jenna's condominium complex. The security guard had her sign a visitor's register, and she noted Jenna's parents' names on the list from the prior day, but no one else. Keera would have to sign out when she left, as well. As she rode the elevator, Keera continued to debate why Jenna would not have mentioned the text messages with Sirus Kohl, and how best to get a truthful answer from her. Keera would not coddle her. When Jenna smelled weakness, she smelled blood. Keera needed to establish further boundaries and consequences if those boundaries were crossed. She would emphasize that she could handle just about anything—if she knew the truth ahead of time. If she did not, she could make no promises.

Jenna, having been alerted by the security guard that Keera was on her way up via the elevator, left her unit door ajar. Keera knocked and stepped inside. The condominium had plate-glass windows and sliding doors with a balcony overlooking downtown Seattle, the Space Needle, and Elliott Bay. This was definitely *not* the King County jail. The front room furniture was spartan. The kitchen appliances and small eating area looked unused and sterile. She noted no personal photographs—not of Jenna or her parents. No friends.

It reminded Keera of Cynthia Talmadge's office, as if Jenna did not want anyone to know anything about her personal life. Or maybe that she did not have one. In all the magazine articles Keera had read about the wonder kid, none had mentioned a significant other, or hobbies for that matter. They'd all applauded Jenna's singular focus, her driven personality, and her ambition to make PDRT and the LINK successful.

Keera had smiled knowingly when she read those articles. The Jenna she knew was singularly focused, but not for any humanitarian reasons. Jenna's driving ambition was to be wealthy—the kind of wealth beyond most people's wildest imagination.

"Jenna?" Keera called out. Marble floors led to beige carpet. The furniture was gray and brown.

"Just a minute," Jenna responded.

Keera stepped to the kitchen island to wait. Moments later, Jenna emerged from her bedroom dressed in jeans and a gray sweatshirt with a large, purple *W* sewn on the front, indicating her alma mater. Her hair was wet, presumably from a recent shower. She wore no makeup and comfortable-looking, camel-colored mule slippers. She looked more like the Jenna Keera had grown up with than the one who had appeared on the cover of business journals.

"Sorry. I didn't get to sleep until very late." She'd rolled her pants up her right leg, revealing the electronic monitoring device. "How do you like my latest fashion statement?"

Keera knew from her time in the prosecutor's office that the bracelet had a Global Positioning System receiver and special software to communicate Jenna's precise location in real time to a wireless monitoring center via cell phone towers. Predefined boundaries or exclusion zones, known as "geofences," had been set up to create a virtual perimeter around her condominium complex. If Jenna left the building, for any reason, or attempted to remove the bracelet, the monitoring center would be alerted. In addition to wearing the ankle bracelet, Jenna was required to call into a number twice a day from the landline in her condominium.

"A prisoner in one's own home," Jenna said. "Never thought it would be literal." She shrugged. "You said it was important."

"It is," Keera said.

"Sounds serious."

"Could be."

"Can I get you coffee? Tea?"

"No. I had a cup of tea earlier. I gave up caffeine. It makes me anxious."

"Welcome to my world," Jenna said. Though the comment was meant to be flippant, it had a ring of truth and sadness to it. Jenna seemed to catch herself and gave Keera a wan smile. Keera decided to let the comment go unanswered.

"Let's go out on the balcony," Jenna said. "It's too nice a day not to enjoy it."

They sat on an outdoor sofa with a round, electric firepit before them. The balcony railing was fashioned from glass panels to showcase the glorious view of Seattle. A warm breeze blew from the south. Elliott Bay was sprinkled with white sails and the wakes from boats.

"I've gone through the police report and the evidence they've accumulated leading to your arrest," Keera said. "I'd like to talk with you about it."

"Keera Duggan, always on point."

"It's my job."

"What I meant was you were always that way. I admired you in high school." Keera sat back, waiting for the cutting comment—or backhanded jab. "I did," Jenna said, perhaps sensing Keera did not buy it. "You always seemed to know where you were headed and how you were going to get there. You were sure of yourself and comfortable in your own skin."

"So were you," Keera said, uncertain where this was going and distrusting.

Jenna shook her head. "Mine was an act. Yours came naturally."

"I don't follow," Keera said, cautious.

"Yeah, you do. You were the one person who always saw through my façade of invincibility. The one person I could never fool."

"Why did you have to fool anyone?"

"Because I wanted them to like me. It was important to me. I don't know why, but it was. You always came off as not caring whether people liked you or not. And yet you were well liked, respected. You never changed or compromised."

Keera remained silent.

"I wanted to beat you, desperately, at just one thing, but I never could," Jenna said, continuing. "Chess, grades, sports. You were always better. I lashed out at you because of it. I'm sorry. I was immature and envious. That time in Chelan . . . I knew you let me beat you at chess, and I hated you all the more for taking pity on me. The calculus exam senior year? I knew I couldn't beat you, so I cheated off Christy Johnson because I couldn't bear the thought of sitting at graduation listening to you give the valedictory address instead of me. I realize I stole that moment from you and your family. I wanted to outski you, but I never could do that either. I know you hurt your knee because of me. Again, I'm sorry."

Jenna had just apologized twice, something Keera had never heard her do before in all the years they went to school, but she remained leery of Jenna's seeming epiphany.

Keera knew from attending AA meetings with her father that steps eight and nine of the recovery process were for the alcoholic to take responsibility for his or her actions by apologizing and making amends to those they had injured. This confessional by Jenna had the same feel, so much so that Keera wondered if Jenna somehow knew about the AA meetings she had attended, just as she somehow knew about Jenna's failed relationship while at the PA's office. As with her father's many apologies for his transgressions over the years, Keera didn't unconditionally accept them, and she wasn't accepting Jenna's either.

"Why are you telling me all this, now?"

"I don't know . . . Maybe because my world is crashing all around me, and it has been for the last five years; maybe because my fate is now in your hands; maybe because I'm wearing this shitty ankle bracelet, and my home will never be my home again. It will always be my jail cell. I just . . ." Jenna shrugged, looking and sounding overwhelmed by her circumstances.

Keera wanted to believe her, but she'd been burned before, and letting go of the past was so very hard.

"Let's talk about the evidence," Keera said, changing subjects.

"See? On point." Jenna smiled, but she was also clearly glad to move away from an uncomfortable topic. "Okay. Do they have some concrete evidence, or is it all circumstantial like the last time?" Jenna asked.

"Circumstantial, mostly."

"What is it you want to know?"

"I received the police report."

"Can I read it? I might be able to provide some valuable insight."

"You can read it," Keera said. "I'll have a copy sent over tomorrow. The bullet that killed Erik Wei and the bullet that killed Sirus Kohl were fired from the same 9-millimeter handgun." Keera watched for a reaction. Jenna showed none.

"Meaning the person who killed Wei also killed Sirus?" Jenna said.

"Probably, but not necessarily. It means the *gun* used to kill Wei was the same gun used to kill Kohl. Could be two people, but I doubt it."

"Can the prosecution make that argument about the two bullets coming from the same gun? I was acquitted of Erik's death."

"No, they can't," Keera said. She explained she'd bring a pretrial motion to prevent mention of the Wei investigation or trial. "I believe I'll win that motion."

"So, it's not going to help them."

Jenna was being obtuse. She knew exactly why Keera had brought up that bit of evidence. "No, but you owned a 9-millimeter handgun, Jenna, and you said it mysteriously disappeared. The State will intimate it did not disappear."

"I didn't say it *disappeared*. I said I left it in the safe at Sirus's home when I moved out. I haven't seen it since." She shrugged. "Am I correct that without the gun, the State can't prove that gun killed either man?"

"You're right. It can't," Keera said. "I want to reconfirm you don't know where your gun is."

"I told you—"

Keera raised her hand. "I don't want that gun to mysteriously show up at trial."

"Can you determine whether the police recovered it?" Jenna asked.

"Nothing in the police file indicates they have."

Jenna looked defiant, her old self returning. "I don't have the gun. I don't know what happened to it after it was placed in Sirus's safe, and I don't know where it is now."

"I can't prepare if I don't know the truth. If I don't know the truth, I can make no promises."

"I don't know what to tell you—"

"The truth," Keera said firmly but gently. "Just tell me the truth, Jenna."

Jenna looked like she was chewing whatever words she'd been about to say and not liking their taste. This was the Jenna of old—defiant when boxed into a corner. "I don't know where that gun is, Keera. I don't have it. I haven't seen it since I left Sirus's house. That is the truth."

If Jenna was lying, Keera couldn't tell, and years of studying her chess opponents' facial expressions and body language had made her astute at reading people and learning their tells. Then again, Jenna was not one of her chess opponents trying to fake a single move. Her masked demeanor and facial expressions had been honed over a lifetime.

"Did you send text messages to Sirus Kohl the night of his murder?" Keera asked without preface, the bluntness intended.

Jenna's brow wrinkled, either in confusion or because she was stalling for time and wondering what Keera knew and didn't know. After a pause, she said with a little too much composure, "Of course not. I haven't had any communication with Sirus since I left his house years ago."

Keera pulled out documents she had copied. "These documents are from the police report. A text string exists on Sirus Kohl's cell phone to a cell phone number assigned to you, according to Adria Kohl. Both burner phones. The PA has obtained the call detail records and confirmed that phone was assigned to you."

Jenna picked up the documents and studied them. After a long minute she said, "I might have used that phone at one time, but I haven't seen it in years and I didn't send those text messages."

Again, Keera detected nothing to indicate Jenna was lying, but she still didn't buy her answer, not completely. "You don't know where the phone is?"

"I have no idea." Perhaps sensing Keera wasn't buying what she was selling, Jenna continued. "Look at the records, Keera. I texted Erik Wei five years ago, then nothing. No calls or text messages to anyone. Why would I text Sirus Kohl after so long a period of time had passed?"

Keera had also noted this large gap in time, as well as a reason why Jenna would have responded in this instance, one that JP Harrison had first postulated—because there was something in it for her to respond, and a strong consequence if she did not.

"Because he texted to tell you he was going to strike a deal to provide evidence to the US Attorney that you knew your representations to the investors were false, and you would naturally want to stop him from doing that."

"Maybe he did. But I didn't get those messages because I don't have that phone. The responses are not from me."

"Then how do we explain the existence of those responses?"

"The same way I explained the gun five years ago. I don't know where the phone is. I must have left it at Sirus's house when I left. Someone else with access to that phone sent those messages to make it appear like I had a motive to kill Sirus, and they might have also used my gun to do it."

"Who would that person be, Jenna?"

"Someone who doesn't like me very much."

"Someone who hates you, Jenna."

She shrugged as if it didn't bother her. Likely it didn't. "At present, that's a lot of people."

"Let's narrow it down. I spoke to certain employees of PDRT. They discussed an oppressive work environment fraught with paranoia and distrust. Could it have been one of your employees?"

"Possibly."

"Any in particular come to mind?"

"Not off the top of my head . . . Well, one, actually. Lisa Tanaka."

Keera tried not to respond to the name, but it seemed an odd coincidence that in a business that once employed over a hundred people, Tanaka would be the one Jenna picked.

"She was our controller. Sirus fired her, and Adria sued her for breach of her employment agreement. It got ugly."

"Ugly how?"

"She threatened to go to our investors and board of directors with sensitive information."

"What sensitive information?"

Jenna again didn't answer right away, as if mulling over what to say. Then she said, "She heard me having sex with the head of my security team in the office late one evening, and she didn't approve."

Honesty. Interesting. Why? "Did she confront you?"

Jenna laughed. "No, but she didn't need to. She saw the afterglow."

"Did she tell anyone?"

"Not that I'm aware of."

Keera couldn't help but sound incredulous. "Nobody ever called you on it?"

"No."

Odd, Keera thought. Adria Kohl had told Tanaka she'd speak to Jenna and to Thomas Martin. Had she not? If not, why hadn't she?

Without prompting, Jenna said, "I didn't love Sirus, Keera." She waited a beat, as if to let the statement sink in, but for what purpose? Then she shrugged and said, "I never did. You want honesty? Fine. I needed his money to keep the company afloat, and I needed his experience to give PDRT credibility."

If she was sincere, it continued an incredibly honest string of admissions, but again Keera wondered for what purpose.

"I truly believed PDRT was on the verge of what would be a great advancement in modern medicine, one that would go down with the invention of vaccines, penicillin, anesthesia, the X-ray, MRI scans. I thought we would pioneer surgery-free repair of damaged organs, cure diseases like Parkinson's and Alzheimer's. I believed it with all my heart. I believed if I could imagine it, it could be achieved. I still do. I pray for my mom's sake someone will figure it out soon."

It didn't sound like a sales pitch. "It was a noble cause, Jenna. It might still happen. But at the moment, I have to ask you some blunt questions."

Jenna nodded. A smile. "I think you already have."

Keera cut to the chase. "You were using Sirus Kohl as a means to an end, then."

"Yes," she said.

"Did you have other affairs, other than with your head of security, while living with Sirus?"

"Yes."

"How many?"

"I don't know."

"Because there were so many affairs, or you just don't recall?"

Jenna smiled but there was nothing malicious about it. "I didn't have time to have *many*. I recall a few."

"Did any of those relationships end badly?"

"Not from my perspective."

"What about from the men's perspectives?"

"They weren't all men," she said coolly. Her blue eyes locked on Keera as if searching for a reaction.

Though surprised, Keera did not physically react. "Did any of these men . . . or women ever threaten you?"

"Woman. Just one. And no, they didn't." She paused. "Have you ever?"

Keera entered that place she once found playing chess, where she locked away her emotions and did not put them on display. "Have I ever what?"

"Had sex with a woman?" Jenna asked.

"No."

"Ever thought about it?"

"No."

"Now who's not being honest?" Jenna chuckled. "I won't say it doesn't have its advantages. She knew how everything worked and didn't need any help or instruction."

"How long did that relationship last?"

"Hardly a relationship. A few months."

"And the other relationships?"

"About the same. Some shorter. One or two one-night stands. As I said, I didn't have time for love."

Keera thought that, if true, it was all incredibly sad, this young woman seeking to change the world, worth billions of dollars on paper, having one-night stands. "How long was your relationship with the head of your security detail?"

Jenna looked out at the view. A breeze picked up and blew back strands of her damp hair. "Off and on for about six months. Maybe longer. I don't recall."

"Was he married?"

"Very. He had two children."

"Did you care for him?"

"What does that have to do with anything?"

"Did you?"

"No. It was just sex, Keera."

"Did he see it that way?"

"I don't know."

"He never said he loved you?"

"If he did, I don't recall it." Another chuckle.

"How did it start?"

Jenna gave the question some thought. "Sirus was older and not exactly spontaneous or adventurous in his lovemaking. I was young when I started PDRT, and I resented the way Sirus controlled me and my day. My affair with Thomas Martin was my chance to rebel, and he was convenient."

"Meaning what?"

"We spent quite a bit of time traveling together. He was someone I could talk to about Sirus and about PDRT. One thing led to another, and the next thing I knew I was in the back seat with my legs in the air and my feet pressed against the ceiling." She shrugged again. "It was exciting, Keera. The kind of sex every woman fantasizes about. You remember the things we used to talk about in high school. Our fantasies?"

Keera did. It had been girl talk. Sex in the back of cars, in elevators, on beaches, at the drive-in. Some of their classmates professed to having experienced such escapades. Some even shared photographs and videos to prove it.

"Thomas gave me the opportunity to experience my fantasies. I once stuck my foot in his crotch underneath a restaurant table, with Sirus sitting right beside me, and felt Martin get off." She smiled. "He wasn't the only one."

"How did it end?"

Jenna gave her a wicked smile and laugh. "With the most exhilarating orgasm of my life after I got home."

"I meant, how did the relationship with your bodyguard end?"

"After I lost my security detail and the opportunities it had once provided, I didn't pursue him."

"Did he pursue you?"

"For a bit."

"Did he call or text you?"

"He never texted. He was very cautious not to put anything in writing. He called, but I told him I wasn't interested. As I said, it was a relationship of convenience, and he was very married . . . with children. He wasn't in a position to force anything."

"Could he have been pissed off enough to do something like this— to kill Wei and Kohl, and try to blame you?"

Jenna gave it some thought. "He'd have the skills, certainly. And access to a weapon. Sirus consulted him before he purchased the gun for me. So he knew it was a 9 millimeter. Would he have the motivation? I don't know."

"I think the question is, could he have hated you that much?" Given Keera's experience watching Jenna lead men on to get what she wanted, she thought it possible. She also knew Jenna could drive men crazy. The kind of sex she described was like any other addiction or craving. When cut off, without explanation, without so much as a goodbye, what did that do to a person? And what would that person do?

"I'd like to think not . . . But . . ."

But Thomas Martin was only human, and people had killed for a lot less.

"Anything else you wanted to discuss?" Jenna asked.

Keera had to refocus. "I know you went to Volunteer Park. Did you go to Sirus Kohl's home to try to convince him not to speak to the US Attorney's Office?"

Jenna glanced at the police report in Keera's hand. "Is there any video or photograph that shows I did?"

"Not to the house, no. Just the photograph of you at Bitchin Burritos, but that could change. Again, I don't want to be blindsided."

"Did CSI find my fingerprints or DNA inside the home?"

Keera felt like she was cross-examining a reluctant witness. "No."

She shrugged. "Then I wasn't there, Keera."

Again, Keera studied Jenna. Again, if she was lying or bluffing, Keera couldn't tell. But she'd been down this road before, and she knew better than to trust her and get burned. Then, again without prompting and not pausing, even for a moment, Jenna said, "And to appease you, I'll swear on my mother's life that I wasn't there."

Chapter 26

The trial judge assigned to Jenna Bernstein's case would not have been Keera's first choice, but he also wouldn't have been her last choice. Judge Johnson Marshall was a jurist with a conservative, but not extreme, bent. Keera couldn't help but think the presiding judge had assigned Marshall for that very reason, as well as his reputation for being unflappable and running a tight courtroom. Given the considerable media attention the trial was generating, Marshall would keep the trial from becoming a circus.

Without Patsy to consult, Keera spoke with other attorneys who had appeared before Marshall and learned the judge preferred legal briefs to be just that. Brief. He read each brief submitted and did not rely solely on his legal clerk's analysis to make his decisions.

When Keera and Walker Thompson entered Judge Marshall's office for the case-setting conference, Marshall swung a golf club slowly in front of a full-length mirror, analyzing his swing. He wore a crisp dress shirt, his tie flipped over his shoulder. "I have the club championship this weekend and haven't had much time to get out and play," he said, setting the club aside. "Golf, like the law, is a jealous mistress. Unfortunately, I don't have free time to devote to her. I don't suppose you've agreed to a plea?"

"No, Your Honor," Keera and Thompson said in unison, but both with a smile.

"Then let's get down to business, eh?"

Marshall slipped behind his desk into an ergonomic chair. Based on what she knew of him from other attorneys, the cleanliness of the judge's desk and the bookshelves behind him, which included pictures of his three children but no spouse, he was divorced and fastidious. Midfifties, and his physical presence was as polished and tidy as his office. His gray hair was clipped short, and his lean physique indicative of a runner. On a wall in his chambers hung a framed photograph of a golf green. A brass plate on the frame indicated he'd recorded a hole in one. He pronounced "about" "a-boot" and slipped in the word "eh," indicating a Canadian background.

As expected, Thompson had submitted a brief requesting that Marshall rescind Judge Greene's decision to grant Jenna Bernstein bail. He had made all the arguments Keera expected. Ella had submitted a brief in opposition. Judge Marshall asked each attorney pointed questions, but it became clear he was not about to undo what Greene had done, at least not without good reason.

"Has there been any indication Ms. Bernstein has failed to abide by the conditions of her bail?"

"None," Thompson admitted.

"Then we'll leave well enough alone, eh?"

Marshall confirmed the State would pursue a first-degree murder charge and seek to have Bernstein sentenced to life in prison—Washington having abolished the death penalty. He also confirmed Bernstein would not waive her right to a speedy trial, then wasted no time setting the case for trial. It was all very efficient.

"We'll have a crowd, but that crowd will be orderly, or I'll have them forcibly removed from the courtroom. I expect your demeanor to be professional and to show respect for the judicial system. The defendant has a constitutional right to a fair trial, and I will ensure that right. If you adhere to my rules, we'll get along. If you don't, your bank account will take a hit. Am I clear?"

In the marbled hall outside the courtroom, JP Harrison reclined on a pew. Among anxious attorneys and their clients waiting to enter courtrooms, he looked like the picture of composure in blue jeans and loafers, no socks, and a blue casual blazer.

"I don't suppose this is a coincidence, you being here," Keera said upon approaching.

"I don't believe in coincidences. Ella told me of your conference. How did it go?"

"Efficient. We have a trial date."

Harrison handed her a multipage document. "Adria Kohl's CDRs from her cell phone."

"Anything of interest? Or can I assume your presence here answers that question?"

"As I said, I don't believe in coincidences. You shouldn't either." He uncrossed his legs and sat up. "Kohl's phone confirms her father's phone call to her the night of his murder."

"Any accompanying text messages?"

"Not that night, but the following morning it seems she tried to reach him by text and by phone. He didn't answer either. However, you will note going through her records that another number also repeats frequently, and those calls started right about the time that Ms. Tanaka threatened to expose Jenna Bernstein's affair with the head of security."

Keera lowered the papers. "Who was Kohl calling?"

"I traced the phone to a warehouse in Auburn, Washington," Harrison said. "It's also a burner phone."

"Is it a business or a residence?"

"Business. TMTP Security."

Keera felt the revelation's weight, dropped onto the bench, and flipped through the pages. "Jenna's security detail."

Harrison nodded. "Would appear to be."

"But Kohl never confronted Jenna about the affair," she said looking up at Harrison. "At least not according to Jenna, though she'd certainly have good reason to do so. Maybe the calls to TMTP were about his relationship with Jenna?"

"Maybe, but it seems doubtful. The calls continued over several months. Not days."

Keera considered the dates and times of the calls. Harrison was correct.

"And I believe you said Martin was not fired."

"No. He wasn't."

"Seems he should have been; doesn't it? Given Jenna was living with Adria Kohl's father."

"One would think he would have been, certainly. What's your thought?" Keera asked, suspecting Harrison, once a homicide cop, was working on a theory.

"My thought is, what if Adria Kohl was also in a relationship with Thomas Martin and, when Tanaka told her what she had uncovered, she learned Martin was cheating on her with Jenna Bernstein? I mean, we both wondered, why would Adria Kohl let her father continue in the relationship, knowing Jenna was having an affair?"

"Why do you think?" Keera asked.

"I've given that question a lot of thought. It's unlikely it had anything to do with Thomas Martin. I mean Adria Kohl was single, so it's not like Martin would have had any leverage over her to keep her from firing him."

"Agree," Keera said. "But why not confront Jenna, or advise her father?"

"Perhaps it had to do with the fact that Adria Kohl's father had invested a hundred and fifty million dollars in PDRT. Most of everything he had, I'm told."

"What do you mean?"

"He was in too deep to just walk away because his girlfriend was cheating on him; wasn't he?"

"You're saying Adria Kohl had no choice but to let it play out and hope the company hit it big, so Sirus might at least get back his money?" Keera said.

"She was his sole heir. No siblings. Mother was out of the picture, and by the way, I've learned the divorce was ugly, and it got uglier after Sirus hit it big. Adria lived with the mother, in an apartment. The mother worked at the courthouse as a secretary. Based upon what I have found, they didn't have much."

"Adds a new wrinkle also to Erik Wei stepping up to say the LINK was just one big con; doesn't it?"

"Indeed," Harrison said.

"Adria Kohl would see no end game if Wei blew the whistle," Keera said. "Her father wouldn't be able to get out his money. It would have ruined his investment."

"And carrying it a step further, Adria Kohl's inheritance. Seems she would need something else to happen. Something that would at least get Jenna Bernstein out of the picture and place the blame for the LINK's failings on her rather than her father."

"By getting Jenna convicted of murdering Erik Wei?" Keera couldn't keep skepticism out of her tone.

"It's a theory to explore," Harrison said. "Might be nothing, but who had access to all the cell phone and computer records at PDRT besides Jenna and Sirus Kohl?" Harrison asked.

"Adria Kohl."

"And who would have access to the safe in her father's house, where Jenna said she last saw him put the gun? Adria was her father's personal attorney, as well as PDRT's general counsel. He would have likely provided her access to his personal records, were anything to happen to him, and he likely kept those records in his safe."

"Possibly," Keera said. "But then why not leave Jenna's gun behind for the police to find?" But even as she asked the question the answer dawned on her.

"Too obvious," Harrison said. "No one leaves the murder weapon behind. It's beyond rare. The police would ask why Jenna would shoot Wei and leave the gun. She's far too smart to do something so stupid."

"True," Keera said.

"Adria Kohl would know from Wei's text message, and the restaurant meeting between Wei and Jenna, that Jenna had a strong motive to kill Wei. That alone, even without the gun, should have been enough to convict her. Except for Patsy pulling a rabbit out of his hat," Harrison said.

"Except for that," Keera said.

"Which brings us to Sirus's murder and the bigger question," Harrison said.

"Why would Adria Kohl kill her father?"

Harrison gave her a look and a shrug. "As I said, she was first on the scene. She could have shot her father, sent those text messages using his phone and Jenna's phone. Then waited and used her father's phone to call herself to make it look like he called to tell her he wanted to go forward with the meeting with the US Attorney."

"But why would she kill him? What would be the animus?"

"Good point," Harrison said. "I'm not yet sure."

Keera wasn't either, but she saw the chessboard pieces sliding, like they did in a chess match when an opponent surprised her, and she had to think of alternatives. Patsy had taught her to be flexible, not to become wed to just one strategy or theory. He said it was too easy to lose when someone blew up that strategy. She had another thought. "Maybe Adria Kohl didn't send those text messages, and maybe she didn't call herself on her father's phone."

"I don't follow," Harrison said.

"We're speculating Adria sent those text messages pretending to be Jenna, then made it look like her father called her so she could tell Rossi and Ford he did so to confirm the morning meeting. But what if her father did send those text messages to Jenna, and it was Jenna who responded? What if, after those text messages were sent, her father didn't call Adria to tell Adria he wanted to go forward with the meeting? What if he called to tell her he wanted to call off the meeting?"

"Why would he do that?" Harrison said, then just as quickly he deduced Keera's possible answer, and they both said at nearly the same time, "Because Jenna convinced him to call it off."

"But after what she did at the Wei trial?" Harrison said. "Why would he even entertain what she had to say?"

"Why would he continue to provide her security services after she had moved out? Why would he send her those texts telling her what he intended to do?" Keera asked.

"He wouldn't."

"Think, JP. You're a man. What would compel him to do that?"

"He wanted to get laid?"

She groaned and shook her head.

"You said to think like a man."

"He was reaching out. He was trying to get Jenna to respond, start a dialogue. Go through Sirus Kohl's CDRs for the past two years and determine the number of times he reached out and Jenna didn't respond. I'm betting it's a dozen or more. What would force her to finally respond?"

"A threat to expose her," Harrison said.

"Yes. But more than to get her to respond, what he truly wants is to see her in person," Keera said, continuing to see the chess pieces sliding across the board. "He wants to ask her what happened to them. Which is why he doesn't capitulate in the text string, and when Jenna can't get him to call off the meeting, what does she do?"

"She puts on a pseudo disguise and goes to his house."

"Which is what he really wants. We both speculated she would do that; didn't we?"

"To convince him not to have the meeting."

"Yes," Keera said.

"But how?" Harrison said, still sounding unconvinced.

"By convincing him that she still loved him, JP. What if she went to convince him they could both be together, that they both could stay out of jail if they didn't testify against each other."

"Why would he believe she loved him after what she did at the Wei trial?"

"Because Jenna made him believe it, like she's always done, and because Kohl did still *love* her. He heard what he wanted to hear, that she did love him and maybe they could still have a future together."

"Then why didn't she respond to his text messages or take his calls prior to that night? Wouldn't he ask that?"

"I'm sure he did." Keera gave his questions some thought. "She could have told him something like . . . if she had taken his calls, or responded to his text messages, or moved back into his house, the police would have thought, just as you did, that Jenna and Kohl had agreed to let her shift the blame to him to get her off for killing Wei. She could have told Kohl that by not responding, she was protecting him from being prosecuted."

"I'm having a hard time with this, Keera."

"Because you don't know her. You've never seen her lie. You have no idea how convincing she can be. Jenna looked me in the eye yesterday and she told me she didn't send those text messages to Kohl. She swore on her mother's life."

"Maybe then she didn't."

"No. She swore because she wanted me to believe her." Keera laughed. She'd been right to have been guarded, but she'd had a lot of practice being skeptical of promises, growing up with Jenna and with an alcoholic father.

"What's funny?" Harrison asked.

"That's why Jenna was being so honest with me when I got to her condominium."

"I don't follow."

She told him about the meeting and Jenna's apologies. "She was trying to soften me up, get me thinking she was being honest, that she'd had some great epiphany because she wanted me to believe she was being truthful when she said she didn't send the text messages." Keera shook her head. "And she was good, JP. I almost did believe her, and I would have, but I'd been fooled before by her, and I wasn't about to let her do it again. It was just another one of her performances and her calculated lies."

"At her arraignment she hardly looked at her parents. She didn't even thank them for putting their home up as collateral for her bail," Harrison said. "That would indicate she doesn't really care about them. But to swear on her mother's life?"

"She cares about them only when she needs them. She repeated this pattern growing up. She used them both to get what she wanted. It meant nothing to her to swear on her mother's life because Jenna does not have the capacity to care about another human being unless she can use that person to her own benefit. She convinced sophisticated business investors with teams of lawyers the LINK would change medicine. It would have been easy for her to convince Kohl to cancel his meeting with the US Attorney."

"Especially if he still loved her."

"Yes. And if he did, it would have enraged Adria Kohl, who would have seen Jenna as screwing up her carefully laid-out plans to save her father and what money he had left."

"Let's assume you're right," Harrison said. "Let's assume this is not just you and me speculating and that's exactly what did happen, or something similar to it. What difference does it make now? You can't very well convince Jenna to testify that she sent the messages to Kohl and went to his house to tell him to call off the meeting. If she did, you could never convince a jury she didn't kill him."

"You're right. I can't. And I'm sure Jenna has known that all along. She knows a jury would never believe it either. Not even Patsy could save her under those circumstances. That's why she denied having the phone—just like she denies having the gun. She denies it because she believes I'll find another way to blame Adria Kohl, or at least confuse the matter enough to create reasonable doubt, the way Patsy created reasonable doubt."

"But you can't point to Adria Kohl if Jenna won't admit she returned the text messages and went to the house and got Sirus Kohl to call off the meeting."

The chess pieces slid again, this time in Keera's favor. "The only way she'll admit it is if she thinks there is something in it for her."

"What would that be?"

"The only alternative to her spending the rest of her life in jail."

Chapter 27

Frank Rossi studied Adria Kohl's CDRs again and felt the strain from reading too many hours on the computer.

"What are you looking at?"

Rossi looked up. Ford stood over him, sipping from a mug of coffee.

"Adria Kohl's phone records."

"Again? What for?"

"I don't know. I'm just . . . still wondering about the flurry of calls to TMTP Security. If she wasn't PDRT's primary contact, why was she calling them?" He pointed to the log of calls on his computer screen. "And at odd hours—late at night and early in the morning. That seem odd to you?"

"Maybe she was just leaving messages, so she didn't forget. People do that."

"Maybe," Rossi said. "But about what?"

"What do you think?"

"I don't know what to think," Rossi said, frustrated.

"I'll call her tomorrow and ask her about it. See if she has an explanation."

"Yeah," Rossi said. "It just . . ."

"Just what?"

He looked again at his partner. "It just seems like one of those cases; doesn't it?"

"One of what cases?"

"You know, where nothing is as it seems. Like Bernstein going out in disguise knowing the security cameras would pick her up leaving her building. Then she walks to Volunteer Park and buys food at the one food truck with a video surveillance camera. It seems like she made it obvious, too obvious." He pointed to the screen. "I get the same feeling about all these calls, like there's something more to them."

"So let's call Kohl. Maybe there's a logical explanation before you get your panties in a bunch."

"Maybe," Rossi said. But he wasn't going to call Kohl. Not yet. Not until he had a better handle on what was going on.

"You heading out?" Ford asked.

Rossi looked at his watch. Five o'clock straight up. "You go ahead. I want to finish a few things."

Ford left. Rossi considered the screen, willing it to give him an answer. "What were all the calls about?" he said.

Maybe Billy was right. Maybe there was a logical explanation. Then he thought of Keera Duggan, and that feeling returned—that feeling that there was something else there. Something more about the phone calls he didn't yet know and needed to explore.

Something he was missing.

Part II

Chapter 28

Keera checked her appearance in the hall mirror of her home. She felt nerves, as always on the first day of a trial, but more so this morning. She'd always attacked in trial and at chess matches, a strategy ingrained in her by her father.

Stay on the attack. Even when you don't think you're winning. Force the issue.

This morning would be different.

Throughout the State's case, she would employ a different strategy, a strategy she had come to realize, after much thought, Patsy had also employed in Jenna Bernstein's first trial. Patsy had lain in wait throughout the State's case, playing possum. Then, in his defense case, he had attacked. Yes, Jenna had insisted she be allowed to testify, and Patsy had allowed her to do so, but not because Jenna had taken advantage of him, as Keera had presumed. Patsy did it because he knew it was his best chance to create reasonable doubt. He had needed Jenna to convince the jury she was innocent, and with his gentle prodding and skill at eliciting empathy-invoking responses to his questions, she had.

Keera's telephone rang. She knew it was her father. He had called to wish her luck the first morning of every trial she'd ever had. Patsy had spent six weeks at the treatment facility in Eastern Washington, five hours from Seattle. He'd spend two additional weeks before he came home. Her mother had moved to a home not far from the facility that Ella had found on Vrbo.

"Hey, Dad," Keera said.

"Hey, kiddo. You knew it was me."

"Trusted my intuition," she said, not mentioning caller ID. "And Mom said when I spoke to her yesterday that they were going to allow you to start making outside phone calls. I knew your first call would be about work."

"I called your mother first. You're my second call. Wanted to wish you luck this morning. I know the Jenna Bernstein trial starts today."

"Your two first loves. Mom and work. I'm glad you got the priority right. I thought they didn't allow any outside news at that facility."

"I've made it to the next step in my recovery. I can watch limited television and read the newspapers. I couldn't avoid the trial if I had wanted to."

"It's gotten a lot of play, that's for sure. We picked a jury Monday. We give opening statements this morning."

"How do you feel?"

"Nervous."

"Good. Nerves are good. It means you're prepared to do battle. I wish I could be at counsel table beside you."

"You will be, Dad. Every step of the way."

"Thanks, kiddo."

"At present you have just one thing to worry about, and that's enough."

"I know."

Keera smiled. It was the first time she could recall her father, following a bender, not trying to convince her he would never drink again, that things would change for the better. "I better get going."

"Good luck, kiddo."

Keera disconnected and stared again at her reflection in the mirror. It was time to look vulnerable.

◆　◆　◆

At Judge Johnson Marshall's invitation, Walker Thompson rose from his chair and approached the lectern in the tightly packed courtroom. The pews in the overflow room next door were also full, and people stood lining the back wall. Jury selection had been arduous and lengthy. So many people in the pool of eligible jurors either knew of, had read about, or had watched reports about PDRT, the Erik Wei trial, and/or Jenna Bernstein. Those persons familiar with the Erik Wei trial were excused for cause, as were those familiar with the US Attorney's pending lawsuit for fraud and conspiracy. Judge Marshall brought in three different jury pools before the two sides either reached agreement on each prospective juror or ran out of challenges to dismiss a particular one without cause. In the end, Keera was satisfied with the seven women and five men. She felt confident in three jurors, and not so confident in another three. The other six could go either way, meaning both she and Thompson had done their jobs well.

At the lectern, Thompson faced the jury. Judge Marshall had given both sides permission to move about the courtroom, but cautioned this was a legal proceeding, not a track meet. If either party wandered too much, he'd rein them back in.

"Good morning, ladies and gentlemen," Thompson said, and they were under way. He thanked the jury for their presence and introduced himself and his co-counsel, Cheryl McFadden. He talked a bit about the State's burden of proof to convict Jenna Bernstein, then he discussed the basis for the State's case.

Motions in limine had been delicate. Thompson had argued to the judge the State should be allowed to discuss the Erik Wei trial so the jurors could understand Jenna's motivation for killing Sirus Kohl. He wanted to tell the jury Jenna had blamed Kohl for the misrepresentations made to investors and to the public, and in response, Kohl intended to provide the US Attorney with testimony, including documents, to implicate Jenna. Keera responded that the documents Thompson sought to admit were noncommittal, and since no deal had been reached with the US Attorney, what Kohl might have said was speculative. Beyond that, she argued the evidence was grossly prejudicial, and the State clearly sought to try Jenna twice for the same crime or, at a minimum, to use the Wei trial as evidence of a prior bad act to convict her in this case. Neither was allowed.

As was typical of Judge Marshall, Thompson won and lost. He won the right to discuss the US Attorney's case, Marshall finding it indispensable to the State's case to show Jenna had a motive, but he denied Marshall's request he be allowed to mention Erik Wei or the trial.

"This case is not complicated," Thompson said, in his relaxed manner, the courtroom as quiet as a church. "Witnesses will sit in that chair and explain to you that Sirus Kohl and Jenna Bernstein were former business partners involved in a romantic relationship. They will tell you Sirus Kohl and the defendant had been indicted by the United States Attorney for committing multiple counts of fraud and conspiracy in the running of their company, Ponce de León Restorative Technology. They will tell you Sirus Kohl had an appointment with the US Attorney handling that case the morning he was found dead, that he intended to provide testimony and documents that Jenna Bernstein had made knowingly false statements to PDRT investors and to the general public about that company's product, the LINK.

"Forensic witnesses will testify that the night Sirus Kohl was murdered, he and Jenna Bernstein had a conversation by text messages in which he revealed to her his intention to meet with and to provide evidence to the US Attorney. Forensic witnesses will show you video evidence that, shortly after the text conversation, Jenna Bernstein walked from her condominium in South Lake Union to Volunteer Park in Seattle." McFadden used her computer to put up a street map on the courtroom screens. Keera made no objection. She would also use the map. McFadden highlighted Jenna Bernstein's path, Sirus Kohl's house in relation to Volunteer Park, and the park easement. "This narrow, unlit easement leads directly to Sirus Kohl's back door," Thompson said.

It didn't, not exactly, but Keera wasn't going to quibble and highlight the easement's proximity to the house even more.

"Finally, ladies and gentlemen, ballistics experts will tell you the person who entered the house that night did so without force. That this person shot Sirus Kohl once, in the back of the head, with a 9-millimeter handgun. Witnesses will tell you that Jenna Bernstein owned such a weapon, but that the gun has conveniently disappeared."

Keera rose. "Objection, Your Honor. Improper opinion."

"Sustained. The jury will disregard the prosecutor's last statement."

Thompson continued. "The State will not put on a witness who saw the shooting, because no witness exists, except for the killer. No cameras filmed what happened inside the Capitol Hill home. Sirus Kohl lived alone. That's the nature of a premeditated, well-thought-out, and pre-planned murder committed by a person who does not wish to be caught.

"The State is convinced that, after you hear the evidence, you will find, beyond a reasonable doubt, that Jenna Bernstein had both the motive and the opportunity, and that she did, with malice aforethought, shoot and kill Sirus Kohl."

Thompson spoke for another few minutes before returning to his chair.

Judge Marshall paused as if contemplating a recess, then leaned forward and spoke to Keera. "Does counsel for the defense wish to make an opening statement now, or reserve? If counsel wishes to proceed now, the court is inclined to take a brief recess to allow the jurors to stretch their legs."

Keera rose. "Your Honor, I'm sure the jurors could use an opportunity to stretch their legs. The defense will reserve giving its opening statement until its case in chief."

"Thank you, Counsel. Then this case will be in brief recess. When we return, the State will commence with its first witness." Marshall cautioned the jurors not to discuss the case during the recess.

The court rose as Marshall descended from the bench.

"What are you doing?" Jenna asked after the jurors had departed.

"What do you mean?" Keera said, playing dumb.

"Patsy told me he never waits to give his opening statement, that he doesn't want the prosecutor's accusations to be in the jurors' heads without some rebuttal."

She was very smart. Always had been. "That was a different trial," Keera said. "This trial requires a different strategy."

"I don't like this strategy. I think you should tell the judge you want to give your opening statement after the break."

"I told you, this trial requires a different strategy. And I told you, I'll make those decisions. We'll play defense until an opportunity to attack opens."

"When will that be?"

"I don't know, exactly. That's the nature of trials. They're fluid. Now, if you'll excuse me, I'm going to use the bathroom." Keera turned away from Jenna. Thompson and his co-counsel, McFadden, were in discussion, but Frank Rossi, who also sat at counsel's table—as the State's representative—stared at Keera, as if he, too, wondered what she was up to.

After the break, Thompson called Adria Kohl to the witness stand. Keera thought choosing Kohl as the opening witness was indicative of a seasoned prosecutor. Thompson wanted to not just set the crime scene for the jurors; he wanted to open with a witness who would evoke empathy, and what better witness than a daughter who would testify that she walked into her father's house and found his dead body?

Kohl wore a conservative-cut, beige suit with a light-blue blouse. The State clearly wanted to soften her image from the hard-charging attorney who had done battle with PDRT employees. Thompson took Kohl through her professional and her personal background and established she was the only child of Sirus Kohl. She described Kohl as a caring father who had paid for her college education and for her postgraduate studies in law, then retained her to serve as his corporate counsel.

What JP Harrison had learned and advised Keera was that Adria Kohl had little to no interaction with her father until she needed money to attend college and law school and struck up a relationship with him.

"What my father truly loved was working with young entrepreneurs with big ideas," Kohl said. "He loved start-up companies, and the energy young people had for their work and their desire to impact the world."

Kohl described her father's interest in biomedical engineering and took the jurors through the start-up companies in which he had invested and worked.

"The company he was most excited about was Ponce de León Restorative Technology," she said.

"Did he say why?" Thompson asked.

"It was everything he looked for in a start-up. He would be getting in on the ground floor. He was excited about the CEO, her vision, and the company's potential to change the medical profession. He talked about curing diseases and about noninvasive means to regenerate and rejuvenate vital organs. He talked about PDRT and the LINK as the Fountain of Youth that would extend human life expectancy by repairing damaged organs with new cells."

Thompson changed subjects to Jenna Bernstein. "Did your father's relationship with Jenna Bernstein extend beyond their being business partners?"

"It did," she said. "Against my advice."

"Why were you against your father and Jenna Bernstein having a personal relationship?"

"First and foremost, it's bad for business for the largest investor in a company to be intimately involved with the CEO. Business executives have a fiduciary duty to act in the best interests of company shareholders, and a personal relationship can be viewed as counter to that obligation."

"Because executives in a personal relationship could do what is in their or their partner's best interests?"

"That's the danger."

"Were you otherwise opposed?"

"Yes. The difference in their ages was also significant. Jenna Bernstein was younger than me. She could have been my father's daughter."

"There have been couples of disparate ages who have had strong relationships, though."

"Certainly, but I didn't like the fact my father was also investing much of his wealth in Jenna's company."

"You didn't believe in the company?"

"I had some doubts, but I was more concerned that Jenna's interest in my father was not honest. I worried she was more interested in the funds she needed to get PDRT off the ground."

"Did your perception of the relationship change?"

"To a degree."

"Can you explain?"

"My father was not going to be convinced otherwise."

"What do you mean?"

"He genuinely cared for Jenna, and he told me she loved him. He said for the first time since his divorce, he was happy. He wanted me to be happy for him."

"But you weren't?"

"I still had reservations. I told my father I'd feel better if I had a role in the company to better monitor his financial investment."

"And he had you appointed general counsel?"

"Against Jenna's wishes."

"Ms. Bernstein was opposed to you being PDRT's general counsel?"

"Very much so. She went so far as to tell me she was against the idea."

"But your father prevailed in spite of her opposition?"

"A hundred and fifty million dollars can be very convincing."

Keera bolted to her feet. "Objection, Your Honor, and move to strike. No foundation for what is an acerbic opinion."

"Sustained," Marshall said. "The jury will disregard the prior answer."

Keera had objected, but only because Thompson would have expected her to. She sensed Frank Rossi, who knew her and her trial skills better than anyone in the courtroom, was already questioning her placid and uncontentious demeanor. Keera was quite pleased with Adria Kohl's testimony that she doubted Jenna Bernstein's interest in her father was genuine, but that her father loved Jenna and wanted his daughter to be happy for him.

"Ms. Kohl, I know this is difficult, but I'd like to take you to the morning you discovered your father's body. What time did you arrive at your father's home?"

"I arrived shortly before six thirty in the morning."

"And can you explain to the jury the reason you were at your father's house so early?"

Adria did so, explaining the US Attorney's lawsuit and the potential ramifications if her father was convicted. She said, "These were serious charges, and my father was facing prison. I was concerned based upon some prior factors—"

Keera prepared to rise and object, should Kohl mention or refer to the Wei matter despite Judge Marshall's decision the subject was inadmissible.

"—that my father might receive the blame for what transpired at PDRT. I had worked hard to find documents to prove he had been attempting to get the company—Jenna Bernstein—to temper representations she was making to investors."

"Can you explain?"

Kohl described the compartmentalization at the company, her father's involvement in the day-to-day business, and Jenna's role as the company face, including securing financing from investors. "My father didn't always know what Jenna was telling investors. These representations were not put in writing. When he found out the extent of her representations, he attempted to get her to pull back, to not be so bold in what she was telling investors and regulators about the LINK. He tried to tell her that while he believed the LINK would someday do all that she was representing, it was not there yet. Further work and testing needed to be performed."

"And where does this information come from?"

"From the documents, and from conversations he had with me alone, and conversations he had with me and Jenna Bernstein."

"And did you also find documents showing Jenna's reluctance to follow your father's advice?"

"Yes and no. As I said, Jenna was careful about what she put in writing."

"Objection," Keera said rising. "There's no foundation for that conjecture."

"Sustained and stricken."

"Did you find documents from Jenna Bernstein in which she expressed reluctance to follow your father's advice?" Thompson asked.

"Not per se, which is why my father's testimony about what Jenna Bernstein knew and what she was telling investors was so important to his meeting with the US Attorney's Office."

It was a strong point by Thompson and Adria Kohl, one that Keera had predicted. By making her father's testimony the linchpin to the deal with the US Attorney, it increased Jenna's motivation to kill Kohl to prevent him from attending that meeting.

"Let's look at some of those documents," Thompson said. He paused, perhaps expecting Keera to object that the documents were not relevant. She didn't. Thompson spent the next half hour displaying some of the documents, and with each passing minute Keera sensed Jenna as increasingly more agitated. The knuckles of Jenna's hands, clasped in her lap, had turned white.

"What was the purpose of the meeting with the attorney from the United States Attorney's Office who was handling the case against Jenna Bernstein and your father?"

"I sought an agreement in which my father would plead guilty and agree to testify against Jenna Bernstein, and for his cooperation he would be given a reduced sentence."

"Had you reached specific terms?"

"No, that was the purpose of the meeting."

"And was your father on board with your intentions?"

"My father called me the prior evening at around 9:30 p.m. to confirm we were going forward with the meeting and asked when I would be at the house the following morning."

Thompson put up CDR records from Adria Kohl's cell phone, asked her to confirm her number, and to identify the call she received from her father that evening. Then he said, "It looks as though you called your father in the morning."

"I called and texted him, several times, but he did not answer. He also did not respond to my text messages. I thought maybe he was in the shower, but when he didn't respond, I decided to drive over."

Kohl went through the process of arriving at and going through her father's rented house, then finding him facedown in the living room, and the aftermath. On several occasions, Thompson offered her a Kleenex. It was, in Keera's experience, a worthy performance.

Thompson's direct examination took up most of the morning. After a recess, Keera rose from her chair and approached Adria Kohl.

"You didn't like Jenna Bernstein very much; did you?"

"I was concerned about my father."

"But you did not like her."

"No. I didn't."

"You thought Jenna used your father for his money."

"That was my concern; yes."

"Because you were the sole heir to your father's wealth?"

Thompson rose. "Objection, Your Honor, without foundation."

"Overruled," Marshall said. "This is cross-examination. Do you need the question repeated, Ms. Kohl?"

"No. I don't. I thought it my responsibility to look after what remained of my father's wealth so he would not be taken advantage of by opportunistic people."

"And you believed Jenna to be one of those opportunistic people."

"Yes. I did."

"You warned your father about this, no doubt?"

"I did, yes."

"Your father valued your advice, I would expect, given he pushed to have you made PDRT's general counsel?"

"He valued my advice."

"But he ignored your advice when it came to Jenna; didn't he?"

Kohl, caught off guard, had to take back whatever she'd been prepared to say. Then she said, "I don't know if he ignored it."

"He didn't follow it; did he?"

"Not everything."

"He had Jenna move into his home; didn't he?"

"Yes, but at Jenna's urging."

"He arranged for a security company to provide Jenna security; correct?"

"He worried about her safety after several magazine articles came out indicating Jenna's wealth based on the company's valuation."

"He arranged for her to be protected; right?"

"He did."

"That was with TMTP Security; was it not?"

"It was."

"Jenna had security to and from work and if she traveled outside of work; correct?"

"Correct."

"Your father also bought Jenna a firearm, a handgun; did he not?"

"He did," Kohl said.

"Where did he keep the gun?"

"I don't know."

"Wasn't it kept in the safe in your father's bedroom?"

"It might have been."

"Didn't your father keep his gun in that safe?"

"I don't know."

"Your father also arranged meals for Jenna and put together a work-out plan for her to follow because he was worried about her physical health working so many hours at PDRT; didn't he?"

Keera knew Kohl was stuck. She couldn't very well say her father did these things as a means to control Jenna, as Jenna had testified during the Erik Wei trial. "He did."

"He doted on her; didn't he?"

"That isn't the word I would use."

"He certainly cared for her."

"I told you he cared for her."

"He cared so much for her that he disagreed with your opinion Jenna was using him for his money; didn't he?"

Kohl pursed her lips. "We had a difference of opinion."

"I'll say," Keera said. "Did you take any steps to ensure Jenna was not taking advantage of your father?"

"I don't understand."

"As general counsel you had access to employee cell phones and their laptop computers. You could monitor emails and text messages, even what internet sites they searched, to be certain employees were not violating company policy on social media and potentially giving away trade secrets; couldn't you?"

"That's true."

"You also assigned the burner phones that PDRT management used; didn't you?"

"I did."

"You assigned Jenna Bernstein's phone to her; correct?"

"Yes."

"So you knew the phone number of Jenna Bernstein's burner phone."

"Of course I did."

"You could monitor employees' phone calls and text messages; couldn't you?"

"That's true, but Jenna and my father were not on that network."

"They were on a separate network for executives, to ensure privacy and confidentiality."

"That's also true."

"And you had access to that network also as general counsel; didn't you?"

"As general counsel, part of my job was to be sure of compliance with company contracts."

"You disliked Jenna so much you were willing to throw her under the bus to the US Attorney's Office; isn't that true?"

"I was looking out for my father's best interests. That's what an attorney does for her client."

"By offering Jenna up as the sacrificial lamb?"

"That was up to the US Attorney. It wasn't my concern."

"But it was; wasn't it? You hated Jenna, and getting her convicted by the US Attorney's Office and sent to prison would get her away from your father and what remained of your inheritance once and for all; wouldn't it?" Keera could have been talking about the Erik Wei trial but made her question specific.

"Objection, Your Honor," Thompson said.

"Overruled."

"I was looking out for my father."

"Both his business interests and his personal interests; correct?"

"Correct."

Keera put up Adria Kohl's CDR records on the computer screens. "Let me direct your attention again to the phone call your father made to you the night he was shot. The one in which you testified that he wanted to confirm the meeting was going forward. That call lasted fifty seconds."

"Okay."

"That's a lot longer than is needed to confirm a meeting; isn't it?"

"We probably discussed other things."

"Such as."

"I don't recall. Personal things. How are you doing? Those kinds of things."

Keera looked at the large clock on the wall. She'd gotten what she could from Adria Kohl. She'd established Kohl had access to Jenna's and Sirus's emails and text messages. She could argue Kohl knew where the safe was in her father's home. She could argue that as his personal attorney he would have given Adria access to the safe. She wouldn't get more, not without potentially alerting Kohl and Thompson to what she intended to do. They would be ultrasensitive to any kind of SODDI defense—Some Other Dude Did It.

"You loved your father; didn't you?"

The question seemed to surprise Kohl. "Absolutely."

"You didn't want to see him hurt."

"No, I did not," she said, now more tentative.

"He'd had his heart broken once, by your mother; didn't he?"

"It was a difficult divorce."

"Initiated by your mother, who was having an affair; isn't that true?" JP had found the information in a court file in Los Angeles.

Thompson rose. "Objection. Relevance."

"Sustained."

"No further questions," Keera said to Judge Marshall. "I'm finished with my cross-examination but request this witness not be dismissed should the defense wish to call her in its case in chief." It was standard for defense counsel not to dismiss certain of the State's witnesses under subpoena, and Keera's request would not make Thompson or Kohl suspicious.

"Ms. Kohl, you are excused but you remain subject to the court's subpoena should the defense wish to call you in its case in chief."

Kohl said she understood and stepped down from the stand.

Marshall, noting the time, dismissed the jury for the day with an admonition not to talk to anyone about the case, and not to read anything written or watch or listen to the news.

Keera returned to counsel's table. US marshals would handcuff Jenna Bernstein and return her to her condominium to resume home confinement until the morning. Before they arrived, Jenna turned to Keera. She looked stunned. "What was that all about?"

"I thought it went well."

"To what purpose?"

"To discrediting Adria Kohl and reducing her emotional impact on the jury."

"By saying she didn't want to see me hurt her father?" Keera nodded. Jenna seemed to study her. "I hope you know what you're doing."

"I do," she said as the marshals approached. "Get a good night's sleep, and I'll see you tomorrow morning."

Chapter 29

Keera fumbled with her chopsticks and extracted a piece of General Tso's chicken from the box along with some rice she had added, working it to her mouth. After not eating all afternoon, the spicy odor of ginger, garlic, and chili oil was intoxicating, as was the taste.

In the background, her Alexa played classical music. Patsy did so when writing his opening and closing statements, believing classical music helped to create a calm and focused environment, without lyrics to distract. Keera did it for those reasons, and because the composition was much like the composition of a good closing and opening argument, with an exposition that introduced the main themes; development, which expanded on those themes; recapitulation, in which the main themes were hammered home; and coda, a concluding section. Having it on now helped her to feel her father's presence.

"A civilized person would use a plate," JP Harrison said across the round table in her office, which was strewn with legal papers, his notepad to the side.

"A civilized person would have time to use a plate. I'm in trial."

Maggie had ordered the food and would each evening. In the past, during trials, their mother would stop by the office to bring a pot roast or stew, but she remained in Eastern Washington with Patsy. In some ways, Maggie's taking care of Keera was reminiscent of Keera's youth, at least before Maggie and Ella went off to college. They had each been mothers to Keera, and while at times it had been suffocating, at other times, like this, Keera was glad to have them.

Ella did the dirty work. She ordered the daily trial transcripts and reviewed them thoroughly, taking notes to help Keera with her opening statement in her case in chief, her direct examinations, and her closing argument. She also was available to respond to or bring trial motions, though this trial was much more civilized than Keera's trial against Miller Ambrose, which had been a bare-knuckle brawl.

Keera had asked Harrison to come into the office after court because she wanted his thoughts on some of her upcoming cross-examinations, like Frank Rossi. Without Patsy to lean on, Harrison became her support.

"How do you feel it went today?" Harrison asked, in between bites of garlic chicken with broccoli.

Keera could hear the band that would play at the Paddy Wagon this night warming up in the bar three floors below. "I'd say it went well, but don't ask Jenna though."

"Do you think she suspects what you're up to?"

"She's suspicious, but that's a way of life for her. I don't believe she knows what I intend to do."

"Can you keep it hidden?"

She shrugged. "I can try."

Harrison took a final sip of his Tsingtao beer and shot the bottle a short distance. It landed with a thump in a recycle basket. "Do you think she's innocent?"

Keera had been negotiating another piece of chicken to her mouth but dropped it. She jabbed the chopsticks into the carton and set it down on the table. "Where did that question come from?"

"I'm just wondering. I don't disagree with your analysis, but it relies heavily on circumstantial evidence and speculation."

"You're concerned because of Vince LaRussa. You're concerned I'm going to free a guilty woman."

"I'm concerned Jenna could be violent, yes."

"We're all capable of violence, under the right circumstances."

"You know what I mean."

She did. "You're asking if she could be a psychopath?"

"That's as good a way as any to put it."

"And my honest answer is: I'm not certain. Cynthia Talmadge thought she could be a sociopath, certainly."

"That's comforting."

"I believe she's a sociopath. Does that make it easier for her to commit violence than it is for anyone else? I don't know."

"Still, not exactly reassuring," Harrison said.

"If I do my job well, I will have provided Jenna with the most vigorous defense I can, which is my only obligation."

He picked up his plate and his chopsticks. "You sound like Patsy." She did.

"Unless you have any additional questions of me, I'll take these to the dishwasher in the kitchen and head home."

"I think we've covered it. Do you feel comfortable with your examination if I need you?"

"Like my dogs sleeping beneath their sheepskin covers."

"Sheepskin? Do you feed them steak too?"

"I'll never tell. See you in the morning."

After Harrison had left, Keera thought further about his question, and about what had happened after the Vince LaRussa verdict. Was Jenna capable of the same physical violence if Keera was able to convince a jury to find her not guilty and set her free?

No one could be truly certain.

But Keera had no intention of giving Jenna that opportunity.

Not if she did her job well.

Chapter 30

Over the next several trial days, Walker Thompson called lay and expert witnesses to the witness stand to establish the scene inside the house, including the location of Sirus Kohl's body. He put on the 911 dispatcher who'd received Adria Kohl's phone call, as well as the first responding officers. Keera opted not to ask questions. Thompson moved on to the CSI experts. Barry Dillard, head of the firearms section, said the bullet that killed Kohl was fired from a 9-millimeter handgun. Keera asked Dillard just a few questions before sitting down. She had just one question of both the DNA expert and the latent fingerprint expert. She asked if either had found Jenna Bernstein's DNA or her fingerprints anywhere in the house.

"No," they each said.

Thompson also put on a blood spatter expert who testified the spatter size indicated Sirus Kohl had been shot at close range, between three to seven feet. Again, Keera asked no questions.

With each witness that she either declined to cross-examine or asked only a few questions, she saw Frank Rossi watching her more and more intently.

Thompson next called Arthur Litchfield, the medical examiner. Thompson established Kohl had been shot once at close range, and he ruled the killing a homicide. He estimated the killing window to be between 8:00 p.m. and midnight, which fit the time frame in which Jenna had done her walkabout to Volunteer Park. Keera asked questions of Litchfield, attempting to reduce his estimated window of time of the killing, but Litchfield, well rehearsed before court, deftly handled her questions. With little to gain, Keera didn't pursue the line of inquiry further.

Jenna grew increasingly unhappy. At breaks in the day, and after court had recessed, she questioned Keera about her trial strategy and asked why she wasn't attacking the prosecution's witnesses, the way Patsy had.

Keera largely deflected the inquiries, telling Jenna this was a different case, and there was little to gain from attacking the witnesses who had been called by the State.

"I think I need to tell the jury why I took the walk, and why I wore the hat and the glasses. If I don't, they'll assume it was to hide my identity and that I walked to Sirus's house."

"It's risky, Jenna."

"I can convince the jury. Your father also told me it was risky, but my testimony is what won that case."

Jenna the narcissist. So predictable. "Let's table this discussion for now," Keera told her. "We can revisit it when we get to our case in chief. By then we'll have all the State's evidence and should be in a better position to make that decision."

Frank Rossi entered the conference room in the prosecuting attorney's office. He felt the strain of trial, though likely far less than Walker Thompson. Rossi's job, as the State's representative, was to largely provide a face for the jury to see every day. Having Adria Kohl in the pew behind the railing also helped in that regard. In addition, Rossi assisted with the evidence, and he kept notes, bringing to Thompson's attention anything the prosecutor might have missed or overlooked as to each witness. So far Thompson hadn't missed a thing. He'd been spot-on. Singularly focused.

Keera, on the other hand, had seemed off her game. This was not the same attorney Rossi knew from the prosecutor's office, or the feisty attorney who fought and beat Miller Ambrose during the Vince LaRussa case. *That* Keera had been more like her father. She brawled with witnesses, if not necessarily to score points, to at least create an impression on the jurors. As a prosecutor, Keera's combative nature had evidenced her belief in the charges brought against each defendant, and the jury absorbed that passionate belief. It was one of the things that made her so formidable.

As a defense attorney in the LaRussa trial, her passion had been just as strong. She established her outrage and intimated the State's case had so many holes it would never float.

While Rossi wondered about Keera's strategy, he didn't for a minute believe she was conceding. He saw this as a new tactic. To what end, he did not yet know.

Walker Thompson entered the conference room in casual clothes. Each day, after the trial, he ran along the waterfront to clear his head and ease his stress, showered at his downtown workout club, and returned to get prepared for the following day. "It's going as well as can be expected," he said to Rossi, who sensed Thompson sought affirmation, perhaps still a bit gun-shy given what had happened in the Wei trial.

"Seems to be," Rossi said. "Though I'm beginning to wonder what Keera Duggan's strategy is."

"What do you mean?"

Rossi told Thompson his prior experiences sitting alongside Keera and across the aisle from her. "She was more like her father," he said.

"She hasn't had much to work with," Thompson said.

"That's true," Rossi said.

"You don't sound convinced," Thompson said.

"It's just . . . unlike her," Rossi said. He didn't add that he'd spent enough time with Keera to understand her personality and her demeanor, that he knew she'd been a chess prodigy as a child and always had more than one response to an opponent's moves. He also didn't say that she adapted better than any attorney Rossi had seen in a court-room, including her father, and she had the ability to make something seemingly out of nothing. Yet she hadn't even tried to do so in this case. Keera had once told Rossi another strategy in chess was to lead her opponent away from where the attack was going to take place, so the opponent wouldn't figure out what she was doing until it was too late to recover. He wondered if Keera was leading Thompson to believe all was well.

While planning an attack somewhere else.

Chapter 31

The following day, Walker Thompson looked to Keera like a man who'd just finished a good meal as he made his way from the lectern back to counsel's table. His direct examination of Frank Rossi had been thorough and well crafted. The lines, mostly scripted, didn't sound rehearsed, a testament to both Thompson's questioning skills and Rossi's credibility. The whole examination had a rhythm to it—the way Keera felt when she was in a zone playing competitive chess. She could see all of her opponent's potential moves and her responses to each before they happened.

One reason for Thompson and Rossi's rhythm was Keera had largely refrained from objecting, except on a few occasions and never vociferously. She wanted the jury to hear from Rossi, especially about how Adria Kohl had greeted them in her father's office. Thompson had also used Rossi to introduce the security tapes, as well as images of Jenna on her walk from her condominium to Volunteer Park. Keera could work with all of that.

"Your witness," Thompson said as he returned to counsel's table.

Keera pushed back her chair, the legs scraping the linoleum. She approached the lectern without notes. She had her arms folded across her chest, watching Frank Rossi. He looked comfortable in the witness chair, but Keera knew him well enough to read his expressions and his body language. Rossi was curious about what she was up to, and maybe a bit anxious about what was to come. He sipped his water and returned the glass to the side table—one of Rossi's tells when nervous.

Jurors liked and respected him. He knew when to laugh and smile and when to be serious. He always respected the gravity of the crime committed, the victim, and the victim's family. All of which meant Keera could not charge at him like a bullfighter with a sword. She had to use a cape—flash it on her left and on her right to keep Rossi off balance and to prevent him from anticipating the direction of her questions, without tricking him. Jurors would not react well if she tricked a likeable witness.

"Good afternoon, Detective Rossi." She unfolded her arms and moved closer to the jury box.

"Good afternoon." He licked his lip. Another of his tells.

"Detective, would you describe Adria Kohl's demeanor when you and your partner, Billy Ford, first arrived at the site?"

"We didn't see her when we arrived at the site. She was inside the house."

Keera considered his answer as if it was new information. "I take it then you spoke to the responding officers and to your sergeant, Chuck Pan, about Ms. Kohl when you arrived?"

"We did."

"And did they discuss her demeanor?"

"I was admiring her car in the driveway, a blue Porsche, and they said she was 'a lawyer.'"

Keera smiled. "Did you understand what was meant by that depiction of her?"

Rossi cleared his throat and did a poor job hiding a grin. Keera took a step closer, not about to lose this moment with the jurors. "It's okay, Detective, we lawyers can take it." Several jurors and others in the gallery chuckled. So, too, did Judge Marshall.

"I took it to mean she was businesslike. She wanted answers and she wanted them quickly."

Keera asked a few open-ended questions, confident she knew the answers. "And where did you and your partner first encounter Adria Kohl?"

"In the office near the main entrance to the house."

"Her father's office?"

"She said it was."

"What was she doing?"

"She was on his computer."

"Doing what?" Keera knew at least part of what Adria was doing because Thompson had produced the computer-printed document in discovery.

"She was making a list of everything she believed was important— such as when she arrived at the scene, what she had done, the prior night's events."

"Businesslike. Hard charging. I can see why you formulated your opinion." Keera walked to counsel's table and picked up the exhibit Thompson had introduced on direct examination. She had it placed on the computer screens and again showed it to the jury for emphasis.

Thompson, after a beat, rose. "Objection, Your Honor. Counsel asked no question and is therefore testifying."

"Sustained. Ms. Duggan?"

"I'm sorry, Your Honor. I was getting to my question." She had not been. She wanted to make a point to the jury and use it in her closing argument. She directed Rossi to the document on the courtroom's computer screens. "This is the list Ms. Kohl put together in her father's office the morning she found his body; correct?"

"Correct."

"She noted she found no gun; didn't she?"

"She did."

"And she specifically told you that; didn't she?"

"She did."

"She wasn't sobbing and lamenting at the computer keyboard; was she?"

"Not that I saw."

"She was businesslike, just as you had interpreted when told she was an attorney; wasn't she?"

"I wouldn't disagree."

"Calculating?"

"I'm not sure I'd go that far." Rossi didn't have to. Keera had done it for him.

"She'd just found her father shot dead on the floor of his home and she was in his office, on his computer, putting together this list of when she arrived and what she had seen and done; is that right?"

"People grieve in different ways."

"That wasn't my question, Detective. Would you like my question repeated by the court reporter?"

"That's what she was doing, yes."

Keera flashed the cape on the other side of her body. "She told you in that conversation, words to the effect that she believed Jenna Bernstein had killed her father and wanted you and your partner, Billy Ford, to drive to Jenna's condominium and confront her; didn't she?"

"She suspected that to have been the case."

"And as the lead detective you sent Billy Ford and another detective to Ms. Bernstein's condominium to question her that morning; correct?"

"I did. I stayed behind as the lead detective to work with the CSI sergeant and his detectives."

"Within minutes of arriving at the scene of this gruesome crime, and without any investigation to speak of, you had already turned your attention to Jenna Bernstein because Adria Kohl directed you to do so; correct?"

"She didn't direct us. We cover every lead. An ex-spouse or girlfriend is always someone we want to talk with."

"But you didn't have a lead; did you? I mean, not until you spoke to Adria Kohl."

"That's true," Rossi said, then forged forward. Keera let him. "We learned from Adria Kohl that Sirus Kohl and Jenna Bernstein had once lived together. We learned Adria and Sirus Kohl had a meeting that morning with the US Attorney to provide evidence against Jenna Bernstein. And Adria Kohl pointed out to us that her father, against her advice, had texted Jenna Bernstein the night before that meeting to tell her his intentions."

"That's right," Keera said, pointing with a pen. "Here, on this document Adria Kohl put together just minutes after finding her father shot and killed, is item number six. 'Text messages between Sirus Kohl and Jenna Bernstein.' Is that what you're referring to?"

"It is."

"And here on this document that Adria Kohl put together is item number seven: 'Police should talk to Jenna Bernstein.' Did I read that correctly?"

"You did." Rossi squirmed a bit in his seat.

"Sounds like a well-thought-out list to direct your investigation; doesn't it?" Keera said, repeating words Thompson had used in his opening statement.

"I considered it informative, not a directive."

"And not calculating either?"

"Informative. But not calculating."

Keera walked back to her counsel table. She set down the exhibit, then turned back to Rossi, leaning on her table. "Ms. Kohl told you her father called her to confirm the meeting with the US Attorney's Office in the morning. That was your testimony; wasn't it?"

"Yes."

"She didn't say her father left her a voice message; did she?"

"No."

"He didn't send her a text message; did he?"

"No."

"She said he called and spoke to her; right?"

"That's what she said."

"And you believed that was in fact the reason for her father's nearly minute-long phone call to Adria Kohl because that's what Adria Kohl told you; didn't she?"

She and Rossi also had a nice rhythm going up to this point. But now Rossi paused, which is what Keera had hoped for. Several jurors turned their heads back to Rossi, like fans at Wimbledon watching two players volley back and forth, until one missed the tennis ball.

"I had no reason to doubt her."

Keera pushed away from the table and approached. "You took her at her word; didn't you?"

"Yes."

"Because you had no way to confirm what Sirus Kohl actually said to her; did you?"

"We confirmed the 9:00 a.m. meeting with the US Attorney's Office."

"You subpoenaed Adria Kohl's call detail records from her cell phone service provider; correct?"

"We did."

"Did those records provide any additional information about the content of her father's phone call?"

"No."

"Because, as we agreed, no voice mail or text message substantiated what Sirus Kohl actually said; correct?"

"Correct. I might add, that by subpoenaing Sirus Kohl's CDRs, we confirmed he made the call at 9:32 p.m."

"Thank you, Detective Rossi. But the fact of the matter is, we don't know that Sirus Kohl actually pushed the buttons on that phone and made that call, and we don't know what he said to his daughter, other than what Adria Kohl says he said; correct?"

Rossi shrugged as if the point she was making was of no import. "That is correct."

"That call lasted fifty seconds; correct?"

"That's what the records indicate."

"They do," Keera said. "Let's pause for fifty seconds; shall we?"

Keera made a point of staring at the clock on the wall, watching the second hand tick. The jurors, and likely everyone in the gallery behind her, also turned their attention to the clock. Rossi looked more and more uncomfortable as the seconds slowly passed.

Finally, at fifty seconds, which felt a lot longer while staring at the clock, Keera said, "That's a long time to confirm a meeting; isn't it?"

"I guess they discussed other things."

"You guess? Ms. Kohl didn't tell you she and her father discussed anything else; did she?"

"I don't know that we asked."

"But she didn't tell you they discussed anything more; did she?"

"No."

"There's no indication in your report that they discussed anything else; is there?"

"No."

"You testified that when you subpoenaed Sirus Kohl's CDR records you confirmed a text conversation between him and Jenna Bernstein the night before the morning his daughter found him; correct?"

"Yes."

Keera put the exhibit documenting the text conversation back up on the computer screen for the jurors. "You never found the second burner cell phone with the number noted on the text conversation; did you?"

"No."

"Adria Kohl told you the one phone belonged to her father and the other phone belonged to Jenna Bernstein; didn't she?"

"She did."

"And you assumed this was accurate; didn't you?"

"We confirmed those numbers were assigned to Sirus Kohl and Jenna Bernstein."

"But you never found the phone Adria Kohl told you belonged to Jenna Bernstein; correct?"

"That's correct."

"So you don't know for a fact that Jenna Bernstein sent the text messages; do you?"

"We presumed it, based on the nature of the text messages on the phone."

Rossi should have known better. Keera pounced. "'Presumed' is just a fancy way of saying you 'guessed'; isn't it? You 'guessed' Jenna Bernstein possessed that phone because Adria Kohl said so; didn't she?"

"We had the text messages, and we deduced Jenna Bernstein had her burner phone that evening."

"'Deduced' is also a fancy word for 'guessed'; isn't it?"

Rossi grinned. "I don't know. I suppose you could check a thesaurus."

"You *guessed* the two of them sent each other these text messages because you couldn't confirm it; correct?"

"We had the CDR records."

"But those records don't tell you who actually pushed the buttons on the phone; do they?"

"No. They don't."

"Did Sirus Kohl's CDRs indicate he sent text messages to Jenna Bernstein prior to that night?"

"Not for some time."

"But between the date PDRT was dissolved and the shooting of Sirus Kohl, he had sent Jenna Bernstein text messages; hadn't he?"

"He had."

"Let's look at some of those; shall we?"

Keera posted a message from Sirus Kohl and its date on the computer screen.

Can we talk?

"That doesn't sound like Sirus Kohl is angry; does it?"

"I can't tell from just three words. He could have wanted to talk about something he was angry about."

"Here's another text message."

I just want to better understand why.

"Did you form any opinions about this text message?"

"No. I didn't note it in any way."

"Here's one delivered just three weeks before the shooting."

I need to talk to you. I just need a few minutes. Please?

"This doesn't sound like a man who was about to testify against a woman he once lived with and cared for deeply; does it?"

Thompson again stood. "Objection. Improper opinion, irrelevant. No foundation."

"Sustained," Judge Marshall said.

"Did you form any opinion based on the language used in this text message, Detective Rossi?"

"Again. No."

"Would you at least agree with me that the word 'please' indicates Sirus Kohl was pleading with Jenna Bernstein?" Keera really didn't care whether Rossi agreed or not.

Thompson pushed back his chair, but Rossi responded before he could object. "Or he was just being polite."

Keera said, "Okay. I can live with that. It certainly didn't convey any animosity, though; did it?"

Rossi, perhaps realizing he'd stepped on Thompson's objection, waited a beat, but Thompson did not rise. "There doesn't seem to be any animosity, no."

"And you found no return texts in response to those text messages; did you?"

"No. I didn't."

"Not one?"

"Not one."

"And the person who had that phone didn't call Sirus Kohl to talk either; did they?"

"We didn't find any calls from that cell phone in Mr. Kohl's CDRs, no."

"Now let's look at the text messages sent that night of the shooting." Keera put the exhibit previously used up on the screen—it had been redacted to remove mention of the Wei trial.

What goes around comes around.

What is that supposed to mean?

You shit on me in ▮▮▮▮▮▮. Time to return the favor.

I don't know what you're talking about.

"You would agree there is animosity in these text messages from Sirus Kohl's phone; isn't there?"

"Again, I was more interested in the text messages as having provided Jenna Bernstein with knowledge Sirus Kohl was going to meet with the US Attorney and provide evidence against her."

"But the text messages don't actually say that; do they?"

"Not in those precise words; no."

"You *presumed* it; didn't you?" she said with a smile.

"I *guess* so," he said, also smiling.

"Assuming Sirus Kohl sent these texts, which you don't know for a fact, and assuming Jenna Bernstein sent these replies, which you don't know for certain either, what if she didn't 'presume' what you presumed? What if she didn't know about the meeting with the US Attorney? Then, using your analysis, she would not have had a motivation to shoot Sirus Kohl; would she?"

"She walked to Volunteer Park right after she sent the text messages," Rossi said.

"But we've established you *guessed* she sent the messages."

"It was her phone."

Keera shrugged as if the response was no big deal. "Let's talk about her walk; shall we? There's no evidence she walked to Sirus Kohl's house; is there?"

"Not to his house, no."

"Her fingerprints were not found anywhere in the house; were they?"

"No."

"Her DNA was not found anywhere in the house; was it?"

"No."

"No photograph exists of her at the house; does it?"

"No."

"So again, you *guessed* she went to his house; didn't you?"

"We made a deduction based on all the evidence."

"You traced a *different* cell phone, that we know for certain belonged to Jenna Bernstein, to her condominium that night."

"We did."

"But Jenna Bernstein did not take that cell phone with her when she left the condominium for her walk; did she?"

"She didn't."

"You thought it curious; right?"

"I did."

"You also testified she wore a 'disguise,' and pointed it out on the video that attorney Thompson played for the jury; correct?"

"I did. And she did."

"A hat and a pair of glasses."

"And baggy clothes."

"Comfortable-fitting clothes for a walk; right?"

"You could say that."

"And perhaps a hat because her hair was dirty?" Keera suggested.

Rossi shrugged. "I don't know."

"A lot of people wear sunglasses when they go out; don't they?"

"Sure," Rossi said.

"But let's 'guess'—as you did—that Ms. Bernstein's outfit was intended as a 'disguise.'" Keera used air quotes. "She had recently been prominent in the public eye; hadn't she?"

"She had been in the news."

"The publicity pertaining to PDRT and her was not positive; was it?"

"It was not."

"In fact, Adria Kohl told you that Sirus Kohl had received death threats; didn't she?"

"We were told that by Adria Kohl, and PDRT's security company confirmed that to have been the case."

"You couldn't confirm it with documents though?"

"No, but I'm not surprised a person would not put the threat in writing."

"Again, you believed what Adria Kohl told you; didn't you?"

"And the security company."

"But it was Adria Kohl who told the security company there had been threats; wasn't it?"

"No reason to doubt her."

"So can I also conclude you *presumed* Jenna Bernstein had also received death threats?"

"I don't know if she did or didn't."

"Because Adria Kohl didn't tell you she did; did she?"

"She didn't."

"If Sirus Kohl received threats, it would make sense Jenna also received threats; wouldn't it?"

"It's possible; though she did not report any to the police."

"Nor did Sirus Kohl; did he?"

"No."

"But if Jenna Bernstein had received death threats, it could explain why she disguised her identity when she went out that night; couldn't it?"

"Speculation," Walker said.

"Overruled."

Rossi shrugged. "It could."

Keera walked back to her computer, and with a few strokes of the keyboard put up the image of Jenna Bernstein purchasing a burrito from Bitchin Burritos. "This is a photograph of Jenna Bernstein buying dinner that evening; isn't it?"

"It's a picture of her in line at a burrito truck; yes."

"You have no other photograph or video of Jenna Bernstein after this one; do you?"

"No."

"Did you find it unusual that someone who you believe disguised their identity would stop off at a food truck with a camera to get a bite to eat?" Keera didn't care whether Rossi did or didn't. She wanted to plant the thought in the jurors' minds.

"She may not have known the camera was there."

Keera put up another photograph JP Harrison took at the food truck. "There's a sign, isn't there, that says, 'Smile. You're on *Candid Camera*.'?"

"Yes."

"But you presumed she didn't see that; didn't you?"

"I don't know if she saw it or not."

"She's looking directly at the camera in this photograph; isn't she?"

"I don't know. It could be the angle of the camera making it appear to be the case."

"So again, you are 'guessing' that, after leaving her building in a disguise, she went to the one food truck in the park that had a camera, bought herself dinner, and . . . What? Wolfed down the burrito, then walked to Sirus Kohl's house and shot him?"

"It was a deduction we made based on all the evidence. I wasn't focused on what she ate as much as the fact that she was in the park, in close proximity to the crime scene."

"That doesn't sound like a 'well-thought-out, pre-planned murder committed by a person who does not wish to be caught'; does it?" Keera said, again using Thompson's words in his opening statement against him.

"I can't tell you what she was thinking."

"I assume you would be open to some alternative presumptions and guesses; wouldn't you?"

"I'm all ears," Rossi said.

"Good," Keera said. Then, without offering a single alternative, she turned to Judge Marshall. "I have no further questions for Detective Rossi at this time. However, the defense asks the court to instruct this witness that he is not dismissed subject to the defense calling him in its case in chief."

Judge Marshall did so.

Keera didn't look at the jurors, but she hoped they looked as they did when Thompson had completed his direct examination. Except this time, she hoped they looked like they had their plates taken away just as they picked up their cutlery, and they were now more curious than ever about what alternative Keera was about to serve them.

Before Keera left the courthouse, Jenna asked to speak to her. Keera arranged to do so in a windowless room down the hall from the courtroom. Keera entered and set her briefcase on the table. The room was warm and the air stale. She'd taken depositions in rooms in the courthouse like this during trials. You couldn't open the door because the voices of people passing in the corridor were too loud, and the court reporter had trouble hearing. It could be oppressive, often what Keera intended.

Jenna remained standing. When she and Keera had been young, Jenna had used her height, as well as her ice-blue stare, to intimidate, but neither had any impact on Keera now. She, too, remained standing, and she wasn't about to speak first. She looked at Jenna as if to say: *You called this meeting.*

"Your cross-examination of Detective Rossi was effective, but to what end? It gained us limited points; don't you think?" Jenna said.

"What do you mean?" Keera asked. She'd also become immune to Jenna's subtle put-downs.

"You didn't really establish anything except that Detective Rossi made presumptions."

"It's a circumstantial case, Jenna. I've told you, that's going to be our best avenue of attack. We can't refute you walked to Volunteer Park the evening Kohl was killed, and a jury is going to presume you went further, to his house. But if you did, why would you stop off for a burrito?"

"I thought that argument was effective, though Thompson will argue I stopped at the burrito truck to explain the purpose for the walk."

"If he does, then I'll argue that if it was purposeful, why wouldn't you have used a credit card so a receipt would prove that's what you did? The jury will also presume you sent those text messages, though no phone has been produced. We don't have anything to refute the phone was assigned to you, or that you sent those texts, except to point out that the information comes only from Adria Kohl's testimony. I'm trying to create reasonable doubt by showing she directed the police investigation to you as a suspect from the very start."

"I can refute the evidence. I can say I haven't seen that phone since I left Sirus's house."

She'd become easy to predict. Again, Keera said, "I don't want to put you on the stand. It's risky." She hoped it sounded forceful.

"Patsy felt the same way, but I handled Walker Thompson then. I can handle him again. I convinced that jury, and I will convince this one. As you said, we don't have any evidence to refute Rossi's presumptions— except me. I can refute them."

Keera blew out a breath and closed her eyes, as if exhausted. After a beat she looked up at Jenna. "We start our case in chief tomorrow.

Let's not make any decisions tonight. Let's see how the evidence from the other witnesses goes in."

"You haven't told me much about our case in chief."

"I'll be recalling several State's witnesses," she said, not being specific. "I think we can score points and continue to create reasonable doubt, which is all we need to do."

"I don't want to just create reasonable doubt," Jenna said, sounding like the insolent child she had been when she didn't get her way. "I want my innocence to be proven beyond reasonable doubt. I have to live in this city. I don't want to be a pariah. I want the jurors and the public to know I am innocent."

"I can't control what others think, Jenna."

"I can," she said. "I can convince them I didn't kill Sirus."

Keera looked away, as if in thought. *Don't give in. Make her think she beat you.*

"You're going to have to trust me, Keera. Just as Patsy trusted me."

Keera paused as if Jenna's reference to Patsy had hit home. It hadn't. She wanted Jenna to testify, but she wanted Jenna to make that decision. "Okay," she said. "If you're sure?"

"I am," Jenna said, and she smiled as she always did when she got her way.

"Walker Thompson will be prepared. He won't make the same mistake again."

"Leave Walker Thompson to me," Jenna said.

Chapter 32

The following morning, when court reconvened, Judge Marshall instructed the jury regarding the defense presenting its case in chief, then invited Keera to give her opening statement. Keera rose and approached the jury box. Over the past two weeks, Keera had established a rapport with the jurors, one advantage of waiting to give her opening statement. They had a better understanding of who she was, and she had a better understanding of who they all were as well—whom she needed to convince. The delay also heightened suspense, and suspense meant she had their attention. It was natural for people to wonder what the defense was going to say, especially when the circumstantial evidence created a presumption of guilt.

Patsy had taught Keera to present a reasoned argument, then challenge the jurors to decide which explanation better fit the facts.

Keera approached the jury railing but did not touch it, giving the jurors deference and respect. She wanted the jurors to know she considered them the most important people in the room. "Ladies and gentlemen, I want to thank you for your patience. The State put on its witnesses and hopes the testimony, and the documents admitted, will convince you my client, Jenna Bernstein, killed Sirus Kohl beyond *any* reasonable doubt. Beyond any reasonable doubt is the highest standard of proof the State must meet in a criminal trial. It means no other logical explanation can be derived from the facts, thereby overcoming a defendant's very strong presumption of innocence. It does not mean no doubt exists, but it does require the State's evidence be so conclusive that you do not have a reasonable doubt."

It was a canned definition she'd learned from Patsy. He'd made a few tweaks, but most prosecutors wouldn't object. If they did, Patsy would make it sound as though they were objecting to the United States Constitution. Thompson had fallen prey to this once. He wasn't going to do so again. He remained seated and silent.

"As the defense puts on its case in chief, I ask you to keep an open mind and remember Jenna Bernstein is still presumed innocent. I ask you to listen to the defense witnesses' testimony and to give their testimony and the documents we introduce due weight. In my cross-examination of Detective Rossi, I noted certain *guesses* Detective Rossi admitted he had made, and which the State hopes you will make."

Thompson stood and objected. "Inappropriate opinion."

"Sustained," Marshall agreed.

Keera ignored both. "The defense will, in our case in chief, provide you with alternative reasons that will not only convince you the State failed to remove 'reasonable doubt,' but prove Jenna Bernstein did not kill Sirus Kohl. Let's get started, shall we?"

The brevity of Keera's opening seemed to catch everyone off guard, including Judge Marshall, who had been moving papers on his desk when he realized she had concluded. The jurors looked like they'd watched a magic act and wondered what happened. Walker Thompson sat back and stretched out his long legs, as some of Keera's older chess opponents did during competitions, confident they had led Keera into a corner, and though the final pieces were not yet in place to achieve checkmate, both he and Keera knew the result was inevitable.

"Very well," Judge Marshall said. "The defense will call its first witness."

Keera faced the bench, keeping her back to Jenna. "The defense calls Lisa Tanaka."

The bailiff left the courtroom for the hallway, where witnesses waited to enter until called, in order to prevent them from being potentially influenced by another witness's testimony.

Keera retrieved her laptop. On it she had composed Tanaka's direct-examination questions.

Jenna leaned forward to block the jurors' view of their conversation. "What the hell is she going to say?"

Keera kept her eyes on the computer screen. "She's going to set up your testimony."

"How?" Jenna asked, intensity permeating the single word.

"Watch," Keera said. She moved to the lectern as the bailiff returned with Tanaka.

Diminutive, Tanaka wore a fashionable blue suit with a skirt that extended below the knee, a beige blouse, and black pumps. She looked nervous. She had told Keera during trial prep she still had misgivings about testifying. Keera told her she would have the chance to testify about the financial projections she created and how it had been Adria Kohl and Jenna Bernstein who inflated the company's value, not her. She told Tanaka that by testifying in court and telling her story of what happened, she would be protecting herself against any insinuation that she misrepresented the company's status in the projections. Keera could have simply subpoenaed Tanaka to testify, but she thought she owed it to the woman to let it be her decision.

After Tanaka took the oath to tell the truth, Keera proceeded slowly, giving Tanaka a chance to relax, though she didn't appear relaxed, which made her credible. Jurors distrusted a witness who looked and sounded calm in this type of high-intensity trial.

Keera gave Tanaka a moment to sip from a glass of water and clear her throat. The smile that followed looked pained.

Keera established the years Tanaka had worked at PDRT as controller. "As the controller, I take it you were part of PDRT's corporate management."

"In theory I was, in reality not so much."

"Let's talk about theory first. As part of corporate management, were you provided a work laptop and cell phone?"

"Company employees were provided work laptops and cell phones."

"Did you take those home with you at the end of the workday?"

"No. We were told the laptops and the cell phones were to remain at work at all times."

"What other restrictions were placed on the use of the cell phones and laptops?"

"The cameras were disabled."

"Were you told why?"

"I was told it was to prevent corporate espionage. PDRT was concerned about competitors stealing its ideas and bringing a product to market that performed what PDRT hoped the LINK would eventually be able to do."

"Were there other such restrictions?"

Tanaka talked about the pervasive corporate paranoia and about how employees were advised their emails and text messages would be regularly reviewed, and any breach of confidentiality would be a terminable offense.

"Were you, as controller, subjected to these restrictions as well?"

"I was, but it wasn't exactly the same."

"How did it differ?"

"Corporate management conversed with one another on a different internal platform than the platform used by company employees. We were also given burner phones so calls could not be traced to certain people."

"And was that internal server for corporate management also monitored?"

"It was."

"How do you know?"

"Because when I was terminated, I was told certain emails and text messages I had sent were grounds for my termination for cause, and that formed the basis of PDRT's refusal to pay my severance and for its lawsuit against me for breach of my employment agreement."

"I'll get back to that. Do you know who monitored the emails and text messages on the corporate internal server?"

"I was told the day-to-day review was performed by Sirus Kohl and by Adria Kohl, general counsel, but Ms. Bernstein also had access to those text messages and emails."

"They all could read what everyone on the management team was emailing and texting to one another?"

"They could. Yes."

"Switching subjects. Did you personally witness interactions between Jenna Bernstein and Sirus Kohl?"

"On many occasions."

"Did you form any impressions about their relationship based on your observations?"

"It wasn't supposed to be public knowledge, or even known within PDRT, but it was a poorly kept secret Sirus Kohl and Jenna Bernstein were living together at Mr. Kohl's home and had a romantic relationship in addition to a business relationship."

"Did you have an opinion about their relationship?"

"Not personally, but as controller for the company I thought it highly unprofessional and believed PDRT's investors would look upon it unfavorably, should they find out."

"Did you tell anyone your opinion?"

"Not then, no. I figured: not my monkey, not my circus." She shook her head and smiled. "Sorry, that's something my daughter says when she doesn't want to get involved. At PDRT we learned to keep our heads down and do our jobs. To be seen but not heard."

"Why?"

"Because the squeaky wheel did not get the oil. The squeaky wheel usually got fired."

Walker Thompson sat up in his chair, scribbled on his legal pad, then nudged the pad to Frank Rossi to read. Rossi slowly shook his head.

"Let's talk about your job as controller. What were your primary duties?"

"I was responsible for managing the accounting department and providing financial information to assist management and its investors in making educated decisions about the company's financial stability going forward."

"Did your duties include providing PDRT financial statements and financial projections to PDRT investors so they understood the company's financial strength?"

"Yes, but I did not have final say about what went into those financial projections."

"Who did have final say?"

"Sirus Kohl and Jenna Bernstein."

"Can you explain what you mean by those individuals having final say?"

"I prepared the financial statements and projections, but they reviewed and edited the projections before dissemination."

"By 'edited,' do you mean they *changed* the financial projections you provided?"

"Yes, in some instances they did."

"Did you agree with the changes?"

"Not all of them, no."

"Why not?"

"Because their changes presented a much rosier financial projection to investors than was reality, especially toward the end of PDRT's existence."

"Meaning what? That PDRT didn't have enough money going forward?"

"Not without a healthy round of new investment."

"Did you voice objection to the management team changing your financial projections?"

"I did."

"And what was their response?"

"I was told to be more of a team player. I was told my statements and projections were too conservative; that I didn't understand the company's progress toward federal approval by regulators, or how close the company was to putting the LINK on the commercial market."

"What was your response?"

"I told them that wasn't my job. I dealt in hard numbers, and the hard numbers before me did not support what investors were being told."

"And was Ms. Bernstein aware of your objections?"

"Intimately. She read and knew every word of my reports and my projections. I had numerous meetings with her in which she made changes, and I told her I could not support the changes to those projections."

"And what was her response?"

"She told me if I didn't sign the statement, she would fire me for not being a team player."

"Did you sign the projections given to investors?"

"Early on I did. I regret that I did, but I needed the job and the income, and early on the statements were not that far off from reality. I was told by both Mr. Kohl and by Ms. Bernstein it was not uncommon, in a start-up, to make projections of where a company hoped to be after its initial formation. They said investors were sophisticated and familiar with this strategy. It was intended to bring in additional investors. They said when the company went public with a commercial product, everyone would make a lot of money."

"You accepted this explanation?"

"As I said, initially I did. In the last year I worked at the company, I did not."

"And were you fired, as Ms. Bernstein said you would be?"

"Yes. I received a text message while at lunch and was told my company pass, needed to gain entry into the building, had been disabled and I was not to return. I was told I was terminated for cause and therefore I would not be paid my severance package, as was called for in my contract."

"Did anyone tell you what constituted 'cause' for your termination?"

"Adria Kohl said in my termination letter that PDRT possessed emails and text messages that violated the terms of my contract, and she made it clear if I didn't walk away, PDRT would sue me and make the litigation financially painful."

Keera entered the letter as an exhibit and put it on the screen. After discussing it, she asked, "What did you do?"

"I brought a lawsuit to recover my severance package," Tanaka said, looking and sounding defiant.

"Did PDRT file a countersuit?"

"Yes. And they made my life hell for months."

"What eventually happened?"

"They paid my severance and dropped the litigation they had initiated."

"Do you know why?"

"I have my opinion; yes."

"And what is your opinion?"

Thompson inched toward the edge of his chair, as if to object, then realized whatever Tanaka said would likely benefit the State's case. Keera saw him glance again at Frank Rossi, who sat looking just as confused.

"PDRT dropped the suit shortly after I told Adria Kohl, PDRT's general counsel, if they did not, I would go to PDRT investors and board members, as well as the newspapers, and I would tell them what I had witnessed at PDRT late one night."

"And what had you witnessed?"

"I was going to Ms. Bernstein's office to deliver some documents, and just as I reached to knock, I heard voices and . . . well, moaning and groaning."

Keera sensed from the silence in the courtroom Tanaka had every-one riveted. "Did you form an opinion about what was happening behind that closed door?"

"I did from the moaning and groaning, and from what I later saw."

"What did you see?"

"Ms. Bernstein opened the door. She stood with the head of PDRT's security, Thomas Martin. He was tucking his shirt back into his pants, and both he and Ms. Bernstein looked like they'd just wres-tled with one another, as my mother liked to say."

Again, her comment brought nervous chuckles from the gallery and from the jury box. Otherwise, the courtroom was silent.

"What did Ms. Bernstein say to you, if anything?"

"She asked me what I was doing at the office so late—a ridiculous question given I was always at the office late, as was she. She said Mr. Martin had just come up to drive her home.

"She said her cell phone was dead, and she'd missed his phone call."

"He had her cell phone number?"

"That's what she said."

"Did you tell anyone about this incident?"

"Yes. I debated whether I should say anything, but ultimately, the next day, I went to Adria Kohl's office since she was our general counsel. I told her what I saw and heard, and I said I thought it was incredibly unprofessional. I said if PDRT investors learned the CEO was sleeping with the head of security, her bodyguard, while living in Sirus Kohl's house as his partner, the entire company could unravel. I said the fallout would be catastrophic."

"How?"

"Obviously, if Sirus Kohl found out, it would create a huge rift. Kohl was the company's largest investor, and if he pulled out over a failed personal relationship, the company would collapse. I even debated whether I should say anything to Adria Kohl, given Sirus was her father."

"How did Adria Kohl take this information?"

"Stoic."

Keera smiled. "Businesslike?"

"I guess."

"Did she say *anything*?"

"She thanked me for bringing it to her attention. She said she agreed with me about it being unprofessional and said she would speak to both Ms. Bernstein and to Mr. Martin, and she would let them know their relationship was unprofessional and could be injurious to the company."

"Do you know if Ms. Kohl did as she represented, whether she spoke to Mr. Martin and Ms. Bernstein?"

"I didn't know. At least not then."

"What do you mean? Did something change?"

"That's what I was getting to earlier. I called Adria Kohl and told her if PDRT didn't dismiss its case and pay my severance, I would bring up what I had seen and heard to PDRT's investors."

"What did she say?"

"Nothing that I can remember, but about two days later I received my severance package in the mail. A day later I received a dismissal of PDRT's complaint signed by Adria Kohl."

Keera put up on the computer screen CDR records obtained from Lisa Tanaka's phone. "Is that your cell phone number?"

"Yes."

Keera directed Tanaka to a specific call made on a specific date and time. "And whose cell phone number is that?"

"That's Adria Kohl's number. The number I called."

"And you assumed what from these actions by PDRT in paying your severance and dismissing the lawsuit?"

"I assumed what I had reported seeing and hearing was accurate, and PDRT did not want the matter to be shared with its investors, board, and general public for all the reasons I've previously stated."

"You believed Adria Kohl and PDRT wanted to keep you quiet?"

"That's exactly what I believe."

Keera thanked Tanaka, then turned to Walker. "Your witness," she said, and moved to her seat beside Jenna.

Walker Thompson looked like a man who had just walked into his own surprise party and couldn't figure out what was going on. When Thompson didn't immediately stand, Judge Marshall prompted him. "Does the State have questions of this witness?"

Thompson turned his head toward Frank Rossi and his co-counsel, Cheryl McFadden, whispering. After several moments, he stood. "The State does not," Thompson said, "but requests Ms. Tanaka not be released from her subpoena should the State wish to recall her in its rebuttal case."

Marshall excused Tanaka, and she stepped down from the witness stand and left the courtroom.

Keera felt Jenna's eyes burning a hole through her and avoided looking over at her.

"Is the defense prepared to call its next witness?" Marshall asked.

In for a penny, in for a pound, Keera thought. "It is, Your Honor. The State recalls Adria Kohl."

Again, Keera saw Jenna stiffen in her seat.

Kohl, who had remained stoic throughout the proceedings, looked less certain as she stepped through the gallery gate for a second time and made her way back to the witness stand.

Judge Marshall said, "Ms. Kohl, you understand you remain under oath to tell the truth, the whole truth, and nothing but the truth?"

"Yes. I do."

Marshall addressed Keera. "Counsel, you may proceed."

Keera stepped forward. "Ms. Kohl, you were in the courtroom when Ms. Tanaka just testified regarding the internal IP server at PDRT for corporate management. Was she accurate in her description of that server?"

"Basically, yes."

"You personally had access to and could monitor all calls, texts, and emails that members of the management team sent to each other; didn't you?"

"I did, but I can't say I looked at them daily, or even regularly. It was meant more as a deterrent—so employees would be cautious about what they put into print."

"But you could, at any time, look up text messages and emails sent between the management team members."

"As I said, I could, but I didn't do it on a regular basis."

"Those text messages and emails remained on the company's server, I assume, indefinitely, or at least until someone deleted them?"

"I assume that's the case. I'm not well-versed in the technology."

"You could look up text messages and emails your father had sent to Ms. Bernstein, for instance."

"My father would usually alert me about an email or text message if it required legal review."

"In that instance, why wouldn't he just copy you on the email string or the text string?"

Kohl shifted in her chair. "Sometimes he did. But sometimes he might not want the person to know he sought legal guidance."

"Fair enough, but you could at any time review any text or email message your father sent in real time, or that he had previously sent to Ms. Bernstein; couldn't you?" she asked again and hoped the jury realized Kohl had not answered the question. If they didn't, Thompson helped them.

"Objection," Thompson said, standing. "The defense is leading her own witness."

"I think we can presume this witness to be hostile, under the circumstances. The objection is overruled," Marshall said. "Does the witness need the question read back?"

"No," Kohl said. She addressed Jenna. "As I previously stated, I had the ability to look at text messages and emails sent between management parties, but I didn't typically do so."

"You testified, when I cross-examined you, that you were concerned about your father's relationship with Jenna Bernstein. You testified you believed Ms. Bernstein was taking advantage of your father for his money. Do you recall your testimony?"

"I recall it."

"As his caring daughter, worried her father was being taken advantage of, are you saying you had the ability to review emails and text messages between him and Jenna, but did not?"

"My father was a grown man. He could handle his own affairs."

"With all due respect, grown man or not, you testified you were worried about his relationship with Jenna Bernstein and about her taking advantage of him. Are you saying you did not sneak a peek at his or Ms. Bernstein's messages to try to discern the nature of their relationship?"

"I've answered your question as best I can."

"You've answered," Keera said. "The jury will decide if it's the best you can."

Thompson stood, but Judge Marshall beat him to the objection. "Ms. Duggan, I will determine what the jury decides, and I will instruct the jury accordingly. Do not cross that line again."

"My apologies, Your Honor." She returned her attention to Kohl. "Ms. Tanaka testified she told you about the encounter she had with Ms. Bernstein and her bodyguard, the head of security."

"She told me about it; yes."

"She told you she believed the encounter between Jenna Bernstein and Thomas Martin, head of security, had been sexual; correct?"

"That's what she believed."

"Did you confront Ms. Bernstein about this allegation?"

"No. I spoke to Mr. Martin."

Keera didn't try to hide her surprise. "You didn't confront Jenna Bernstein?"

"No. Because I spoke to Mr. Martin, and he said Ms. Tanaka was mistaken, that he had been in Jenna Bernstein's office because her phone was dead, and he wanted to determine how late she planned to work because he was to drive her home."

"Did you ask him about the moaning and groaning Ms. Tanaka heard in the office?"

"He said he was helping Ms. Bernstein move some furniture, and that must have been the sounds Ms. Tanaka heard."

Keera smiled and couldn't keep a chuckle out of her voice. "And you believed him?"

"I didn't have further information, so . . . ," Kohl said, voice trailing off.

"Did you ask him why he was tucking his shirt back into his pants when he came through the door, or why he and Ms. Bernstein looked as disheveled as Saturday-morning wrestlers?"

This drew chuckles from the jurors.

"I don't think Ms. Tanaka told me that."

"Ms. Tanaka came to you and told you she believed the CEO of PDRT was having a sexual encounter in her office with PDRT's head of security, and you didn't ask her what evidence she had to support her allegation?"

"I asked her, but I don't recall her saying anything about his tucking in his shirt or the two of them looking disheveled."

"You agree, though, it was a matter for your attention as general counsel of PDRT; don't you?"

"It was, and I handled it."

"By talking only to Thomas Martin?"

"Yes."

"But not firing him."

"No."

"So you believed him, and you did not believe Lisa Tanaka."

"I believe Lisa Tanaka was mistaken."

"PDRT sued Ms. Tanaka for breach of her employment contract and dismissed her for cause, without paying her a severance package; did it not?"

"We did."

"PDRT—you—as its general counsel, pursued litigation for almost five months, did you not?"

"I don't recall how long the litigation proceeded."

"Let me remind you with documents." Keera put up the complaint by PDRT against Tanaka, then the dismissal on the computer screen. "Does that refresh your recollection?"

"It does. It looks like the suit was just over five months."

"So we can assume that PDRT did not file lawsuits indiscriminately and felt strongly that it was correct in suing Ms. Tanaka in this instance; can't we?"

"We believed we had legal grounds, otherwise we would not have filed suit."

"Do you recall Ms. Tanaka calling you directly and telling you if PDRT did not dismiss the lawsuit, she would tell PDRT's investors about Jenna's sexual encounter with Thomas Martin in the office?"

"I don't recall any such call," Kohl said.

"Let me refresh your recollection again," Keera said. She put up on the computer screen CDR records obtained from Lisa Tanaka's phone. "You were in the courtroom when Lisa Tanaka confirmed this was her cell phone number; were you not?"

"I was."

Keera directed her to a specific call made on a specific date and at a specific time. "That is your cell phone number; is it not? I believe we confirmed that your father called that number—you—the night he was shot; didn't we?"

"It's my number. Yes."

"That call from Lisa Tanaka lasted for a little more than six minutes."

"Yes."

"So she did call you after PDRT initiated suit and just three days before PDRT dismissed the lawsuit and paid her full severance package."

"It looks like she did, but we did not dismiss the case because Ms. Tanaka made a threat to blackmail us."

Keera simply paused, with a look like a parent disbelieving their child's excuse for why they were late getting home. She wasn't about to let Adria Kohl explain away the obvious by asking her an additional question. The jurors' expressions made clear they did not buy Kohl's explanation either.

Thompson, perhaps sensing Kohl in trouble, objected. "Relevance, Your Honor. This is getting very far afield from the matter at hand."

Marshall looked like he wanted to say: *Seriously?* Then he said, "Overruled."

"Getting back to the matter at hand," Keera said, tweaking Thompson. "You were concerned about your father's relationship with Jenna Bernstein, but you told this jury you did not confront her with Ms. Tanaka's allegation she had a sexual encounter with Thomas Martin in her office?"

"I told you I didn't."

"Surely you told your father about it?" Keera was taking a chance with an open-ended question, because she believed she knew the answer. No texts or emails existed between Adria and Sirus Kohl about the allegation.

"No."

Keera widened her eyes. "You didn't say, *Dad, I hate to tell you this, but the woman who you gave a hundred and fifty million dollars, and who is living in your house and sharing your bed, is having a sexual relationship with the head of security?*"

"I told you Thomas Martin denied the encounter happened. I didn't want to hurt my father with an unsubstantiated rumor."

Keera shook her head. "Did you know your father texted Jenna Bernstein even after PDRT dissolved and after she had moved out of his house?"

"I didn't know that; no."

"Didn't the fact that Jenna Bernstein moved out of the house after PDRT had dissolved convince you she didn't love your father?"

"I can't say that," Kohl said.

"And that she maybe never did love him, as you suspected?"

"I don't know."

"Did it cross your mind?"

"I don't know what I thought."

Keera pointed to Bernstein. "And you didn't monitor your father's text messages or emails to make sure he didn't get entangled with Jenna Bernstein again?"

"As I said, my father was a grown man and could handle his private affairs."

"But not grown enough for you to give him the bad news Jenna was sleeping with PDRT's head of security?"

"I didn't see it as the same."

"Isn't it true, Ms. Kohl, that you hated Jenna Bernstein for what you perceived she did to your father?"

"I've already admitted I didn't like her," she said, unapologetic. "But after PDRT dissolved, my father and I concentrated our efforts on getting his one-hundred-and-fifty-million-dollar investment loss minimized and preparing for the US Attorney's case against him."

"And what you intended was to have your father provide the US Attorney's Office testimony and documents you hoped would prove its case against Jenna Bernstein for misrepresentations made to PDRT investors and to the general public; correct?"

"That was what we intended, yes."

"To send Jenna Bernstein to prison; right?"

"What ultimately happened would not be up to me."

"And was your father on board with your strategy?"

"He said he was."

"So you're saying you both intended to put Jenna Bernstein in jail for a very long time?" Keera said.

"If that was the consequence of my father's decision to provide testimony," Adria Kohl said with a shrug.

"And your intent," Keera said again.

"My intent had nothing to do with it," Kohl said.

"Maybe your intent had nothing to do with the plea deal agreement," Keera said. "But it certainly had everything to do with putting Jenna Bernstein in jail for years; didn't it?"

Thompson rose quickly. "Objection, Your Honor. Argumentative."

Marshall paused a beat, then said, "Cross-examination. Overruled."

Adria Kohl remained defiant. "It was a potential quid pro quo to my father's deal with the US Attorney, had we the chance to make that deal. We never had that chance."

Chapter 33

Keera returned to her seat and again avoided looking at Jenna Bernstein as Walker Thompson conducted a brief cross-examination of Adria Kohl. The air between her and Jenna crackled, as if charged, so much so that Keera felt the hair on her arms beneath her jacket sleeves standing. She sensed Jenna had figured out what Keera was up to and what she intended to do.

Thompson asked Adria Kohl questions because the jury expected him to do so, though Keera doubted he knew yet what was going on. Keera was certain her direct examinations of Lisa Tanaka and Adria Kohl had flummoxed him, though he didn't visibly show he was confused to the jury. He was trial tested, a pro, and he knew better than to reveal any confusion to the jury. He still tilted a bit to one side, like a man with one leg a fraction shorter than the other, and his drawl seemed more pronounced, folksy, as did the inflections in his voice. When finished, he lumbered back to his chair, but Keera caught him glancing at Rossi as if to say, *What the hell is going on?*

Throughout Thompson's questioning, Keera kept one eye on the clock on the wall. The minute hand had ticked past the 3:00 hour, then steadily inched its way over to the one, past the two, the three, and settled on the four by the time Thompson had finished. She did not want the court to recess for the day before she called her next witness. If the court recessed, Jenna would have more time to think about what was happening, and though Keera believed her strategy was the only way to save her client from a life in prison, Jenna was just stubborn enough and arrogant enough to disagree. She still believed she was the smartest person in the room and, if given the chance, that she could again lie her way out of this situation.

Keera wasn't about to let Jenna get on the stand and perjure herself.

Judge Johnson Marshall considered the clock on the wall. "Counsel, we're nearing the end of the day."

Keera stood. She tried not to rush, not to look desperate, or like she was pulling a fast one on the prosecution. She kept her voice calm and spoke deliberately. "Your Honor, the defense wishes to call one more witness before we break for the day. I understand it's been a long week for all of us. I'm sure the jurors could use a head start to their weekend, but the direct of this next witness will be brief."

Thompson stood. Like a fighter who'd taken shots to the head and was now unsteady on his feet, he welcomed the sound of the bell and a reprieve. "Your Honor, we've been going strong for the entire day, and week; I'm sure the jury could use a break. Also, I might point out the defense has no other witnesses expected to testify today."

Thompson no doubt was thinking first and foremost about the Erik Wei trial and Patsy's unorthodox moves, and he did not want a repeat performance. Rossi may have also gotten in his ear. He might not have known exactly what Keera was doing, but he had watched her in trial enough to know no move Keera made was without purpose.

"Your Honor, it is certainly not the defense's intention to wear out the jury," Keera said with what she hoped was a touch of humor. "But counsel is wrong in his assertion the defense has no other witnesses. Moreover, the defense will conclude with its next witness, and that is worth a final push before we break for the weekend. Perhaps a five-minute break to allow the jurors to stretch their legs, then a brief final examination before we break?"

Marshall spent a few moments seeming to debate the matter. Keera hoped he didn't ask her whom she intended to call. She didn't technically have another witness listed on the witness list, but the defendant was always a possibility. After consideration, the judge said, "We'll take a short break and come back for one more witness."

Jenna stood. For one frightening moment Keera thought she might speak, then realized she had stood in deference to the jury departing the courtroom. Murmurs rose from the gallery, whispers at first, then increasing both in volume and intensity. Everyone was wondering what they had just witnessed, and what more was to come.

"I don't know what you're playing at," Jenna said, speaking softly but with clenched teeth and anger in her voice and on her face.

Keera would have none of it. "Conference room," she said. When Jenna did not back off, Keera leaned in closer and said, "We have five minutes." She made a show of checking her watch. "Less than that. I'd suggest you move, now."

Jenna straightened, turned, and moved toward the door. Keera advised the bailiff she needed to speak to her client in confidence, and he escorted them down the marbled hallway to the windowless, adjoining room, then stood outside the door. As soon as the door had closed, Jenna said, "You are deliberately throwing me under the bus. If I am convicted, I will—"

"Shut up," Keera said softly.

She spoke two words Jenna had likely rarely, if ever, heard before. They knocked Jenna back on her heels. She was going to hear what Keera had to say, or she was going to spend the rest of her life behind bars. Keera didn't much care, but she took her job and her reputation seriously, and she would not allow Jenna to tarnish it.

"We have less than five minutes, and for once in your life you're going to shut up and listen to someone other than yourself."

"You have no right to speak to me that way."

"I have every right to speak to you as your attorney. And as your attorney, I am telling you that if you don't want to spend the rest of your life in an eight-foot-by-ten-foot cell doing chores for less than a dollar an hour and eating starchy food, you're going to shut up and listen."

Jenna tapped the table with her finger. "I will bring a motion for ineffective assistance of counsel, and everyone in that courtroom who witnessed what transpired this afternoon will agree with me."

"You bring that motion, but you'll be in jail until you have the chance to have that motion heard, which will take months, and when you lose, you will be in prison long after that. Are you so arrogant and petty that you'd throw away your freedom just to get the better of me? I'm giving you the chance to get off on this charge, which is my only responsibility to you—the best defense I can provide. I can get you off. I can clear your name in the killing of Sirus Kohl and Erik Wei."

"Your father already—"

"Do you want to hear what I have to say? Or do you want to keep talking and use up the precious few minutes we have remaining?"

Jenna stared, defiant. Keera waited. She thought Jenna's ego and her arrogance might just keep her from being quiet.

It was time to get to the truth. JP Harrison and Keera had speculated about what had happened, and based on Jenna's reaction to both Lisa Tanaka's testimony and Kohl's testimony, Keera knew her theory was more than speculation. "I know Sirus Kohl sent you those text messages, and I know you responded."

"I told you—"

"A lie." Keera slapped her palm on the wooden table. The sound reverberated on the scratched and scarred lacquered surface. "You lied to me, after I told you that if you did, I would walk. I can still do that. Sirus Kohl sent you those texts because he sought a response from you. Up to that point you had ignored every one of his overtures. He wanted the chance to speak to you because he didn't want to give you up to the US Attorney, as his daughter was urging—even after you had testified that he had the greater motivation to kill Erik Wei. He sent you those text messages because he knew that threatening you was the only way to get you to respond."

Jenna remained silent.

"Tell me that I'm wrong, Jenna."

She did not.

Jenna stepped back from the table, arms folded, head tilted. Her jaws undulated like she was chewing on something distasteful and couldn't bring herself to swallow.

"Adria Kohl painted you into a corner in the US Attorney's suit, and you did what you've always done. You pivoted, and you schemed, and you figured out a way that you could still change his mind—if you could just speak to him without Adria present. That's why you didn't text him and say you were going to meet him at the house. It's why you didn't call him. You didn't want Adria to know. You didn't want to give her the chance to scuttle your plans. You didn't have time to come up with a perfect scheme. The meeting was first thing in the morning. You also knew there were security cameras in your building, as well as street cameras. You decided not to drive. You knew the police could more easily track your car as well as your cell phone, so you left both at home. You knew they would find the messages Sirus sent you and your responses. So, you did the opposite of a well-thought-out plan. You deliberately left the building in something far less than a perfect disguise, and you walked to Volunteer Park knowing that street and business cameras were picking you up. If they weren't, you made sure one would when you stopped at a food truck that would capture you on video. Because even then you anticipated a potential trial, and even then you wanted to give Patsy the argument that you never would have been so blatant, so obvious, if you had planned to kill Sirus." She looked at her watch, then directed her attention back to Jenna. "Again, stop me if I'm wrong, Jenna."

Again, Jenna didn't.

"You walked to Volunteer Park in a disguise but not really a disguise. And you left your phone at home purposefully, and you stopped at the burrito truck and purchased something not because you were hungry but because you wanted to be photographed, because you deliberately wanted to be obvious. You did this because you knew who was behind the deal with the US Attorney to put you in jail for a decade or more. You knew it was Adria Kohl because you knew Adria Kohl hated you.

"The easement in the park leads to Sirus Kohl's back door and, probably after some tense moments, you somehow convinced him that you still loved him. You likely told him that if you remained a united team, you could both defeat the US Attorney's charges. You likely told him the documentary evidence—without his testimony to explain it— was inconclusive because you had been careful to make it look like you'd been kept in the dark. He likely asked you about Erik Wei, about your testimony at that trial. Did you tell him that you did what you had to do because you were fighting for your life? Did you say that he would have done the same thing? Maybe he asked you why, if you still loved him, you left his home? Likely he asked you why you hadn't responded to any of this phone calls or text messages. And, again, you did what you do so well. You lied. What did you tell him, Jenna? Did you tell him that if you had immediately moved back into his home, the police would have thought you and Sirus had schemed, and that they might have charged him for Erik Wei's murder? Did you tell him you were protecting him? Again, stop me if I'm wrong, Jenna, and I will walk out that door and you can fire me and seek another attorney."

Jenna did not speak. Keera again considered her watch. They had less than a minute to get back into court. "But before you answer, let me make one thing perfectly clear. Do not open your mouth and lie to me again. I told you once, and I'm telling you for the last time, that if you lie to me, I will walk and you will be convicted, and you will spend the rest of your life in jail."

Jenna exhaled. Her nostrils flared. She shut her eyes and spoke softly. "How is this going to help me?"

She looked for the first time like that young girl when forced to do something she didn't want to do yet couldn't find a workaround.

"It provides me with a motive to pin the killing of Sirus Kohl on another person."

"How—"

The marshal knocked on the door, then opened it and stuck his head into the room. "Bailiff says Judge Marshall is prepared to retake the bench. He wants you back in court. If not, he says he will recess for the day."

"We're on our way," Keera said. When the door shut, she spoke to Jenna. "We're out of time, and you're out of options. Are you going to trust me?"

"What do I have to do?" Jenna said, still a hint of defiance in her voice.

"You convinced the Wei jurors you were innocent by telling them lies. I watched you do it from the courtroom gallery. You made them believe you. You're going to have to make this jury believe you by doing something you've never done in your life. You're going to have to make them believe you're telling the truth—by telling the truth."

"If I tell the truth, that I knew the representations regarding the LINK were fraudulent, I'll go to jail in the US Attorney's case."

"Probably. But we're talking about a medium-security facility for ten years, likely less given good behavior. The alternative, if I can't get you off, is life behind bars in a maximum-security prison."

"You said you were already creating reasonable doubt."

"I said that was my intent. I'm not sure we're there yet. Maybe I have. Maybe I haven't. But if I haven't, I go home to my next case. Do you want to gamble with your life that I have?"

As soon as Keera and Jenna returned to counsel's table, Judge Marshall climbed the steps and retook his seat on the bench. Those seated in the gallery quieted and sat. Marshall looked over at the clock. Keera thought he might bang his gavel and adjourn for the day. "The bailiff will bring in the jury, please."

Keera exhaled, but she was a long way from finishing what needed to be done. She couldn't get there alone, and she remained uncertain Jenna Bernstein was even capable of telling the truth.

The jurors came into the courtroom and retook their seats, looking eager about what was to come. The murmurs from the gallery indicated those present were like bettors at a horse track trying to predict what was going to happen in the next race.

With the jury in place, Judge Marshall wasted no time. "Ms. Duggan. Call your next witness."

Jenna rose. "Your Honor, the defense calls Jenna Bernstein."

The gallery crowd's noise increased and the jurors shifted in their seats, giving each other looks. Thompson turned and leaned toward Frank Rossi and McFadden. Adria Kohl slid to the edge of her gallery pew to be part of their conversation.

Jenna rose from the table, her movements languid, poised, and composed. It impressed Keera because she knew behind the façade Jenna simmered, but it didn't surprise her. Jenna had been acting her entire life. This would be another performance, only this time her performance would be without scripted lines or a dress rehearsal to perfect her voice intonations and inflections.

Jenna stood a head taller than the bailiff as he administered the oath to tell the truth, the whole truth, and nothing but the truth. She said, "I do."

They were about to find out.

Keera approached the lectern. She needed to keep her questions tightly worded and not inadvertently stray into other topics. Thompson's cross-examination questions, by law, were limited to the topics on which Keera questioned Jenna, though Keera intended to ask questions right up to the four o'clock hour and hopefully prevent Thompson from cross-examining Jenna before the weekend.

Keera didn't waste time on preliminaries. She had read the transcript of Patsy's questioning of Jenna in the Erik Wei trial, and she would take a page out of his examination. She had meant it when she told Patsy he would be at trial with her.

"Jenna, tell the jury your position while at Ponce de León Restorative Technology," Keera said.

"I was the company CEO."

"What were your duties as CEO?"

"I set PDRT's strategy, built the executive team, and reported to the board of directors. I met with potential investors and with the media."

"You were the face of PDRT to the general public; is that correct?"

"You could say that; yes."

"And during your time as CEO of PDRT, did you have a personal relationship with Sirus Kohl?"

"Yes."

"A romantic relationship?"

"Yes."

"Did you move into and live with Sirus Kohl in his house?"

"Yes."

"Did you love Sirus Kohl?"

Jenna shifted in her seat. "No."

You could have heard a leaf fall on snow.

"As the CEO of PDRT, did you knowingly make misrepresentations to investors about the development of, and the capabilities of, the LINK?"

Jenna's eyes watered, probably not from regret, but from anger, but either way it made for good theater. She appeared sympathetic, maybe even empathetic, for the first time Keera could recall. "Yes," she said.

"Did Sirus Kohl know you were making these misrepresentations to investors?"

"Yes, he did."

Keera walked to the end of the jury box and folded her arms. The jurors turned their heads and watched her. "Did Sirus Kohl text you on the night he was shot and killed?"

"Yes."

Keera stepped deliberately toward her computer and struck a key, putting up the text message string on the courtroom computer screens, redacted as previously agreed. She wanted to use every minute left before the break.

What goes around comes around.

"Is this the first text message Sirus Kohl sent to you that night?"
"Yes."
"Did you respond?"
"Yes."
"Is this your response?"

What is that supposed to mean?

"Yes."
"Did he also send you this text?"

You shit on me in ███████. Time to return the favor.

"And is this the text you sent in response?"

I don't know what you're talking about.

"Yes."
Keera paused, then said, "Did you walk from your condominium in Lake Union to Volunteer Park on the evening Sirus Kohl was shot and killed?"
"Yes."
Now the jurors leaned forward. Their chairs creaked.
"Did you stop and purchase a burrito in Volunteer Park?"
"Yes."
"After getting the burrito did you continue to Sirus Kohl's home on Capitol Hill?"
Walker Thompson, McFadden, and Frank Rossi also leaned forward, like swimmers on the blocks awaiting the starter's gun.
"I did. Yes."

The gallery murmurs grew louder. Judge Marshall looked up and reached for his gavel but did not rap it. Keera again paused to let the jurors absorb what they had just heard. She then said, "Why did you walk to Sirus Kohl's home on Capitol Hill?"

Jenna bit her lower lip. "I wanted to convince Sirus not to testify against me in the US Attorney's case for fraud and conspiracy."

"Is that what you interpreted he meant from the text string we just discussed?"

"Yes. It was."

"Can you tell the jury the substance of the US Attorney's charges against you?"

"The US Attorney is alleging Sirus and I knowingly made misrepresentations to our investors and to the general public, then conspired to hide the truth about the LINK's progress and capabilities."

"What is the penalty if you were convicted in that case?"

"I don't know."

"Would you go to jail?" Keera believed it was important for Jenna's credibility for the jurors to know that Jenna's admission could result in her conviction in the federal case.

"I assume I will go to jail if I am convicted; yes."

"Can you tell the jury the conversation you had with Sirus Kohl in his home that evening?"

Jenna cleared her throat. "I told Sirus that I still loved him."

"What was his response?"

"He asked why I had ignored his phone calls and text messages after moving from his home."

"What did you tell him?"

"I told him I didn't respond because I was protecting him, that I didn't want the US Attorney to think we were colluding. I told him that the documentary evidence in the US Attorney's case was weak, but if we both attacked one another, we would make the US Attorney's case for her and we would both go to prison."

"Were you lying then or telling the truth?"

"That was the truth."

"Did he agree?"

"Not right away, no."

"Eventually?"

"Yes."

"How did you get him to agree?"

Jenna again sighed. "I told him if we stuck together, that once we put the federal case behind us, we could move away and start a life together."

"Were you telling him the truth?"

"No."

"Were you lying to him?"

"Yes."

"Why?"

"To convince him not to go to the meeting in the morning and provide evidence against me," she said, matter-of-fact.

This was the extent of what Keera knew from her brief conversation with Jenna in the windowless room, but she was confident of what had happened next. "Did Sirus Kohl ultimately agree to cancel his meeting with the US Attorney?"

"Yes. He said he would call his daughter and have her call off the meeting to give us more time to talk and to discuss our trial strategy."

"What did you say?"

"I told him to make the call. He didn't want to because he knew it would make Adria angry. He said she had worked hard to put the deal together."

"Did Sirus Kohl make a phone call to his daughter Adria Kohl in your presence that evening?"

"Yes. He called her between nine fifteen and nine thirty."

"Were you present when Sirus Kohl spoke to his daughter, Adria Kohl?"

"Yes."

"Why did you wait?"

"I wanted to be sure Sirus didn't change his mind, or that Adria didn't change his mind. I knew he wouldn't, not while I was present, but . . ."

"How did you know he wouldn't?"

"Because I knew he still loved me."

"What did Sirus Kohl tell his daughter, Adria Kohl, in that phone conversation?"

"He told her he wanted her to cancel the meeting with the US Attorney to have more time to discuss trial strategy."

"Could you hear Adria Kohl's response?"

"Yes. I had asked Sirus to put the call on his speakerphone so I could hear what he said and Adria's response."

"What was her response?"

"Adria was angry. She told him she had worked hard to set up the meeting. She told him she had worked hard to keep his ass out of prison. She told him he was going to throw it all away because he was a lovesick puppy."

"You said she was angry. How did you know?"

"She screamed at him. She called him weak and said I was using him. She told him I didn't love him, and that I would take everything he had left. Then she got quiet and said, 'She got to you; didn't she? Jenna got to you.' She asked if he had called me. She asked if he had emailed or texted me about the deal. When Sirus didn't respond, Adria said, 'She's there; isn't she? She's with you at the house now.' When Sirus again didn't respond, she said, 'I'm coming over there.' Then she swore and disconnected the call."

"Did you wait for Adria Kohl to arrive at the house?"

"No. Sirus and I agreed it wouldn't be healthy for me to be there when Adria arrived—when she was so angry—that it would only make her angrier if I was present."

"Did you discuss anything else with Sirus Kohl before you left?"

"I told him to remain calm and to explain that he was worried the meeting could backfire because I could present evidence against him, that I had documents that were definitive about what he knew about the LINK. I also told him to call me after Adria left his house."

"What was his response?"

"He kissed me and said he would."

"Did he call you?"

"No."

"How did you learn Sirus Kohl was dead?"

"Two detectives showed up at my condominium door early the following morning and began asking me questions about where I had been the prior night."

"Did you answer them?"

"No."

"Why not?"

"When two homicide detectives show up at your door, you have a pretty good idea someone has died."

"Who did you think had died?"

"Sirus. I knew it was Sirus."

Keera looked at the clock on the wall just as the minute hand clicked forward one tick. Four o'clock.

"One last question," Keera said. "Did you shoot and kill Sirus Kohl?"

"No," Jenna said. She turned to the jury. "I absolutely did not."

Chapter 34

As Keera had predicted, Walker Thompson did not protest when Judge Marshall moved to adjourn. Knowing he'd get just one chance to cross-examine Jenna Bernstein, and not knowing with certainty what had just transpired, he no doubt welcomed the recess to regroup, to talk to Tanaka, Adria Kohl, and perhaps Thomas Martin before he took a shot at Jenna.

After Judge Marshall released the jury for the weekend and departed the bench, what remained of the courtroom decorum disintegrated. Those in the gallery no longer whispered or tried to hide their astonishment. Most of what was said was lost in the cacophony of voices.

Mr. and Mrs. Bernstein stood at the gallery railing looking concerned and confused. "Keera," John Bernstein said above the din, anger in his tone. "Keera? Keera, I want to talk to you. Keera!"

Beside and behind John Bernstein, reporters pressed to the railing to ask questions, but Keera wasn't about to talk to Bernstein, the reporters, or anyone else. Not here and not now. She quickly packed her computer and slid the briefcase strap over her shoulder to free her hands. She picked up a box of trial materials and spoke to Jenna. "Don't say a word to anyone. Not a word. Do you understand me?"

Jenna didn't answer, but her look of hatred spoke volumes.

Keera glanced across the courtroom. Thompson had his back to her, speaking to Rossi and to Adria Kohl, but Frank's gaze found her over the prosecutor's broad shoulder. Rossi didn't have the same perplexed look as everyone else in the courtroom. He looked as if a light had illuminated a darkened room, and though his eyesight had not yet completely adjusted, the fuzzy shadows were becoming more detailed.

Marshals reapplied Jenna's ankle bracelet and led her out the courtroom door behind the bench as Keera escaped and took the stairs down to the underground tunnel to the administrative building. Outside, she felt the fading warmth of the day and the light breeze blowing up from Elliott Bay. Traffic lined the city streets, and workers commuting home waited to cross at the intersections. She walked down the hill toward the water but had no intention of going to her office. She wasn't going to get near her desk—or her phone. John Bernstein would not be content with Keera having ignored his questions. He'd want answers. He'd call Ella to tell her what he'd just witnessed, and he would demand to know Keera's strategy. Ella would also want to know what the hell had happened. Maggie's interest would be prurient. Nothing got Maggie going like a good bit of juicy gossip, though she soon would be unhappy being inundated with phone calls and not being able to reach Keera.

Keera smiled. Payback for ruining Keera's vacation.

Maggie's evening would be a bitch.

Keera entered the Paddy Wagon and smelled fried and grilled food from the kitchen, chicken and hamburgers and the aroma of salted French fries, but she had no appetite. Liam, waiting on tables near the long mahogany bar, glanced over at her, smiled, and approached.

"You've been busy, I see from the newspapers," he said, raising his lyrical Irish accent to be heard over the sound of the band Nirvana playing from the ceiling speakers. The bar turned up the music Thursday, Friday, and Saturday nights and welcomed local bands as well. "Let me take that box for you."

"I have had a little bit on my plate," Keera said, also raising her voice as she handed him the box. She didn't add, *Wait until you see the headlines in tomorrow morning's newspaper.*

Jenna's testifying would be streamed across the front page.

"Coming in to get a bite to eat before you put your nose back to the grindstone?" Liam asked, leaning in close.

She pointed to the back of the bar, keeping her voice up. "I'd like the owner's booth in the back. Is it open?" Keera had, on occasion, used the booth to escape her phone and emails when under the gun to file a motion, write a brief, or just needing a moment of peace. The owner's table was down a narrow hallway at the back of the restaurant and afforded privacy and, except on nights like this, quiet.

"I'm sure it is," Liam said. "Will you be dining with us, then?"

"I don't think I'll have time," she said. "I'm hoping to meet some-one here."

Liam did his best not to look disappointed, but he couldn't mask his expression entirely. "'Hoping to'? Who'd be crazy enough to stand you up?"

"Work related," she said.

He nodded, then led her past busy tables and a crowd gathered at the bar, kick-starting their weekends with a drink before they headed home, or to downtown restaurants, or the theater. He set her box on the brown leather seat in the horseshoe-shaped booth dimly lit by a single wall sconce affixed to the mahogany panels.

"Just a drink then?" he asked, his voice back to normal volume.

"Club soda," she said.

She slid into the booth beneath the framed photographs that told a pictorial history of Seattle dating back to the days when the wharf was filled with gambling and prostitution houses, and the city had almost as many bars as churches. Photographs depicted shoe-shine boys working their booths, sailors walking with young ladies on their arms, newspaper boys hawking daily papers on street corners, and tourists at the Pike Place Market lined up three rows deep watching fishmongers tossing a giant king salmon. The Paddy Wagon's owner had told Patsy the booth had been used for clandestine meetings—when the mayor, the police chief, and the politicians were all as guilty as the sex workers for taking money for favors. At least the sex workers were honest about it and had earned it.

Keera took out her phone. It was blowing up with messages and emails. She ignored them and sent the text message. Now she'd wait.

Liam returned with her drink. "You're sure I can't tempt you with just an appetizer?"

"Not at the moment, Liam, thank you."

"I'll leave you to it, then."

Keera sipped her club soda and checked and rechecked her phone for a response. She alternately told herself all the reasons he would call, and all the reasons he would not.

He didn't call.

He showed up at the table instead.

"Expecting an important message?" Frank Rossi asked.

She smiled and set down her phone. "One never knows."

Rossi slid into the booth across the small table. "You do," he said. "You knew I would come."

She shrugged one shoulder. "I suspected you might."

"Bullshit," he said quietly. "You knew."

She smiled. "Yeah. I did."

"Am I that predictable?"

"You're a good cop. A good detective. A good detective wants to know the truth. After what happened in court this afternoon . . . You'd come."

"Flattery. You must want something. Is that what Jenna Bernstein gave us on the witness stand this afternoon, the truth?"

He sounded skeptical. He had a right. "She did."

"A cynic might argue you're taking a page out of Patsy's playbook, putting her back on the witness stand."

"No," Keera said. "I'm not."

"Writing your own playbook?"

"Something like that."

"So then why should I believe her this time? Seems that woman has made a habit out of lying."

"She has. Her whole life has been a lie. And she isn't telling the truth this time because she found God or has a guilty conscience."

"No? Why then?"

"Because I explained to her it's to her benefit to tell the truth. And that is the only thing to ever motivate Jenna Bernstein."

"Why didn't she just tell us the truth from the start?"

Keera made a face. "It's complicated, Frank. If she told you what she just said on the witness stand, would you have believed her when she said she didn't kill Sirus Kohl?"

Rossi sighed and shook his head. "No. I would have arrested her on the spot. And for the record, I'm not convinced she didn't kill Sirus Kohl."

"Fair enough. My point, though, is she couldn't tell you. She needed someone—Patsy originally, but when she found out he wasn't available, me—to figure out what happened and provide you with the evidence to prove she didn't kill Sirus."

"Why didn't she just tell you what happened?"

"Again, would I have believed her, even if I didn't know her?"

"Okay. Have you figured out what happened?"

"I'd say I'm seventy-five percent there. I need you to prove the rest."

Rossi shrugged, but he still looked skeptical. "Okay. I'm listening." He sat back against the leather and folded his hands in his lap.

"I think I established who had access to the PDRT's corporate management emails and text messages, and that included Adria Kohl as general counsel. Which means, she would have known when Erik Wei sent the text bomb to Jenna Bernstein that night, or not long after."

"Doesn't prove Adria Kohl looked at it."

"She did."

"A little late for that now; isn't it?"

"Just listen. That's part of the twenty-five percent. She looked at that text message, and I can prove it."

"How?"

"A witness."

"Who?"

"I'll get to 'who' in a moment. Adria Kohl looked at the text and she had two thoughts." Keera raised a finger. "One, her father was going to lose a hundred-and-fifty-million-dollar investment if Erik Wei went public with information that the LINK was fraudulent." She raised a second finger. "And two, Wei had met with Jenna Bernstein to tell her what he intended to do. In other words, it was the perfect setup she needed to save her father and get rid of Jenna."

"To kill Wei and place the blame on Jenna? I follow the bread-crumbs, but the information about PDRT and the LINK being a scam was going to come out eventually. Adria Kohl couldn't prevent that. And her father wasn't going to recoup his investment. She couldn't change that either."

"Maybe. Maybe not. Maybe she saw an exit strategy for her father. Regardless, she could protect the money he still had, which she had an interest in doing as his only child—if she could get Jenna convicted for Wei's murder and thereby get Jenna away from her father."

"It's thin," Rossi said. "And you can't prove it."

"Saving her father wasn't her only motivation."

"Okay, what else?"

"She hated Jenna Bernstein."

"Yeah, I know, but that came after Bernstein testified and tried to place the blame for Wei's killing on her father."

"No. It came before. You heard her testify she knew Jenna was using her father and his money. She knew Jenna didn't love him, and she believed Jenna was manipulating him and spinning him around like a top."

"Knew?"

Keera shrugged. "She clearly suspected it at the start, and Lisa Tanaka confirmed it when she came forward with proof Jenna was having an affair with Thomas Martin."

"The exact opposite of what Jenna testified to at the Wei trial. She said Kohl was manipulating her."

"Another setup, convincingly delivered—the young, naïve entrepreneur taken advantage of by the older, sophisticated investor. The jury bought it."

"Was that Patsy's doing?"

"No. That was all Jenna."

"How do you know she's not lying now?"

"Because I grew up with her. I witnessed her performances far too often."

"Again, you don't have hard evidence."

"Stay with me, Frank."

He smiled but looked like he was biting his tongue. "Okay."

"Who had access to the safe Sirus Kohl kept in his bedroom, which held the 9-millimeter handgun Sirus bought for Jenna?"

"Jenna."

"Be practical, Frank. If Sirus Kohl was hit by a bus, or dropped dead of a heart attack, who would be the logical person to have access to the safe in his bedroom where he likely kept his will and trust and every other important document?"

"I followed your line of questioning in court," Rossi said, "though I can't say I knew exactly why you did it."

"Adria Kohl knew Jenna received the text message from Wei, and she knew Jenna had left to meet with Wei. She had access to Wei's personnel file, and therefore knew his home address, and she had access to Jenna's gun."

"So, you're speculating that she took the gun, drove to Wei's home, and killed him?"

"You weren't at that Wei trial. You didn't hear her testify—"

"I read the transcripts."

"Then you know Wei didn't put up a struggle. No forced entry. No forced entry at Sirus Kohl's home either. Both men opened the door and let the person in."

"Both men knew Jenna Bernstein."

"And both men knew Adria Kohl." They stared at one another. Keera said, "I don't know if she went to Wei intending to kill him. I would like to believe she went to Wei and told him she had spoken with Jenna, and they were taking his text bomb seriously. Likely she told him that she and her father didn't know the extent of the misrepresentations Jenna had made to investors, but that they would handle it. Maybe she tried to reason with him—told him they were going to pull the LINK from the market. I don't know. Maybe Wei told her it wasn't enough, that it was too late, that people's lives could be at stake. Again, I don't know for certain, but I think she saw everything unraveling, all because of Jenna, and when Wei relaxed and turned his back, she shot him."

"With Jenna's gun."

Keera nodded.

"You sound like you speak from experience . . . about things unraveling."

Keera did. She felt empathy for Adria Kohl because she had been in her shoes. So many times Jenna schemed and manipulated situations to Keera's detriment, and her frustration had built to a point that she had wanted to lash out verbally and physically. She saw Adria Kohl's killing of Wei and attempt to blame Jenna more as an act of self-preservation, not just for her but primarily for her father, who had clearly fallen under Jenna's spell.

Rossi shook his head. "You're making a lot of leaps here, Keera. Grand Canyon–size leaps I'm not sure I can make."

"I can help you."

"Okay. What's the next step?"

"Adria Kohl shoots Erik Wei, and all the evidence points to Jenna Bernstein. SPD thinks they have her dead to rights, but they don't know her. Jenna doesn't give in that easily. She knows somebody has set her up, and that really bothers her. Jenna has never liked anyone to get the better of her, at anything."

"Who does she suspect? Sirus?"

"No. She knows Sirus still loves her and never would have set her up. She suspected she knew who did kill Wei and why, but she also knows she doesn't have the evidence she needs to prove it. She knows that person likely has her gun, the text message from Wei, and that person also knew Jenna had her security team take her to meet with Wei at the restaurant the night he was killed."

"She hires the Irish Brawler to defend her and find the evidence."

"Patsy was considered the best defense attorney in the city, and Patsy owed the Bernsteins a favor."

"Why?"

"Long story. Not relevant. But Jenna knew Patsy owed her parents and would feel obligated to them and to her, and therefore that she could manipulate Patsy by playing the young girl he knew growing up."

"Did she? Manipulate him?"

"I thought she did, but no, I was wrong. Patsy knew what Jenna was all along. Yes, he owed the family a favor, but knowing my father, that isn't why he represented her."

"Why then?"

"Because he had empathy for her parents, for what they were going through because of Jenna."

"Did he know she lied on the witness stand in Wei?"

"No. He would not have let her testify if he had known she was going to lie. Patsy was a brawler, but he always did his brawling inside the ring and within the rules."

"Some in the prosecutor's office would dispute that, but . . . Jenna got acquitted."

"Exactly. She survived, but PDRT did not, and given her testimony at that trial, everyone now knew of the misrepresentations concerning the LINK, including the investors, and they wanted blood. But then Covid hit and the world, including the courthouse, shut down. When it started back up, PDRT's investors—powerful and influential men and women—knowing they had been duped, pushed all the right buttons to get the US Attorney to file a federal complaint for fraud and conspiracy.

Adria sees another opportunity to save her father and put Jenna behind bars and quickly seeks to make a deal with the US Attorney."

"So why would she kill her father? If that is indeed where this is going."

"It is, and as with Wei, I don't believe she went to the house that night intending to kill her father, Frank. I believe she went because she needed her father to testify about the documents she had gathered to put Jenna in prison. But as I've said, Jenna was not going to make it that easy."

"You're saying Jenna gets the text messages from Sirus Kohl, shows up at his house, and works her black magic to get him to call off the meeting with the US Attorney, and when he calls his daughter and she realizes Jenna is manipulating him, again, she gets angry, and one thing leads to another."

"Exactly. I think Sirus's murder was a moment of escalation. I think Adria went to his house that night furious with him for allowing Jenna back into his life and giving her another chance to ruin Adria's well-thought-out and executed plan—everything she had worked so hard on—to protect her father and what money he had left. I think her father's refusal to go forward with the meeting put Adria over the edge. So what does she do? She's a lawyer, Frank. She knows evidence. She knows Jenna has been to the house. She knows her father's text messages to Jenna will establish Jenna knew about the meeting in the morning with the US Attorney, which means Jenna had a motive to kill Sirus. And maybe Adria was also banking on human nature."

"What human nature?"

"That the PA's office, believing Jenna got away with Erik Wei's murder, would be just as intent on putting her behind bars. Go back and read how many times Walker Thompson and Dan Butcher said after that trial that Jenna Bernstein wasn't found innocent, that she was found not guilty beyond reasonable doubt. This was another bite at the apple, Frank. I'm not criticizing you, or your investigation, or Walker

Thompson. I'm just saying Walker Thompson wanted another shot at Jenna Bernstein and at the Irish Brawler. Am I wrong?"

Rossi stared at Keera for a long moment. *This could go any number of ways,* she thought, but she was banking on the Frank Rossi she'd come to know. Reasonable. Rational. Willing to admit when he was wrong, or at least not quite right. Someone who didn't let his ego get in the way of the truth. Plus, she had one last thing to hopefully tip the scales. Keera reached into her briefcase and removed documents an inch thick, clipped together in the right corner.

"What are these?" Rossi asked.

"These are Adria Kohl's phone records. Her CDRs."

"You've already established her father called her. Seems to me what was said in that conversation is a she-said-she-said situation between Adria Kohl and Jenna Bernstein."

"No. Look at the other number I highlighted that Adria Kohl repeatedly called."

"I already have," he said. "It's Thomas Martin's number."

"Right. Weren't you curious about all those calls?"

"I was, yeah."

"Look at the date. They started after Lisa Tanaka stumbled onto Jenna screwing Thomas Martin in her office and told Adria Kohl about it."

Rossi took a moment and considered the dates of the calls, then returned his attention to Keera.

"But Adria Kohl didn't go to her father and tell him Jenna and Martin are screwing. Why not?" Keera asked. "If she wanted to have something to make her father realize Jenna was a fraud and using him, a way to get rid of her, why wouldn't she go to him with this incriminating evidence?"

"I don't know. I've been asking myself that same question."

"Because she couldn't, Frank. Because, as I said, Jenna has always been a master manipulator, and Sirus Kohl wasn't the only one she was manipulating. She was also manipulating Adria Kohl."

A light bulb flickered behind Frank Rossi's eyes. Or maybe the bulb had always been there. He had just needed Keera to illuminate it. "Why didn't you call Martin to the stand and get him to tell you the substance of the calls?"

She smiled. "Come on, Frank. He wasn't going to admit it. He's married with kids."

"All right, you called this meeting. What do you suggest?"

"Just do what you do best, Frank. Bring in Thomas Martin and lean on him a bit. Question him about his affair with Jenna Bernstein."

"And if he denies it?"

"Tell him you know about the two of them screwing in the car. Tell him you know about Jenna giving him a foot job under the table in a restaurant, with Sirus sitting at the table."

"Seriously?"

She nodded. "Question him about these records, and all these calls from Adria Kohl. Get him to admit Adria Kohl called him repeatedly because she was blackmailing him, threatening to expose his affair with Jenna to his family and to his clients to destroy his personal life and his business if he didn't do as she said."

"And if he still doesn't admit it?"

"Then I'll put him on the witness stand Monday and do my best Perry Mason impersonation, then take my chances that I've created reasonable doubt with at least one juror."

"You already think you've convinced them; don't you?"

She shrugged. "Maybe not all of them."

"But one or two." He studied her. "So why not just let the case go to the jury?"

"Patsy always taught me to never rely on a jury, that when you think you know you've won, that's when you're in real trouble. If you can get your client a good deal and avoid the jury, take it. Don't let your own ego—your desire to win—be injurious to your client."

"But that's not the only reason; is it?" he asked.

Keera wasn't trying to make herself look magnanimous. "Walker Thompson is a good man and a good prosecutor. He's not Miller Ambrose," she said.

"You're giving him a chance to save face, not lose another case the public and the PA's office thought he should win."

"I'm not interested in rubbing anyone's nose in the dirt."

"Does that include my nose?"

It did. Keera had thought of Frank Rossi before she thought of anyone else. She'd always liked him. And a part of her, were things different, would have pursued her feelings. "I'm just doing what's in the best interests of my client."

Rossi nodded but looked disappointed. "You realize the consequences of her testimony today, that she knew she made misrepresentations about the LINK to investors and regulators. It's admissible in the US Attorney's action."

"I do and so does she. She's not innocent in this, Frank. She's responsible for everything she put in motion, for those two lost lives. She didn't pull the trigger, but she might as well have."

"So she chose the lesser of two evils."

"I spelled it out for her. It's the right deal for all of us."

"And you think all of this started because Jenna Bernstein was sleeping with Thomas Martin, and Adria Kohl was upset because she was also sleeping with Martin, and blackmailed him?"

Keera thought back to the meeting she'd had in Jenna Bernstein's condominium. She thought Jenna had steered that conversation to get a rise out of her, which was not unlike Jenna, but Jenna hadn't said what she'd said for that purpose. She'd said it to lead Keera to find the critical evidence everyone was missing, why Adria would be vengeful.

"No," Keera said. "Not because she was sleeping with Thomas Martin."

Chapter 35

Keera rang the doorbell and waited. She had to sign into the register at the desk in the lobby, and the guard on duty called and announced her, but she still had doubts that Jenna would let her in. She heard the deadbolt disengage, and the door pulled open. Jenna stood dressed in sweats. She'd clipped her hair atop her head and wore glasses. Keera had never seen her wear glasses.

"What are you doing here?" she asked, her tone flat.

"We need to talk."

"You couldn't leave the courtroom fast enough this afternoon," Jenna said.

"You want to do this in the hall?"

Jenna stepped aside and Keera stepped in, closing the door behind her. She heard the television on in the other room, the local news. Most people in Jenna's position would have avoided the news. Jenna wasn't most people. Far from it. On the counter were a wine bottle and a glass of white wine.

"I had to take care of something before speaking with you."

"What?"

"Leading the police to the evidence I need to negotiate a deal for you."

"I'm not taking a deal." She picked up the glass of wine and walked into the living room.

Keera followed. "I haven't made one yet. As I said, I'm waiting for certain things to transpire. If everything goes as I hope they will, I suspect I'll be able to make a deal to have all charges against you dismissed with prejudice."

"With prejudice?"

"It means the prosecution could not retry you. But I need to ask you a couple more questions."

"What questions?"

"I didn't put it together right away because I thought you intended it just to get a rise out of me."

"Put what together?"

"Why Adria Kohl hated you so much."

"You're going to have to be a little more specific," Jenna said.

"The other morning, when I came here, you told me about a sexual relationship you'd had with a woman while living with Sirus Kohl. Why?"

"You asked about affairs. I told you about my affairs."

"Why didn't you tell me her name?"

Jenna shrugged.

"Because you wanted me to figure it out on my own and find the evidence to prove it. You wanted me to figure out why it was significant." When Jenna did not answer, Keera said, "That woman was Adria Kohl." It wasn't a question. Keera intended it to be rhetorical. "It's the reason she didn't tell her father about you and Thomas Martin, the reason why someone who hated you so much didn't use your affair to convince her father to get rid of you. She didn't tell him because she feared what you would tell her father about the two of you. If she betrayed you, you would betray her. You had her over a barrel. You had the ultimate way to hurt her father. But you made one mistake."

Jenna admitted and denied nothing. She asked, "What's that?"

"You didn't realize who you had manipulated. You didn't realize Adria Kohl would play your game even nastier than you."

After a beat of silence, Jenna said, "You spoke of a deal? What kind of deal?"

"The kind of deal that requires you to again tell the truth about why Adria Kohl would want to put you behind bars."

"There's no reason for me to do that. You've established reasonable doubt. You've established Adria Kohl had the opportunity to kill her father, and that she had access to a weapon."

"I don't have a motive."

"Greed. She wanted what was left of her inheritance."

Keera smiled. Jenna, smarter than everyone else. "Not strong enough."

"Why not?"

"It doesn't explain the entire story. I told you in the conference room, Jenna, it's a gamble to take this to the jury. Maybe I've created reasonable doubt. Maybe I haven't." Keera shrugged. "Juries are always a crapshoot. Patsy would tell you the same thing and give you the same advice. If a good deal can be made, take it."

"And if I don't take it?"

"Then, if I didn't create reasonable doubt, you're going away for the rest of your life at a maximum-security facility. You said it wasn't enough for me to have a jury find you not guilty beyond a reasonable doubt. You wanted me to prove your innocence."

"But not by destroying my reputation."

Keera, despite all her experiences with Jenna, still marveled at her lack of self-awareness. Jenna still believed, despite everything that had happened, that she could rise from these ashes. "That ship sailed when you testified in court this afternoon, Jenna. I don't know what you're thinking, but you're not going to walk away from this and start another company or convince other investors to give you money. That part of your life is over, Jenna."

Jenna lowered her gaze, and Keera saw the young girl and woman still trying to find an end around. Jenna had obscured the truth so often she could no longer find it. She finally understood what JP had meant when he said Jenna hadn't won anything, that she'd lost everything, including herself. Jenna was like Jay Gatsby in F. Scott Fitzgerald's novel *The Great Gatsby*, one Keera had read in high school but which now, ironically, had deeper meaning. Jenna had pretended for so long to be someone she was not, she no longer knew who she was. She had become the person consumed by the pursuit of money and status and willing to do almost anything to get it and to keep it. But she would never be rich, and she would never be the person she pretended to be, the person she desperately wanted to be, a person of power and influence.

She would never be admired.

She would never be respected.

She would be pitied. Much like Gatsby.

And maybe that's what Jenna feared even more than spending her life behind bars, why she wanted desperately to be found innocent. She still thought she could find a way out of her predicament. She still thought she could win.

She couldn't.

Not this time.

"You're going to jail, Jenna. Your testimony ensures you'll be convicted in the US Attorney's case. It won't be the state penitentiary, and it won't be for the rest of your life, but you will be a convicted felon. So you can forget about starting another company or becoming rich or being on the cover of any more business journals. Maybe, instead, you can think about ways to rebuild your credibility and your life, and find out who you really are."

Jenna drank the remainder of her wine. Her eyes got that sharpened blue focus, and her voice that convincing tone Keera had heard too often to be fooled again. "You created reasonable doubt. You can win this case, Keera. It will be a huge feather in your hat."

Keera smiled. "You just can't stop; can you?"

"No, Keera, listen to me. You win this case, and you'll have clients begging for you to represent them. You'll be like Patsy once was—the best there is."

"I don't want to be like Patsy. I just want to be me." She started for the door, then turned back. "Maybe I was wrong."

"About what?"

"Maybe you're beyond rehabilitation. That's up to you. I did my job." Keera pulled open the door but glanced back again. "Ironic; isn't it?"

"What?"

"You spent a lifetime lying and manipulating others to get what you wanted, and you've ended up with nothing. And now the only thing that will prevent you from spending the rest of your life in a prison . . . is to tell the truth. I'll need your answer first thing tomorrow morning."

Chapter 36

Rossi wasn't surprised when Thomas Martin told him he preferred to meet at TMTP's offices in Auburn, though it meant hearing Billy grumble about fighting traffic on a Friday night. Rossi had given Martin the courtesy of a telephone call, also to Billy's chagrin. Ford wanted to go in with guns blazing and haul Martin downtown to answer questions in the hard-interrogation room, which wasn't much larger than a prison cell, and watch the heat warm his ass until he squirmed.

"You're a hard-ass," Rossi said to his partner. "Sometimes you get more bees with honey."

"And sometimes you get stung by that bee."

"I don't want to raise any red flags and have him clam up before we even get him talking."

Rossi told Martin that some things had come up during trial, things that Rossi needed help understanding. Martin sounded curious, as expected, but also perhaps concerned. He initially told Rossi it wasn't a great time—one of the kids had the flu.

Rossi told him the meeting had to be tonight and suggested they meet at TMTP so as not to disturb Martin's wife and children. "Wouldn't want your wife to worry that anything was wrong" was how Rossi had put it.

Either Martin got some religion, or he got the point. The interview was going to take place. Rossi was willing to let him pick his poison on the location. Martin picked TMTP.

The gate rolled back. This time the security guard on duty never left his booth, just waved Ford and Rossi through. It being after hours, they had to buzz the intercom. Rossi smiled at the security camera posted over the door, just to be polite. The door buzzed and Ford pulled it open.

Martin met them in the lobby. He did his best to smile, but it looked forced and uncomfortable. Rossi wondered if he'd already spoken to Adria Kohl. "Sorry you had to come all this way," he said.

"Not a problem. Billy and I like to spend our Friday nights in traffic on the freeways." Rossi smiled. A subtle way to let Martin know not to waste any more of their time.

Ford remained silent. He didn't smile.

"Must be important," Martin said.

"It is," Rossi said. "Would you like to do this here or in your office?"

"Come on back," Martin said, sounding even less confident.

When they reached his office they retook their positions, Martin behind the desk. But this time neither Ford nor Rossi took a seat, and Martin took the hint. He remained standing.

"We don't intend to be here long," Ford said, another not-so-subtle way of saying they expected to get straight answers.

"How's your little boy?" Rossi asked.

"I'm sorry?" Martin said.

"Your son with the flu."

"Oh. Yeah. He's fine. Just a temperature and a runny nose."

"Unusual time of the year for the flu; isn't it?" Ford said.

"You know kids. They're always getting sick," Martin said.

"I don't have kids. Not married." Rossi held up his hand and showed Martin his ring finger. "Hope to someday. Must be nice to have someone to go home to, raise a family, do all those fatherly things. You sure love it; don't you, Billy?"

"Wouldn't throw that away for anything in the world," Ford said. "All you really have is your family."

They stood in silence. Martin blinked first. "You said on the phone it was important."

Rossi said, "Lisa Tanaka testified in court today."

"Who?" Martin said.

"Don't do that," Ford said.

"What?" Martin said.

"Don't act like you don't know who she is," Ford said.

"It's been a few years, Officers."

"Detectives," Ford said. "Violent Crimes."

"She was PDRT's controller," Rossi said. "She worked late quite a bit. I understand Jenna Bernstein did also, and we've already established that you waited at night to drive her home."

"That's right."

"She'd call you on your cell phone when she was ready to go home?"

"Usually, yeah."

"Was there some other way she'd let you know she was ready to go home?" Billy asked, sounding perturbed.

"No."

"So she would call you," Ford said. "Not usually. *Always.*"

"Okay. Always."

"Unless you happened to be in her office," Rossi said.

Martin chuckled and shook his head. "Tanaka," he said. "Yeah. I know who she is now."

"Tell us," Ford said.

"She was working late one night, and I was in Jenna Bernstein's office helping her move some furniture. She knocked on the door and when Jenna answered it . . . well, she saw us not exactly put together and came to the wrong conclusion. She even told Adria Kohl about it."

"Moving furniture?" Billy said, arching his eyebrows. "Late at night. I've never heard it called that before. You, Frank?"

"That's a new one for me," Rossi said. He looked at Martin. "Jenna Bernstein also testified today, under oath."

"Yeah?" Martin asked, trying to sound surprised, though Rossi suspected he knew that already, either from the news or from Adria Kohl.

"Yeah. And she said Tanaka did in fact catch you both doing the dirty deed in her office. Are they both lying? Under oath?"

Martin lost the smile. "Am I in some kind of trouble here, Detectives?"

"I don't know," Rossi said. "Are you?"

"But lying to us isn't going to help your situation," Ford said.

Martin let out a breath. "Okay."

"Okay, what?" Ford said.

"Okay, Tanaka was telling the truth."

"That wasn't the only time you and Jenna Bernstein had sex, though; was it?"

"No."

"There were times in the back of the car, and once in a restaurant. I believe she put her foot in your crotch under the tablecloth, while Sirus was present."

"Ballsy," Ford said. "No pun intended."

"Am I right?" Rossi asked.

"Yeah," Martin said, sounding tired and defeated.

"How long did you and Jenna Bernstein have the affair?"

"I don't know. Months."

"Did anyone reprimand you?"

"No."

"Adria Kohl didn't call you to discuss what Tanaka claimed she had seen?"

"She called."

"And what did you tell her?"

"I told her that Tanaka was mistaken, just what I told the two of you."

"And then what happened?" Rossi asked.

"Nothing. That was the end of it."

"Nothing?" Rossi asked.

Martin shrugged and shook his head.

Rossi looked at Ford, then back to Martin. "Let me get this straight. You were screwing Jenna Bernstein, who at the time was living with Sirus Kohl, and his daughter called you up and you said you were moving furniture and that was the end of it?"

"I don't know what to tell you, Detective."

Rossi reached into his jacket and pulled out the CDR records from Adria Kohl's phone showing the numerous telephone calls between her phone and Thomas Martin's cell phone. He'd highlighted the calls in yellow for emphasis. "Do you know what those are?" Rossi asked.

"They're call detail records," Ford said. "Tells us every call Adria Kohl made, every text she sent, on what date, and to what number."

"And these are CDRs from your cell phone," Rossi said, holding up another packet, also highlighted. "Same thing. So on the night that Lisa Tanaka caught you and Jenna Bernstein screwing in the office, Adria Kohl called you."

"I told you she did."

"But you didn't tell me that she continued to call you, multiple times, sometimes at very odd hours of the night. Feel free to take a look at the records. They don't lie."

"I didn't think it relevant."

"No?" Ford said. "Were you also sleeping with Adria Kohl, and these calls were maybe her expressing that she wasn't very happy to find out that the cheater was also cheating on her?"

"No. No, I wasn't sleeping with Adria," Martin said. "Did she tell you we were sleeping together?"

"We haven't talked to her yet. Is she going to tell us something different?"

"No," Martin said. "We . . . we weren't sleeping together."

"How about this call?" Rossi pointed to a call he had highlighted in yellow. "Did you think this call was relevant?"

Martin looked at the highlighted call. "I don't know."

"That was the night Erik Wei was shot and murdered. That was the night that you brought Jenna to the restaurant to meet with Erik Wei, then brought her home to Sirus Kohl's house. Why would you call Adria Kohl, who you already said wasn't your regular contact at PDRT?"

Martin paled. He was gripping the desk like he was holding on to keep himself upright. "I think I'd like to speak to an attorney."

Rossi nodded. "Okay. Anyone in particular you want to call?"

"What do you want from me?"

"The truth," Rossi said. "That's all we've ever wanted. Just tell us the truth."

"Can I get in trouble? I mean just for reporting in."

"That's up to you," Rossi said. "And what were you reporting in?"

Martin looked to be measuring what he was about to say next. "What if I told you I think I know who killed Erik Wei and Sirus Kohl?"

"I'd tell you that if you know who did it, or think you do, you'd better tell me, or you really will be in trouble."

"Obstruction of justice," Ford said.

"Conspiracy to commit murder," Rossi said.

"What about some kind of deal?" Martin said quickly. "Immunity for my telling you what I know."

"We can call a prosecutor and we can all wait an hour for them to get down here and then you can tell them, and they can then decide whether what you have to say is worth a deal, but isn't your wife going to start to wonder where you are and what's taking you so long to get home?" Rossi asked.

"Start with telling *us* the truth, and if you do, then we'll lobby the prosecutor to make you a deal, if you're willing to go on the record with what you have to say and it has merit," Ford said.

Martin blew out another breath. Again, he looked to be weighing his options. He dropped into his chair. Ford and Rossi sat in the chairs across from him. Ford took out his phone and hit the record button, then set the phone on the desk.

Then he and Rossi sat back and listened.

Chapter 37

Keera returned home to await Frank Rossi's call. She considered her chessboard and thought about getting involved in a game online to distract herself, but she knew it wouldn't work. In prior times she might have had a Scotch, but she had no alcohol in the house and no desire for a drink. Instead, she sat on the sofa reading a book, but she had to restart the same page several times and finally set it down.

Shortly after ten o'clock, Keera heard a sharp, no-doubt-about-it police officer's knock on her front door. Frank Rossi.

She pulled open the door. "I thought you were going to call?"

"Phone calls can be traced, as you well know." He arched his eyebrows. "Can I come in?"

"Yeah. Sure." She stepped aside. After shutting the door, Keera followed Rossi into her living room.

"Nice place," he said.

"I'm just getting a screaming rental deal from an appreciative client of Patsy's. Can I get you anything?"

He shook his head. Then noted the chess table. "I knew you didn't give it up."

"Yeah?"

"You try cases the way you told me Patsy taught you to play chess. Bold. Unpredictable. Instinctual. After this trial I'd add you bluff well too."

She motioned to the dining room table. They sat across from one another. "Billy and I paid a visit to Auburn and spoke to Thomas Martin."

"And?"

Rossi told her Martin initially denied having a sexual tryst with Jenna Bernstein, that Lisa Tanaka had been mistaken, and denied having an affair with Adria Kohl.

"And?"

"And he began to change his tune when I gave him some specific details." Rossi said he also pointed out the calls Martin made to and received from Adria Kohl the night Erik Wei was murdered. "Then he started asking about a deal."

"What kind of deal?"

"The kind of deal where he gives us evidence to solve both the murder of Erik Wei and the murder of Sirus Kohl, and he walks free."

"What kind of evidence?"

"That's what I asked."

"Come on, Frank," Keera said.

He smiled. "Voice recordings."

"Of . . ."

"Telephone calls he had with Adria Kohl, as well as some photographs and videos of her at TMTP Security. He had quite the elaborate system, as one would suspect of a security professional. You weren't wrong, but you also weren't right. Not exactly."

"No?"

"All those phone calls between Martin and Adria Kohl weren't just threats. They were also a proposition."

"What kind of proposition?"

"You know that saying about the enemy of my enemy is my friend?"

"Jenna?"

"After Kohl learned from Tanaka that Martin and Jenna were having an affair, she visited Martin at TMTP. She said she knew about them, and she wanted his cooperation. If he chose not to cooperate, she'd fire him and let his wife and all his clients know he was sleeping with one of his clients who he was supposed to be guarding. End of marriage. End of business."

"So I was right."

"About that, yeah."

"What did Adria Kohl want?"

"Initially she wanted Martin to let her know everything Jenna Bernstein did. Where she went. Who she met with. What they discussed."

"So he kept up his relationship with Jenna?"

"While Jenna continued to live with Sirus. Must have made for an interesting living arrangement. It also brings up another adage," Rossi said.

"Keep your friends close. Keep your enemies closer," Keera said.

"Exactly. On the night Wei sent his text message to Jenna about the LINK, Martin drove Bernstein to meet with Wei. While Jenna Bernstein was in the restaurant with Wei, Martin called Adria Kohl and told her what was going on, just as he said. She asked to be kept informed. He called again later that night and told her what Bernstein said happened at the meeting, about Wei threatening to blow the whistle on the LINK, and he'd taken Bernstein back to Sirus Kohl's mansion and they'd had a fight. He said Jenna had stormed out, and while in the car she told Martin she was not going down with the ship. She was not going to take the fall. He drove her to an apartment she kept. The next day he learned Erik Wei had been shot and killed, and Jenna Bernstein had been arrested. He said he didn't know whether to believe she had done it or not. He said he thought Adria Kohl might have had a hand in the murder, but he couldn't prove she did because he had no evidence, and he wasn't about to say anything to anyone while Kohl could ruin him."

"And the voice recordings?"

"Confirm the blackmail, though Kohl was too smart to say anything about the murder of Wei."

"He'll testify to this?"

Rossi smiled. "He'll testify, but as I said he wants a deal."

"What kind of deal?"

"I'm sure he'll start at something in which he walks completely. Since we can't really nail him on much, maybe obstruction of justice. Thompson and Butcher are working with his lawyer now."

"What about Adria Kohl?"

"I have an unmarked car sitting on her place of residence in case she somehow gets wind of all this and tries to run. We know she has access to Sirus's bank account. His fortune isn't what it was, but it's still more money than I'll ever see. We've also obtained an arrest warrant and a search warrant. Hopefully we'll find Jenna Bernstein's gun."

"Will Walker Thompson and Butcher agree to drop the case against Jenna?"

"I don't know. You'll have to talk to them, but I suggested a few things."

"Such as?"

"Bernstein admits she had an affair with both Adria Kohl and Thomas Martin, which is what set everything in motion. Martin admits Adria Kohl called and blackmailed him. Told him she wanted to know everything Bernstein did and in exchange she wouldn't upset his marriage and his business. Martin also admits he called Adria Kohl and told her about Erik Wei's text message and Jenna's meeting Wei in the restaurant. He also has a recording of Adria Kohl admitting she hated Jenna Bernstein. Thompson will call you in the morning. I think he realizes you have reasonable doubt and he is willing to pivot to Adria Kohl, assuming Jenna Bernstein will testify to what you say she will. Will she?"

"Again, if there is something in it for her."

He nodded. "By the way, Thompson won't say it, but he knows what you're doing, not rubbing his nose in the dirt. I do too."

"Just looking out for my client," Keera said.

Rossi chuckled and pushed back from the table, though with a touch of resignation. "I know. Just doing your job."

Keera stood also. "I appreciate you letting me know, Frank."

At the door he turned back. "Just so you know. Some of us miss not having you working for the good guys."

Keera smiled. "At times, I do too."

"Cases like this?" he said.

"Cases just like this," she said.

"Certainly not a grounder."

"More like a line drive back at the pitcher," Keera said.

"You know baseball."

"Used to watch the Mariners with my father. Still go to a handful of games a year."

"Me too. I love baseball."

"Maybe we can catch a game."

He smiled. "Maybe. Do you think your client understands how close she came to being the person killed?"

"I doubt she'll ever admit it to me, or herself."

"Maybe sitting in a prison, even a medium-security prison, will give her some time to think about it."

"Maybe," Keera said, though she couldn't keep skepticism out of her voice.

"You don't think so?"

"I don't know what I think, Frank. One never knows with Jenna Bernstein."

"Have a good night, Keera." He turned for the door.

"Frank?"

He turned back.

"You want to play a game?" She motioned to the chessboard.

He smiled, but it faded. "And get my ego further bruised? I'm no dummy."

Chapter 38

Monday morning, Keera appeared in court, this time without the jury present. Given the magnitude of the case and the plea deal they were about to enter, Walker Thompson and Daniel Butcher insisted that Jenna's statement be attached to the deal and entered in open court, before Judge Marshall and the general public. Spectators packed the gallery, including local and national reporters, who sensed or had heard rumors that something was up.

Rossi had advised Keera early that morning that as a result of the statements of Jenna Bernstein and Thomas Martin, Adria Kohl had been arrested in the murders of Erik Wei and Sirus Kohl and a search conducted of her car and place of residence. The gun had not yet been found, but the police had learned that Kohl also maintained several safe deposit boxes and were in the process of obtaining search warrants to search those as well.

Jenna was escorted into the room still in handcuffs, the ankle bracelet removed. Jenna had done what she'd always done when Keera brought her the prosecutor's deal. She'd probed around the edges, and she sought to have the charges dismissed before she testified under oath, but Thompson and Butcher wouldn't have it. Eventually, with little choice, Jenna had capitulated and gave a statement before a certified court reporter. Thompson pushed her in his questions about her affair with Thomas Martin, which she had admitted. He asked her about her relationship with Adria Kohl, and she told him she'd used Adria to keep her from poisoning her relationship with Sirus, whose money she needed to keep PDRT afloat. She'd even kept text messages, on two different burner phones, between her and Adria, should she ever need to use them.

She did.

It was the Jenna that Keera knew, always scheming, always using others to get what she wanted or needed.

Marshall took the bench looking like he'd just taken a shower after a long run. He wiped beads of perspiration from his brow with a handkerchief and drank from a water container emblazoned with the phrase "The Buck Stops Here."

"Counsel, I'm told a deal has been reached between the State and the defense?"

Thompson and Keera both stood. "It has, Your Honor."

"Will the State read the agreement into the record, please."

Thompson lifted a sheet of paper and read the preliminary legalese, then the terms of the agreement. The State agreed to dismiss all charges against Jenna Bernstein, with prejudice. In exchange, Jenna Bernstein had provided the State with testimony, taken under oath and after being sworn to tell the truth, the whole truth, and nothing but the truth, that she had a sexual relationship with the head of PDRT's security, Thomas Martin, as well as with Adria Kohl, providing the estimated dates of each relationship. Thompson went on to detail everything Jenna had told him under oath, and to provide half a dozen documents obtained from Jenna and from Thomas Martin to substantiate what she had to say.

Predictably, the gallery came to life with the mention of Adria Kohl's name, and it buzzed until Thompson finished reading the concluding legalese into the record. Reporters would get the documents online.

"Ms. Bernstein," Judge Marshall asked, "do you acknowledge the terms of this plea agreement?"

Jenna stood beside Keera. "I do, Your Honor."

"And does it represent a true and accurate statement of the agreement you have reached?"

"It does," Jenna said.

"Counsel, do these terms accurately represent the agreement reached between the State and the defense?"

Again, Keera and Thompson acknowledged they did.

"Then the matter of the State of Washington versus Jenna Bernstein, case number C-061625, is hereby dismissed, with prejudice. Ms. Bernstein, you are free to go. Counsel, we are adjourned. You are free to meet with the jury, should you desire to do so, after I advise them what has transpired. They will be very interested to learn what has happened this morning."

Keera asked JP Harrison to meet with the jurors and determine which way they were leaning. Her statement to Jenna that the jury was always a crapshoot had not been a bluff. She sensed she had a few holdouts that might have prevented the prosecution from obtaining a guilty verdict, but that was never a given.

Marshall rapped his gavel once, adjourned, and quickly descended from the bench. Keera turned to Jenna, but Jenna had turned her back to her, speaking quietly with her parents. Apparently, they weren't interested in talking to Keera either.

Keera hadn't expected a thank-you, and she wasn't going to get one.

Walker Thompson crossed the aisle and shook her hand. "I'd say the leaf doesn't fall far from the tree, but I suspect you've heard that before."

"A few times."

"Well then, let me say, having tried a case against both you and your father, I'd say you're much more than a fallen leaf. I'd say you've set down your own roots. Why in God's name did we ever let you go?"

Keera smiled. "Thanks, Walker."

Thompson departed. Jenna refused to meet with the press, though Keera had suggested it might be best to rip off the Band-Aid with one press conference; she thought she couldn't move on without it. She also couldn't leave Seattle given the US Attorney's indictment and pending trial. When that matter was resolved, she'd be headed to prison. Where, and for how long, would be up to her attorneys and whatever deal they could reach with the Department of Justice, if Jenna agreed to another deal. That was also unknown, though, again, Jenna did not have a lot of leverage.

If she thought she'd been a pariah before . . .

Keera slipped from the courtroom and the court. Outside, she headed down the hill to the office. When she stepped from the elevator onto the third floor, Maggie was not seated behind the reception desk, though the phones were predictably ringing off the hook. Maggie had turned on the answering service.

Keera walked down the hall toward Ella's office. Voices, intimately familiar to her, drifted down the hallway. She pushed open the office door. Ella sat behind her desk. Maggie stood to the side. Her father and her mother sat in the two chairs across from Ella's desk.

"Hey, kiddo," her father said.

She smiled, as she always did when her father called her that, and she crossed the room to hug and greet both her parents. She looked to Ella, then back to Patsy. "I was told you were coming home this morning. Sorry I couldn't be here to greet you."

Patsy said, "Sounds like you've had enough on your plate. Ella was just filling me in."

"Did you get it done?" Ella asked Keera.

"It's done," Keera said.

"Did you speak to the jurors?" Patsy asked.

"I asked JP to talk to them."

"Your father is not supposed to be working for another month," her mother said.

Her father looked like he'd lost weight. He also looked tired, bags under his eyes. "That doesn't mean I can't listen," he said. "You got a dismissal with prejudice?"

"That's the gist of it. Don't expect the Bernsteins to refer us any more business, however, or a thank-you."

"Maybe they won't need to, again," Patsy said.

"I wouldn't be so sure," their mother said. "Trouble always follows that girl."

"You want to talk?" Patsy asked.

"No," Keera said. "You should listen to what the rehab people are telling you, Dad. We can talk later."

"Hey, I'm not talking about partner to partner. I'm talking about father to daughter."

Again, Keera smiled. "I could always use my father's opinion."

Her father stood and walked to the door. "Say no more. My office."

"No business," her mother called after them.

They walked to Patsy's office, though it didn't look like his office. All the paper, files, and most of the knickknacks that had once cluttered his desk had been removed and the shelves rearranged and organized. The desktop shone, reflecting the ceiling lights.

"This place is so neat I won't be able to find a damn thing," he said.

"Took Maggie with a bulldozer to clean it up," Keera said.

"Ella told me." He settled into his chair, just like old times. "What's going on?" he asked. "You seem troubled. Is it the deal?"

Keera went through the evidence with him and told him the deal terms.

"Sounds to me like you did your job. Sounds to me like the Bernsteins should be worshiping the ground you walk on."

"That is not going to happen. This is far from over for them or for Jenna. The federal case is just getting started, and from what I'm told, based on Jenna's testimony, she's looking at ten or eleven years, with time off for good behavior."

"Sounds like Jenna can use some time to reflect on what she did wrong."

"I thought so, too, but I doubt that is going to happen. We both know that. People like Jenna are incapable of change." Keera yawned. The adrenaline of the past few days had subsided. She was beat. "But it's not my monkey and not my circus."

"What?"

"An expression I heard. It means, I don't have to think about her anymore."

"I know a restful place for a retreat in Eastern Washington."

She smiled. "No thanks, but I did check with Ella, and she and the new attorneys have things under control, so I'm going to take that vacation I missed out on. Would you please tell Maggie not to bother me?"

He smiled. "I can tell her, but as you said, some people are incapable of change."

Keera laughed. "I'm going to head down to the Paddy Wagon and get a bite to eat. You and Mom want to come?"

"No. Thanks, kiddo. I'm looking forward to getting home."

"I imagine you are," Keera said and moved toward his office door.

"Was I right?" her father asked.

She looked back at him. "About?"

"About defending Jenna. Did you learn something about yourself?"

Keera had. Jenna was proof of that old adage about money not buying happiness; that life wasn't about how much money you made, the car you drove, or the size of the house you lived in. It was about getting up in the morning and loving what you do and the people you do it with and, along the way, stopping to smell the roses. Keera's life wasn't perfect, but she was happy in her career and her family, as dysfunctional and challenging as the members could be. Her life was also far better than Jenna's, and always had been, but she also no longer wanted to compare herself to Jenna or anyone else.

Jenna had no idea who she was.

Keera did. She was a defense lawyer. A damn good one.

"I think I did, Dad. Thank you."

Her father nodded. "Remember, next Sunday is the first Sunday of the month."

Keera laughed. "Then I am definitely taking a vacation somewhere outside the country," she said and left his office.

"Your mother won't be happy. Those dinners are sacrosanct," he called out.

Keera continued down the hallway to the reception desk, where Maggie again answered the phone lines, which rang incessantly. She looked harried as Keera passed reception in the direction of the lobby.

"Keera," Maggie said. "Keera. Keera!"

"I'm on vacation, Maggie!!!" she said, and imagined multiple exclamation points at the end of her sentence.

"What am I supposed to do with all these calls for you?"

She entered the elevator without answering her sister, though she could think of several retorts.

On the ground floor she stepped from the elevator and crossed to the Paddy Wagon. She told the hostess she wanted to sit outside, in the sunshine, breathing the fresh air.

The hostess seated her, and a young waiter handed Keera a menu. "Can I get you something to drink?"

She didn't open the menu. "Are you still serving breakfast?"

"Until 11:00 a.m."

"I want the country-style breakfast. Eggs over easy. Bacon *and* sausage. Hash browns and wheat toast. And I'll take two pancakes on the side with extra butter and syrup. And a glass of orange juice."

"Got it." He looked at the other table setting. "Are you expecting someone?"

She smiled and thought, *I wish.* "No. I'm not."

After the waiter departed, Keera looked into Occidental Square at the men playing chess. She might just take a few of them on after breakfast, but for the moment she was happy to shut her eyes and not think of Jenna Bernstein, the law, or anyone or anything else.

She sensed a shadow, like when clouds pass across the sun. She opened her eyes expecting the waiter. She looked up into the bright light, unable to see the person hovering over her. She shielded her eyes with her hand.

"Are you meeting someone for lunch?" Frank Rossi asked.

Keera thought of all the food she'd ordered. "You had breakfast yet, Frank?"

"Just left the courthouse."

"You like bacon and pancakes?"

"Prefer sausage."

Keera stretched out her leg under the table and pushed back the chair across from her. "Take a load off, Frank. I'd say we both earned it."

Acknowledgments

One of the fun parts of this job is the research I get to do when I have a new idea. I'm always dependent on many for their help.

I've been fascinated by sociopaths ever since I encountered one when I practiced law. I'm sure there were others, but this one stood out. He was incredibly bright and manipulative. He was also incredibly convincing. It was hard to determine when he was lying, and I thought he must have been terrifying for our clients to work with when they realized that things were not as they seemed.

I've done research into sociopaths for other novels I've written. In this book, I wanted a person who ran her own company with an incredible upside that would attract investors. The story of Sam Bankman-Fried was fascinating to me. I have no idea if he has an antisocial personality disorder. All I know is that he had the ability to get other very bright individuals to invest in his company. Bernie Madoff was the well-known person I researched for the first Keera Duggan book, *Her Deadly Game*.

For this novel, I wanted a fictional company that was on the edge of possibly breaking through and finding a cure for, or a different way of treating, insidious diseases like Alzheimer's, Parkinson's, and dementia, which impact so many people and their families. I called on my good friend Dr. Dan Brzusek, and, as always, he was right there with information to help me craft a cutting-edge company on the verge of going public with a new treatment. Dr. Dan introduced me to nanotechnology and nanotransfection, which is a revolutionary treatment currently being studied. The testing is, to my understanding, limited to laboratory rats, and while we may be a way off from testing in humans, the work alone is awe-inspiring because of the potential ramifications.

Let's hope it is developed soon.

In the interim, I thought it would be a good technology for a young entrepreneur with an antisocial personality disorder because Jenna Bernstein is literally preying on the hopes and dreams of so many seeking a cure or a treatment.

It is a fascinating world. I hope you enjoyed it.

Luckily, I had a great team to help me.

As with all the novels in the Tracy Crosswhite series, I simply could not have written *Beyond Reasonable Doubt* without the help of Jennifer Southworth from the Violent Crimes Section of the Seattle Police Department, and Allan Hardwick, a retired law enforcement officer. Allan and Jennifer never hesitate to assist me with police procedure and point out where I've made mistakes. If there are any mistakes in the police aspects of this novel, those mistakes are mine and mine alone.

If there are any mistakes with respect to emerging medical technologies or the legal aspects of the novel, they are mine and mine alone. In the interests of telling a story—and hopefully keeping it entertaining—I have condensed certain timelines, such as the time it takes for a case to go to trial.

Thanks to Meg Ruley, Rebecca Scherer, and the team at the Jane Rotrosen Agency. I rely on their guidance for so much, and they never hesitate to assist me. I'm blessed to have them on my team. They make my life easier so I can focus on writing, which is what I love the most.

Thomas & Mercer at Amazon Publishing also has a great team of individuals. I've written a number of books and series with them, and they are so good at managing and promoting all of my novels. Their support and guidance, again, allows me to do what I do best—write the next novel and hopefully make it engaging for the reader. People ask me how I'm putting out more than one novel a year. The simple answer is I work every day and I love what I do. But I also get a lot of support from my writing team at the literary agency and at Amazon Publishing. The team at Thomas & Mercer has made each novel better with their edits, comments, and suggestions. I take each suggestion seriously.

Once the novel is published, I'm always in awe of the marketing and promotion Amazon Publishing devotes to selling and promoting my novels all over the world. The teams from the UK, Ireland, France, Germany, Italy, and Spain are full of hardworking people for whom I am so very grateful. I've seen several of my novels on billboards in Times Square in New York City and in the *New York Times* Sunday book section, as well as all over the Amazon pages. My publicity team is always on the cutting-edge of promotion and marketing.

Thanks to Nicole Burns-Ascue, production manager, and Jarrod Taylor, art director. I love the covers and the titles of each of my novels. The Amazon PR team, which now includes Megan Beatie at Megan Beatie Communications, is always available when I call or send an email with a need or a request. Thank you, Megan, for all your hard work.

Thanks also to the marketing team, Andrew George, Erica Moriarty, and Andrea Mendez for all your efforts and creative ideas. I'm indebted to each of you. Thanks to Amazon Publishing's publisher, Julia Sommerfeld, for creating a team dedicated to their jobs and allowing me to be a part of it. I am sincerely grateful—and even more amazed with each additional million readers we reach.

I am especially grateful to Amazon Publishing's associate publisher, Gracie Doyle. Gracie is terrific at managing each of my series so that readers never have to wait too long in between the next Tracy, Keera, or stand-alone novel. She and I work closely from my initial ideas to print. It was Gracie who suggested I write legal thrillers again and let me do so in my own unique way, with family dynamics, police procedure, and legal aspects.

Thank you to Charlotte Herscher, developmental editor. All of my books with Amazon Publishing have been edited by Charlotte—from police procedurals to legal thrillers to mysteries and literary novels—and she never ceases to amaze me with how quickly she picks up the storyline and works to make it better. Thanks to Scott Calamar, copyeditor, who I desperately need. Grammar has never been my strength, so there is usually a lot to do.

Thanks to Tami Taylor, who creates my newsletters and some of my foreign-language book covers. Thanks to Pam Binder and the Pacific Northwest Writers Association for their support.

Thanks to all of you tireless and loyal readers, who discover each new novel, for your incredible support of my work all over the world. Hearing from readers is a blessing, and I enjoy each email. None of this would be possible without your continued support. Thank you.

Thanks to my mother and father for all their encouragement. They led by example that hard work and persistence pay off. I couldn't think of two better role models.

Thank you to my wife, Cristina, and to my two children for all their love and support.

I couldn't do this without all of you, nor would I want to.

About the Author

Photo © Douglas Sonders

Robert Dugoni is the *New York Times, Wall Street Journal, Washington Post,* and Amazon Charts bestselling author of several series, including Tracy Crosswhite, Charles Jenkins, David Sloane, and Keera Duggan. His stand-alone novels include *Damage Control, The 7th Canon, The World Played Chess,* and *The Extraordinary Life of Sam Hell,* which was named *Suspense Magazine*'s 2018 Book of the Year and won Dugoni an AudioFile Earphones Award for his narration. The *Washington Post* named his nonfiction exposé *The Cyanide Canary* a Best Book of the Year. Dugoni is the recipient of the Nancy Pearl Book Award for fiction and a multi-time winner for best novel set in the Pacific Northwest. He has been a finalist for many other awards. Dugoni's books are sold in more than twenty-five countries and have been translated into more than thirty languages, reaching over ten million readers worldwide. He lives in Seattle. Visit his website at robertdugonibooks.com.